Cindi Myers is the author of more than fifty novels. When she's not crafting new romance plots, she enjoys skiing, gardening, cooking, crafting and daydreaming. A lover of small-town life, she lives with her husband and two spoiled dogs in the Colorado mountains.

Nichole Severn writes explosive romantic suspense with strong heroines, heroes who dare challenge them and a hell of a lot of guns. She resides with her very supportive and patient husband, as well as her demon spawn, in Utah. When she's not writing, she's constantly injuring herself running, rock climbing, practicing yoga and snowboarding. She loves hearing from readers through her website, www.nicholesevern.com, and on Twitter, @nicholesevern

Also by Cindi Myers

Investigation in Black Canyon
Mountain of Evidence
Ice Cold Killer
Snowbound Suspicion
Cold Conspiracy
Snowblind Justice
Saved by the Sheriff
Avalanche of Trouble
Deputy Defender
Danger on Dakota Ridge

Also by Nichole Severn

The Fugitive
The Witness
Rules in Blackmail
Rules in Rescue
Rules in Deceit
Rules in Defiance
Caught in the Crossfire
The Line of Duty
Midnight Abduction

Discover more at millsandboon.co.uk

MOUNTAIN INVESTIGATION

CINDI MYERS

THE PROSECUTOR

NICHOLE SEVERN

MILLS & BOON

First Published in Great Britain 2021
by Mills & Boon, an imprint of HarperCollins*Publishers* Ltd,
1 London Bridge Street, London, SE1 9GF

www.harpercollins.co.uk

HarperCollins*Publishers*
1st Floor, Watermarque Building,
Ringsend Road, Dublin 4, Ireland

Mountain Investigation © 2021 Cynthia Myers
The Prosecutor © 2021 Natascha Jaffa

ISBN: 978-0-263-28324-2

0221

MIX
Paper from
responsible sources
FSC™ C007454

This book is produced from independently certified FSC™ paper to ensure responsible forest management.

For more information visit: www.harpercollins.co.uk/green

Printed and bound in Spain
by CPI, Barcelona

MOUNTAIN INVESTIGATION

CINDI MYERS

For Lucy.

Chapter One

DEA officer Mark "Hud" Hudson liked his work. He liked having a job he believed in, one that stopped people from doing bad things and protected innocent people. A few times people he had arrested had even turned their lives around, and he liked to think he had had a hand in that.

But he didn't like dealing with people like the man in front of him right now. Dallas Wayne Braxton was a big, belligerent man whose bigness and belligerence had been only slightly diminished by the broken arm, two broken ribs, broken nose and two black eyes he had suffered. He stared out of his swollen face with the eyes of an angry animal, but spoke like a whiny child. "He just came out of nowhere and attacked me," he said, addressing Hud and fellow Ranger Brigade officer Jason Beck. "He's a dangerous lunatic. You people need to stop him."

"Him" was Dane Trask, an environmental engineer who had disappeared in Black Canyon of Gunnison National Park six weeks before, after sending his late-model pickup truck over the canyon rim. Since that time, Trask had been accused of embezzling large sums of money from his former employer, TDC Enterprises; stealing food and other items from campers in the park; and evading capture despite a large-scale manhunt involving officers from every law enforcement agency in the county.

"What were you doing in the park, Mr. Braxton?" Beck asked.

"I was hiking. This guy came out of nowhere and attacked me."

"You were hiking with a Ruger semiautomatic pistol in a shoulder holster under your jacket," Hud said. The park rangers who had responded to Braxton's call for help had relieved the injured man of the weapon.

"It's been all over the news how dangerous this Trask character is," Braxton said. "He's already murdered that girl hiker. I have a right to protect myself."

"Dane Trask did not kill the woman who was murdered in the park last month," Hud said. "That was another man." Though Trask may very well have killed, the Rangers had no proof he had committed murder. "And carrying a weapon in a national park is illegal."

"You're going to give me a hard time about that when this man almost killed me?" Braxton tried to sit up in his hospital bed, but fell back with a groan. "I'm not believing this. Whose side are you on?"

"Tell us again what happened," Beck said. "Just so we're sure we have all the details."

Braxton stuck out his lower lip, and Hud thought he was going to argue some more, but instead, he said, "I was hiking along, enjoying the nice day, and this guy jumped me. He came at me from the side of the trail, grabbed me around the neck and started whaling on me with a big stick. Kind of a club, you know? He broke my arm and my ribs. I swear, he was trying to kill me."

"But he didn't kill you," Hud said. "Why not, do you think?"

"Something must have scared him off," Braxton said.

"Did you draw your weapon?" Beck asked.

"I didn't have time. I tell you, he came out of no-where."

Hud consulted his notes. "The park ranger said he found your gun lying on the trail."

"It must have fallen out in the struggle." Braxton wouldn't meet Hud's gaze.

Hud nodded to Braxton's right arm, swathed in a cast. "Are you right-handed?"

"Yeah. So are a lot of people. What does that have to do with anything?"

"I was just thinking that if Trask wanted to kill you, the fastest way would have been to shoot you," Hud said. "We have reason to believe he's armed."

"He's crazy. Who knows why he does what he does?"

"Or maybe you saw him first," Beck said. "You drew your weapon and he struck your arm, breaking it and preventing you from shooting him. Then he punched you and broke your nose. You broke the ribs when you fell back. Then Trask ran away."

"Are you calling me a liar?" Braxton's face flushed, a pulse pounding in his temple.

Hud met and held his gaze. "Did you go to the park today looking for Dane Trask?" he asked.

"What if I did? There's no law against that. And there's a $25,000 reward for his capture. Why shouldn't I get that money?"

Hud bit back a groan. That reward had caused nothing but trouble for law enforcement since TDC Enterprises had offered it. TDC had bombarded the media with an-nouncements about the reward and plastered the town with posters, bringing every would-be bounty hunter to the park to stalk the trails and campgrounds, causing at least as much trouble as Trask ever had. TDC ostensibly wanted Trask found because he had embezzled $50,000 from them, but it seemed a lot of time and effort to expend when TDC made millions, or even billions, in profits every year.

"We don't have any other records of Trask attacking hikers, or campers, or anyone in the park or out of it," Hud said. "So I'm asking you again—what happened on that trail?"

Braxton looked away. "I had him dead to rights. I was on the trail and he stepped out in front of me."

"How do you know it was him?" Beck asked.

"I asked him! I drew my Ruger, told him to stop right there and I asked him. 'Are you Dane Trask?' He fit the description and the pictures on the posters, but I wanted to be sure. I'm not stupid."

Doubtful, Hud thought, but kept that opinion to himself. "What did he say?"

"He said 'Yes, and you need to go away and leave me alone.' Like that was going to happen. I told him he needed to come with me, then he took the big walking stick he had and went after me. It's lucky I'm still alive."

If Dane Trask, a former army ranger, had wanted to kill this man, he would be dead, Hud thought. "Is there anything else you'd like to tell us?" he asked.

"When you find him, you charge him with assault and attempted murder and grievous bodily harm. And I'm going to sue him for everything he's got."

"In the meantime, you'll be charged with carrying a concealed weapon without a permit and possession of a firearm within a national park."

Braxton's shouts of rage followed them down the hall and out of the hospital. Hud stopped beside the Ranger Brigade cruiser to inhale the non-antiseptic smells of hot asphalt and blooming lilacs. "If this keeps up, someone is going to end up dead," Beck said. "What does Trask think he's doing, running around in the park like Sasquatch or something?"

That was the question they'd been asking ever since park rangers had discovered Trask's late-model pickup at the bottom of the canyon, without Trask in it. A man with a good job, a good reputation, family and friends, had abandoned it all to hide in the wilderness, reappearing sporadically to send cryptic clues that seemed to implicate his former employer, TDC Enterprises, in some kind of shady goings on. But none of the clues were very clear, and the game had long since gotten old for everyone, it seemed, but Trask.

BAD THINGS COULD happen any day of the week, but when they happened on Mondays, somehow that made them worse. Audra Trask thought this when she saw the woman waiting outside her office that Monday morning, the first of June. A parent, though Audra couldn't put a name to the face this early in the day, and not a happy one, judging by the stiff posture and deep frown lines on the woman's otherwise attractive face.

It could be worse, Audra reminded herself, gathering herself for whatever confrontation was to come. Instead of a parent waiting for her, it could have been police, with more bad news about her father. Dane Trask had been missing—and wanted by the police—since mid-April. Every day Audra dreaded hearing he had either been found or was dead. Sometimes, she didn't know which would be worse.

"Good morning," Audra said as she moved past the woman to unlock her door. "What can I do for you?"

"It's what you need to be doing for my little girl," the woman said. She followed Audra into her office. "I enrolled her in this school because my friends raved about you. I had my doubts when I saw how young you were, but I decided to give you the benefit of the doubt, but now I see you clearly don't have any idea how to manage young children."

"Mrs. Patrick, please sit down and tell me what's wrong." Thank goodness, the woman's name had popped into Audra's head. "Has something happened with April?" April Patrick was in the four-year-old class with Jana Kepler as her teacher. Jana was new to the preschool, but she had come highly recommended.

"April is being bullied!" The word burst from Mrs. Patrick like a bullet from a rifle. She pressed her lips together, eyes shining with unshed tears. "I knew she'd been acting a little different these past two weeks, but I thought she was still recovering from the cold she had over Easter break. But when I picked her up Friday evening, she was crying. It took me two days to get her to tell me what was wrong."

"I promise you, we take bullying very seriously," Audra said, struggling to keep her voice calm. "I want you to tell me everything you know and I will get to the bottom of this."

Thus unfolded a story of another girl, Mia Ramsey, who had begun teasing April. At first it was simple mimicry, repeating everything April said in a whining tone. Then Mia began calling April names, and taunting when April cried. This progressed to pinching and hair-pulling—but only when no one else was around to see.

"Did April tell Mrs. Keplar about this?" Audra asked.

"She says she did, but Mrs. Keplar accused her of tattling and of being too sensitive."

Audra sat up straighter. If she had been a cartoon character, smoke would have come from her ears. "I will talk to Mrs. Keplar, and I will talk to Mia and her parents," she said. "I'm appalled that April had to endure something like this, and I'm also upset that this is the first I'm hearing of it. No child should ever have to experience something like that—especially under my care."

Mrs. Patrick's shoulders had relaxed, though she continued to frown. "I hope so. I decided to keep April home today. She's with my neighbor, who used to sit for me before we enrolled in day care. I do think it's good for her to be around other children, but not if she's bullied."

"I promise I'll get to the bottom of this," Audra said.

She escorted Mrs. Patrick out of the office, but Audra's hands were still shaking when she sat behind her desk again. She pictured April, a pale, timid little girl who was smaller and quieter than most of her other classmates, exactly the sort who made an easy target for bullies. Audra had been a child like that, the girl who never fit in, who was teased and called names and made the butt of every joke. She had been older than April during the worst of it, but the scars had shaped her. She had had to fight for every bit of self-confidence she now possessed, but the conversation with Mrs. Patrick brought the old inner demons roaring back. Of course she wasn't capable of running this preschool, if she couldn't see a situation like this when it was right under her nose. Who did she think she was?

She took a deep breath and silenced those old tapes. She was capable of running this school, and she was exactly the person to handle this problem. She picked up her phone and called her assistant. "Brenda? Go to Mrs. Keplar's class and tell her I need to speak to her immediately. You can watch her class while she's with me."

"Sure," Brenda said, drawing out the word in a way

that conveyed her curiosity over this unusual summons, but Audra didn't offer any details.

A few minutes later, Jana Keplar stood in Audra's open doorway. A tall, strong-featured woman in her early forties with short dark hair streaked with gray, Jana had started working for the school in January, replacing a teacher who had decided to remain home with her new-born twins. Audra had been impressed with Jana's experience and with her enthusiastic teaching style, which students—and parents—seemed to love.

"This couldn't have waited until lunch?" Jana asked before Audra could speak. "It's very disruptive to my class to ask me to leave in the middle of a lesson."

"I didn't feel this could wait. Please, shut the door behind you and have a seat."

Jana shut the door, but she remained standing, "What's the problem?" she demanded.

"April Patrick's mother came to see me this morning," Audra said. "She told me April is being bullied. Naturally, she was very upset."

"April is entirely too sensitive," Jana said. "If she didn't cry every time anyone looked at her sideways, the other children wouldn't pick on her so. I've told her she should stand up to them, or at least ignore them, but she doesn't listen."

"Sit down." Audra was firm. "Please."

Jana hesitated, then sat, perched on the edge of the chair, back stiff, hands on her knees as if she was prepared to leap up again at any second.

"Mrs. Patrick said Mia Ramsey in particular targets April," Audra said.

"Mia is a very bright, outgoing girl who is very popular with the other children," Jana said. "I think April is jealous of her. She exaggerates the things Mia says and takes offense where none is intended."

"Mrs. Patrick says April told her Mia pinches her and pulls her hair. You know that is strictly against the rules."

Jana did not roll her eyes, but Audra had the sense she wanted to. "I've examined April and questioned Mia several times," she said. "But she swears she never touched April, and I couldn't find a mark on the child. If Mia really pinched her, it would leave a mark, don't you think?"

"It's important to take accusations like these seriously," Audra said. "We have a zero-tolerance policy when it comes to bullying."

"And it's just as important not to brand an innocent, perfectly pleasant child as a bully simply because some sniveling ninny is trying to get attention." Jana's voice rose and her knuckles blanched white as she gripped her knees.

"I won't allow you to label any child that way." Audra spoke sharply. "If I hear it again—and especially if I hear it in front of the children—you will be dismissed."

Jana paled and bowed her head. "I'm sorry. I'm frustrated with this whole situation and I let my frustration get the better of me. It won't happen again."

"I hope not," Audra said. "Perhaps it would be helpful if I talked to the girls."

Jana leaped up. "You don't need to do that. I was teaching children when you were still in diapers," she said. "I think I know how to handle a group of four-year-olds."

"Then handle it," Audra said, outwardly calm, but inwardly seething. She had long suspected that Jana, who had operated her own day care center in Kentucky, where she had lived before her husband transferred to Colorado, resented working as a teacher under someone so much younger. "Instead of telling April to ignore Mia, tell Mia to ignore April. Separate the children as much as possible. And keep an eye on them. I don't want any more complaints."

Jana glared at her. "Is that all?"

"Yes, that's all."

She left, closing the door very firmly behind her. Audra sighed. She didn't have a sense that anything she had said had changed Jana's mind, but then again, she didn't know the woman very well. The school she had run in Kentucky had gotten rave reviews. One of the parents Audra had contacted when checking Jana's references had even cried as she talked about how much her little boy missed his former teacher. That kind of experience had to count for something.

A knock on the door interrupted her musings. "Come in," she called.

Brenda stuck her head around the door. "Everything okay?" she asked.

"Everything's fine. How was the class?"

"Oh, they're a great bunch of kids," Brenda said. "They were learning a new counting song and the cutest little girl—Mia Ramsey—volunteered to teach it to me. Such a sweetie."

Audra's stomach clenched. A "sweetie" who might very well be a bully. But what if Jana was right, and April *was* making things up, or at least exaggerating, in order to get attention? Shy, awkward children, so used to being overlooked, did sometimes act out as a way to be noticed. Audra had done it herself.

Brenda had come all the way into the room now, and was watching Audra, looking apprehensive. "Is there something else?" Audra asked. Another Monday problem to tackle?

"Did you watch the news this morning?" Brenda asked.

Another knot in Audra's stomach. Since her father's disappearance, she avoided the news. "No. Why?"

Brenda winced. "There was a story about a man attacked in Black Canyon of Gunnison National Park. I guess he was hurt pretty bad. He says your father attacked him."

Audra held herself very still, keeping in all the emotions that battered against her insides. Her father, the man she had loved and depended on all her life, was now some wild man, lurking in the wilderness and doing crazy things. She didn't understand any of it. She hated all of it.

"I'm sorry," Brenda said. "I hated to tell you, but then I thought if one of the other teachers or a parent, or even a child, said something, you ought to be prepared."

"Thank you."

She expected Brenda to go then, but she didn't. "There's another reason I felt I should tell you," she said.

"Yes?" Could this really get worse?

"There's an officer out front who wants to see you. He didn't say, but I'm pretty sure it's about your father."

Audra closed her eyes. Of course the police wanted to talk to her about her father. It was that kind of Monday.

Chapter Two

Audra remembered Officer Mark Hudson as having a smile that would melt chocolate and a laugh that had set up a butterfly flutter in her chest. Add in thick blond hair and sky-blue eyes, and the sum was a man who, under other circumstances, Audra wouldn't have minded seeing again. But the handsome cop wasn't smiling now, and unlike the other times when he had questioned her about her father, today he seemed more forbidding than friendly. He entered her office and stood beside her desk, frowning down at her, the way a teacher might confront a student who had misbehaved.

She shook off the notion, straightened her back and spoke first. "I heard there was a news report that my father attacked someone in the park. Is that true?"

The frown lines on Hudson's forehead deepened. "A man was attacked early this morning. He says the person who attacked him was your father."

She curled her hands into fists, her fingernails digging into her palms. "That doesn't sound like Dad at all," she said softly.

Hudson pulled the visitor's chair closer to her, alongside the desk instead of across from it, and sat, the various items attached to the belt at his waist softly clanking and creaking as he did so. She caught the scent of his aftershave—something clean and woodsy—and felt disoriented. This man was hunting her father. He wasn't her friend, so she shouldn't be thinking about how good he smelled and looked.

She forced herself to look into his eyes. "Why are you here?" she asked.

"We need to find your father before more people are hurt," he said. "Or before someone hurts him."

She gasped. "What do you mean?" She had visions of officers going after her father with orders to shoot to kill. "I don't care what you say, I can't believe my father would deliberately hurt anyone. He's not like that."

"I'm sure he isn't like that with you," Hudson said. "But remaining on the run in the wilderness is the act of a desperate man. One who might do anything to avoid being caught."

"Then tell me why he'd attack a stranger," she said. "What does he possibly have to gain by that? Are you even sure it was him? After all, people thought he killed that hiker, Marsha Grandberry, and it turned out to be someone who was trying to frame him for the crime."

The murderer, Toby Masterson, had kidnapped her father's former girlfriend, Eve Shea, and tried to use her to lure Dane from hiding. After Masterson died, some people whispered Dane had killed him in order to save Eve, but that wasn't the same as the kind of unprovoked attack Officer Hudson was talking about.

"The man who was attacked says he asked the man he encountered if he was Dane Trask and the man said he was," Hudson said.

"So they had this conversation and then Dad just attacked him?"

"The man had a gun. I think he was injured when your father disarmed him. Your father did hurt him, but I believe he acted in self-defense. He probably could have killed the man if he had wanted to, but he didn't."

The relief that surged through her made her eyes sting with tears. "Why are you doing this?" she asked. "Why are you hunting him, like...like some wild animal? Why can't you just leave him alone?"

"Until we have him in custody, he won't be safe," Hudson said. "The reward TDC is offering for his capture has raised a lot of interest. People are coming into the park just to look for your father. The man he fought with today isn't the first one of those people to be armed. It's against the law to carry a weapon in a national park, but that hasn't stopped everyone."

"Then make TDC end the reward offer," she said.

"We don't have the authority to do that. They aren't breaking any laws. They may even think they're helping."

"I still don't see why you're here." She sat back, trying to put more distance between them. "You're wasting my time and yours."

"Are you sure your father hasn't been in touch with you?"

"No. I'd tell you if he had. Why are you even asking?"

"I'm asking because he contacted his former administrative assistant, Cara Mead, and his former girlfriend, Eve Shea. You're his daughter. It would be very natural for him to turn to you for help."

"I don't know why he hasn't contacted me, but he hasn't." Part of her was hurt that her father had turned to others for help instead of her. But she was also relieved. Whatever he was involved in, how could she possibly help him? She wasn't a lawyer or a cop. She ran a preschool for a living. "Look, Officer Hudson. I understand why you think I must have heard from my father, but I'm telling the truth."

"Call me Hud," he said. "Everyone does."

She looked away, unsure how to respond. He was being friendly, but how could he be her friend? "Maybe he hasn't contacted me because he's always been the one to help me," she said.

"How did he help you?"

She shrugged. "Just, you know—Dad things. He gave me advice. He lent me money when I needed it." *He drove me to rehab and paid for lots of therapy.* But that was personal, not anything the cops needed to know.

"He and your mother never married, is that right?"

He knew this. They had been over everything the first time he talked to her, right after her dad disappeared. But the cops always asked the same questions over and over, as if double-checking her answers. "My mother was Dad's college girlfriend," she said. "He offered to marry her, but she said no." She had asked her mother once why she'd said no. "We were young and stupid and we certainly weren't in love," her mother had replied. But she had gone on to marry two other men, and had, at least eventually, not been in love with them, either.

"Was he around much when you were growing up?" Hudson asked.

"All the time. He and my mom shared custody. For a while in high school I even lived with him full-time." Her mom had been married at the time to a man who didn't like Audra. The feeling had been mutual. "He was always there for me," she added.

"And it hurts that he's not here now."

She stared at him, stunned at his perception. "Yes." She swallowed. "Yes, it does. Which is why I'd do anything to help you find him if I could."

He nodded, though whether to confirm that he believed her or because she had given an answer he liked, she couldn't tell. "I've been thinking a lot about how he's managed to pull this off," Hud said. "I think he must have planned this ahead of time. He may have cached food and water in the park, and other supplies. Maybe he scouted out caves and other places he could use for shelter. Others have told us he spent a lot of time hiking in the park."

"It was one of his favorite places," she agreed.

"When did he go there?" Hudson asked. "How often?"

"He went on weekends or after work, but I don't think it was that often. Maybe once a month. It could have been more. I mean, we each had our own place, and we didn't see each other every day."

"Tell me again about the last time you saw him."

"I told you all this before," she said. "Don't you have it written down somewhere?"

"I do, but it's helpful to go over it again. You might remember something you didn't mention before, or something might stand out for me that I didn't pay attention to before."

"All right." She stared at the desk, trying to bring that day over seven weeks ago back into focus. "We had dinner the night before I left for vacation in Paris," she said.

"You went there to see friends, right?"

"Right. I'd been planning the trip for a couple of years, so I was really excited to go. I think that's why I don't really remember a lot about that night. Dad seemed normal to me, but if he wasn't, I might not have noticed. I wasn't really focused on him."

"What did you talk about at dinner?"

"We talked about Paris. He went there once, when he was in the military. He was stationed in Germany and went there on leave. He told me about the museums he visited and talked about places I planned to go. We talked about the friends I visited—Denise and Richie.

Dad had met them a couple of times." She paused, then added, "We talked a little about the new school TDC is building near their headquarters. I won the contract for the on-site day care and preschool, and I was really excited about that."

"Did you father work on that project?" Hudson asked.

"I think he did the initial environmental assessment. Or someone in his department did, anyway. That happens way before construction, though, so he didn't have anything to do with the project once they broke ground."

"You mentioned before that he told you to be careful before he left you that night."

"Well, yeah. But I didn't think there was anything odd about it. He was always telling me to be careful. Parents do that. But then he said it again, and it did strike me as odd that he would say it twice, and so intently. I even joked about it, and asked him if he had some kind of presentiment that something terrible was going to happen."

"What did he say, exactly?"

"He said, 'I mean it, you be careful—in Paris, and after you get home.'"

"Anything else?"

"No." His expression of disappointment made her feel awkward, as if she'd failed him somehow.

"Did your father have a favorite place in the park?" he asked. "A place he liked to camp or hike?"

"No. That wasn't something we shared."

"You don't like to hike or camp?"

"I enjoy it, but I'm not into it the way Dad is. I thought it was fun for a night or two, but Dad would camp for a week or more." She stopped to fight back another wave of emotion. "I wonder if he thinks it's so much fun now."

"Maybe he enjoys the challenge. He trained for this kind of thing in the army."

"Maybe." She glanced at the clock, astonished to see it was after ten. "I really need to get to work," she said.

He stood and moved the chair back in front of the desk. "Thank you for your help," he said. "If you think of anything else, call me. Do you still have my card?"

"Yes." She had it tucked inside her billfold. Not that she intended to ever use it, but she liked knowing it was there. She stood also. "I have to get to playground duty," she said.

"You run this place and you have to do playground duty?" he asked.

"It's important for the students to get to know me, and it's a good opportunity to observe their interactions with one another and with the teachers. You can't really run a business if you sit behind a desk all day."

"Did your father teach you that?"

She smiled. "Yes, he did."

"We're not hunting him," he said. "Not like an animal, or like a criminal. When we find him, we want to help him. Only a desperate man would do what he's done."

"Why is he so desperate?" she asked.

"That's what we have to find out."

HUD SHOULD HAVE been reviewing the case on the drive back to Ranger Brigade headquarters, but instead he found himself focused on Audra Trask. Barely five feet tall and fine-boned, she struck him as the sort of person others might underestimate on first meeting. Then again, maybe the real clue to her spirit lay in the abundant dark hair that swirled like a storm cloud about her head, the thick curls refusing to be tamed.

Of all the people associated with this case, she was the one he felt for the most. Of all the people Dane Trask had hurt with his disappearing act, Audra struck him as the most bereft, more confused than devastated just now, but if Trask continued these dangerous games, Audra might be the one who was most damaged by his actions.

He turned off the highway onto the road leading into Black Canyon of Gunnison National Park. The high desert of this part of southwest Colorado struck most first-time visitors as flat and uninteresting, without the majesty of the distant snow-capped peaks or the lushness of river valleys only a short drive away. The canyon that gave the park its name revealed itself with stark suddenness to those who parked at one of the many scenic overlooks along the roadway and took a short walk to the canyon rim. The chasm that opened at their feet split the earth like a knife gash cut into a lavish confection, layers of crimson and shell pink and silver plunging over three thousand feet to the slender silver ribbon of Gunnison River.

It was this wilderness—approximately 130,000 acres, including the park and two adjacent national recreation areas—that Dane Trask had chosen as his hideout. This was also the territory of the Ranger Brigade, a unique, multiagency task force designed to fight crime on these vast public lands.

Hud didn't know if Trask had committed any crimes, but the man had disappeared in the Rangers' jurisdiction, so they were the ones tasked with finding him. The longer this one man eluded them, the more frustrating the case became.

He turned into Ranger headquarters, a low-slung building just inside the park entrance, and parked out front. He had scarcely exited his car when a man hailed him from across the parking lot. "Officer Hudson!"

An athletic man with windblown sandy hair trailing

past his shoulders jogged over to Hud. "Roy Holliday," he said, offering his hand.

Hud didn't accept the handshake. He didn't know this man, and letting a stranger get you in his grip could be a recipe for trouble with the wrong person. "What can I do for you, Mr. Holliday?" he asked.

"I'm working on a story on the Dane Trask case. I wanted to ask you a few questions."

"I can't help you." Hud turned away, but Holliday kept pace with him as he strode toward headquarters.

"What about the attack on Dallas Wayne Braxton this morning?" Holliday said. "Braxton says Trask attacked him without provocation, but I heard his gun was found on the trail and his right arm was broken. That suggests to me that Braxton drew the gun and Trask broke the arm to keep him from firing. What do you think about that?"

He thought someone had probably spoken to the reporter who shouldn't have. One of the park rangers, maybe? "No comment," he said.

"What about Audra Trask?" Holliday asked.

Hud stopped. "What about her?"

"She's Dane Trask's closest relative. She must know something she's not telling. Do you think she's covering for her father? Have you questioned her?"

"Ms. Trask doesn't know anything," Hud said. "You need to leave her alone."

"It's my job to talk to people," Holliday said.

"There's a fine line between talking and harassing," Hud said. "If you cross it, you'll have me to answer to."

"That's a mighty strong answer," Holliday said. "Do you and Ms. Trask have some kind of personal relationship?"

Hud cursed his inability to keep his mouth shut. "I'd say the same about any witness in this case," he said.

"So you admit that Audra Trask is a witness." Holliday pulled out a notebook. "Can I quote you on that?"

They had reached the door of the office. Rather than dig the hole he was in any deeper, Hud yanked open the door, ducked inside and shut it in Holliday's face.

"Your turn to run the gauntlet, I see." Officer Carmen Redhorse gave Hud a sympathetic smile. A slender woman of Ute descent, Redhorse had been with the Ranger Brigade since its inception two years ago and had grown up in the area. She'd been generous in sharing her knowledge with newcomers like Hud.

"Don't we have someone who's supposed to deal with the press?" Hud asked.

"I already gave him an official statement." Sheriff's deputy Faith Martin, the Ranger Brigade's official media liaison, looked up from her desk across the room. "I can ask him to leave, but you know I can't keep him off public property."

"I don't remember seeing him around before," Hud said. "Who's he with?"

"He's a freelancer," Martin said. "He's the one who broke the story this morning about the attack on Dallas Wayne Braxton."

"Beck told us you think Braxton went after Trask and Trask fought back," Redhorse said.

Hud nodded. "I'm sure part of Trask's army training was in disarming the enemy. Braxton is a blowhard who thought he had the upper hand because he had a Ruger in his hand. Trask probably broke his arm with one blow, then socked him in the face to send a message. Then he got out of there. If he'd wanted to kill the man, he could have. But he didn't."

"What did his daughter have to say?" Redhorse asked.

Hud shook his head. "She's worried about her father, but she doesn't know anything."

"Not anything she'll tell us, anyway," Redhorse said.

"I really think she doesn't know. Which doesn't do any of us any good."

"Trask seems to have it in for his former employer," Martin said. "All these cryptic clues he's left us—the environmental reports from the Mary Lee mine and the press release he tried to get his former girlfriend to give to the press—have to do with that mine. But how are a bunch of reports that may or may not be right be worth throwing away your whole life for?"

"You could say that TDC has it in for Trask, too," Redhorse said. "They've accused him of embezzlement and are offering that big reward for his capture."

"Whatever is going on, I wish they could have settled it with mediation or something sensible," Hud said. "How much time and money are we wasting, chasing after this guy?"

"There has to be more going on," Redhorse said. "Everything about Dane Trask's past says he's a smart, sensible guy."

"He's not acting smart or sensible now," Martin said.

Was Trask behaving so out of character on purpose? Hud wondered. If his own daughter had no explanation for his actions, how did the cops have a hope of figuring him out?

Chapter Three

Tuesday, Audra made a point of greeting April Patrick and her mother at drop-off that morning. "Hello, April." She squatted and looked the little girl in the eyes. "We missed you yesterday. I'm glad you're back."

April flushed and stared at her shoes. Audra turned to Mrs. Patrick. "I've spoken with April's teacher, and we'll be keeping a close eye on the situation."

"Thank you." Mrs. Patrick addressed her daughter. "Remember what we talked about," she said. "You're my wonderful girl."

Audra turned away, blinking back tears. Her father used to say that to her when he dropped her off at school in the mornings.

"Hello, Mrs. Patrick. April." Jana stepped between Audra and the girl. "How about I walk you to class?" She took April's hand and left, but Jana glanced back once, as if to say "See, I've got this."

April remained on Audra's mind the rest of the morning. At noon she walked down to the lunchroom, arriving just as Jana's class of four-year-olds filed in. April was easy to spot, lagging behind the others, head down. She sat at the end of the table farthest from Jana, an empty seat on either side of her. Audra's heart twisted at the sight of the child. She took the seat next to her. "Hello, everyone," she said.

"Hello, Ms. Trask," the children chorused. Jana merely frowned from the other end of the table.

"Hello, April," Audra said to the child next to her.

"Hello." April spoke so softly, Audra had to lean forward to hear.

"I thought you might like to come and eat lunch with me today," Audra said.

April stared at her, eyes wide. "Am I in trouble?"

"No, of course not." Audra looked at the other students. Everyone at this table, and those nearby, was watching. "I'm starting something new," Audra said, loud enough for everyone to hear. "I'm going to have lunch with a different student every week, in order to get to know you all better. We'll have a special table, over there." She pointed to a table in the far corner of the room. The only thing special about it was there was no one else seated at it. She stood and began gathering April's lunch things. "Come on, April, we'll have fun."

The little girl followed, head down, clearly less than delighted. Audra signaled to Mrs. Garibaldi, the lunchroom manager, and after a brief, whispered discussion, Mrs. Garibaldi hurried away, and Audra led April to the table. A few moments later, Mrs. Garibaldi returned with a tray that held two glasses of fizzy water with slices of oranges and lemons, a rose in a bud vase, and two little containers of vanilla ice cream. Ordinarily, the students had ice cream for dessert on Fridays, so Audra hoped this was enough of a special treat to ease April's fears that she was in trouble.

Audra unpacked her own sandwich and fruit. "Let's talk while we eat, okay?" she suggested.

April nodded and picked up her sandwich—peanut

butter and strawberry jelly. A classic. "You remind me of me when I was a little girl," Audra said.

April stared and nibbled at the edge of her sandwich.

"I was very quiet," Audra said. "There's nothing wrong with being quiet, but sometimes the other children didn't understand. Sometimes they picked on me."

April put down the sandwich but remained silent. "Do other children ever pick on you?" Audra asked.

A shrug.

"When someone picks on you, they're being a bully," Audra said. "Have you heard that word before?"

April nodded.

"Bullying is wrong," Audra said. "I don't want any bullying in my school, so if anyone bullies you, I want you to promise to tell me. You can ask to be excused and come to my office anytime." That might be asking too much of the little girl, but Audra hoped just knowing she was ready to listen if April found the courage to talk to her might help.

"Okay," April said. She picked up her sandwich and studied it. "Sometimes the other girls call me a baby."

"You're the same age they are, so you obviously aren't a baby," Audra said.

"They mean I act like a baby, because I cry a lot."

"It's hard not to cry when you're upset about something," Audra said. She resisted the urge to tell the girl to try harder not to cry. Adults had told Audra that over and over when she was a child, and it only made things worse. "Crying just makes you human, it doesn't made you a baby."

April looked as if she didn't quite believe this. "None of them cry as much as I do."

"Some people talk more than other people," Audra said. "Some people have a harder time sitting still in class. Some people are really good at running, while others can sing or tell stories or read better than everyone else. Some people like peanut butter and other people like tuna fish. Everyone is different. The world would be really boring if we were all alike."

"I guess."

Audra stifled a sigh. She didn't really blame the girl for not being persuaded. When you were a child, the adults around you had plenty of advice, but the only thing that really helped was to teach everyone to be kinder and more understanding. Audra could work on that. There were probably lots of anti-bullying programs out there. She'd find one and implement it at her school.

She checked her watch. Lunch was almost over. "Eat your ice cream before it melts," she told April.

"But I haven't finished my lunch," the girl said.

"That's okay. Today, if you want, you can eat the ice cream first."

To her delight, April smiled, a toothy grin that transformed her from pale and sullen to pink-cheeked and happy. Maybe, sometimes, ice cream worked better than talking.

AUDRA WASN'T SURPRISED when Jana came to her office after classes that day. "If you're going to take a child out of my class, you need to talk to me about it first," she said without preamble after Audra greeted her.

"I didn't take her out of class. I took her to another table at lunch."

"So you could get her away from me and talk." Jana dropped into the visitor's chair. "I asked her what you talked about, and she said you talked about bullying. Didn't you believe what I told you before?"

"This isn't about you," Audra said, trying to keep the

frustration out of her voice. "I wanted April to know that if she has any problems, I'm another adult she can talk to."

"I'm her teacher. If she has a problem, she should come to me."

"Of course. But she needs to know there are other sympathetic adults in her life. I thought I would have lunch with Mia another day and hear her side of things."

"There's nothing wrong with Mia," Jana said. "She's just a strong-minded child who doesn't suffer fools gladly."

"Are you calling April a fool?"

"I didn't mean that and you know it," Jana said. "But people are too quick to label someone a bully. There's too much political correctness. Instead of babying children and catering to every whim, we ought to teach them how to deal with adversity."

"April and Mia are four years old!"

"They're privileged and spoiled. A few challenges in life would only do them good."

"That is for their parents to decide, not us."

Jana looked away. When she faced forward again, her expression was more composed. "Speaking of challenges, why was that cop here yesterday?"

"That doesn't really concern you," Audra said.

"It doesn't look good for the school to have cops hanging around. You ought to know that."

"I'll take care of the school. You take care of your class." Audra met the older woman's cold gaze with an icy stare of her own. Jana was older and more experienced and thought she knew better, but Audra sensed if she yielded to her, Jana would end up taking over. In that way, she was just another kind of bully. "You can go now," she added.

Jana went, and Audra waited a moment, collecting herself before she followed the older woman out the door. *You'd have been proud of me just now, Dad*, she thought as she walked to her car. *Please come home so I can be proud of you.*

ONE OF THE things that had struck Hud the most when he first became a law enforcement officer was how many people weren't glad to see him when he walked in the door. Most of them never said anything, but he had learned to recognize the averted eyes and shrinking back that signaled they'd be happier if he left. He had naively imagined that people would be grateful to him for keeping them safe and riding to their rescue. His first few weeks as a rookie had taught him otherwise.

But it stung a little more when the person averting her eyes or shrinking away was a woman he was attracted to. A woman like Audra Trask.

He was returning from transporting a prisoner to the county jail that evening when he spotted Audra's car ahead of his. When she signaled a turn onto a side street, he followed, and parked behind her when she pulled to the curb in front of a neat, stucco-sided duplex. She waited beside her car as he approached her. "Is there a reason you were following me?" she asked.

At five feet ten inches, he wasn't a tall man, but he felt oversize and clumsy next to her. She was so petite, but there was nothing childlike in the hard look she gave him. "I saw your car and I wanted to make sure you were all right," he said.

"Why wouldn't I be all right?" she asked.

"Other women who were close to your father have been threatened." Cara Mead had been. So had Eve Shea.

"No one's threatened me," she said. "Why would they?"

"One of the many, many unanswered questions in this case," he said.

She folded her arms in front of her. "You don't need to follow me," she said. "I'm fine."

"I wasn't following you." He took a step closer. "I just saw you and thought it might be nice to have a conversation that wasn't about your father."

"That's a line I haven't heard before. It's original, I'll give you that."

"It wasn't a line," he said.

"Wasn't it?" Her eyes held a challenge. He shifted his gaze from her dark brown eyes to her lips—full and tinted a dark pink. He felt a rush of heat that had nothing to do with the weather and thought of stepping back. Instead, he moved closer.

She didn't back up. Instead, she uncrossed her arms. In her right hand, she held her house keys. "You might as well come in."

He waited while she unlocked the door, then followed her into the western half of the duplex. The rooms were small and simply furnished, with white-painted walls and lots of green plants. The place was neater than it had been the first time he'd interviewed her, but then she had just returned from two weeks in France. She dropped her purse and briefcase on a table at the end of a red-upholstered sofa. "Would you like a glass of water?" she asked. "Or I could make tea."

"Water is fine." The kitchen was also small, but glass-fronted cabinets and a large window over the sink made it appear larger. She took a pitcher of water from the stainless refrigerator and filled two glasses, then handed him one. He waited for her to speak, but she didn't. He let the silence stretch until it was uncomfortable. "How was your day?" he asked.

"It could have been better," she said. "I'm dealing with a child who's being bullied, and that's upsetting."

"Is that a big problem in preschool?" He would have thought bullying was something older children faced, not toddlers.

"Sometimes. This child is the sort of shy, awkward girl that some kids target."

"A lot of bullies are hurting and lash out," he said.

"I see you've read the literature," she said. "Was that part of your law enforcement training?"

"Not exactly. What are you going to do about it?"

"I'm going to talk to both of the girls and try to help them. They're very young, so stopping this kind of behavior now can save a lot of trouble in the future."

"So you believe bullies can change."

"Some can. Some never do. You see it every day, in politics and business, on television. People who seize on the weakness of others, who are cruel in order to make themselves feel better." She set her half-empty glass on the kitchen counter behind her. "What makes a person decide to become a cop? I would think it would be a dangerous, often unpleasant job."

Was she equating cops with bullies? Or just trying to change the subject? "I'd hate sitting in an office," he said. "I liked solving problems and helping others. People don't always believe that, but most cops do." He drained his glass, then set it aside. "What makes a person want to teach preschool? It may not be dangerous, but I'm pretty sure it's unpleasant at times."

"Oh, very unpleasant," she agreed. "We still have children in diapers. And stomach flu season is always fun."

She laughed at the horror that must have shown on his face. "Don't tell me you'd rather face down bullets than a dirty diaper."

"Can I have another choice?"

"You're going to make a great dad someday."

"I hear it's different when it's your own kid."

"And I've heard that's a lie."

"Then I guess I'll learn to live with the disappointment."

Her eyes met his, and he felt that *zing!* of heat again. This was such an ordinary conversation, in a sunlit kitchen on a late spring afternoon, nothing stronger than water at hand, and yet it felt intimate, as if they were confiding deep secrets.

The doorbell rang, the chime overly loud in the stillness. "Are you expecting someone?" he asked.

"No."

He followed her to the front door. A woman dressed all in brown, like a UPS delivery person, but without the brown truck, stood on the top step. "Are you Audra Trask?" she asked Audra.

"Yes."

"This is for you." The woman pressed a large white envelope into Audra's hands. "You're being sued. All the details are in that packet." Not waiting for a response, the woman turned and walked away.

Audra held the envelope by the edges, staring at it as if afraid it might bite. Hud eased it from her hands. Audra's name and address were neatly typed on the label affixed to the front, but there was no return address. "Do you want me to open it?" he asked.

She shook her head and took the envelope from him, then tore open one end. She pulled out the papers and studied them. He leaned closer and read the ten-point legalese.

"Terrell, Davis and Compton are suing me," she said. "Me and my father. For fraud and libel and misappropriation of funds, and a lot of other legal terms I'm too stunned to make sense of right now." She shoved the papers back into the envelope. "Or ever. None of this makes sense. If my father did all the things they said he did, then fine, sue him. But I didn't have anything to do with any of it."

"Let me see that." He held out his hand, and she gave him the envelope. He read through the papers. "I'm not an attorney, but it appears to me they're saying you have knowledge of your father's dealings that you refuse to divulge. They're suing, I think, in an attempt to get you to tell what you know."

"I don't know anything," she said. "Why does TDC think I do?"

"I don't know." Was this an especially bold gambit on TDC's part, or merely a desperate one?

"Maybe this isn't about what TDC wants you to reveal," he said. "Maybe it's about what they think you know that they *don't* want you to say."

She pushed her hair back from her forehead, a distracted gesture. "I don't understand what you're getting at."

"Everything TDC is doing—the charges against your father, the big reward, the publicity—those are the actions of an organization that is desperate to find your father."

"Because they want to stop him from talking?"

"I could be wrong, but I think so."

Most of the color had left her face, but she remained strong. "That sounds dangerous," she said. "A lot more dangerous than diapers."

"You don't have any idea what TDC might be worried about?" he asked. "It could even be something your father mentioned to you in passing."

"He didn't talk to me about his work. He knew I wasn't interested."

"What did you talk about?" Maybe the answer lay there.

"What I was doing. What was going on in my life." She shrugged. "Sometimes we talked about music, or movies, or books. Travel—that was something we both enjoyed. There was nothing secret or mysterious or having anything to do with TDC."

"If you think of anything else, call me." It was what he always said to people involved in cases, but he hoped she really would call him.

"I will." Did he detect annoyance in her voice?

"What will you do about the lawsuit?" he asked.

She looked down at the white envelope. "I'll contact my attorney. The whole thing is ridiculous. And annoying." She shifted her gaze to him at the last word. Maybe a signal for him to go.

"I'll let you know if I hear any news," he said, moving toward the door.

"Thanks."

"Try not to worry," he said, then added, "I'll protect you." Because it was the right thing to say. Because it was his job.

Because he realized nothing was more important to him at this moment.

Chapter Four

Audra was eating breakfast the next morning when her doorbell rang again. Heart in her throat, she tiptoed to the door, half expecting to see the brown-suited woman again, delivering another sheaf of dire-sounding legal documents. The first set sat on a table by the door. Audra would need to contact her attorney about them, but for now she was treating them like something contagious.

The man who stood on the steps wore a dull green windbreaker, jeans and dark blue athletic shoes, and had sandy blond hair that hung past his shoulders. He smiled at the peephole. "Is this Audra Trask's place—the woman who runs Canyon Critters Daycare? I'm sorry to bother you at home, but this was the only time I could see you."

A parent, she decided, relief flooding her. She undid the chain and opened the door. "What can I do for you?" she asked. "Do you have a child at Canyon Critters?"

"It's Roy," he said. "Roy Holliday. Can I come in?"

The name sounded familiar. Maybe he had recently put in an application. She opened the door a little wider. "If this is about a new admission, I'm afraid we won't have any new openings until we move into our new facility this fall."

He slipped past her, into the house. "Excuse me," she said, flustered by the move. "What is it you want?"

"You have the contract for the space next to the new elementary school, don't you?" he asked.

"That's right. Is this about a new enrollment?"

"Not exactly." He looked around her small home as if he were taking notes.

"Then why are you here?" she asked.

"Did your father help you get the contract at the new school?" he asked. "Since TDC is building that facility and he worked for them?"

"My father? Who are you? Why are you here?" She grabbed her phone off the table by the door. "You need to leave or I'm calling the police."

"You invited me in," he said. "You can't call the police."

"Oh, yes, I can." Hands shaking, she dialed 911.

He took the phone from her. "Don't do that."

She ran into the kitchen. He followed, not running, but walking fast enough to catch up. By the time he reached her, she stood on the other side of the room, a large chef's knife in her hands. "Oh, don't be like that!" he protested. "I just want to talk to you. I'm a reporter. I'm working on a story about your father."

"I don't want to talk to you," she said. "You need to leave."

Instead of leaving, he leaned back against the counter and took out a notebook. "What was it like, growing up as Dane Trask's daughter?" he asked. "Did he take you hiking in Black Canyon National Park with him? Did you have any idea he was planning to disappear this way?"

"Leave!" she shouted. What had he done with her phone?

He ignored her, scribbling in his notebook. He studied the pictures on her refrigerator. "Hey, is this you, with your dad?" He plucked a photograph from beneath a magnet, one that showed her and her dad together two Christmases ago.

"Put that back!" she said.

He laid the photograph on the counter, pulled out his phone, took a picture, then turned back to her. "You don't look that much like your dad. I assume you take after your mother. What was she like? How did it feel, knowing your parents never married?"

Audra looked at the knife in her hand. She might defend herself with it, but she wasn't going to walk up and stab this guy—even if that might be the only way to make him leave. He was twice her size, so she couldn't shove him out the door. He clearly wasn't afraid of her.

If he wouldn't leave, she would. She walked out of the room and collected her purse and briefcase from the table by the sofa. She found her phone on the back of the sofa, but instead of dialing 911, she punched in Mark Hudson's number. "There is a man here who says he's a reporter and he refuses to leave," she said. "He says his name is Roy Holliday."

"What's he doing?" Mark asked.

"He's standing in my kitchen, making notes."

"Are you okay?"

"I'm really annoyed. If I opened the pantry and started throwing cans of soup at the guy, would that really count as assault? I think that might persuade him to leave."

"Don't do anything. If you're uncomfortable, go out and sit in your car with the doors locked."

"I'm not going to leave him alone to wander around my house at will," she said.

"I'm on my way."

He ended the call, and she tucked the phone in her pocket and headed back to the kitchen. "Mr. Holliday!" she called. "You had better not be snooping in my cabinets."

But Holliday was gone. The back door stood open, and the only other sign that he had been there was the photograph of her and her father, lying on the counter by the refrigerator.

Hᴜᴅ ʀᴀɴ ʜᴏᴛ all the way into Montrose, lights and sirens clearing his path down the highway. When he hit the city limits, he slowed and shut off the fireworks, aware that he was no longer in his jurisdiction. Better not to alarm the locals, unless he needed their help.

He parked at the curb in front of Audra's house, and she met him at the front door. "He's gone," she said. "When I got off the phone with you, he wasn't there. The back door was open, so I guess he went out that way."

"How did he get into the house?" Hud asked.

She flushed. "I let him in, sort of. I was holding the door open to talk to him and he just slipped past. He caught me off guard. I thought he was a parent wanting to talk about enrolling a child in school. I mean, I jumped to conclusions, but he let me believe them."

"Audra!"

"I know, I know. It was very stupid of me. But he looked so harmless. And he was, I guess." She led the way back into the house. "I tried to call you back and let you know you didn't need to come all the way out here, but your phone went to voice mail."

"I was driving."

"Oh. Right."

"What did he do while he was here?" Hud asked.

"He looked around. He asked a lot of questions about my dad. I didn't answer them. He took a picture of a photograph of the two of us that I had on my refrigerator." She rubbed her shoulders. "It was calm and kind of ridiculous and really creepy, too."

"Don't let anyone else inside who you don't know," Hud said.

She nodded. "I know. It's just—this whole situation is so bizarre. My father, the lawsuit and everything."

"Have you talked to anyone about that lawsuit?" he asked.

"I have an appointment with my lawyer this afternoon." She checked her watch. "And I really have to go. Thank you for rushing all the way out here."

"I never mind an excuse to see you." He turned toward her. "You could make it up to me by having dinner with me tonight."

That blush again, her cheeks rose pink, her eyes bright. "Officer Hudson, are you sure…"

"Like I said before, call me Hud. Everyone does."

"All right. Hud. Are you sure it's, well, ethical to get involved with someone who's part of a case you're working on?"

"You're not a suspect or even a witness to a crime. You're the daughter of a missing person we're searching for."

"That's all my father is to you—a missing person? Not a desperate fugitive or a fleeing criminal or any of the other descriptions I've seen on the news?"

"He's a man who went missing in our jurisdiction, so we're trying to find him." He also might be a fugitive and a criminal, but they didn't know that yet. There were a great many rumors circulating about Dane Trask, but thus far Hud had seen very little proof of anything truly criminal about the man.

"Thank you for saying that, even if it's not true."

"Does that mean you'll have dinner with me?"

"I'll think about it."

He'd have to be satisfied. She picked up her purse and briefcase. "I'll walk out with you."

She locked the door behind him, then he followed her to her car. As she opened the driver's-side door of the black RAV4, she froze. "I know that wasn't there last night," she said.

Hud moved around her to examine the note tucked under the driver's side windshield wiper. He slipped on a pair of gloves, then carefully lifted the note from beneath the wiper blade and spread it out on the hood of the car. Audra leaned in beside him, pressed against him as they read.

You need to be careful who you talk to, or you'll be next.

"THE NEXT WHAT?" Audra asked for the third time as she sat across a table from Hud, Officer Beck and a woman who introduced herself at Officer Redhorse at the Ranger Brigade headquarters. Reluctantly, she had agreed to come here and give her statement before going into work. She had telephoned Brenda and let her know she would be late, though she had avoided her assistant's attempts to find out why.

"The next person hurt?" Officer Redhorse suggested.

"The next person to disappear?" Beck offered.

"You're not making me feel any better about this," Audra said.

No one pointed out that it wasn't their job to make her feel better, so she was grateful for that, at least. Hud was trying to soothe her frazzled nerves. She remembered him saying he had become a cop because he wanted to help. She was beginning to believe that. "Could Roy Holliday have left that note?" he asked.

"Why would he?" she asked. "He got into my house

and was talking to me. He didn't even have to threaten me to get me to let him in." The more she thought about the way she'd behaved with the reporter, the more like an idiot she felt.

"Maybe he wasn't sure he'd get you to let him in, so he left the note before he rang your doorbell," Beck said. "Did you see where he was parked?"

"No." She paused, trying to re-create the scene in her head. "I looked out the peephole and he was standing on the steps. He apologized for coming to my house so early and said he needed to talk to me. I asked if it was about a student and he didn't say no."

"You say he left out the back door," Officer Redhorse said.

"When I returned to the kitchen, the back door was open and he was gone," she said. "I didn't actually see him leave."

"Did you hear him leave?" Beck asked.

"No. I was on the phone with Hud—with Officer Hudson. I wasn't listening." She should have been listening. What if he had tried to sneak up behind her? "Why don't you call him and ask him about the note?" she asked. "If he's a reporter, you should be able to get in touch with him."

"He hasn't answered my calls," Hud said. "I left a message."

"He probably thinks you're going to give him a hard time about being at my house," she said. "He won't call back."

"Who else would threaten you?" she asked.

"No one," Audra said. "I run a day care center. I don't make enemies."

"You have employees," Beck said. "Are any of them upset with you? Are any parents angry?"

She thought of Jana, who resented taking direction from a younger woman. But Jana was a good, dedicated teacher. In her shoes, Audra might feel the same. Jana had had a successful day care of her own that she had had to give up when her husband transferred. Now she was working for a much younger woman, used to making her own decisions but unable to do so. So yes, Jana resented Audra, but why make dire threats against her?

As for parents, April's mother wasn't happy at how her child's bullying had been dealt with, but Mrs. Patrick struck Audra as being as gentle and harmless as her little girl. "I can't think of anyone," she said. "Truly."

"You don't recognize the handwriting?" Redhorse asked.

"It's just block printing. No, I don't recognize it."

"What about the paper?" Beck asked.

"It looks like a sheet of plain copy paper." She shook her head. "Maybe this is someone's idea of a sick joke. I mean, that threat is so vague. It doesn't say what is going to happen or who I'm not supposed to talk to or give me any idea what I'm not supposed to say."

"TDC Enterprises sued you," Hud said. "They think you know something your father also knows."

She had tossed and turned half the night, trying to make sense of that lawsuit. "The papers I was given don't say that," she said.

"No, but it's implied," Hud said.

"But why would someone from TDC leave a note on my car?" she asked. "I think they sent a clear enough message with the lawsuit." She shook her head. "The more I consider this, the more I think this is just a bad joke." She frowned at the piece of paper.

"Has anyone from TDC contacted you since your father disappeared?" Redhorse asked.

"No."

"Does that surprise you?" Redhorse asked.

"Not really. I hardly knew anyone at that office. And I'm baffled as to why they're dragging me into this lawsuit. There's absolutely nothing I can tell them."

They all fell silent. "Any other questions?" Hud asked.

"No," Redhorse said. "Thank you for coming in."

"Yeah, thanks," Beck said. They all stood.

"I'll walk you out," Hud said.

He didn't say anything else until they stood by her car. "Are you okay?" he asked. "This kind of thing can really shake a person up."

"I'm okay," she said. "I guess I don't scare so easy. It seems more ridiculous to me than anything—that silly confrontation with that reporter, then this vaguely threatening note. It's ludicrous."

"Are you sure? Do you want me to come sleep on your couch tonight?"

She didn't know whether to be flattered or amused by the offer. There was definitely some attraction between them—she'd felt it at their very first meeting, right after she had learned of her father's disappearance. Sometimes, it almost felt as if he was coming on to her. Other times, she was sure he saw her as just another link to her father, a man he was trying to find. "That won't be necessary. I'm fine, really." She unlocked the car and opened her door, deciding as she did so that now was as good a time as any to clarify where she stood with this man. "But I will take you up on your other offer."

"What offer is that?" he asked.

"I'll go to dinner with you."

When he grinned, he was even more handsome. "When?"

"Why not tonight? Then you can take me home and see for yourself that everything is just fine."

"It's a date."

"Good." And if someone happened to be lurking around, it wouldn't hurt for them to see that she had a capable cop in her corner.

CHERYL ARNOTTE HAD hair the red-brown of pine bark and intense gray eyes. She also had a little girl and a little boy who attended Canyon Critters, and a reputation as a good civil attorney. From time to time, she handled legal matters for the day care center and had agreed to meet with Audra Wednesday afternoon. "While I'll want more time to review this completely, I can see two motives for this suit," Arnotte said after the two women had visited briefly. "One, they're hoping word gets back to your father that they've involved you and he'll come out of hiding in order to protect you. Or two, they think you have money or information or something that this suit will bring into the open."

"The Ranger Brigade think TDC is digging for information they believe my father shared with me," Audra said. "He didn't tell me anything, but maybe someone thinks he did. In any case, whatever sent my father into hiding, I doubt he'll come out just to protect me from an annoying and baseless lawsuit."

"Even baseless suits can be time-consuming and expensive," Arnotte said. "If we're unlucky and can't find a judge to dismiss this, this could drag on for a very long time."

"I have to fight them," Audra said. "I don't have a choice."

"All right. Then I'll proceed. Have you spoken to anyone at TDC about this?"

"No."

"Don't. If anyone tries to contact you, refer them to me."

Audra signed papers, wrote out a check and left the office, feeling drained. She debated calling and canceling her date with Hud, but that would leave her home alone all evening to brood, and that thought was even more depressing.

At home, she was changing clothes when she heard a car door slam. She checked the clock: six forty-five. She and Hud had agreed to meet at seven. She gave him credit for being eager, but they'd have to have a talk about why it wasn't a good idea to show up before your date had time to get ready. She cinched on her robe and went to the front window and peered out.

The sun had just dipped behind the roofs of the houses across the street, casting her side into deep shadow, but it was still light enough to see there was no one parked at the curb. Angling her head, she spotted a dark shape behind her car, blending into the shadow cast by a tall pine. Maybe Hud had realized he was too early and was sitting out there now. She started to open the door and call out to him, but remembering her earlier mistake with the reporter, pulled out her phone instead.

Are you sitting in my driveway? she texted.

No answer. She watched the car in her driveway. The shape didn't look like a Ranger Brigade cruiser, but then, Hud would probably bring his personal vehicle, wouldn't he?

The crunch of gravel made her jump. Was that footsteps? Every hair on the back of her neck stood on end, and she shrank from the window.

Her phone pinged. I'm on my way there. About ten minutes out.

Hurry! she answered.

The phone vibrated in her hand. She scrambled to silence it and retreated into the kitchen, searching for the same knife she'd used to defend herself against Roy Holliday. "Audra, what's going on?" Hud asked when she answered.

"There's a car parked behind mine in the driveway." She spoke softly, just above a whisper. "At least, I think it's a car. It's really dark over there, so I can't tell much. But I was in the bedroom getting dressed and I thought I heard a car door. I thought you were here early."

"Call 911," he said. "Now. I'll be there as soon as I can."

Chapter Five

Audra dialed 911, gave her name and address to the dispatcher, and explained what was going on. "We'll send a car right over," the man on the other end of the phone said.

He offered to stay on the line with her, but she declined, instead pocketing the phone, then tiptoeing through the house, double-checking the locks on all the doors and windows. That took two minutes. Another seven before Hud would be here. She didn't want to look out the window, but she couldn't stop herself. The vehicle was still there, a bulky shadow crouched behind her RAV4, menacing in its indistinctness.

She carried a kitchen chair into the hall and sat where she had a view of both doors, but she doubted anyone could see her. She leaned forward, straining to catch any sound, and thought she heard a scraping like a shoe on concrete.

Then lights lit up the front of the house. Heart pounding, she jumped up, almost knocking over the chair. Men shouted and feet pounded against pavement. Car doors slammed, followed by a racing engine and the squeal of tires. She reached the front window in time to see a Montrose Police Department cruiser speeding away.

A second patrol car pulled to the curb, followed by

a dark pickup. The vehicles parked, and Hud emerged from the truck, a familiar, comforting figure. She opened the door as Hud and two Montrose police officers approached her. "Are you all right?" Hud called when he was halfway up the walk.

"I'm fine."

"Ma'am, would you put the knife away, please?" one of the officers said.

She stared down at the knife in her hand. She'd forgotten she had it. "Sorry," she mumbled, and laid the knife on the hall table.

Hud walked up and embraced her. She hadn't realized how much she needed that embrace until his strong arms encircled her. She wanted to bury her face against his shoulder and stay there until her heartbeat slowed and this panicked feeling subsided.

But she was acutely aware of the two police officers standing in front of her, so she remained standing straight and faced them. "Thank you for getting here so quickly," she said.

"We have a unit in pursuit of your trespasser," said the older of the two officers, gray at the temples of his curly black hair and lines etched deeply in his mahogany skin. "Can you give us a description of the vehicle or the person driving it?"

She shook her head. "I'm sorry, I can't. It was parked over there, in the shadow of that tree." She indicated the spot. "I had the impression it was dark and fairly large, like a larger SUV. Bigger than my RAV4. And I never saw the driver. I only heard footsteps outside."

The officer's radio crackled and a voice announced they had lost the vehicle they were pursuing. "We'll search the area for shoe impressions and other evidence," the younger officer, red-haired and freckled, said.

Only after they left did Audra remember she was wearing just her bathrobe and underwear, her feet bare and her hair uncombed. "I should get dressed," she said, pulling the robe more tightly around her.

"All right," Hud said. "I'll wait in the living room."

Instead of the dress she had planned to wear for their date, she pulled on leggings and a long T-shirt. Clothes that were comfortable and comforting. When she walked into the living room, she found Hud standing before her bookshelf, studying the titles there. "Do you like to read?" she asked.

"I do." He tapped the spine of a J. D. Robb novel. "I love this series," he said.

"Yeah. Me, too."

They talked about books for a while, and she began to feel calmer. Then the two Montrose officers returned, and Hud sat beside Audra on the sofa while she gave her statement to the officers. After they left, he gathered her close and held her for a long moment, not saying anything. "I'm all right," she said after a while, and sat up straight. "Really. But I don't know if I'm up to going out for dinner."

"How about we order a pizza?" he suggested.

"That sounds perfect."

"Do you want to get a bottle of wine to go with it?" he asked.

"No, thanks. I'm not much of a drinker. I have some sparkling water and some sodas."

"A soda sounds great."

She appreciated that he didn't question her decision not to drink. It had been a problem with other men she dated. It had become a kind of test for her—if he objected too much, she knew he wasn't the man for her.

When the pizza arrived, they sat on the floor in front

of the coffee table and ate. Audra began to relax. Hud wasn't in uniform tonight. He wore gray cargo pants and a blue T-shirt and light casual jacket. She could almost forget he was a cop. It helped that he didn't ask her more about what happened tonight. She had gone over everything with the Montrose police and didn't want to relive those frightening moments anymore.

"How did it go today with the lawyer?" he asked instead.

"It went okay. She thinks we have a good chance of getting the suit dismissed." She licked pizza sauce from her fingers. "She thinks TDC may have filed the suit to try to draw out Dad. They think he'll come out of hiding in order to protect me."

"Do you think that will work?"

"No. If he hears about it he'll be angry. And maybe even a little worried. But he taught me to stand on my own two feet." She wiped her hands and tossed the paper napkin beside the remains of the pizza. "And he knows I don't need protection against a nuisance lawsuit."

Hud moved closer. He wasn't much older than her, she guessed, but he had fine lines at the corners of his eyes and the weathered skin of a man who spent a lot of time outdoors. If you didn't know what he did for a living, you might mistake him for a surfer or a snowboarder. "There are other things you might need protection against," he said.

"Oh? Like cops with big guns?" She shifted her gaze to his biceps, which stretched the fabric of his shirt.

"I was thinking of whoever was sneaking around out there tonight."

She looked away. She should have known they couldn't stay away from this topic for long. "Maybe it was that reporter."

"Maybe. But he walked right up to you before. Why not do that again?"

"Because I know him now. He knows I wouldn't let him in."

"I've been watching the news. I haven't seen any more reports from him."

"He said he was working on a story about my dad. That could be a pretty complex story at this point. Dad has been away weeks now, and there are all kinds of wild rumors flying around about him."

He rubbed her back, gently, the heat of his palm penetrating the thin fabric of the T-shirt. "I'm worried about you here alone."

She resisted the urge to lean into his touch and straightened her spine. "I have good locks and a cell phone. And I know not to open the door to strangers, even friendly looking strangers. That's why I called you tonight, instead of stepping outside to see who was there. At this point, I wouldn't open the door for a Girl Scout selling cookies."

He took his hand away. "Are you sure you're only twenty-three? Because you sure have it more together than I did when I was twenty-three."

"How do you know I'm only twenty-three?" He made her sound impossibly young.

"I know everything about you." He shrugged. "Well, everything that's part of the public record."

"Most people just google their dates," she said.

His smile took some of the sting out of his words. "Cops go the extra mile."

"Hmm." She wasn't sure how she felt about that. He probably knew about the traffic ticket she got for speeding in a school zone when she was sixteen, but he clearly didn't know everything.

"Did you google me?" he asked.

She shook her head. "Only because I haven't had time." She tilted her head, considering him. "How old are you?"

"I'm twenty-eight."

"Oh, an old man. Wise in the ways of the world."

"A law enforcement career has a way of maturing a person in a hurry."

"Is that another way of saying you're jaded?"

"We weren't talking about me, we were talking about you." He leaned toward her, not touching, but close enough she could sense the heat from his body and distinguish individual golden eyelashes. "Are you just naturally precocious? I'll bet there aren't many twenty-three-year-olds with their own successful businesses."

"And I think that's a bet you'd lose. Let's just say my parents encouraged independence." She had lived a lot in her twenty-three years, not all of it good, but all of it part of who she was today. She stifled a yawn.

"Is that a not-so-subtle way of telling me it's time for me to go home?" Not waiting for an answer, he heaved himself to his feet and began clearing the remains of the pizza.

"It's been a long couple of days," she said. "But thanks for coming over. And thanks for the pizza."

"I'll leave, but don't be alarmed if you see my car circle the block a couple of times. I just want to make sure the coast is clear."

"I feel safer already."

She kissed him goodbye at the door, a deep, languid kiss that set every nerve tingling and could have led to more, if she had let it. But she pulled away, smiling, savoring the delicious tension and tantalizing anticipation, like an enthralling novel whose last page read "to be continued…"

IN THE FOLLOWING DAYS, Hud knew he was falling for Audra. All the signs were there—the intense focus on her when they were together, the desire to know everything about her and most of all the difficulty of keeping her out of his thoughts. He'd be compiling a spreadsheet of evidence in a case and find his mind wandering to an image of her slim figure, clad only in her bathrobe. Or he'd be studying footage of a crime scene and find himself thinking about something amusing she had said, or a joke he wanted to share with her later. The distractions were maddening, yet he didn't want them to stop. He wondered if she thought about him even half as much.

She probably didn't. She seemed to enjoy their time together, but he sensed she was holding back. She had secrets—some pain in her past she wasn't yet ready to reveal. She didn't know yet how patient he could be. When she was ready to open up to him, he'd be there, willing to hear what she had to say and to give whatever she needed.

Friday, two days after Montrose police responded to the call at Audra's house, Detective Marty Burns contacted Hud. "We caught the man who was snooping around your girlfriend's house," Burns said. "You want to observe while we question him?"

Hud didn't correct Burns's assumption that Audra was his girlfriend. "Thanks. I'd like that."

So it was that an hour later, Hud stood behind a one-way mirror, looking in on a gray-walled interrogation room at the Montrose Police Department at a slight man with close-cropped white hair and a soul patch, who fidgeted restlessly as he sat alone at a metal table that was bolted to the floor. "The officer who pursued him got a partial license plate and the make and model of the vehicle, and we were able to track him down that way," explained Detective Burns, who had the heavy jowls and thick body of a man who worked too many hours and ate too much fast food. "His name is Richard Salazar, and he's a private detective."

He left Hud alone behind the mirror and went to question Salazar. After the preliminaries for the recording, Burns got down to business. "What were you doing parked in the driveway of 122 Zane Court on the evening of June 3?" he asked.

"I wanted to talk to the woman who lives in the house." Salazar's tone was dismissive, annoyed that the police were wasting his time this way. "I knocked, but she didn't answer my knock. I was on my way back to my car when the police showed up, hit me with a spotlight and started yelling like I was an ax murderer or something."

"Do you know the woman who lives in that house?" Burns asked.

"Audra Trask. I've never met her before. I wanted to talk to her on behalf of a client."

"Who's your client?"

Salazar smirked. "That information is confidential."

Burns remained impassive. "Ms. Trask says you never knocked on her door, and you didn't ring the bell."

"She must not have heard me."

"She telephoned the dispatcher at 6:47 to report a strange car parked in her driveway. The first officer arrived on the scene at 6:56 and spotted you at the corner of the house, some fifteen feet from the front door. What were you doing for the nine minutes between the time Ms. Trask saw your vehicle and the time police arrived?"

"I was looking around."

"Were you looking for a way into the house? An un-locked window or a door you could force?"

Salazar frowned. "I'm a private detective, not a thief."

"You were trespassing," Burns said. "I could have your license revoked for that."

"I was doing my job."

"You were a stranger to Ms. Trask, prowling around her yard in the dark when you weren't authorized to be there. Ms. Trask is prepared to press charges for tres-passing."

"I was doing my job," Salazar said, louder this time.

"Why did you run when the patrol car showed up?" Burns asked.

"I was afraid. The way they were shouting and carry-ing on, I figured they were going to shoot me. That hap-pens all the time these days."

Burns looked wearier than ever. "Try again. Why did you run?"

"I told you, I was scared."

"You were scared we'd find the baggie of heroin stuffed under the front seat of your vehicle," Burns said.

Salazar drew back as if slapped. "I don't know what you're talking about!"

Burns stood and leaned over the table, his face close to Salazar's. "Who hired you to 'investigate' Ms. Trask?"

Salazar remained mute.

"I'll be contacting the state licensing board as soon as I leave this room," Burns said. "And recommending no bail on the drug charges."

"I was hired by a guy named Lawrence," Salazar said.

"That's all I know. He paid cash, and there's an email I'm supposed to send my report to."

"Is Lawrence his first name or last name?"

"I don't know. He just said to call him Lawrence."

"What did he look like?"

"I never saw him. He called me and sent the money via PayPal."

"You didn't think that was unusual? Maybe even illegal?" Burns asked.

"There was nothing illegal about it. And some people don't want other people to know they hired me. Divorce cases, for example." He shrugged. "He paid cash and didn't argue about the price."

"What did he want to know about Ms. Trask?" Burns asked.

"He just said he wanted me to find out everything I could about Audra Trask."

"Why?"

"He didn't tell me his reasons, and I didn't ask."

"What did you find out?"

"Enough." Salazar sat back. "And that's all I'm going to stay. You may think my standards aren't very high, but I have some."

Burns looked at him for a moment, then left the room. Another officer entered and escorted Salazar away. "Any ideas on who hired him?" Burns asked Hud when he rejoined him.

"TDC Enterprises has filed a bogus lawsuit against her and her father," Hud said. "Maybe they wanted to do some anonymous snooping."

"Her dad is Dane Trask, right? The guy loose in the national park?"

"Yeah. It's a tough situation for her."

"If we find out anything else, I'll let you know," Burns said. "Do you want to notify Ms. Trask, or should we?"

"Let me do it," Hud said. He didn't like being the bearer of bad news, but Audra had proved she wasn't easily shaken.

SHAKEN WAS NOT the word Audra would have used to describe how she felt when Hud told her about Richard Salazar and the mysterious "Lawrence." "Forget the kitchen knife," she raged, pacing back and forth across her kitchen in agitation. "If that man shows up here again, I'll brain him with my cast-iron frying pan. How dare he!"

"That man will be in prison for the next little while," Hud said. "The Montrose cops found heroin in his car when they arrested him."

Some of the anger leaked away, replaced by a pang of sympathy. "He probably bought it with whatever Lawrence paid him," she said. "Maybe prison will be a good thing. Maybe it will help him kick the habit."

"Maybe." She felt Hud's gaze on her, full of questions, so she changed the subject. "I haven't heard anything from my lawyer yet. I called her office and left a message, but I haven't heard back."

"People talk about swift justice, but in my experience the process usually takes time," he said. "You should tell your lawyer about Salazar and Lawrence, though. There might be a connection to TDC."

"You mean 'Lawrence' might be someone with TDC, trying to dig up dirt on me?"

"I can't imagine what kind of dirt he thinks he'll get on a woman who runs a day care center." Hud kissed her cheek. "I have to go. I just stopped by for a minute to give you the news."

"Thanks."

After Hud left, Audra continued to pace her office. Usually when she struggled with something like this, she called her father for advice. He had a knack for listening, asking questions and helping her plot the right course. Unlike her mother and various girlfriends she might have confided in, her father had no patience with avoiding confrontation or sitting around hoping things would resolve without her intervention. "Problems seldom get better if allowed to fester," he said. "If you want a solution, you have to tackle the issue head-on. Fighting is better than fidgeting any day of the week."

She took out her phone and called Cheryl Arnotte's office again. A pleasant female voice invited her to leave a message. She ended the call without leaving a message, then stared at the photograph of her and her father that sat on the credenza behind her desk. "If you knew you were going to leave, you might have left something more useful behind," she said. "A letter or a diary, or some explanation for all of this."

She still loved her father, but right now, she had never felt more abandoned.

Chapter Six

"The Park Service reports that Dane Trask sightings have dwindled to only three in the past two weeks." Ranger Brigade commander Grant Sanderlin addressed his officers at Monday morning roll call. The FBI special agent had assumed command of the Rangers only a few weeks before Trask's disappearance, and it seemed to Hud that the frustrations of the case had added a few more strands of silver to Sanderlin's sandy hair.

"How many confirmed sightings?" second-in-command Lieutenant Michael Dance asked. A veteran with the Rangers, Dance had deep shadows beneath his dark eyes these days, a testimony to sleepless nights as father to a new baby girl.

"No confirmed sightings," Sanderlin said.

"He's been quiet since that attack on Braxton," Rand Knightbridge said. Knightbridge, along with his Belgian Malinois, Lotte, were an expert tracking team, though they had had no luck locating the elusive Dane Trask. "Maybe he's moved on."

"Maybe." The commander sounded doubtful.

"Maybe he's dead," Ethan Reynolds said. A man who listened more than he spoke, Ethan studied psychology and talked of one day becoming a profiler. His talents had come in useful more than once for the Rangers.

Hud hoped for Audra's sake her father was still alive, but death was a definite possibility. The wilderness where Trask had chosen to hole up was filled with hidden canyons, steep drop-offs and miles of roadless backcountry. A minor slip that resulted in a broken bone could be deadly for a man alone.

"If he's still out there, I don't think he'll remain quiet for too much longer," Sanderlin said. "All of his communications to this point have made some kind of accusation against TDC Enterprises, to little effect. He wants something, and I think he'll keep agitating until he gets it."

"TDC's big reward hasn't gotten any results yet," Jason Beck observed. "They may make a new move soon, too."

Hud thought of the lawsuit TDC had filed against Audra and her father. He had reported the lawsuit at an earlier meeting. If TDC had hoped to draw out Trask with the suit, they hadn't succeeded. Hud wasn't sure how Trask did it, but he seemed to keep up with the news. Did he have a volunteer on the outside who was funneling updates and supplies to him? Audra would be the most likely candidate, but Hud believed her assertion that she hadn't been in touch with her father.

"Officer Hudson, did you hear me?"

Hud started, and his face heated. "Sorry, sir. I was thinking."

"Stop, before you hurt yourself," Beck quipped.

"The Forest Service has hired a contractor to clear the illegal construction dump site in Curecanti Recreation Area," Sanderlin said. "They're going to start work tomorrow. I want someone on-site in case they turn up anything new. Beck will take the morning shift—you can relieve him at noon."

"We've combed through all that like it was an archaeological dig," Dance said. "We came up with nada."

"We have a child's drawing, a man's work glove and a key to a standard padlock," Reynolds corrected. These items had been dutifully tested, tagged, bagged and placed in the Rangers' evidence lockers, but had yielded no information that pointed to who had dumped hundreds of yards of construction debris in the middle of the wilderness.

"The Forest Service is anxious to get it cleared out," Sanderlin continued. "We'll continue to run regular patrols out that way for the next few months, in case the original dumpers decide to try again."

"It's not like there aren't miles of other places they can use as their free disposal site," Redhorse said. "People do it all the time."

"Yeah, but they dump a single refrigerator or a television set," Knightbridge said. "Maybe a junked car. It took weeks, and truckload after truckload, to dump everything at that site."

"And they did it right under our noses," Hud said. That grated more than anything.

"The Forest Service has submitted a proposal for drone patrols to monitor wildlife populations," Sanderlin said. "But they could also look for illegal dump sites like this one. If funding is approved, it has the potential to curtail problems like this one."

"Maybe the drone can find Dane Trask," Knightbridge said. "He can't hide from the eye in the sky."

Hud wasn't so sure about that. Trask operated by his own rules, and Hud was beginning to believe the man wouldn't be found until he was ready to reveal himself.

THE ARREST OF twelve people in a local burglary ring dominated the papers and television news, so for the next couple of days no stories about Dane Trask appeared. He didn't leave any more mysterious messages or tangle with any hikers, and while Audra continued to worry about him, she was glad he wasn't causing more trouble.

She began to relax a little, to focus on her job and her growing relationship with Mark Hudson. She thought her dad would probably like him. Dane invariably intimidated her dates—a former army ranger who could still run rings around men twenty years his junior could do that. But she thought Hud wasn't the type to be easily intimidated. The idea pleased her.

But life wasn't all romance and optimism. Monday morning brought an unwelcome phone call. "Ms. Trask, Superintendent Wells would like to see you in his office at ten thirty." The woman on the other end of the line didn't identify herself, but she didn't have to. Audra recognized the voice of the woman who was the assistant to school superintendent Vernon Wells.

"Why does he want to see me?" Audra asked.

"I'm sure I don't know, but it's important. Can I tell him you'll be here?"

Audra thought of several things the assistant could tell the superintendent, but thought better of all of them. "Of course I'll be there."

Audra had just enough time to finish her coffee, comb her hair, freshen her lipstick and drive to the school district offices. The assistant—Maeve or Mavis or Madge or something like that—wore her customary smirk, sweeping a judging look over Audra's neat gray slacks and purple blouse, pausing in her survey to frown at the small stud in Audra's nose.

Mr. Wells didn't look happy to see her. A large man with abundant chins and thinning hair, he studied Audra from behind black-framed glasses. "What did you need to see me about?" Audra asked as she slid into the chair across from the superintendent's desk. Maybe he had a report on the construction project at the new school, or he needed her input about some furnishings for the day care center.

"I'm very concerned about the negative publicity surrounding you," he said.

Audra blinked. "I'm not aware of any negative publicity about *me*."

"There are wanted posters for your father all over town. He's in the news constantly. I hear now he's attacked a hiker in the park and almost killed the man."

She couldn't believe that just when she thought public interest in her father was dying down, *this* happened. "My father is not me," she said. "You can't blame me for things he may or may not be doing."

"People see the name Trask and they associate it with bad things," he said.

"I have no control over what people think," she protested.

"Still, there are people who have suggested that we shouldn't have the Trask name associated with our new preschool and day care."

What people? she wanted to ask. But that was the kind of question people like Wells never answered. "My preschool and day care isn't a school facility," she said. "It's an independent business that happens to lease space from the school. It's an innovative model that will benefit parents, students, employees of nearby TDC Enterprises and teachers with children who will now have on-site day care." That was a direct quote from the bid she had submitted when she had first learned of the plans for the new buildings. A bid that had persuaded the school board to vote unanimously to award her the contract. "We have a contract," she added.

"The contract has a morals clause."

She flushed. "I haven't done anything immoral."

He shuffled papers on his desk, avoiding her gaze. "I wanted to extend you the courtesy of letting you know where the board's thinking is leading," he said.

"What do you expect me to do about it?"

"I don't know. But perhaps you could think of a way to separate yourself from your father. To demonstrate your fine character so that parents will feel comfortable trusting you with their children."

"Parents already feel comfortable trusting me with their children," she said. "My school is at full capacity."

"Maybe some testimonials from those parents would help," he said. "It's worth considering."

Audra had no memory of leaving the superintendent's office, or of the drive back to her school. Rage blotted out everything else—rage at Superintendent Wells for blaming her for her father's actions, closely followed by rage at her father for running away and acting like a wild man.

Maybe he really was ill, she thought. Maybe something in her dad had snapped, and that was why he was living in the wilderness doing inexplicable things. In that case, he needed to come home so she could help him. He definitely didn't need to be there, ruining her life from a distance.

By the time she pulled into the parking lot she had calmed down a little. She had a job to do, and she needed to focus on that and worry about the rest later. Walking down the hall toward her office, she spotted Jana Keplar and her class of four-year-olds filing into the lunchroom and detoured toward them.

When Audra took her seat at the end of the lunch table, Jana frowned at her. "Hello, Ms. Keplar," Audra said. "Hello, children."

"Are you going to eat lunch with us again today?" a little boy with a shaved head asked.

"I'm going to eat lunch with Mia today." Audra focused on Mia, a sturdy girl with long brown hair and hazel eyes.

Mia smiled back and bounced in her seat in excitement. "Do we get ice cream?" she asked.

"Yes, you do," Audra agreed.

"Can I have chocolate?" Mia asked as she walked beside Audra to the table in the corner. The staff had placed a vase of fresh flowers on the table, and Mrs. Garibaldi soon arrived with their sparkling water and ice cream—chocolate for Mia.

Audra had to spend a little time getting some of the children to relax and talk to her, but she didn't have to work at all with Mia. By the time Mia had eaten half of her turkey sandwich, she had told Audra about her baby brother; her dog, Sam, and her cat, Pumpkin; her ballet class; and her favorite subject—art. She smiled and laughed and was the picture of a sunny, friendly child.

Only when she stopped to eat her ice cream was Audra able to get a word in edgewise. "I especially wanted to have lunch with you today, Mia," she said, "because I think you can help me with something."

Mia's eyes widened. "Of course I'll help you, Ms. Trask."

"It's your classmate, April. I'm afraid she has a hard time making friends, and I'm hoping you'll be her friend."

Mia's bright smile faded. "I don't like April," she said.

"Why don't you like her?" Audra asked.

"She's such a crybaby. My baby brother cries less than she does. I'm almost five and I never cry. At least, not about things that aren't important. I mean, you can't even look at her and she cries. Plus, she's a tattletale. If

I so much as bump into her in line, she runs to tattle to Mrs. Keplar."

Audra listened to this outburst in dismay. From Mia's point of view, April's behavior did sound tiresome. She carefully considered her next words. "You're very lucky, Mia," she said. "You find it so easy to talk to people and to make friends. Not everyone is made that way. Some people are shyer. They don't know what to say to other people, and being in new situations frightens them."

"I am very lucky, Ms. Trask," Mia said, her face serious.

"I think April is shy," Audra said. "She doesn't know what to say, and maybe she's even afraid. It would help so much if you could be nice to her."

"I'm not mean to her," Mia protested. "She even called me a bully, and that wasn't right. That's calling names."

"It's calling names when you say she's a crybaby," Audra said gently.

Mia pressed her lips together. "Try to be April's friend," Audra said. "For me? I believe you could really help her."

"She can't be my best friend," Mia said. "That's Maddie Friar."

"April doesn't have to be your best friend. Just…try to say one nice thing to her every day."

Mia sighed with the drama only an almost-five-year-old can manage. "I can try," she said.

"Thank you." Audra held up her glass of sparkling water. "Let's drink a toast to that."

Mia grinned, and the two clinked glasses. Audra's mood lightened. This was why she had opened her day care center, not to please bureaucrats like Superintendent Wells, but to make a difference to children like Mia and April.

"WE'RE NOT UNCOVERING anything the crime scene team might have missed, but the men know to keep a lookout for anything that might identify who dumped all this." Officer Jason Beck had to shout to be heard over the roar of the front-end loader that was scooping up mounds of construction debris and depositing them in the back of a big dump truck when Hud arrived at the dump site Tuesday afternoon.

Hud nodded and squinted in the bright sunshine at the piles of old timbers, rock and gypsum board scattered across an acre of sagebrush scrub. An aerial search for Dane Trask a couple of weeks ago had discovered instead this illegal dump, located on federal land just outside of the national park boundary. "I talked to every major construction outfit in a hundred-mile radius," Beck said as the front-end loader moved farther away, making conversation more possible. "And some not-so-major ones. They all swear they had nothing to do with this. A lot of them offered to show me their dumping receipts for the last three months."

"The guilty party isn't likely to confess," Hud said. "And I bet dumping receipts can be faked easily enough."

"Whoever did this, they stopped as soon as we started watching the place," Beck said. "They're either really wary or really lucky."

"Maybe our patrols or the drone surveillance the Forest Service is proposing will help," Hud said.

"At least we can be pretty sure Dane Trask didn't have anything to do with this," Beck said. "As much as that man has been a thorn in our sides, at least there's that."

"He's like our own bigfoot, a boogeyman people can scare themselves with," Hud said. For a while there had been almost daily reports from hikers who had claimed to have seen Trask or been chased by him. Almost all of them had turned out to be either attempts to gain attention or people scaring themselves into seeing what wasn't there.

"Hey, I almost forgot to show you this." Beck pulled out his wallet and took something from it. "Cara brought this home yesterday. Someone was selling them at the bookstore downtown." He handed over what turned out to be an oval white decal, the words *Free Dane Trask* filling the oval.

"People can't decide if he's a criminal, a myth or a folk hero." Hud returned the decal, then both men turned as shouts rose from across the open ground. The man operating the front-end loader shut down the machine and leaned out of the cab, waving frantically.

Hud ran, Beck right behind him. The worker pointed toward the front of his machine. A few steps from the bucket, Hud halted. A man's body lay half out of the debris, mouth open, one arm flung over his head, like a drowning man emerging from a tumultuous sea.

"He hasn't been there long," Beck said. He looked up into the bright blue sheet of sky. "No ravens circling."

"I just saw him last week." Hud took out his phone to summon help, then slipped it back into his pocket. No cell service out here. "That's Roy Holliday," he said. The reporter must have asked too many questions of the wrong person.

Chapter Seven

Audra arrived at her office after lunch Tuesday to find a Free Dane Trask sticker on her desk. Brenda came in and found her staring at it. "Who put this here?" Audra asked.

Brenda shrugged. "I don't know, but I've been seeing them around town. Kinda cool, huh?" She laid a stack of mail on Audra's desk and returned to the outer office.

It was nice to think that not everyone saw her father as a criminal, but was this just another way of portraying him as someone outside the law?

"Knock, knock."

She turned, and her mood lifted at the sight of Hud. He looked rumpled and windblown, but all the more handsome for it. But when he didn't return her smile, some of her happiness abated. "What's wrong?" she asked.

He stepped into her office and pulled the door closed behind him. "We found Roy Holliday," he said. "Or rather, we found his body."

"He's dead?" How could that be?

Hud took her arm and led her to the chair behind her desk, then handed her the water bottle from the corner of the desk. She drank, then pulled herself together. "That's a shock," she said. "Can you tell me what happened?"

"The coroner thinks he died six days ago."

She did the math. "But that would have been Wednesday. The day he was at my house."

"Yes. That's one reason I'm here. You may have been the last person to see him alive."

That sounded ominous. She took a deep breath. "Maybe go back a little and tell me everything. Where was he found? And when?"

"He was found at an illegal dump site a couple miles off Highway 50, in the Curecanti National Recreation Area. Someone—we don't know who—dumped a couple hundred yards of construction debris there a few weeks back. The Forest Service hired a contractor to haul everything away, and they found Holliday's body underneath a pile of broken drywall."

She made a face. "How horrible. If he's been out there five days—" Even in June, daytime temperatures could climb into the nineties, and there was so much wildlife out there...

"He hadn't been there five days," Hud said. "He may have been there only a few hours."

"Where was he before that?"

"We don't know for sure, but the coroner thinks he might have been kept in cold storage."

"In a refrigerator?" She couldn't even wrap her mind around the idea.

"Or a morgue or somewhere similar."

She shuddered. "That's bizarre. How did he die?"

"He was shot in the head. Small-caliber bullet. I need you to go over again everything he did and said when you saw him last Wednesday."

"Right." She rested her hands on her knees and thought a moment, then said, "When I opened the door to him, I don't remember another car parked on the street or in my driveway. I wasn't looking for one. But I think

I would have noticed if one had been there. My house isn't set that far off the street and though it was early, it was quite light."

"What was his manner?" Hud asked. "How did he seem?"

"He was very relaxed. He apologized for coming to the house so early, but he really needed to talk to me. I asked if this was about a new enrollment and he asked again to come in and talk." She flushed, remembering how naive and vulnerable she had been. "He introduced himself as Roy Holliday, and I thought the name sounded familiar, but I thought I must have seen it on an application for enrollment. We've been getting a lot of those, now that word has gone out that we're moving to the new elementary school and doubling our capacity."

"When did you realize he was a reporter?" Hud asked.

"He said he was working on a story about Dad. He wanted to know if Dad helped me to get the contract for the new center, since TDC was building the facility. He asked me what it was like growing up with Dane as a father, and if I had any idea what he was planning when he disappeared. I felt really foolish for letting him in."

"Did he act aggressive at all?"

"Not really. He took my phone away when I tried to call 911, but he just laid it on the back of the sofa. He was really very relaxed. Confident. When I told him I was leaving, he didn't try to follow me. He probably thought it would be a good opportunity for him to snoop around."

"Did you hear him leave?"

"No, but I was on the phone with you. When I got back into the kitchen and he was gone, I was surprised, but I guess he heard me on the phone and didn't want trouble."

"Did you think it was odd that the back door was standing open?"

"Not really. I figured he was in a hurry, and sometimes the latch doesn't catch all the way. You have to pull it hard until it clicks into place." She pictured that back door again and gasped. "Do you think someone *took* him from the kitchen?" she asked. "They forced him to leave and then killed him?"

"We're going to interview all the neighbors around the house and on the adjacent streets," Hud said. "Maybe one of them saw something."

"I can't believe all this is happening," she said. "It was bad enough when Dad pulled his disappearing act, but lately, every time I turn around, something horrible is happening." She put her head in her hands. "I'm ready for it to stop."

Hud rested his hand on her back. "What else has happened?" he asked.

She straightened. "Oh, it's more of a nuisance than anything. At least, I hope that's all it is."

"What?" He pulled the visitor's chair around beside her and sat.

"Oh, yesterday I got a call from the school superintendent, summoning me to his office. My day care and preschool are a private concern, not part of the school district, but the new elementary school is district property. TDC donated the land for the new school and gave them a big break on the construction costs. Rather than operate their own day care and preschool, the district decided to award a contract to a private concern. I'll actually be leasing my classroom space from the school district."

"What did the superintendent want to see you about?"

"He—Vernon Wells—was upset about what he termed all the negative publicity about me. I got him to admit the publicity was about my father, not me, and that I had nothing to do with it. But he said it looked bad to have the Trask name associated with this project."

"You have a contract, don't you?" Hud said. "There would be consequences for pulling out."

"Yes, and believe me, I'll fight him all the way if he tries to back out on the deal. But he said the contract has a morals clause and he could exercise that."

"On what grounds?"

"I don't know." She chewed at her lower lip, gut churning. "But he might find a reason." She clasped her hands tightly together, wishing she could as easily contain the anxiety within her. "Have the police had any luck identifying 'Lawrence'?"

Hud shook his head. "I haven't heard anything. Any word from your lawyer?"

"No. She's filed some motions, and we're waiting on the judge."

He slipped his arm around her. "What you need is a night out. You still owe me a dinner out."

"I do, don't I?"

"A movie and Thai food?"

"I want to see something funny. I need a good laugh."

"I think we can manage that."

THEY SAW A comic mystery that was both silly and fun. Sitting next to her in the dark theater, laughing at outrageous situations, Hud felt transported to another world, one where pain and trouble couldn't intrude, where he and Audra could be more than a cop and a crime victim, but friends.

Over pad thai and pineapple fried rice, Audra told him about the Free Dane Trask sticker someone had left on her desk. "It's probably one of the teachers," she said.

"Depending on who it is, they're either trying to cheer me up or giving me a hard time."

"I've seen those around," Hud said. "Apparently your dad has fans."

"I don't get it," she said. "The media have made him out to be so horrible."

"Some people like to root for the underdog. And he has a lot of friends in the community—veterans he helped through the veterans' group he founded."

"Welcome Home Warriors was very dear to his heart. He helped so many men and women to find jobs or get counseling, or simply to find friends with others who shared common experiences." She rested her chin in her hand, a wistful expression on her face. "Those people were really his tribe. I was more shocked that he left them behind than that he left me."

The words tugged at his heart, and he searched for something he could say to comfort her. But Audra wasn't looking for sympathy. She squared her shoulders. "Enough of that. I'm not going to get all maudlin, I promise. Tell me about your family."

So he told her about growing up with a younger brother and sister, a father who worked in marketing and a mother who ran a women's boutique. "They don't understand why I wanted to be a cop, but they never tried to talk me out of it. My other brother works in marketing like my dad, and my sister works for a big corporation in sales. When we get together at the holidays, the four of them have a lot more to talk about than I do." He shrugged. "It's okay. I like my life, even if it's not the one they wanted for me."

"My dad never put any expectations on me," she said. "I think my mother would have liked if I had married money, or done something more glamorous than teach toddlers how to tie their shoes, but she's too involved in her own dramas to worry much about mine. My dad always said he just wanted me to be happy."

"I like him better, the more you tell me about him."

"I think he'd like you, too," she said.

If they ever met, it might be with Hud pointing a gun at Trask and ordering him to accompany him back to the station. He probably wouldn't like Hud much then, but there was always hope they could get past that.

He took Audra home and kissed her good-night at the door, a lingering kiss full of passion and promise. He wanted to stay with her, but he wouldn't press. When she was ready, she'd let him know.

He had just turned onto the highway leading out of town when his phone signaled an incoming text message. He pressed the button to have his car's system read the text out loud.

"From Audra," the mechanical voice intoned. "Come back. Spend the night."

He did a U-turn in the middle of the highway. "Text Audra I'm on my way," he ordered.

She met him at the door, dressed in the same silky robe that had so distracted him when he arrived the evening when the private detective had trespassed. "What took you so long?" she said, pulling him inside and shutting the door behind him. Then she slipped her arms around him and kissed him, a kiss that pulled him under, out of the real world of unsolved crimes and petty annoyances into a universe where the two of them were the only things that mattered.

He broke the kiss and pushed back the edge of the robe, the sight of her nude body stirring him more than all his fantasies. He pulled her to him, smoothing his hands down her sides, then bringing them up to cup her breasts. He looked into her eyes, watching her pupils widen and darken as he brushed his thumbs across her nipples, a deep pull in his groin as the tips hardened and pressed into his palm.

"Oh, yes," she whispered, arching to him. He bent to take the tip of one breast in his mouth, swirling his tongue around the areola, the tension inside him building as she gasped. She smelled of peaches and vanilla and tasted slightly sweet. She clutched at his head, fingers digging into his scalp, the softness of her breast against his cheek. He closed his eyes, determined to savor the moment, determined not to lose it in a rush of need and heat.

He slipped his hand between her thighs, her skin warm and softer than any satin. He entered her with one finger, then two, feeling her tighten around him. She rocked forward, pressed against him, making incoherent sounds of pleasure as he dropped to his knees and sealed his mouth over her center, tasting sweet and sour and female.

He teased with his tongue, fingers still stroking inside her. She moaned, the sound resonating through him, his erection pulsing in response. He experimented with different rhythms and pressures until she rocked against him, impatient. Demanding.

He smiled against her, delighting in her pleasure, delight building and expanding as she came, thrusting hard against him, spasming against his fingers. She sagged against him, and he stood, gathering her close once more and leading her to the bedroom.

They lay down together and she opened her eyes and looked up at him, eyes still dark with desire. "Oh, that was very good," she said. "But you and I are just getting started."

Chapter Eight

Audra had lit candles in anticipation of Hud's arrival, and now she watched him undress in the golden light, revealing a lean, muscled body, strong legs and arms, and an erection that made her tighten in anticipation, desire building once more. He slid under the sheets beside her and reached for her, and she rolled on top of him, reveling in the feel of him along her full length.

Then she broke the kiss and straddled him, smoothing her palms along his shoulders and down his chest, his erection hot and eager at the junction of her thighs. He reached up to cup her breasts, gently pinching her nipples until she gasped with pleasure. "Do you like that?" he asked.

"Oh, yes." She wrapped both hands around the length of his erection, stroking until his eyes lost focus, then leaned across to take a condom from the bedside drawer, unwrap it and roll it on.

He grasped her hips and guided her as she slid over him, and he arched up to drive deeper, beginning a rhythm that she quickly modified, a thrust and parry that satisfied them both. When he reached one hand down to fondle her, she silently thanked whoever had taught him that move and abandoned herself to pleasure.

She didn't know how long they rode that wave of pleasure, but when she climaxed for the second time that night she would have said she had never enjoyed anything more.

They fell asleep in each other's arms. When she woke again, sunlight was just streaming through the gap in her bedroom curtains, and the shower was running. She smiled and wrapped her arms around her herself. She loved that Hud was so passionate and intense, but he was also so much fun. She loved his bad jokes and flippant remarks, his silly faces and even his off-key singing in the shower.

She might even be falling in love with the man himself, but she pulled back from examining those feelings too closely. They had plenty of time to explore and see what developed. No sense rushing and maybe ruining everything.

HUD DIDN'T KNOW if he had the strength to leave a naked Audra in a warm bed, but by the time he was out of the shower, she was up and dressed and had coffee going. "The day starts early at a day care center," she told him after she kissed him good morning. She handed him a mug of coffee. "What time do you have to be at work?"

"Early, too." He sipped the coffee and welcomed the bitter jolt. "I'm going to try to interview Roy Holliday's live-in girlfriend today, to see if I can figure out what he was doing that got him in trouble with the wrong people."

"I don't envy you your job," she said.

"And I don't envy you yours." He shuddered. "I'd rather face down armed criminals than a room full of two-year-olds."

She laughed. "There are days when I would, too, come to think of it."

Hud might have taken the two-year-olds over the

grieving woman he faced two hours later. Renee Delaware was pale and shaken, silent tears streaming down her face despite her efforts not to weep. "I'm sorry I'm such a mess," she kept apologizing. "I just can't believe he's gone. We were talking about getting married in the fall, and now that's never going to happen." She bit her lip, her face crumpling again.

Hud waited while she pulled herself together. "I'm sorry to have to bother you at a time like this," he said. "But I'm trying to get a picture of what he was working on, what enemies he might have."

"Anything to help find the person who did this." She blotted her eyes with a tissue and sniffed. "Ask me anything."

"What was Roy working on in the weeks before he died?" Hud asked.

"He was writing about Dane Trask. Anything he could find about the man. He was fascinated by him, and the news outlets were hungry for more stories, so Roy was giving them everything he could. He talked to people Dane worked with and veterans at Welcome Home Warriors, people who said they'd seen him at Black Canyon—anybody who could give him a new angle on the story."

"Was there anything in particular he was excited about?"

She nodded. "When he left here Wednesday morning, he said he had a hot tip that could blow the case wide open."

Hud sat forward on the edge of the sofa. "Did he say what the tip was?"

"No. He just said it was big, and that he was going to talk to Dane's daughter, to see if she had more information."

"What did he work on?" Hud asked. "Did he have a laptop, or a desktop here at the house?"

"He had a laptop," she said. "He carried it with him almost everywhere. He had it with him when he left the house the morning…" She swallowed hard. "The last time I saw him. The officer who came here to tell me they'd found…they'd found his body…said they didn't find the laptop. And I guess they're still looking for his car."

Hud nodded. "Maybe the laptop will be in the car when we find it." Though he wasn't holding out much hope of that. "So he didn't have a computer here at the house where he might have kept some of the files?"

"No."

"What about backup?" he asked. "Did he use a flash drive, or back up to the cloud?"

"The cloud. I think he had some kind of program that automatically backed up everything."

"Do you remember the name of the program?"

She shook her head. "I'm sorry, I don't."

There weren't that many. Hud had copies of the more common ones on his unit at Ranger headquarters. "Do you know his log-in information?" he asked. "His username and password? Maybe something he used for most things?" Most people didn't bother having very many different log-ins and passwords.

"I'm sorry, I don't."

"Was there somewhere he would have written them down?"

"I don't know." Her eyes filled with tears again. "I really want to help you, but I don't know. His work was his work, you know?"

"No, you're doing fine," Hud said. "Did he keep a diary or an appointment book or anything like that?"

"It was all on his phone," she said. "The officer said they haven't found that, either."

"We'll get records of his calls from his carrier," Hud said. "Do you know which one he used?"

"Yes. We both have Verizon."

That would make things a little easier. "The call record will help us figure out who he was working with." And maybe who he had talked to before he was killed. It might even be his killer.

"The officers who came here searched his desk." She nodded toward an old oak desk in the corner of the living room. "They took a few things, but there wasn't much here. And I found a few more things I saved for you."

She stood and collected a box from the kitchen table and handed it to him. "It's copies of a lot of the articles he wrote about Dane Trask, and a few other things he wrote recently. And I wrote out what I remembered about what he had been doing in the days before he disappeared."

"That's great," Hud said. "That will be really helpful." Later, Hud would read through these and build a database that could help him figure out who might have wanted the reporter out of the way. He stood, the box tucked under one arm. "If you think of anything, call me, anytime." He handed her one of his cards. "Especially if you think of that log-in information. Even if you're not sure it's for his backup files, it might be useful to us."

"I will," she promised, and walked him to the door.

She stood in the doorway and watched as he walked to his cruiser, a slight, sad figure, alone as only the grieving can be. He felt sorry for her, but told himself the best thing he could do was find the person or persons who had killed her fiancé.

Instead of going back to Ranger headquarters after his visit with Renee, he stopped by Canyon Critters Daycare. He spotted Audra on the playground, surrounded by a group of toddlers, and walked over to join her. The children stared, wide-eyed, at his uniform and weapon and, aware of their audience, Hud didn't kiss Audra, though he wanted to.

"Is something wrong?" she asked, anxiety in her eyes.

He supposed he couldn't blame her, since the only other times he'd stopped by her workplace had been to deliver bad news. "Nothing's wrong," he said. "I was in the neighborhood and thought I'd say hello."

"That's nice." The warmth of her smile took away the sting of her earlier wariness. She turned to the toddlers still gathered around her. "Everyone go play while I talk to Officer Hudson."

The children moved away in groups of two or three, some toward a play structure with swings and a miniature climbing wall, others to where two teachers were organizing a game with plastic balls and bats. "It was such a beautiful day I couldn't stand sitting in my office another minute," Audra said.

"It is," he agreed. "I may have to find an excuse to hike out into the park this afternoon."

"That shouldn't be—" But a wail from the play structure stopped her in mid-sentence. They both turned to see a thin child with long white-blond hair sitting in the dirt, bawling.

"Get up, you big baby." Another little girl, with long brown hair and rosy cheeks, stood over the first child.

"You pushed me!" the first girl sobbed.

"I did not. You're just clumsy. Ugly and clumsy." The dark-haired girl scuffed her shoe in the dirt, the resulting dust settling on the crying child.

Audra rushed to the girls, arriving at the same time as an older woman with short, graying hair. "April, get up," the older woman ordered. "You're not hurt."

"How do you know she's not hurt?" Audra squatted beside April. "Honey, are you hurt?"

"I scraped my elbow." The child displayed a bleeding elbow.

"Come on, then, let's get you into the office and clean you up." Audra took the child's arm and helped her up.

"I'll see to it." The older woman took hold of April. "You get back to your visitor." She sent Hud a narrow-eyed glance.

"April, go with Mrs. Keplar," Audra said.

Mrs. Keplar pulled April toward the building. Audra turned to the other little girl. "I didn't push her," the child said before Audra could speak. "I was trying to do like you said and be her friend and play with her, and she's so clumsy she can't even do that right."

"Mia." Audra spoke quietly. "Calling April clumsy and a crybaby is not being her friend."

"But she is clumsy and she is a crybaby." Mia's face was flushed. She looked at the children who had gathered around. "I don't want to be friends with her and you can't make me." She stalked away, half a dozen others following her.

Hud walked over to stand by Audra. "Little April looks like she'll be okay," he said. "No broken bones."

"I'm afraid there's more to this than a fall off the play structure," she said. "Mia—the girl who just left—has been bullying April. April is very shy and timid and I'm afraid that's made her a target for Mia." She turned to him, her face a mask of anguish. "I don't understand why anyone would want to bully someone else. And Mia and April are both so young. What is this kind of behavior going to do to both of them?"

Her distress pinched at him, and he struggled for something to say to ease her frustration, but as much as he was used to being in charge and having all the answers, he had none now. "I'm sorry you're having to deal with this," was all he could manage. "I can see how much it upsets you."

"Of course it upsets me. It should upset anyone." She touched his shoulder. "I really need to go in and check on April."

"No problem." He took a step back. "I'll talk to you later."

He returned to his cruiser, a dull ache in the middle of his chest. Of course Audra disliked bullies. Anyone would.

Would she dislike him if she knew he had been a bully? He thought he had put all that behind him a long time ago, but maybe there were some mistakes you could never entirely live down.

AFTER AUDRA LEFT the playground, she found April with Jana in the four-year-olds' classroom. "Hold still. I know it stings, but I need to clean it up. And will you please stop crying?" Audra heard Jana's scolding before she reached the room.

Both April and Jana looked up when Audra entered. "I've got this under control," Jana said, tossing aside a cotton ball and reaching for a bandage.

"It sounds to me like you're losing your temper," Audra said, her own voice calm. "Finish up here and I'll stay with April while you see to the other children."

"I don't need—"

"And I need you to see to the rest of your class while I stay with April." Audra put more steel in her voice. Jana made a face, but stuck the bandage on April's elbow, then stood and stalked out of the room.

"How are you feeling, honey?" Audra asked. She began to put away the first aid supplies.

April sniffed. "Okay, I guess."

"What happened before you fell?"

More sniffling, then April said, "Mia asked me if I wanted to play on the swings. I said yes, and she offered to push me. But she pushed too hard and the swing went too high. I was scared. I told her not to do it and she just laughed and said we were playing and I had to play nice. I was really scared, so I tried to get off the swing and I fell. And she called me a crybaby."

Audra held back a sigh. Had Mia set up the situation to frighten April? Or did she simply not know how to play with a timid child? Audra was debating how best to approach this when Brenda rushed into the room. "You have a phone call you need to take," she said.

"Take a message," Audra said. "I have something else I need to see to."

"I really think you need to take this." Brenda glanced at April, then leaned closer. "It's April's mom," she whispered.

Audra frowned. "All right. You stay with April until Mrs. Keplar returns with the other children."

Audra shut the door to her office, took a deep breath, then answered the phone. "Hello, Mrs. Patrick," she said. "What can I do for you?"

"You can tell me why you continue to allow my daughter to be bullied. Why there wasn't proper supervision on the playground this afternoon. Why my daughter was put into a situation where she could have been badly hurt."

How had Mrs. Patrick already heard about this incident? Someone must have telephoned her, but who? Brenda? Jana? Now didn't seem the appropriate time to ask.

"I was on the playground this afternoon, Mrs. Patrick," she said. "April and Mia were playing on the swings and appeared to be having a good time—and then April was on the ground crying. I take it she jumped out of the swing because she was afraid."

"You shouldn't have let her anywhere near that little bully," Mrs. Patrick. "What if April had broken her arm? I can't believe this. I'm coming over there right now and I'm withdrawing April from your school. I want her ready to go, with all her things, and I expect a full refund of this month's fees."

Not waiting for an answer, Mrs. Patrick hung up. Audra dropped into her desk chair. She didn't blame Mrs. Patrick for being angry. Maybe Audra was even partly to blame, for encouraging Mia to befriend April. If she'd opted to separate the two girls instead of trying for reconciliation, maybe this never would have happened.

Resigned, she returned to the four-year-olds' classroom. April sat in a beanbag chair in the reading nook, curled in on herself, while the rest of the class gathered around Jana, who was laying out items for what Audra thought was a science experiment. Audra cleared her throat and Jana looked up. "I just need a moment of your time," Audra said, and returned to the hallway.

Jana joined her a moment later. "What is it?" she asked. "I just got the children settled. I decided it was better to leave April to herself than to try to do anything with her."

"April's mother is coming to pick her up soon," Audra said. "I need you to gather all her belongings and have them ready to go. Mrs. Patrick is withdrawing her from school."

"That's probably for the best," Jana said. "I don't think April has the social maturity for a school like this."

Audra didn't want to hear Jana's opinions on the matter. "Did you call Mrs. Patrick?" she asked.

"A parent should always be contacted immediately if their child is injured at school."

"Then I'm the one who should have contacted April's mother."

"I'm her teacher. I saw it as my responsibility." Her clipped tone and the stubborn set of her jaw made it clear she wouldn't change her mind about this.

"Gather April's things, and I'll take her to the office with me to wait for her mother."

Jana returned to the classroom, and Audra leaned against the wall beside the door to wait. She couldn't help feeling judgment behind everything Jana said to her. Was that because the judgment was really there, or because of Audra's own insecurities?

If her father was around, she would call him and ask his advice. He had always done a good job of bolstering her spirits and helping her see solutions to problems. If he had died, she'd be grieving his departure. Instead, she felt a confusing mixture of anger and loss. He had sent messages to other people since his disappearance—why hadn't he made it a point to contact her?

April emerged from the classroom a few minutes later, backpack on her shoulder and her arms laden with a box that appeared to contain school papers and supplies, a water bottle, a bunch of paper flowers and a box of tissues. Audra forced cheerfulness into her voice. "Your mom's coming to pick you up. You can wait in my office until she gets here."

"Am I in trouble?" April asked, freckles standing out against her pale skin.

Audra melted in sympathy for the child. She'd been so focused on her own troubles without thinking about how April must feel. "You're not in trouble," she said, one hand on the girl's shoulder. "Not at all. Your mom just thought you might need a break."

April nodded. "Yeah. I do."

Mrs. Patrick arrived fifteen minutes later, tension radiating from her slender body. "Are you okay?" she asked April, accepting the box of belongings from her.

"I'm okay now." April displayed her bandaged elbow. "Mrs. Keplar fixed me up."

"I should hope so." Mrs. Patrick glanced at Audra, then looked away again. "I'm very disappointed things have come to this," she said. "But I hope you understand why I can't allow April to remain here, where she doesn't feel safe."

"I'm very sorry, Mrs. Patrick," Audra began. "I—"

"After reading the papers this morning, I was already thinking that this school was not the place for my girl." Mrs. Patrick slipped the backpack from April's shoulders as she spoke. "But after this, I'm sure of it."

"What do you mean?" Audra asked. "What was in the papers?"

Still the woman didn't look at her, fussing with smoothing April's hair. "I'm not saying you had anything to do with the murder of that young man, but it doesn't look good, does it? Come on, April, we need to go." She took her daughter's hand, then at last returned her gaze to Audra. "I'll expect that refund."

Then she was gone, leaving Audra stunned. Were the papers saying that she had something to do with Roy Holliday's death? Or had someone else died? She thought of calling Hud and asking him if he knew what Mrs. Patrick was talking about, but told herself that was silly. She could figure this out easily enough on her own.

She gathered her purse and her keys. "I have to leave

early today," she told Brenda as she passed through her assistant's office.

"Are you okay?" Brenda rose from the chair behind her desk, her expression filled with concern. "You don't look well."

"I'm sure it's nothing. I just… I just need to get home." She all but ran from the building to the safety of her car. On the way home, she stopped at a convenience store and bought a copy of each of the two papers for sale—the *Denver Post* and a local paper. She didn't look at them until she was home, her door locked and her shades drawn. Then she sat at the kitchen table, took a deep breath and opened the local paper first. She stared at the bold black letters of the headline:

Holliday May Be Trask's Latest Victim—Trask's Daughter Last to See Reporter Alive.

Chapter Nine

Hud read the article that filled the front page of the Montrose paper, anger growing as he read. The piece reported how freelance reporter Roy Holliday had been found on public lands just outside Black Canyon of Gunnison National Park, a single gunshot wound to the back of the head. Holliday had been reporting on the Dane Trask disappearance, and Trask's daughter, Audra Trask, had been the last person Holliday was known to have spoken to before he died.

The article went on to detail Trask's disappearance and repeat the worst rumors about him—that he was accused of embezzling money from his former employer, TDC Enterprises, that he had been the chief suspect in the murder of a female hiker and was suspected in several other attacks on hikers, as well as theft from campers in the park. The writer concluded by alluding to unidentified "authorities" who "are not ruling out a link between Holliday's visit with Audra Trask and his death."

When he finished reading, Hud sat back in his chair, fury growing. He wanted to punch somebody for filling the public's heads full of lies and speculation. Searching for a target, he spotted Faith Martin across the room. As the department's liaison with both the press and the Montrose Sheriff's Department, Martin would be most familiar with the players in this fiasco. He stalked to her desk and tossed the paper onto it. "How do reporters get away with lies like this?" he asked. "And who are the 'authorities' he's quoting?"

Martin, a petite woman whose brown curls fought to escape the bun at the nape of her neck, removed her ear-buds and looked up at him, then, registering his anger, studied the paper before her. Frown lines formed between her neatly shaped eyebrows. "The official statement I is-sued from this department said nothing about Dane Trask or Audra Trask."

"Then someone leaked the information about Audra."

"It could have been someone from the Montrose po-lice," she said. "They responded to the call at her house the day Holliday disappeared. Or maybe the reporter saw the item on the police report and put two and two together."

"It's all speculation and innuendo," Hud said. "Dane Trask isn't a suspect, and Audra didn't have anything to do with Holliday's death."

Martin shrugged. "It's the kind of thing that sells pa-pers."

"It's wrong."

Martin looked up at him, her brown eyes calm. "It's upsetting, but there's nothing we can do about it. We have more important things to focus on."

Right. He returned to the desk but didn't sit, still trying to calm down. He wanted to call Audra, but she'd still be at school. She wouldn't appreciate the interruption, and clearly, when he talked to her earlier she hadn't known about the article. He'd call later and break the news gen-tly, just so she'd be prepared tomorrow.

He read the article again. The story didn't say any-thing about Roy Holliday's body being kept in cold storage before it was dumped. That was a heavy point in Trask's favor. Not only had he had no motive to kill the reporter, it was doubtful he had access to anyplace to stash the body.

As Hud flipped through the rest of the paper, searching for any further mention of Trask or Audra, he began to calm down. Martin was right. The paper had been featuring the Dane Trask story at every opportunity for weeks now. Readers were obviously hungry for this local mystery.

On page six of the paper he focused on a small article near the bottom of the page. TDC Fined for Falsifying Reports.

The EPA has levied fines in the amount of $350,000 against TDC Enterprises in connection with the cleanup of the Mary Lee mine earlier this year. TDC, which was awarded the contract to mitigate heavy metals and other contaminants at the former gold and silver mine in the Curecanti Wilderness outside of Montrose, has been found guilty of falsifying some of its reports showing lower-than-actual levels of contaminants. Though TDC has since corrected the reports, and the mine site has been deemed satisfactorily mitigated, the EPA issued a statement saying, "It's important that mistakes like this not go unpunished. The public is entitled to accurate data about the projects its tax dollars are funding."

TDC vice president Mitchell Ruffino told reporters at a press conference Tuesday morning that the reports were falsified by former employee Dane Trask, who is himself subject to a massive manhunt in Black Canyon of Gunnison National Park since

*disappearing there six weeks ago. "TDC and its
employees take pride in the work we have done to
completely clean up the contamination at the Mary
Lee mine," Ruffino said. "We're disappointed that
the EPA sought to blame us for the actions of one
clearly troubled man, but as good public citizens,
we will pay the fines and continue to set the kind
of environmental example we hope other corpora-
tions will follow."*

Hud sat back, digesting this information. From the
very first, Dane Trask had tried to focus attention on
the work TDC was doing at the Mary Lee mine. The day
his truck was found at the bottom of Gunnison Gorge
in the national park, he had left a flash drive for his former administrative assistant. Hud himself had analyzed
the contents of that flash drive, which contained parts
of environmental assessments from the Mary Lee—reports showing much higher levels of contaminants than
TDC had reported.

Later, Trask had mailed a press release to his former
girlfriend, asking her to give it to reporters she knew.
The press release—which had never been published—
alleged that TDC had falsified the reports about the
mine. Samples Trask's former admin collected from
the site seemed to back up this assertion, but only a
short while later, TDC held a ceremony to announce
the mine was "fully mitigated"—and that appeared to
be the case. So who was lying? Or was everyone shad-
ing the truth?

"What are you scowling about?"

Hud looked up to see Jason Beck standing at the corner of his desk. He straightened. "What's up?" he asked,
ignoring his friend's question.

Beck sat on the corner of the desk. "I've been reinterviewing construction people, trying to establish some kind of connection to that dump site or Roy Holliday, but getting nowhere. What about you?"

"I talked to Holliday's girlfriend this morning. She said he was working on something big to do with the Dane Trask story. He'd been talking to everyone who knew Dane, searching for new angles to report, since the local paper was hungry for more stories from him. The girlfriend said Holliday had a 'hot tip' he wanted to talk to Audra about."

"No idea what the tip was?" Beck asked.

"None."

"Then we need to talk to the people Holliday talked to," Beck said. "One of them must have given him this tip—and it may be what got him killed."

Hud blew out a breath. "You're right. And I did get some names from her. We can get others from the stories he filed."

"Let's divide the list," Beck said. "I'd like to solve a case for a change, instead of beating ourselves up chasing Dane Trask."

"Did you see the latest edition of the local paper?" Hud asked.

"No, why?"

Hud showed him the articles about Roy Holliday's murder and the EPA fine against TDC Enterprises. "It doesn't really help us, does it?" Beck said. "You don't think there's really a link between Audra and Holliday's death—other than he wanted to ask her about something that might be related to his killer."

"I don't think that, but the public might," Hud said. "I guess I worry about how this might affect her. She's having a hard enough time, with her dad constantly in the news."

"So—something going on between you two?" Beck asked.

Hud shrugged. "Something." He wasn't ready to define his feelings for Audra. Not yet. Better to keep things loose and see what developed. Maybe it was a cop-out. Or maybe it was good protective instincts.

His phone buzzed, and he pulled it out to answer. His heart sped up when he saw Audra's name on the screen. Beck waved and walked away, and Hud turned his back on the room and answered the call. "I was going to call you later," he said.

"Do you think you could come over to my house? Now." No missing the strain in her voice.

He headed for the door, digging out his keys as he walked. "What's wrong?" he asked.

"Nothing. I mean, I'm not in any danger or anything. There are just a bunch of reporters here and I'd feel better if I wasn't alone."

"I'm on my way."

AUDRA HAD TRIED to be polite with the reporters. That was her first mistake. There were three of them—two women and a man. They had identified themselves and who they worked for, knocking on her door only minutes after she finished reading the article about Roy Holliday's death. She immediately forgot everything they told her in the shock of seeing them there, as if they had been waiting out of sight to pounce when she was most vulnerable.

Perhaps they had. She tried to tell them she had no comment, but they continued to fire questions at her, the words as stinging as gravel thrown at her. Finally, on the verge of tears, she had retreated into the house, where she sat now, huddled in the darkness, feeling foolish and ashamed. She hated cowering in here, as if she truly had something to hide. Her father, she was sure, would not have put up with such behavior. But she wasn't as strong as Dane was. All she wanted was to go to sleep and to wake up tomorrow to find her life was back to normal, with her father home and plans for her new school moving forward.

Voices rose, and she moved to the front door and risked a peek outside. Hud was making his way up the walkway, shoving past the reporters—who had been joined by two more people now. They shouted questions at Hud, who moved past them, stone-faced.

She opened the door and stepped outside. As one, the group around Hud left him and surged toward her. "Why are the police here?" one of the women demanded. "Does this have anything to do with Roy Holliday's death?"

Hud reached her and took her arm. "Let's go back inside," he said, speaking softly but firmly.

She shrugged out of his grasp. "No," she said. "Maybe if I say something they'll leave."

"I don't think—"

But the reporters had moved in. "What was your relationship to Roy Holliday?" one asked.

"I didn't know Roy Holliday," she said. "He came to my house pretending to be the parent of one of my students and after I let him in he questioned me. I refused to talk to him and called the police. When the police arrived, he was gone. That's the whole story and that's all there is to it."

"Do you think your father killed him?" another reporter asked.

"No. Why would my father kill him?"

"To protect you from being harassed," someone said.

"That's ridiculous. My father didn't have anything to do with Roy Holliday or his death. In fact, he hasn't done half the things you people insinuate he's done. For you to try to make him out as a murderer is disgraceful."

She probably could have said more, but Hud succeeded in pushing her inside and closing the door behind her. She pressed her back to the wall and closed her eyes, fighting tears, waiting for her heart to slow. When she opened her eyes again, Hud was watching her. "I imagine that will all be in the paper tomorrow, with some sensational headline," she said.

"Probably." He held out his arms. "Come here."

She sighed as he wrapped her in an embrace, and she rested her head on his shoulder. "I know I shouldn't have talked to them, but I couldn't listen to them say those things about my father. He doesn't have anyone else to defend him."

"It's okay," he said. "Maybe it helped to get some things off your chest."

"It did help, some." She pulled back far enough to look into his eyes. "Thanks for coming over. Part of me wishes I were strong enough to stand up to this myself, but the rest of me is really glad you're here."

"There's no weakness in relying on your friends," he said, but the tenderness in his eyes made her wonder if he was thinking of himself as more than a friend. Was she?

She pulled away and walked into the kitchen, where she poured a glass of water. He followed. "How did it go after I left the school this afternoon?" he asked. "With the little girls?"

"Not good." She took a long drink of water, then set the glass on the counter. "April's mother withdrew her from school. She's furious that this happened with a bunch of adults standing around, supposedly watching.

I guess in her shoes I'd feel the same. But the worst of it was, as she was leaving, she said something about how, though she didn't believe the things the papers were saying about me, it didn't look good, did it? I rushed right out and bought a paper, then came home. I had just read the article in the *Daily Press* about Roy Holliday and my and my dad's supposed role in the murder when those reporters showed up."

"Did you see the other article in the paper?" he asked. "About TDC?"

She groaned. "There were others? What did they say?"

"The EPA is fining TDC for falsifying environmental reports about the Mary Lee mine—the very thing your father was accusing them of."

"That's something, I guess," she said. "I hope Dad sees it, whatever he's up to."

"Except TDC places the blame on him," Hud said. "They say he falsified the reports."

She shook her head. "He wouldn't. The thing people don't realize—can't realize unless they know him—is that my father doesn't lie. He just doesn't. And he'd have no reason to do so in this case." Agitation bubbled up again. "I can't stand people saying all these bad things about him and there's no way to defend him. It's not just what they say—it's how it feels. Like I'm a little girl, being bullied all over again. The name-calling and lying—it feels the same."

"Words can hurt as much as blows," he said. "We don't always think about it, but they can."

"I hate bullies!"

She wanted him to pull her to him once more. Instead, he took a step back, mouth tight. A chill settled between them. "What is it?" she asked. "What's wrong?"

He shook his head. "Nothing. But if you think you'll be okay now, I have to go."

"Oh. Of course. But I don't understand. Did I say something to upset you?"

"It's okay." He smiled, but it wasn't convincing. "If you need anything later, just call."

Then he was gone, the door closing softly behind him. She followed and locked the door, listening to the reporters outside calling out questions, which he didn't answer. Something had happened just now to change the whole mood between them. She had said she hated bullies—but why would that upset him? Of course she didn't really hate a little girl like Mia—she hated the child's behavior. If Hud didn't like her word choice, why didn't he say so?

That moment when she had been in his arms had felt so warm and comforting. Now she felt more desolate and alone than before.

"WHAT AN IDIOT!" Hud cursed himself as he drove away from Audra's home. The look on her face when he'd left her made him feel like more of a jerk than ever. He'd overreacted to her declaration that she hated bullies—as if she had declared she hated him. But what would she think if she knew he'd once been the number one bully in his high school—a boy so cruel and relentless he had driven a fellow classmate to attempt suicide?

His stomach still knotted at the memory. He had come a long way since his mixed-up childhood, but would Audra believe that? Would her history as the object of a bully's taunts allow her to see past how truly awful he had once been?

He was still preoccupied with these thoughts when he returned to Ranger headquarters. "There's someone here to see you," Officer Reynolds said as he walked in. He nodded toward Hud's desk, where Renee Delaware sat, focused on the phone in her hand.

"Ms. Delaware, how can I help you?" he asked, approaching her.

She looked up and slid the phone into the back pocket of her jeans, then dug a piece of paper from the front pocket. "I found this when I was going through the drawer of the nightstand on Roy's side of the bed," she said. "I think it might be his log-in username and password."

Hud studied the series and numbers and letters scribbled in blue felt-tip pen on the paper. H0liday95 and 164951225. "What makes you think this is his log-in and password?" he asked.

"His birthday is…was… April 16 and he was born in 1995. Christmas is 12-25—his favorite holiday and a play on his last name." She pressed her lips together, clearly reining in her emotions.

Hud nodded. "Thanks," he said. "And thank you for stopping by. This could be a big help."

"Nothing can bring him back," she said. "But I think it really would help if you could find out who killed him. I know people didn't always like him asking questions, but that was his job, and he was good at it. He didn't deserve to die because of it."

"We'll let you know if we find anything," Hud said. "Thank you again for coming in."

She nodded, then stood and left.

Hud settled behind his desk and pulled up an automatic data backup program he knew to be common with journalists. He was entering Roy Holliday's log-in information when Reynolds approached his desk. "You're working on the Holliday murder, right?" he asked.

Hud nodded, still focused on the computer.

"Delta County Sheriff's Department found his car this morning," Reynolds said. "Abandoned behind some storage units out in Whitewater."

"Oh?" Hud looked up, alert. "Did they find anything in it? His computer?"

Reynolds shook his head. "I sent you a copy of the report, but the gist of it is the car was stripped, the interior gutted. They even removed the seats, then set fire to what was left."

"Whitewater is a long way from where Holliday's body was found," Hud said.

"Less than an hour's drive," Reynolds said. "There aren't any neighbors near the place, so they haven't been able to determine when the vehicle showed up there."

"That was Holliday's fiancée who was in here just now," Hud said. "She found a username and password that may get us into the cloud storage where Holliday backed up his computer files."

"Let's hope his killer didn't get there first," Reynolds said.

Hud nodded and went back to work. He typed in the password, pressed Enter and waited. A thrill shot through him as the screen filled with a file directory. "Did you get something?" Reynolds leaned in closer.

"Yeah." Hud began typing, sorting the files by date, most recent to oldest. "It looks like over a hundred files here. This could take a while."

"Then I'll leave you to it." Reynolds clapped him on the back.

Hud didn't hear him leave. He was already deep into the hunt for anything that might lead them to a killer.

Chapter Ten

Audra arrived at work the next morning, prepared to deal with Jana and Mia and the whole bullying situation. She'd decided to implement a school-wide anti-bullying curriculum, and had located some age-appropriate resources the teachers could use in the classroom. She would take the sad situation with April and turn it into a program everyone involved could be proud of—a model for other schools like hers to follow, even.

But she forgot all of this when a pale and anxious Brenda met her at the front door. "Have you seen the papers this morning?" Brenda asked. "Or watched the news?"

"No." Audra didn't like to start her day with strife and bad news, so she kept her television off and her radio tuned to her favorite music station on her drive in to work.

Brenda clutched her wrist. "It's bad," she said. "I'm so sorry, but it is. I've already had calls from two parents, saying they're going to withdraw their children from school. I put the phone back to the answering service after the first two. I didn't know what else to do."

"What's going on? Why do they want to withdraw their children?" Audra's hands shook as she opened the door to her office.

"I left a copy of the paper on your desk." Brenda bit her lip. "I don't even know if what it says is true, but people believe it's true, and I guess that's just as bad." Then she turned and hurried from the room, as if determined to outrun a storm.

Audra shut the door behind her and stared at the paper on the desk blotter. Even upside-down, she could read the headline: Dane Trask's Daughter Defends Father, Despite Their Troubled Past.

She frowned. She and her father didn't have a troubled past. They'd always gotten along well. He had always been a part of her life, and he had always been the one person in the world she could count on. With growing dread, she moved around the desk and sank into the chair. Then, as if she were approaching a poisonous snake, she cautiously leaned forward and began to read.

The beginning of the story wasn't bad—a rehash of yesterday's encounter with the press outside her house, and a somewhat garbled quote in which she said people calling her father a murderer was disgraceful. But the second paragraph sent a stabbing pain through her. "To some, Audra Trask's defense of her father might come as a surprise, considering that in her late teens, her father had her forcibly committed in an attempt to deal with her out-of-control drug addiction. Since then, others close to Trask say Audra has drifted in and out of his life, Trask always stepping forward to bail her out of trouble when needed. Most recently, Trask may have played a role in his daughter being awarded the contract for a new preschool and day care facility on the campus of a new elementary school TDC Enterprises is constructing in the northeast part of the county. At the time of Trask's disappearance, his daughter admitted she hadn't spoken to her father for two weeks."

She struggled to breathe, to overcome the red mist of rage that clouded her vision. The paper made her sound like a junkie whose father had had to send her away in a straitjacket—a spoiled daughter who only turned to Dad when she needed money or help out of trouble. Yes, she had become addicted to prescription painkillers in her late teens and yes, her father had persuaded her to go to rehab, and had paid for the treatment, or at least the portion not covered by his health insurance policy. But there had been no force involved. Audra had been desperate for help, and so grateful her father had come to her rescue at a time when she felt so powerless.

As for the rest, it was all lies. She had not been "in and out" of her father's life. She hadn't spoken to him in the two weeks before he disappeared because she had been visiting friends in France. And he had nothing to do with her getting the contract with the school district—Dane was an engineer with TDC, not someone with any kind of influence over the local school board.

Steeling herself for more bad news, she continued reading the article. After a summary of Dane's disappearance and the various accusations against him, her gaze landed on a quote attributed to Jana Keplar. "Since taking a position as a teacher at Canyon Critters Daycare, it's become clear to me that Ms. Trask has some problems she needs to address. I think the school district will be reassessing whether she is really the person they want operating their new day care and preschool."

Audra made a strangled sound in her throat, then sucked in a deep breath. *Think*, she reminded herself. What was she going to do about this? There were so many things wrong with this article. She needed to address them all. There was Jana, of course. Should she fire the woman for speaking against her? No—she wanted to fire her, but that would only cause problems, not the least of which is she didn't have anyone to take over Jana's class. And the students and parents clearly loved her. If Audra fired Jana, she'd come off looking vindictive and immature. Not the sort of person anyone would want to trust. So she'd leave Jana be for now.

What else? She probably needed to contact the school superintendent and persuade him that she was capable, stable and exactly the person he wanted for the new facility. But how could she do that when he was already upset about her father? This article wasn't going to help her standing in his eyes. She needed to find someone who had more influence than she did to speak up on her behalf. She'd have to think about that one.

She scanned the article once more. Who were these mysterious "others close to Trask" who had said she was "in and out of his life"? Not his former girlfriend, Eve Shea. She and Audra had always gotten along great. She didn't know of any other women her father had dated recently. Was it someone from Welcome Home Warriors? The men and women who were part of the veterans' group Dane had founded didn't really know her. But she had attended events there when her dad invited her, so they would have seen her with him and realized how close they were.

Coworkers? A sensation went through her as if a nerve had been touched. Ever since her father had disappeared, TDC Enterprises had done everything they could to discredit him. Was this simply one more way to get back at her father, by lying about his relationship with her?

She folded the newspaper and tucked it away. In the background, the phone rang, falling silent after three rings as the answering service picked up. She'd have to deal with those calls from disgruntled parents soon, mustering every bit of confidence possible to persuade them that the article was filled with lies and exaggerations, and their children were in good hands with her.

Her father had taught her to stand up for herself. When people went after you, you didn't sit back and take it— you fought back. But how was she going to fight back against this onslaught, when she wasn't even sure who her enemy was?

HUD FELT SICK to his stomach as he listened to two newscasters discuss Audra Trask's "sad history" of drug addiction and her stormy relationship with her father. "An old familiar story," the male newscaster said. "One many parents have dealt with."

"But one that has captured the public's interest, now that Dane Trask is the most wanted man in the county, if not the state," his female counterpart concluded.

Hud switched off the television and sank back in his chair. Audra had been an addict? It shouldn't surprise him. Drug addiction cut across all socioeconomic levels. As a DEA agent, he dealt with the ugly side of addiction—people who stole from their parents, who prostituted themselves and broke ties with everyone who loved them, at the mercy of their addiction. Good for her getting past that—so many people didn't. And he was pretty certain he'd know now if she was hiding any current addiction. The woman didn't even drink!

As for her relationship with Dane, she had always spoken of her father warmly. If they had had their difficulties in the past—and what parent and child hadn't?—she didn't consider them significant enough to share with him. That part of the news story had been more speculation than fact, the word "allegedly" liberally sprinkled in the reporting.

He tried to call Audra's cell, but his call went straight to voice mail. She was probably getting calls from the press and most of the people she knew. Fine. He'd go to her. He was supposed to continue working his way through Roy Holliday's computer files, but so far that had turned up nothing. Whatever was in there to be discovered would have to wait a little longer. Things had been awkward between him and Audra when he'd left yesterday—all his fault. He'd find a way to make it up to her now. She didn't need to be facing this alone.

Everything at the school looked normal to him—no crowds of reporters or irate parents. The playground was empty, but kids didn't have recess all day, did they? But inside, things were definitely more tense. The phone rang and rang, and when Hud entered the office, Audra's assistant scarcely looked up from her computer. "Audra isn't here right now. You'll have to come back later," she said, in the tone of voice of someone who had repeated the same phrase over and over all morning.

"I'm Officer Mark Hudson," he said in his sternest voice.

The woman's head snapped up. She stared at him, wide-eyed. "Is something wrong?" she asked. "Is Audra in more trouble?"

"She's not in trouble," he said. "Where is she?"

"Can I help you with something, Officer?" A tall woman with gray streaks in her short dark hair stepped out of Audra's office. She looked familiar, but Hud couldn't remember her name.

"Who are you?" he asked.

"I'm Jana Keplar." She moved toward him. "I'm helping Brenda since Audra isn't in."

"Where is Audra?" he asked, annoyance giving a harder edge to his voice.

Jana's expression, which he would have labeled smug, didn't change. "I think she went home. With a headache."

The constant ringing of the phone was enough to give anyone a headache. But things must have been very bad for Audra to leave the school. She didn't strike him as one who would abandon her post. "I'm surprised she left," he said.

"Oh, she didn't want to go." The assistant spoke from behind him. "Jana and I had to talk her into it. With the news reports and everything, it's been a little wild here. No one can get anything done. We decided if she wasn't here, there would be no one for the parents and reporters to talk to, so they'd give up and leave us alone." She looked toward the phone, which, after a brief respite, had started up again.

"Is that working?" Hud asked.

"It worked with the people who came in person," Brenda said. "We're letting the calls go to voice mail."

"We'll be lucky if we don't have to close the school after this," Jana said. "But maybe it would be for the best, in the long run."

Hud didn't wait to hear more. He left and drove to Audra's house. The relief that washed over him when he spotted her car in the driveway surprised him. He hadn't been able to admit to himself that he was half-afraid she might do something drastic, such as confronting reporters, or worse, that she might try to harm herself.

He had to ring the bell twice before she answered. She looked pale and a little drawn, but if she had cried about this, she had done so earlier. "I didn't answer right away because I thought you might be a reporter," she said, leading the way into the living room.

"I heard the news reports," he said. "How are you doing?"

"I've been better."

"You should have called me right away. You shouldn't have to deal with this alone."

She shrugged. "I thought maybe you wouldn't want to see me again."

The words hurt, but he couldn't say he didn't deserve them. "I know I was a jerk last time we spoke," he said. "I'm sorry."

She faced him at last. "You're sorry? I'm the one who should be apologizing, for not being honest with you about my past. I did struggle with drug addiction—but it was nothing like the papers made it out to be. And everything they said about my relationship with my father was a lie." She dropped onto the sofa, elbows on her knees, face in her hands.

Hud sat beside her, close, but not touching. "Your past is your past," he said. "Where you've been tells me a lot about you, but it's not as important as where you are now—who you are now."

She sat up straighter but didn't look at him. "What does my past tell you about me? That I was a low-life addict? Someone with no self-control who used drugs as an escape?"

The harshness in her voice was like a barb under his skin. "It tells me you had real pain in your life," he said. "Pain you tried to overcome, maybe the only way you knew how. But you got past that. You found the strength to overcome an addiction that a lot of people struggle with. I think that probably made you wiser and more empathetic than a lot of people."

The tears came then, sliding down her cheeks, though she didn't make a sound. He took her hand in his, and she leaned over until her head rested on his shoulder. He fished a handkerchief from his pocket, and she took it. Neither of them said anything, but he felt some of the tension ease from her body. After a while, she began to talk. "I was nineteen. I tore my knee up skiing and had to have surgery. The doctor gave me Vicodin for the pain in my knee, but it made me feel better in other ways, too. I'd just broken up with my first serious boyfriend. My mom had married again, and that put some distance between us. But the pills made me feel like I could cope." She shrugged. "I guess that's how a lot of people get hooked. I thought I could handle it. It wasn't like I was out on the street trying to score heroin or something. But I wasn't handling it. I wasn't handling anything."

"But you got help," he said. "You overcame the addiction."

"Dad is the one who saved me. He knew a lot about addiction—he worked with a lot of veterans who struggled through the group he founded here—Welcome Home Warriors? Anyway, he got me the professional help I needed and paid for rehab, but mostly, he just listened." She sat up and angled toward him. "You know how in AA, people have sponsors—someone they can call, night or day, when they're feeling tempted? Dad was that for me."

"That's why you don't drink alcohol, isn't it?" he asked.

She nodded. "In rehab I learned that people with drug addiction problems also have a greater likelihood of becoming alcohol-dependent. I don't want to take a chance." She dabbed at her eyes, then returned the damp handkerchief. "So now you know my dark secret."

He looked down at the handkerchief, a smudge of her pink lipstick on one corner. "You're not the only one with secrets, you know," he said.

She stared at him. "Don't tell me you did drugs, too."

"No. I think maybe what I did was worse."

It was her turn to take his hand, her fingers soft and cool, twining with his. "No judgments," she said.

"Yeah, well, the reason I left the way I did yesterday was because you said you hated bullies, and I was a bully."

Confusion clouded her eyes. "You? But you're one of the nicest, most patient—"

"I was a bully," he repeated. "In high school. There was a kid in one of my classes—one of those awkward kids who doesn't fit in. He tried to be friends with me, and I lashed out. And I didn't just do it once. I made him a target. I teased him and humiliated him." He swallowed hard. Even after all this time, it was hard to talk about. To think he had had that kind of darkness in him. "I don't know why I did it. I think—I think I was afraid of being like him. Of being the weak kid no one else liked. So I lashed out. It made me feel stronger. Safer." He bowed his head and squeezed his eyes shut, telling himself he wasn't going to break down. Not after all this time.

Her fingers traced gentle circles across the back of his hand. "What happened to change you?" she asked, her voice just above a whisper.

"The boy—his name was Cameron—tried to kill himself. His father found him. He'd…he'd tried to hang himself."

"Oh, Hud." She leaned her head on his shoulder once more.

But the worst was out. He felt stronger now. "Cameron told his parents what was going on. They told the school. I was expelled, and my parents put me in counseling, and the counselor referred me to a program for bullies. There were a couple of cops who volunteered with the program, and they got me interested in police work. I was lucky, really."

"You changed. I can't tell you how hopeful that makes me." She sounded as if she meant it.

"I was thinking about that little girl at your school. Mia," he said.

Audra nodded. "She's not a bad child. I know that. And I tried talking to her parents, but they refused to see that there was any problem. Her teacher is convinced that the whole problem was with April. Now that she is no longer enrolled, there won't be a problem. But I'd like to do what I can to address situations like this from both sides. In fact, I spent half the night looking up resources and planning a curriculum that would address bullying for all ages. It was going to be a model program. And then the news about my past addiction came out. I had parents calling all morning, wanting to withdraw their children, or at least demanding to know if what they had read was true."

"Your assistant told me they sent you home as a stalling tactic," he said.

"You went by the school?"

"When you didn't answer your phone, I checked there first."

"How was it? I hated to leave Brenda to deal with things alone, but under the circumstances, my presence there was only fanning the flames. I'm hoping, given a few hours, some of the most heated emotions will cool, though I'll have to address the situation one way or another."

"The phone was ringing a lot, but there were no parents, and no reporters, at the school when I was there. But your assistant—Brenda—wasn't alone. Jana Keplar was in the office with her."

Audra straightened, color flooding back to her face. "Jana had no business being in the office. She has a class to see to. And after what she said about me to reporters, she's lucky to have a job."

"I only heard the story on the television news," he said. "What did the papers say?"

In answer, she got up, retrieved a folded newspaper from her bag and thrust it at him. He scanned through the article, then shook his head. "Where do they get all this about your relationship with your father being rocky?"

"I don't know," she said. "But I'm guessing TDC. Anyone he worked with could claim to be close to him, and ever since he left, they've been doing everything possible to discredit him. This is just one more way to embarrass him."

He tossed the paper aside. "I'm sorry you're having to go through this," he said. "What can I do to help?"

She sat beside him once more and wrapped her arms around him. "You're already doing it," she said. "Right now."

IT WAS WELL after noon before Hud made it to Ranger headquarters. He'd called in earlier, claiming he needed to see to a personal matter and would be in late. Thankfully, no one had questioned him too closely. Audra had assured him she was fine, and while he wanted to get back to her as soon as possible, he knew he'd be working late, going through the rest of Roy Holliday's computer files.

So far he'd read through numerous drafts of articles Holliday had written—many about Dane Trask, but also features on Black Canyon of Gunnison National Park, and one profile of TDC Enterprises that delved into the history of the company, its principal officers and its current projects, which included the elementary school where Audra was scheduled to relocate her business.

Other files consisted of transcripts of interviews, though Holliday had a maddening habit of identifying the people he interviewed only by their initials. Sometimes Hud was able to figure out that MC in one interview was Michael Carter quoted in an article Holliday had written, but other times the identities of the interviewees remained a mystery.

A third set of files seemed to consist of to-do lists, which included everything from "change oil" to "meeting with RJ 2:15." Using these lists and the dates the files originated, Hud was able to construct a rough schedule of Holliday's activities in the weeks prior to his death. He focused on appointments, most of which were either for interviews or research for articles, or with editors with whom Holliday worked.

He found a note that said "see AT" dated the day before Holliday disappeared. Was this a reminder to himself to stop by Audra Trask's house to try to interview her? The day before that was a note to "call MR" but Hud had not been able to determine who MR might be, and had found no reference to anyone with those initials in the files, and no interview or other notes about such a person. He was still waiting on Holliday's phone records.

Hud sat back and studied the schedule he had made of Holliday's activities in the days before the reporter died. He believed Holliday had made some kind of contact with the person or persons who killed him during that time. He had met up with them again shortly after he left Audra's house Wednesday morning. He and his car had been taken, Holliday killed and his body put in cold storage, then dumped, and his car and everything in it destroyed and dumped. Why? The most obvious answer was that in the course of his reporting, Holliday had come across information his killer or killers didn't want made public.

Holliday had primarily been working on the Dane Trask disappearance at the time of his death. Had he learned something about Trask?

He groaned and tried to rub the kink out of his neck. Time to share what he'd learned with the rest of the team. Maybe other eyes would see what he hadn't. Even though Holliday was dead, there was always a sense of urgency in a murder case. Too often, the murderer would strike again. Hud wanted to stop him before that happened.

He was on his way to the commander's office when his cell phone rang. "Officer Hudson," he answered.

"Martin Burns from Montrose PD. You're working on the Dane Trask disappearance, aren't you?"

Hud remembered the MPD detective who had questioned Richard Salazar. "I am," he said. "What's up?"

"Someone broke into Trask's house this morning. I figured someone from the Ranger Brigade would want to take a look."

"I'll be right over." Dane Trask's home had sat empty for seven weeks. Had the vacant property been too tempting for thieves, or was someone after something in particular?

Chapter Eleven

"A neighbor saw someone over here and called it in." Detective Burns met Hud in front of Dane Trask's home. Hud had been to the modest but elegant cedar-sided home once before, to collect Trask's electronics and search for anything that might aid them in discovering his purpose in disappearing. The Ranger Brigade's searches hadn't turned up anything of value, and they had left the house much as they found it, orderly but lifeless.

This time, someone else had been searching for something, and had destroyed any sense of order. Furniture had been overturned, the cushions and undersides of chairs and sofas slashed open. Books from the bookcases lay twisted on the floor, and the pots from dead or dying houseplants had been emptied onto the carpet. Every drawer and cabinet had been emptied, every picture taken from the wall and cut from its frame. A forensics team dressed in white coveralls and booties moved through the mess, taking photographs, dusting for fingerprints and searching for evidence.

"Whoever did this left behind an expensive watch and high-end electronics," Burns said as he and Hud followed a carefully marked path through the chaos. "Though it's impossible to tell if they took anything else."

"Is every room like this?" Hud asked. They were in

the kitchen now, broken dishes and opened packages of pasta and coffee littering the floor.

"Every one," Burns said.

Hud shook his head. "Then I don't think whoever did this found what they were looking for."

"What were they looking for?" Burns asked.

"I don't know." Was it someone from TDC, trying to find something to further discredit Trask? Was it the mysterious "Lawrence" who had paid the private detective to dig up information about Audra? Or someone else entirely, someone the Rangers weren't yet aware of?

"Detective! We've got something here." One of the forensics team, a tall woman with a braid of blond hair, approached, a plastic bag in her gloved hand.

Burns studied the bag, then leaned over and sniffed. "Heroin?" he asked.

"I think so," the young woman said.

"We'll test it to be sure," Burns said, and the woman left the room with the bag.

"Have you found anything to indicate Trask was into drugs?" Burns asked Hud.

"No," Hud said. "And we searched this place, and his office at TDC, right after he disappeared. We didn't find anything."

"So whoever was trashing the place left it behind?" Burns scratched behind his ear. "That's not something you just casually drop—especially since they haven't left so much as a hair behind, at least that we've discovered to this point.

"Maybe it was a clumsy attempt to discredit Trask," Hud said.

"Clumsy, all right." He looked around the room, then back at Hud. "I can't figure this guy out. He had everything going for him—great job, respect in the community, a good relationship with his daughter. Yet he chucks it all to play hide-and-seek in the national park. You're pretty sure he's still there, right?"

Hud nodded. "Pretty sure." Dallas Wayne Braxton had been definite in his identification of the man he had encountered on the hiking trail, and it didn't seem likely Trask would have stuck it out living rough for so many weeks and suddenly decided to move on.

"If we get any more information here, I'll let you know," Burns said.

"Thanks. I'll pass on anything we uncover on our end." And now he'd have to tell Audra about this latest development. He didn't want her deciding to drop by her father's place and discovering this mess.

They headed toward the door, but Burns paused to look back at the chaos. "Whatever Trask is up to, he sure ticked off somebody," he said.

Hud needed to find Trask—or the person who was after him—before Audra ended up the chief casualty of the battle.

WHEN AUDRA RETURNED to work after lunch, the phones had stopped ringing off the hook and, while a few students had been kept home by their parents, only one child had been officially withdrawn. Audra breathed a little easier, believing she had weathered the worst of the latest crisis. People had realized their children were well cared for and happy and getting a good education at her school, and that mattered more to them than something that had happened in the past. Now if she could persuade the school district to think the same way, everything would be back on track again.

But that still left the problem of what to do about Mia and bullying. Her conversation with Hud had made her want to dig deeper and try to help the girl before a minor problem became a serious one. So she sent Brenda to fetch the child from Jana's classroom.

Brenda returned a few moments later, Mia, looking frightened, at her side. "Am I in trouble?" Mia asked as soon as she saw Audra.

"No," Audra said firmly. She looked at Brenda, who was still standing by Mia, taking all of this in. "Thank you, Brenda. Mia and I will be fine now."

"Then why did you call me out of class?" Mia asked after Brenda had left and shut the door behind her. "Mrs. Keplar said I shouldn't have to go to the office if I'm not in trouble."

Jana Keplar needs to keep out of this, Audra thought, but she said, "I wanted a chance to talk to you about what happened with April. But I promise, you're not in trouble. I want to hear your side of the story."

Mia slid into the chair next to Audra, her feet not touching the floor. She sat very straight, her hands in her lap. She was a pretty child, with an alert expression and an easy manner. An easy child to like. "I tried to be friends with April, like you asked," Mia said. "But the other girls made fun of me for hanging out with a baby."

And of course it was tough for a little kid to stand up to that kind of criticism, Audra thought. Children could be cruel. Then again, adults could be, too. "Sometimes, doing the right thing is more important than being popular," she said gently.

Audra's interpretation of the look Mia sent her was "adults can be so dumb." Okay, time to try another approach. She searched her memory for everything she knew about Mia. "You have a little brother, don't you?" she asked.

Mia nodded.

"Why doesn't he come to day care, too?"

"Mama says he can't come until he's out of diapers."

"But we take infants," Audra said. Was Mia's mother unaware of this?

"I know. I told her that, but she said the extra charge for babies is too high, so she's going to stay home with him." She pouted, yet still managed to look adorable. "I don't see why I can't stay home, too, but she said no. So she gets to be with him all day, while I have to be here."

Audra caught a glimmer of understanding. "That must be really hard," she said.

Mia swung her legs and looked away.

"I guess sometimes it's hard for you to be happy here at school, then, when you wish you were home," Audra said.

Mia shrugged. "I like school. But I miss my mom, too."

Audra wanted to pull the little girl close and rock her in her arms, but she wasn't sure how Mia—or her mother—would view that. Instead, she patted Mia's shoulder. "Thank you for talking to me," she said. "Starting soon, we're going to have some lessons that talk about being kind to everyone and not calling names. I think you'll be able to help your classmates with those lessons."

Mia looked relieved. "So I'm really not in trouble?"

"Not at all." What Mia had done to April was wrong. But the adults in her life were at fault, too, for not doing more to help her, as well.

When she was alone again, Audra called Mia's mother. "Mrs. Ramsey, this is Audra Trask, from Canyon Critters Daycare."

"If you're calling about Mia, I don't want to hear it," Mrs. Ramsey said. "I won't have her being made a scapegoat for other people's bad behavior."

"I am calling about Mia, but not because she's done anything wrong," Audra said. "She's a very sweet, smart child."

"Oh." Audra could almost feel the woman on the other end of the line deflating. "Then why are you calling? Are you fundraising or something?"

"No. I had a conversation with Mia this afternoon I thought would interest you."

"What has she been telling you?"

"Mia loves you very much. And she loves her little brother."

"Well, of course. She's a very loving child. And we love her."

"I know you do. But I think she's feeling a little left out, with you staying home with the baby all day and her coming here."

"Day care for infants is more expensive, and I was able to work out an arrangement with my employer to work from home, so it makes sense for me to be here with the baby. But trying to work with two children underfoot, especially one as lively as Mia, would be impossible."

"I understand. And I'm not calling to persuade you to put your son in day care. Not until you're ready."

"Mia loves going to school. She has so many friends there, and she's learning a lot. She's already in the second-grade reader."

"She's a very bright child. But bright children can also be very sensitive. I know you're sending Mia to school, even though you could keep her home, because you see the benefits to her. But to her four-year-old mind, she just sees herself being sent away while the baby gets all your attention."

"Are you saying this behavior of hers, with that other

little girl, April—was just acting out because she's upset about the baby?"

"It could be," Audra said.

"Then what do you suggest I do?"

This was the opening Audra had been waiting for. "You could try keeping Mia home a couple of days a week. Just as an experiment. We offer that option for parents with flexible schedules."

"That would certainly save us money. But do you really think it would help?"

"It might. I think after a few weeks, Mia might decide on her own she wants to come to school every day. But it will be her decision then, not something forced on her."

"She's only four. It's my job to make decisions for her."

"Of course. But I really do think this could help."

"Then I'm willing to try. And thank you. I may have spoken a little harshly before."

Audra smiled. "You love your daughter, so of course you were sensitive to criticism of her."

"Thank you for understanding."

Audra ended the call and hung up the phone. One victory. If only every problem could be solved with a little thought and conversation.

Hud FILLED IN the rest of the team about the break-in at Dane Trask's home. "There was no heroin in that house when we searched it," Knightbridge said. "Lotte would have found it." At the sound of her name, the Belgian Malinois at his side looked up, alert.

"Didn't you say Montrose PD found heroin in that private detective's car?" Dance asked. "Could there be a connection there?"

"Richard Salazar is still in county jail," Hud said. "I checked."

"Maybe the connection is Trask's daughter," Redhorse said. "She had an opiate addiction."

"To prescription painkillers," Hud said. "Not heroin. And she's been clean for years." Painkiller addicts did sometimes turn to heroin for a cheaper fix, but Audra showed none of the signs of addiction.

"Has she been to her father's house since we searched it?" Dance asked. "She probably has a key."

"I don't think so, but I'll ask her." He wanted to protest that Audra didn't have anything to do with this, but he bit back the words. Dance's question wasn't unreasonable. They needed to rule out Audra's involvement if they were going to find the real culprit.

"Have you discovered anything useful in Roy Holliday's records?" Commander Sanderlin asked.

"I've created a time line of his last days, and a list of everyone he noted speaking to," Hud said. "Though he usually identified people only by their initials. I haven't figured out all the names yet."

"Share what you have, and let's see what we come up with," Sanderlin said. "And talk to Audra Trask. Maybe she can shed light on that heroin and where it might have come from."

"Heroin?" Audra stared at Hud, trying to make sense of this latest development. She'd been pleased when he met her at her home after work, anticipating a pleasant evening together that was sure to take her mind off her troubles, at least for a few hours. Then he'd shattered that happy fantasy with the news that someone had broken into her father's home. "Dad didn't do drugs," she said. "Ever. He would never have had heroin in his home. Someone else must have put it there after he was gone."

"I have to ask, just to make sure I'm covering every

base." Hud looked as upset as she felt. "Have you been in your father's house since he disappeared?"

Did he think *she* had put heroin in her father's house? That she had anything to do with heroin? The words hurt more than she would have thought possible. "No," she said. "I wouldn't do that."

"I never thought it was you," he said. "But I had to ask."

Maybe that was true, but the knowledge didn't lessen the sting of his words. As a DEA agent, would he always think of her as a former addict—someone who might relapse at any moment? She forced her mind back to the break-in. "Was anything stolen?" she asked. "My dad had some really nice electronics, and guns and stuff that I think were valuable."

"It doesn't look like they took anything," Hud said. "But I think they were looking for something." The pained expression returned. "They really trashed the place. They slashed cushions and emptied out cabinets. I can give you some names of companies who will go in and deal with the mess after the police release the scene. It's not something you'll want to tackle yourself."

She tried to picture the scene he described, but couldn't. Her father was an orderly man who shelved his books by topic and arranged his furniture at ninety-degree angles. The idea of someone destroying that order hurt. "What were they looking for?" she asked.

"I was hoping you'd have an idea," he said. "What would your father want to hide? Did he keep money in the house, or important documents?"

"He has a safe in the bedroom closet for that sort of thing."

"The safe wasn't disturbed."

"Then I don't know what to tell you."

"He must have run into veterans in the Welcome Home Warriors group who struggled with addiction," Hud said.

"Yes. And he always tried to help them." The way he had helped her.

"What if they wouldn't accept help?"

"I think he kicked people out a couple of times, if they were disruptive. But no one recently. At least not that I knew about."

He pulled her close, and she didn't resist. "I hate to always be the bearer of bad news," he said.

"Better you than someone I don't know." She pulled back enough to meet his gaze. "I know you have to ask hard questions sometimes," she said. "But I want you to trust me."

"I trust you," he said. "And I don't say that lightly."

She nodded and moved out of his embrace. "All right, then. You can help me cook supper, then we'll watch a movie. We both need a break from this case." She needed to step back from worry and stress for a while and focus on being young and navigating a relationship with a man who could be both lover and accuser.

THE NEXT DAY, Hud focused on reviewing Roy Holliday's files yet again. He couldn't shake the feeling there was something in them that was vital to this case. Was MR Mitch Ruffino, TDC's vice president in charge of the Montrose facility? If so, then the reporter had contacted him, most likely in relation to research Holliday was doing on Dane Trask. Had his questions led Ruffino to believe Holliday knew something damaging to TDC or Ruffino himself? But what was that information?

Holliday's body had been dumped in the same area where construction debris had been illegally deposited. Though the Rangers had investigated TDC as the possible culprit, they had found nothing to link the company with the debris. But why had Holliday's body been left there?

He looked again at the list of evidence they had collected from the dump site. The one item that stood out to him was the children's drawing, signed "Max." Hud pulled up the scan of the drawing of a boxy, broad-shouldered figure scrawled in red crayon, with an oversize head and a wild tangle of black hair. He had seen no connection to the Dane Trask case or TDC when the drawing had been discovered at the dump site, but now it seemed so clear. A small child had made this drawing. TDC was constructing a new elementary school, which would also be the site of Audra's new day care and preschool. Was Audra the link between TDC and the dump site? And even Roy Holliday's murder?

He printed a copy of the scan, then checked in with the commander. "I'm going to show this to Audra Trask," he said. "It's possible it was made by one of her students."

"Didn't Beck check the roster of her school for a student named Max?" Commander Sanderlin asked.

"Yes, but maybe this is a student's sibling," he said. "Or maybe Max isn't the student's name, but the name of the person in the drawing."

"Better check it out," Sanderlin said.

He found Audra in her office, frowning at her computer screen. The frown didn't fade when she turned to greet him. "Another student was withdrawn from the school this afternoon," she said. "The mother said it was because she had made other arrangements for care, but I worry it's the influence of the news stories."

"I'm sorry to hear that," Hud said. "Let's hope the media finds something else to latch on to soon."

"I hope so. In the meantime, what can I do for you?"

He pulled a chair up to her desk and sat, then handed

her the copy of the child's drawing. "What do you make of that?" he asked.

"Um, it's a copy of a kid's drawing?" She squinted at the name in the corner. "We don't have a Max here at the school. Where did you get it?"

"It was found at an illegal dump site on public land. I'd like to show it to your teachers. Maybe one of them will recognize it as their student's work."

"All right." She studied the paper again. "Some of the three-year-olds and most of the four-year-olds can write their names," she said. "We'll start with the fours."

"That's Jana Keplar's class, isn't it?" he asked, following her from the office and into the hallway."

"Yes. The threes are with Trina Guidry."

Jana was reading a story to the assembled children when Audra and Hud entered and took a seat at the back of the room, Hud perched awkwardly on a tiny blue plastic chair. Every child swiveled to stare at him, and though Jana continued to read for several minutes, she finally gave up and closed the book. "Addison, you and Mia get the modeling clay, and we'll work on shapes and numbers as soon as I'm done talking with our visitors."

She joined Audra and Hud near the door. "It's very disrupting, barging into my classroom this way," she said.

"This will only take a few seconds," Hud said. He passed over the drawing. "Do you recognize this?"

She glanced at the drawing and handed it back. "No. I've never seen it. What's this about?"

"I'm just trying to figure out who drew this," he said.

"Why?" Jana turned to Audra. "Are you involved in another crime? What is wrong with you?"

Audra gripped Hud's arm and dragged him from the classroom. She all but vibrated with anger, her face flushed, her eyes blazing. He was glad he wasn't the object of her ire. "I'm going to advertise for a new teacher starting today," she said as she headed down the hallway once more. "I don't care how much her parents and students love her, I can't work with that woman one day longer than necessary."

She stopped outside a door painted bright orange, with a large 3 on the front. "This is Trina Guidry's classroom," Audra said. "I think you'll like her."

The young African-American woman who looked up when they entered wore a colorful scarf around her long dreadlocks and a dress printed with sunflowers. She and a group of children were gathered around a wire cage against the wall. "Come on in," she said. "The children and I were just feeding the guinea pigs."

"Their names are Gilda and George," a little girl said.

"Officer Hudson just needs a few seconds of your time," Audra said. "The children can tell me about George and Gilda while you're talking."

"George is the boy!" said a child with a great many freckles.

Trina followed Hud to the door. "Is something wrong?" she asked.

"Nothing's wrong," he said. "I'm just hoping you know who did this drawing." He handed her the paper.

She smiled. "Oh, I think that's one of Mason's drawings," she said.

"Mason?" He squinted at the scrawled letters at the bottom of the page. "This looks like it says Max."

"Yes. Some days he likes to be called Max. Would you like to meet him?"

"Yes."

"Mason, come say hello to Officer Hudson."

The boy with the freckles hurried to join them. Hud

squatted down until he was eye-level with the child. "Do you remember drawing this?" he asked.

Mason/Max pushed out his bottom lip as he studied the drawing. "I remember," he said. "It's a man who is singing and playing the guitar. And the people who are listening really like the song."

Hud nodded. Questioning a three-year-old was more challenging than interrogating a thirty-year-old. "Do you remember when you drew it?"

Mason shook his head.

"Do you remember where you drew it?"

Mason's quizzical look clearly communicated that he thought this was a dumb question. "No."

Hud looked up at Trina. "Do you know?"

"I really don't know. We draw almost every day. It's one of the children's favorite things to do."

"Are we going to draw now?" Max asked.

"In a little bit," Trina said.

Max handed the drawing back to Hud. "You can keep this," he said, then ran to rejoin his classmates around the guinea pigs.

"What do you think?" Hud asked Audra when they had left the classroom.

"I can't imagine how that drawing got from here—if it was done here—to that dump site," she said.

"Who are Mason's parents?" he asked. "What do they do?"

"His father is a soldier, currently stationed in Afghanistan. He's been there for six months now, I think. His mother is a stay-at-home mom with three other children, all a little older than Max."

"I'll have to dig a little deeper."

"This dump site—is that where Roy Holliday's body was found?"

"Yes," he said.

"Then do you think this drawing ties someone here at the school to his murder?"

"No. The drawing was found long before Roy died."

She put a hand to her chest. "You don't know how relieved I am to hear that. I hate anyone thinking I or anyone else here had anything to do with that poor man's death."

"I'm going to go back out to the site and look around more," he said. "It's officially a crime scene, now that Roy's body was found there, so that halted the cleanup efforts."

"Can I go with you?"

Her request startled him. "I want to see it," she said.

"Why do you want to see it?"

She pressed her lips together, then said, "I guess I want to see if I have any sense that my father has been there."

"It's not a part of the park he's been spotted in. It's not even in the national park, but on public land just outside the park."

She looked away. "I'm being silly, I guess. I just—I know he's out there and I wish I could reach out to him, some way."

"I don't think he's there," Hud said. "But you can go with me. Maybe you'll see something I haven't." And maybe it would help her to deal with everything she was going through right now. If he could do that for her, it would be something.

BY THE TIME Hud's Ranger Brigade SUV bumped down miles of rocky dirt road and pulled over in the shade of a large rock formation, Audra felt as if she'd been transported to another planet. She stepped out of the vehicle into an alien landscape of gravel, sagebrush and red-

and-gray rock monoliths casting long shadows over the mostly barren ground. The sun beat down with a blinding brilliance, and heat radiated off the rock, alleviated only a little by a hot wind that tugged at her clothes and whipped her hair back.

"This is certainly remote enough," she said. "How far are we from the highway?"

"Only about two miles," he said. "But yeah, it's remote. That's why whoever did this was able to get away with it for so long."

"This" was mountains of trash dumped haphazardly across the landscape in front of her—broken concrete, pieces of lumber, rocks, sections of drywall and sheets of plastic, tipped out like sand from a child's bucket onto the beach. "It must have taken months to haul all of this out here," she said, following him along a path marked by yellow flags into the debris field. He had warned her in the car to only walk where he walked and to avoid touching anything.

"It wouldn't have taken that long," he said. "A few big dump trucks could have probably deposited all of this in only a few days."

She put up a hand to shield her eyes and stared toward an area cordoned off with yellow-and-black plastic tape. "Is that where they found Roy Holliday?" she asked.

"Yes."

She tried to recall Holliday's face, but her encounter with him had been so brief she had no recollection of him. "Where did you find Mason's drawing?" she asked.

"Over there. There's still a flag marking the spot." She stared in the direction he was pointing and was able to make out a bit of blue plastic on the end of a wire stuck in the ground. "It was mixed in with some rock and broken concrete."

"It doesn't make any sense that one of my students' drawings ended up out here." She shook her head.

"I haven't figured that out yet, either," Hud said. "But I'm working on it. But what about this place—do you think this is someplace your father would come?"

She turned slowly, until her back was to the garbage, and she had a view of barren hills, piles of rocks and the blue, blue sky. "Dad liked places like this," she said. "Wild places. Open places where he said he had room to think."

"My dad used to take me camping, too," he said, moving up beside her. "Well, my mom, too. I sometimes think she liked camping and the outdoors even more than he did. But we always camped in the woods, near water. We fished and canoed and hiked. It was fun, but I was always glad to get home to my room and my stuff and my friends."

"Oh, yeah, that was me, too," she said. She squatted and sifted the gravelly soil through her fingers. "When I was little, Dad would take me camping, and he would always tell me to stop and look around my feet. He'd ask me to describe what I saw. No matter how many times he had me do that, I was always amazed at everything that was going on down at ground level." She studied a small beetle who carried a piece of leaf across the ground in front of the toe of her right shoe. "That was Dad—looking at the little details. Seeing what other people ignored." She looked up at Hud. "I'm afraid that's what got him in trouble. He noticed something TDC, or someone else, didn't want him to notice, and he had to run for his life."

Hud held out his hand. She took it; his fingers were warm and strong as he pulled her to her feet. "I'm worried about Dad," she said, continuing to scan their surroundings, as if she expected her father to step out from behind one of the piles of debris. "Even though I always thought he could do anything, I'm not so sure. Maybe he can survive in the wilderness, but what else is he up against? Is it TDC or someone else?" She turned and put her hands on Hud's shoulders. "I want you to meet Dad. I think you'll like him."

"But will he like me?"

"I'd make him like you."

He kissed her, and she closed her eyes and surrendered to the kiss. It didn't quell the nervousness that made her insides feel as if she'd swallowed broken pottery, but it helped. It made her feel a little safer and a lot less alone.

Then Hud shoved her violently to the ground. Pain shot through her as her knees slammed against the rocks, and her eyes blurred with tears. Then she heard the explosive sound of gunfire. Hud eased off her and pushed her toward a boulder. "Get behind that rock," he ordered.

She lurched toward the rock shelter on her hands and knees, heart in her throat, terror driving her forward. Once behind the rock, she peered out to see Hud scooting backward toward her, pistol in hand. Then he was beside her, firing up into the rocks above them, and the only thought that pushed past her fear was, *I don't want to die.*

Chapter Twelve

The sniper was aiming at them from a ledge high above, bullets striking close enough to explode shards from the rock they were hiding behind. A single shooter, Hud thought. He must have been up there awhile, watching them. But why stake out this remote location? And why wait until they were about to leave to fire on them?

"Who is up there?" Audra whispered. She was pressed against his back, so close he could feel her trembling.

"I don't know." He hadn't noticed any other vehicles on the way in, though someone could have parked farther up the road and he wouldn't have known. It would take a while to hike up to that ledge, though.

Audra shifted behind him. "I've got my phone to call for help," she said. "But there's no service."

"There's no service anywhere here until you get to the marina at Blue Mesa Reservoir," he said.

"Then we're trapped here." She sounded calm. Maybe she was in shock. He shifted to glance back at her and went cold all over.

"You're bleeding." He put a hand to her cheek, which was wet with blood.

She put her hand over his, then probed the spot. "It's not a bullet," she said. "Just a piece of rock, I think."

He dug out his handkerchief and pressed it over the

wound. "Hold that there," he said. "Press down to stop the bleeding."

"You're bossy when there's danger." But she said the words with a hint of a smile. He wanted to pull her close, but forced his attention back to the sniper. Whoever was up there hadn't fired for a while. Was he repositioning to get closer? Would he try to come up behind them?

"What's he doing up there?" Audra asked.

"I can't tell." Should he try to draw the shooter's fire? Carefully, he picked up a rock and tossed it into the bushes about six feet away. Nothing. Their assailant wasn't falling for that trick.

He kept his gaze fixed on the spot the shooter had been firing from, but could detect no movement. The spot was too far away for him to have any hope of hitting the guy with a pistol. He should save his ammunition in case the sniper moved in closer. But Hud needed to know the shooter's position. Taking aim at a spot just below the ledge, he fired. A puff of dust marked his shot, but only silence answered.

"Maybe he's gone," Audra said.

Or maybe he was moving closer. Moving in for the kill.

Hud considered his options. The cruiser was parked on the road, about two hundred yards away, across open ground. There were a couple of piles of boulders between here and there that offered some shelter, and his body armor gave him a better chance of surviving a hit, provided it wasn't a head shot. But that would mean leaving Audra alone here, where she was possibly more vulnerable.

In the car he had a rifle, a shotgun and a Taser, plus more ammunition. And water—he was conscious of being very thirsty. The sun beat down on the rock, radiating heat. They couldn't stay here too many hours before they might be in real trouble. The rifle would even the odds a little if he could retrieve it. He also had a radio that might or might not enable him to call for help, depending on how well the repeater system worked here. When he was here with other members of the Rangers before, it hadn't worked at all.

They could wait awhile and hope someone else came along—but that wasn't very likely. The Rangers all had assigned duties, none of which would bring them to this remote location today, and this wasn't a place tourists were likely to wander.

"How long do we just sit here?" Audra asked.

"A little longer," he said. "Listen for anyone moving around up there." Even the stealthiest person was bound to scrape a foot in the loose gravel at some point.

At first, all he heard was his own breathing, but as that slowed and quieted, he became aware of the wind rattling the branches of a dead piñon and stirring the tall stems of wild lettuce and bear grass. A lizard scurried over the boulder they hid behind, tiny claws gripping the rock, the drag of its tail a whisper in his ear.

Audra shifted, probably trying to get comfortable. "I don't hear anyone," she said.

Neither did he. "We should wait a little longer." Move too soon, and it could cost them their lives.

Audra lowered the handkerchief from her face. "I think the bleeding has stopped," she said.

"That's good. I'm glad you weren't hurt worse."

"I'm tougher than I look." Another slight smile, which made him feel momentarily light-headed. No matter what else happened, he couldn't afford to lose this woman.

He sat up straighter, aware of some change around them. "Do you hear that?" he asked.

She raised her head. "Is that a car?"

"I think so." He strained his ears, and the sound of a rumbling engine and tires on gravel grew louder. But the car wasn't coming from the highway—it was traveling from farther up this gravel track. It continued to move closer, growing in volume and speed. He shifted position and could see a small section of the road through a gap between boulders. A cloud of dust appeared, almost obscuring the white SUV it engulfed. Hud couldn't tell anything about the driver through the heavily tinted windows.

As the SUV passed the dump site, it picked up more speed, the back wheels fishtailing in the gravel, great plumes of dust rolling up like smoke from a wet bonfire, until the only clue that a car lay within was the dull red glow of the brake lights as it navigated a sharp curve.

"We should have jumped out and waved," Audra said. "We should have tried to stop them."

"No, it's good that we didn't do that," he said.

"Why not? Maybe they could have helped."

"I think that might have been our sniper," he said.

She gaped at him, then sagged back against the rock. "How can we find out?" she asked after a moment.

"I'm going to go out there. If he's still up there, I'll draw his fire."

She grabbed on to him, fingers digging in hard. "No! You could be shot."

"I don't think I will be. And I'm wearing body armor."

"You don't have armor on your head! Or your legs and arms! What am I supposed to do if you're hurt?"

"It'll be okay," he said. He wasn't at all sure of that, but who else would have been parked down this road? Who else would speed up passing a law enforcement vehicle, to make sure he and the vehicle he was driving couldn't be identified later?

He leaned down and drew the small revolver out of his ankle holster. "Do you know how to fire a gun?" he asked her.

She nodded. "Dad took me to the shooting range. He taught me gun safety and made me practice." She frowned. "It's not something I really kept up with."

"Take this." He handed her the revolver. He'd feel better knowing she wasn't completely defenseless if something did happen to him.

"All right." Dried blood stood out against her pale cheek, and he could read the fear in her eyes.

He kissed her cheek. "It's going to be okay," he said, and then sprinted out from the shelter of the boulder.

He ran a zigzag pattern toward the next grouping of rocks, shoulders tensed for the bullet he half expected to come. But no shots sounded, and only the rasp of his own ragged breathing accompanied him to his cover.

The next sprint was longer, and the third longer still, but with each one, he gained confidence. Whoever had been firing at them earlier was gone. He reached the cruiser, climbed in and started it, then guided it over the rough ground to Audra's hiding place.

As soon as he stopped the vehicle, she hurried out from cover and into the passenger seat. She leaned back, eyes closed. "I've never been so terrified in my life," she said.

"Yeah." He reached back and pulled two bottles of water from the cooler on the floorboard, and handed one to her. "I need to report this and get some people out here to investigate," he said. "Do you want me to get someone to take you home?"

"No." She opened her eyes. "I'd rather stay here with you."

"I'd rather have you here." For a little while longer, at least, he needed to see her, to know for sure that she was all right.

"Why do you think he left?" she asked.

"I don't know. Maybe he never intended to kill us, only to scare us away. Maybe he got cold feet about killing a cop. Or a woman."

She hugged her arms across her stomach. "Scare us away from what? We haven't figured out anything."

"And someone wants it to stay that way."

THE BLUE AND RED revolving lights of law enforcement vehicles cast eerie shadows across the rock monoliths and sagebrush-covered slopes around the illegal dump site. Spotlights bleached all color from the construction debris and sent long shadows up the sides of the surrounding cliffs. Audra huddled in the passenger seat of Hud's cruiser, a square of cotton gauze taped over the gash a shard of rock had cut in her cheek. The wound ached, and her whole head throbbed, but the EMTs who had arrived with three cruisers of Rangers in response to Hud's call for help had decided she didn't need stitches or further medical attention.

Mostly, she wanted to go home, but she was too afraid to go there by herself. That unknown shooter, firing on them from the hills, had felt somehow personal. As if her enemies—her father's enemies?—wanted her not only disgraced, but dead. And why? Why send a private investigator after her? Why smear her reputation in the newspapers? What had she ever done to hurt anyone?

She had been sitting here for hours, as the last light faded from the sky, waiting for Hud and Lieutenant Dance to return from their climb into the hills, to the place where Hud thought the person who had fired on them had been hiding. When she saw him walking toward her through the harsh glow of the spotlights she sat up straighter, some of the weight lifted from her shoulders. "What did you find?" she asked when he reached her.

"Someone was up there, all right," he said. "We found some spent brass, some scuff marks. And we found where he parked the car, off the road behind the remains of an old corral."

"He must have driven in ahead of you and waited," Dance said.

"He let us wander around here for a while before he ambushed us," Hud said. "Was he waiting to see what we would do?"

"Maybe he was moving into position." Dance addressed Audra. "Who knew you were coming here with Hud this afternoon?"

"No one," she said. "We met up after work, and I didn't tell anyone where I was going."

"We talked about it at your school," Hud said. "Maybe someone overheard."

She considered this. "We were standing in the hallway. There wasn't anyone else there."

"Could someone in a classroom have heard us?" Hud asked.

"Maybe, if they were listening at the door. But who would do that? And why?"

"I don't know, but I think we'll look into your staff a little more closely," Dance said.

The idea of any of the people on her staff—all women—climbing up into the hills and trying to kill her and Hud with an assault rifle was so absurd, she wanted to laugh. But her cheek and her head hurt too much to allow laughter. "Do what you have to do," she said. "But I don't think this was someone on my staff."

"Any other ideas who might want you out of the way?" Dance asked.

Who might want me dead? She suppressed a shudder. "What about the private detective—Salazar?" she asked. "Maybe you should talk to him again, and ask about the person who hired him."

"We've been trying to track down Lawrence," Dance said. "Salazar has been cooperative, but Lawrence hid his tracks well. But we'll keep digging."

She nodded. "I'm so exhausted, I can't even think."

"Hud can take you home," Dance said. "We've done all we can here for now."

She would have said she was too keyed up to relax, but once in the comforting darkness of the cruiser, the radio murmuring softly in the background, neither she nor Hud speaking, she drifted off, unconscious until he gently woke her in the driveway of her home.

"I think I should stay here tonight," he said.

She touched his cheek, feeling the rough stubble from where he needed to shave. "I think you should," she said. They could comfort each other and escape, for a little while, all the hurt that crowded in too close during the day.

HUD ENDED UP spending much of the weekend with Audra, working at a laptop on her sofa while she did paperwork at the kitchen table. Though the events of the past week were never far from her mind, the weekend felt like a return to normalcy, or rather, a new normal, one where Hud was part of her everyday life.

By Monday morning, her cheek had turned an ugly purple, though the cut itself was small enough she hoped it wouldn't leave a scar. "How do you feel?" Hud asked, examining the wound after she emerged from the shower.

"It's pretty sore. And I'm vain enough to be self-conscious about it."

"You're still beautiful." He brushed back her hair and kissed her bruised cheek.

She wrapped her arms around him, wishing they had time to go back to bed. Loving him was the only thing that made her forget herself and her troubles these days. But life didn't stop just because she wanted it to. "Do you think I'll frighten any children?" she asked.

"Oh, probably not too many." Laughing, he danced out of the way. He had her smiling through breakfast, and by the time she arrived at work, she was feeling more optimistic. As horrible as last week had been, today was bound to be better.

Brenda hadn't arrived yet when Audra pulled into the parking lot, the admin's reserved space still empty. So she was surprised when she walked into the administrative suite and saw the door to her office open. She stepped inside and stared at Jana, who sat in Audra's chair, the desk drawers pulled open. "What are you doing?" Audra demanded.

Jana looked up. "What happened to you?" she asked. "You look terrible."

"Never mind about me." Audra moved forward and put her bag and purse on the desk. "What are you doing going through my desk?"

"I wasn't going through your desk. I was looking for a pen."

Audra grabbed a pen from the mug on the corner of the desk. "Then why didn't you look here?"

"Thanks." Jana tugged on the pen, but Audra refused to release it. "Why were you going through my desk?" she asked again.

"I have to get to class." Jana stood and tried to move past, but Audra blocked her.

"You're not going anywhere," Audra said. "You're fired."

"You can't fire me."

"I can. Now you have ten minutes to collect your things and leave."

"What are you going to do with my class?"

"I'll take it this morning, then I'll call in a sub." She had a short list of moms who would fill in as needed, in exchange for a break on their children's tuition.

"You can't do this," Jana said, her face reddening. "I'll sue."

"I caught you, red-handed, riffling through my desk," Audra said. "That's grounds for dismissal."

Jana glared, and Audra wondered if she was going to have to call the police to escort the woman off the premises. But after a few tense seconds, Jana stormed out of the office. Audra followed, watching as Jana collected her purse and a tote bag of books and papers and other items from her classroom. Then the older woman marched out.

Brenda was coming in as Jana was leaving. "Is Jana sick or something?" she asked, watching Jana's red Toyota screech out of the parking lot.

"Jana is fired," Audra said. "I came in this morning and caught her riffling through my desk."

"What?" Brenda's eyes widened. "Did she take anything?"

"I don't know." Audra tried to remember if she had anything in her drawer worth taking. "But going through my personal belongings is grounds for dismissal."

"What are you going to do about her class?"

"I'll take it this morning. Call the subs until you find someone who can come in this afternoon. Don't tell them why we need them—just that we have a teacher who's going to be out for the next few days. I'll draft an ad for a new teacher."

Chapter Thirteen

Audra spent the morning with the four-year-old class. Being with the children, focusing on them, calmed her. Jana had planned a science lesson about plants, with examples of bark and ferns and leaves for the children to feel and examine, then they read a story about animals that lived in the forest, and drew pictures of trees. By the time the substitute showed up to take the children to the lunchroom, Audra was feeling more relaxed. She decided to walk to a nearby park for lunch and enjoy the warm weather.

The letter was waiting on Audra's desk when she returned from lunch. A fine linen envelope, with the embossed return address of the Superintendent's Office of the Montrose School District. Stomach churning, she slit open the envelope and unfolded the single sheet of paper:

Dear Ms. Trask,

This letter is to inform you that your contract with the school district is now declared null, according to Article 17b of your contract with us. We will no longer require your services as director of a day care and preschool facility in conjunction with Canyon Creek Elementary School.

Her eyes blurred as she scanned the following lines of legal jargon. She set the letter aside, took a deep breath, then picked up the phone.

"Ms. Arnotte is unavailable at the moment," the woman who answered the phone at the attorney's office said. "May I take a message?"

"This is Audra Trask. I just received a certified letter informing me that the school district is canceling the agreement for me to manage the day care and preschool at their new Canyon Creek Elementary campus. I need to know if they can do that, and what we can do to fight it."

"I'll give her the message."

Audra ended the call. The initial numbness upon reading the letter was fading, replaced by a growing rage. She punched another number into the phone.

"Superintendent's office. This is Maeve."

"Maeve, this is Audra Trask. I need to speak to Superintendent Wells."

"Superintendent Wells is not in. But I was told if you called to tell you that the decision is final and there's nothing we can do to help you." And then she hung up before Audra could say another word.

Audra was still staring at the phone in her hand when it rang. "Hello?"

"Audra, this is Cheryl Arnotte. What's going on?"

"I received a certified letter from the school district. Let me read it to you." She read the letter. For a long moment, Cheryl didn't say anything. "How can they do this?" Audra asked. "We have a contract. That's legally binding, isn't it?"

"They're invoking the morals clause. They have the right to cancel the contract if they feel your behavior jeopardizes the reputation of the school district."

"I haven't done anything. Certainly nothing that would violate a morals clause."

Another long pause.

"What is it?" Audra asked. "Do you think I've done something immoral?"

"Not necessarily immoral," Cheryl said. "But your name has been linked with a murder, and my girls tell me there have been law enforcement officers at the school several times recently. That concerns me as a parent, so I can understand how it would concern the school district, too."

"I'm not a suspect in any crime," Audra said. "The police have questioned me, but only as a possible witness."

"A school's first mission has to be to protect the children in its care," Cheryl said. "I think most courts would consider them justified in exercising an abundance of caution."

"Are you saying you agree with what they've done?"

"I'm saying I understand what they've done. I can file an appeal if you want me to, but I would caution against it. I don't think you'll win, and it could be very expensive."

"Do you plan to withdraw your children from Canyon Critters?" Audra asked.

"Certainly not right away. But when the new school opens, it will be so convenient for me to drop off all the children at a single location. I'm sorry, but I'm just being honest with you."

Audra didn't answer. What did you say to a remark like that—thanks for nothing?

"I understand this must be extremely upsetting for you," Cheryl said. "Don't rush to do anything right now. Wait a few days and consider your options. Then get back to me."

What options would those be? Audra wondered after

she ended the call. She had put everything—all her savings, all her credit, all her experience and training—into Canyon Critters. Once the new school opened, she doubted many parents would opt to stay with her. The new location was much nearer TDC Enterprises, where many of them worked. Those with older children, like Cheryl, liked the convenience of having all their children on one campus. Others simply wouldn't want to be associated with someone as notorious as Audra Trask.

She couldn't have said later how she made it through the rest of that day. She closed her office door and pretended to work on her computer, but she lost long minutes staring vacantly into space. She wanted to call Hud, but he was working. And she didn't want to be that needy girlfriend who was always calling to cry on a man's shoulder. She kept telling herself this wasn't the worst thing that could have happened to her. She wasn't dying of cancer. No one she loved had died. So many people had dealt with true tragedies. She was only in danger of losing a business she had poured her life into.

Okay, so maybe that wasn't cheering her up. But she wasn't aiming for cheerful. She just had to find a way to keep going. To stay standing until she could figure out a better way forward.

After work, she got behind the wheel of the car, intending to drive home, cry her way through a long, hot shower, then put on her pajamas and eat her feelings with a pint of ice cream. Or a bottle of wine. Or both.

Instead, she found herself driving to what would have been the future home of Canyon Critters Daycare and Preschool. Late-afternoon light bathed the construction site in a soft golden glow, warming the red stone of the emerging buildings to the same shade as the surrounding rock. The construction crews had left for the day, and she parked and walked across the gravel that would one day be a paved parking lot.

She had stood in almost this same place the day of the groundbreaking. She and her staff had brought all the children to watch the ceremony, the little ones excited at the prospect of a field trip and by the sight of all the construction machinery ringing the area. Audra had stood with the other people involved as the ribbon was cut and the first shovel of dirt removed. Then a backhoe had moved in to start digging the foundation. She could still see the children, wide-eyed and thrilled to watch the big machines. Some of them had drawn pictures and waved them like little banners.

"Oh!" The cry escaped her involuntarily as another memory surfaced, clear as if she had just witnessed it. Mason stood behind the ropes that separated the children from the construction zone, a crayon drawing in hand. The wind had caught the drawing, whipping it from his hand and into the path of the backhoe. He had cried and had to be restrained from running after it, but had soon been distracted, watching the backhoe bite into the earth, imitating the movement with several other boys, roaring like a monster.

The paper with his drawing had fluttered away, soon buried in a shower of construction debris from one of the backhoes.

HUD WAS WALKING out of Ranger Brigade headquarters when Audra's RAV4 pulled into the lot. He jogged over to the vehicle as she turned into a parking space. "What is it?" he asked. "Is something wrong?"

"I just remembered something," she said. "Something important."

"What is it?"

"It's about that drawing—the one Mason did. I know how it ended up in that dump site."

"Come on." He took her arm. "Let's go inside so the whole team can hear."

Beck, Dance, Reynolds and Redhorse, as well as the commander, were still at headquarters when Hud returned with Audra. "Audra has some new evidence for us," Hud said, and led the way to the conference room.

He set up the recording equipment as the others piled in, then sat across from Audra at the table. "Tell us what you know," he said.

"The day of the groundbreaking for the new elementary school, we took the Canyon Critters students to see the ceremony," she said. "The kids were really excited about seeing all the heavy equipment. Some of them were carrying drawings they had made that morning. I remember Mason dropped his drawing. The wind picked it up and carried it into the path of a backhoe, which dumped some rocks and concrete and stuff on it."

"You're sure about this?" The commander leaned toward her.

"Absolutely sure," she said. "I was at the construction site this afternoon and the memory came back to me, clear as if it had just happened."

"What were you doing at the construction site this afternoon?" Redhorse asked.

Her expression grew more troubled. "I received a letter from the school district this afternoon informing me they were canceling my contract for the new day care and preschool on the elementary school campus. I was upset and wanted to see the place one more time."

"Can they just cancel a contract like that?" Hud asked.

"They invoked a morals clause. Apparently, they

think my involvement in this case could be damaging to their reputation."

He wanted to vent his own rage at this turn of events, but had to maintain his composure for the tape and in front of his coworkers. "I'm sorry to hear that," he said. "I imagine that was upsetting."

"I'm not so upset now," she said. "That drawing proves TDC dumped that construction debris illegally on public land."

"I interviewed the construction supervisor for the elementary school," Jason Beck said. "He showed me receipts for dumping all the construction debris and talked about how committed TDC is to green practices."

"People lie and receipts can be faked," Reynolds said.

"This ties TDC to the dump site," Sanderlin said. "But it doesn't prove they actually dumped that debris. A contractor could have dumped it illegally."

"It's not enough to get a warrant to inspect their accounts," Dance said.

"Even if we got a warrant, they've probably covered themselves," Hud said.

"How much money do you reckon they pocketed by charging for waste disposal and dumping it on public land instead?" Beck asked.

"It could be as much as $250,000," Dance said. "Construction debris costs about $500 a ton to dispose of, and the national forest techs estimated that dump site has five hundred tons or more."

"They gave the school district a big discount on the construction of the school. This was a way to get a little back."

"It's pocket change for someone like TDC," Audra said. "They lost more paying those fines to the EPA."

"They're contesting those fines," Sanderlin said.

"They say Dane Trask faked the reports to get them into trouble."

"My father wouldn't do something like that," Audra said.

"Then maybe Trask caught them lying and threatened to blow the whistle," Hud said. "They threatened him or his family and he decided to run away and hide out instead."

"Then why not go to the press or someone at the EPA to begin with?" Redhorse asked. "Why disappear and leave a lot of cryptic reports for other people to figure out?"

"Because that was too dangerous," Audra said. "I know my father. It would have to be something really risky to keep him away this long."

"It would help if we had someone inside TDC," Beck said.

"Dane Trask was on the inside, and it didn't help him," Hud pointed out.

"Can we put more pressure on Mitch Ruffino?" Dance asked.

"We can question him," Sanderlin said. "But that doesn't mean he'll tell us anything. And I imagine he has plenty of lawyers to make sure he doesn't say anything to incriminate himself or the company."

"Let's try," Dance said.

"I'll see if I can reach him at his office," Hud said. "We can go over there now."

He expected an assistant to put him off, but when he identified himself and asked to speak to the TDC vice president, he was put right through. "I was just about to call you people," Ruffino said, without any preamble.

"Oh? What can we do for you?" Hud asked. He looked up and found everyone else in the room leaning forward in their chairs, listening intently. Now he wished he'd thought to put the call on speaker.

"We've had a break-in at TDC headquarters," Ruffino said.

"When did this happen?" Hud asked.

"Very early this morning. And I'm sure the culprit is Dane Trask."

Chapter Fourteen

Mitch Ruffino met Hud and Commander Sanderlin in his office on the sixth floor of the TDC office building, four miles outside the national park boundary. TDC's vice president had a fringe of snow-white hair around a bald spot and an expression that hinted at chronic indigestion or a dissatisfaction with life in general. "I don't know why it is taking you people so long to stop this man," Ruffino began as soon as they were admitted to his office. He stood behind a massive desk, arms crossed, radiating belligerence. "You're supposed to be an expert group, but this one man is making you look like clowns."

"You're working late this evening," Sanderlin said, ignoring the outburst.

"It's not unusual for me to work late," Ruffino said. "It's a requirement for the job, but one I don't mind. I do some of my best work after most people have left the office."

"Tell us about this break-in," Sanderlin said. "You said it took place early this morning?"

"At 3:52 a.m., according to the time stamp on the security footage," Ruffino said.

"Did you call the sheriff's department to report the break-in?" Sanderlin asked.

"No. I was going to call you people, but you contacted me first." He frowned. "Why was that?"

"We wanted to ask you some questions," Hud said.

"Those will have to wait until after you deal with this break-in."

The commander moved in closer to Ruffino, his lean figure towering over the VP. "Why did you wait so long to report the crime?"

Ruffino looked away. "We needed time to review the security footage, and we wanted to determine what might have been taken."

"And in the meantime, you were conducting business as usual," Sanderlin said.

"Of course. We are a multinational company with many projects to oversee."

Sanderlin didn't hide his annoyance. "Which means any evidence we might have gathered if you had reported the break-in immediately has been compromised."

"That's your problem, not mine."

"What was taken?" Hud asked.

"Thankfully, nothing. But the footage shows he was clearly looking for something."

"We'd better have a look at the footage," Sanderlin said.

Ruffino picked up his phone. "Send Larry in with the video footage," he said.

Seconds later, as if he had been waiting right outside the door, a middle-aged man with thinning blond hair and wide blue eyes entered, a compact disc in hand. "I have the footage right here, Mr. Ruffino," he said.

"This is Larry Keplar," Ruffino said. "He's head of our IT department."

"You're working late today, too," Hud said. "Is that usual?"

"Mr. Ruffino asked me to stay, to talk to you," Keplar said.

"Any relation to Jana?" Hud asked as Keplar fed the disc into a computer drive.

Keplar looked up, clearly startled. "Jana's my wife," he said. "How do you know her?"

"She works at Canyon Critters Daycare," Hud said.

"Yeah, she does." He turned his attention back to the computer. "Okay, it's going to play right now."

Hud and Sanderson leaned in closer as a grainy black-and-gray image appeared on the screen. A time stamp in the corner clearly showed 3:52 and that day's date. The figure—little more than a shadow at times—moved around a room, opening and closing file drawers, then riffling through a desk. At its clearest, the image appeared to be a slender man, over six feet tall, dressed in dark clothing. The search took about ten minutes, then the room was empty again.

"Is this the only footage?" Hud asked. "Do you have any of the man entering the building or searching anywhere else?"

"No, we don't," Ruffino said. "But how much more do you need? He's clearly not supposed to be snooping around like that at almost four in the morning."

"How did he get in?" Hud asked.

"Obviously, he used a key card," Ruffino said. "Anything else would have set off an alarm."

"You didn't deactivate his card after he left?" Sanderlin asked.

"Of course we did. But he must have gotten hold of another one."

"Run it again, please," Hud said. He watched the figure carefully, but could find no identifying marks. The man kept his head down, obscuring his features.

"What makes you think this is Dane Trask?" Sanderlin asked when they had reviewed the footage a second time.

"Who else would it be?" Ruffino asked.

"It could be almost anyone," Hud said. "The image quality on this footage is so poor we can't make out his features—not to mention, he's avoiding looking toward the camera. It's like he knows it's there."

"Exactly!" Ruffino said. "Dane Trask knows our security system and he knows how to avoid it. It's why we don't have footage from anywhere else in the building."

"Where is this footage from?" Hud asked.

"It's from the file room on this floor," Ruffino said.

"He avoided all those other cameras, but didn't avoid this one?" Sanderlin asked.

"He was too focused on looking for whatever it is he wanted," Ruffino said.

"Do you have any idea what he was looking for?"

"I don't know. Maybe confidential documents or proprietary information he thought he could use against the company. He's made it clear he wants to destroy us."

Hud thought it was clearer that TDC wanted to get rid of Dane Trask, but he remained silent, watching the video repeat. He turned to Keplar. "What about motion sensors? Don't you have those?"

"We do, but—" Keplar looked to Ruffino.

"They were shut off," Ruffino said. "Which is another reason it had to be Trask. He knew how to bypass our system."

"Didn't Trask work as an engineer?" Hud asked. "How

would he have known how to bypass your security system?" He looked at Larry again. "I would imagine it's a pretty sophisticated system."

"Well, yes," Keplar said. "I don't really know how he could have bypassed it."

"Clearly, the man is not an idiot," Ruffino said. "And he was somehow able to bypass our system."

"We can't identify the man and nothing was taken," Sanderlin said. "There's not a lot we can do."

"That is Dane Trask!" Ruffino stabbed a finger at the screen. "At the very least, he's trespassing."

"I suggest you file a complaint with the Montrose County sheriff," Sanderlin said. "This is their jurisdiction, not ours."

"But the Ranger Brigade is in charge of the hunt for Dane Trask," Ruffino said. "This is your problem. I want to know what you're going to do about this."

"We're continuing our investigation," Sanderlin said.

Ruffino leaned toward them, finger upraised as if he intended to poke Sanderlin in the chest. He refrained. "You've questioned Trask's daughter, haven't you?" he asked. "She must know something."

"Ms. Trask has cooperated fully with our investigation," Sanderlin said.

"And what has she told you? Does she know where her father is hiding? Has he told her what he has against us? How he plans to smear our name?"

"The details of our investigation are confidential," Sanderlin said. He turned to Larry. "We'll need a copy of that footage," he said.

"Of course." Larry ejected the disc and handed it to Hud.

"Why do you think Dane Trask has targeted TDC Enterprises?" Sanderlin asked.

"Because he embezzled from us and he's trying to deflect the blame," Ruffino asked. "He has the mistaken belief that by trying to make us appear in the wrong, it will lessen his own guilt."

"What, exactly, is he trying to make you appear wrong about?" Hud asked. "Was it just the false reports about the levels of contaminants removed in the mine cleanup, or is there something else?"

"Dane Trask faked those reports." Ruffino's voice rose. "We did nothing wrong."

"What about the construction debris that was illegally dumped on public land?" Hud asked. "Could some of that come from TDC?"

"Is that what Trask is saying now?" Ruffino asked. "It's absolutely untrue. And I believe one of your men already talked to our construction superintendent about that and we were cleared."

"Where were you Friday, about six thirty?" Hud asked.

Ruffino glared at him. "Why are you asking?"

"Where were you?"

"I was here, at the office. I told you, it's not uncommon for me to work late."

Ruffino didn't have to have been the sniper who fired on Hud and Audra. It would be more his style to hire a professional to do the job for him.

"I expect you to report back with your findings," Ruffino said as they turned to leave.

Sanderlin made no answer. When he and Hud were back in the cruiser, he asked, "What do you make of that security camera footage?"

"I would expect a company like TDC to have better quality security cameras," Hud said. "I noticed on the way in, they have cameras at the entrances, in the lobby and in the elevators. Even if the intruder knew to take the stairwells, and for some reason TDC doesn't have security cameras there—which would be a big oversight—I don't see how he avoided being caught on film everywhere but that one spot."

"Maybe he really was able to bypass the system," Sanderlin said.

"I'm not convinced that was Trask in the video," Hud said. "And for all the guy was going through drawers, it didn't look to me like he was searching for anything in particular. The whole thing felt staged to me."

"Staged for TDC, or staged for us?"

"Staged for us. I think Ruffino wanted an excuse to get us to his office so he could try to find out whatever we know about Trask." He frowned. "He seemed particularly focused on Audra." That really bothered Hud. Could Ruffino and TDC be behind the bad press Audra had suffered lately?

"Take a closer look at that video footage and see if you find anything significant," Sanderlin said. "From what I've learned about Dane Trask, he might very well be capable of bypassing a security system. But if he got into TDC headquarters to steal something in particular, I don't think he would have abandoned the task after ten minutes."

"What are you going to do about Ruffino?" Hud asked.

"Nothing for now. But we'll keep a close eye on him."

Hud would be keeping an eye on Ruffino, too—and looking for anything that might link him to Audra's woes. An attack on her was beginning to feel very personal.

AUDRA WAITED UP for Hud to return from TDC headquarters. She hadn't objected when he had suggested he spend the night with her again. She felt more vulnerable lately than she had in years, and having him with her eased her fears somewhat. Plus she was anxious to know what he had learned from Mitch Ruffino.

It was after eleven when his cruiser pulled into the driveway. She met him at the door, but only offered a hug and a kiss, resisting the urge to pepper him with questions. He shed his gun and utility belt at the door, then went into the bedroom, where he removed his body armor and uniform and changed into sweats from the bag he had brought with him. "Are you hungry?" she asked. "I could make eggs or something."

"Somebody ordered in pizza at the office," he said. "So I'm good." He opened his arms. "Come here."

He hugged her tightly, and she wondered at his ardor. "What's wrong?" she asked, searching his face for some clue to his emotions.

"I can't prove anything," he said. "But I don't think it's a bad idea for you to be wary of anyone and anything having to do with TDC."

She pulled away. "What did you find out?" she asked. "Did Mr. Ruffino say anything about me?"

"He asked if we had questioned you. He said he was sure you knew something about your father and his 'plans.' He's definitely convinced your dad has it in for the company—and maybe for him personally."

"But he didn't threaten me or anything, did he?" Her stomach trembled at the thought.

"No. But he's a man who's used to having a lot of power and using it to get what he wants."

"Did my dad break into TDC headquarters?"

Hud put an arm around her shoulders, and together they moved toward the living room. "Someone was on a security tape they showed us. There was a lot suspicious about the footage, which I won't go into. But there's no way to tell it's your dad. I don't think it is. I think the whole thing was an excuse to get us to his office so Ruffino could try to find out what we know. He ended up disappointed."

"TDC could have paid that private investigator to dig into my background," she said. "Then they leaked my past to the news media. And I wouldn't put it past them to have put pressure on the superintendent to drop me from the school contract. They donated the land for the school, and that probably bought them some influence." She sank onto the sofa. "Or I could be imagining all of it."

"What can you tell me about Jana Keplar?" Hud asked.

"Jana?"

"Her husband, Larry, works for TDC. Did you know that?"

"I think she might have mentioned it. Lots of the parents who have children in the school work for TDC. It's one of the largest employers in the area. Did you meet her husband?"

Hud sat beside her. "Yes. He's head of the IT department. He's the one who gave us the security footage. I thought he looked nervous, and was clearly watching Ruffino for cues." He rubbed her back. "What happened with you and Jana? Did you fire her?"

"Yes. We never saw eye to eye on the whole bullying issue, or anything else, really. But this morning, I got to my office a little early, and she was there, going through my desk." Anger rose as she remembered the scene. "I caught her red-handed and she didn't even try to deny it. Instead, she accused me of overreacting and tried to change the subject. Obviously, she wasn't happy about being fired, but I stood up to her."

"Who will teach her class?" he asked.

"I have a couple of moms with teaching experience who have agreed to fill in. And an ad will start running tomorrow for a new teacher." She turned to meet his gaze. "Why? Do you think she's the link between me and TDC? Or her husband?"

"I don't think anything. I was going to warn you to be cautious, since she was working for you. Now that she's not around, it shouldn't matter."

"When I got home this evening, I had a message on my phone from Brenda, my assistant. She said Jana is already talking bad about me all over town. She also said she heard a rumor that the school district has awarded Jana the contract for the new day care and preschool."

"That has to hurt," he said.

"I'm getting past hurt and moving on to anger. Now I wonder if Jana might be the one who hired the investigator and told the media about my addiction history." She hugged a pillow to her chest. "Or maybe I'm being paranoid and it's all coincidence. No one has made me a target. It's just my turn for bad luck."

"It's not all bad," he said.

"No." She tossed aside the pillow and put her head on his shoulder. "Meeting you has been good. Whatever happens, I'm not going to regret that."

THE NEXT MORNING, Hud ran through the video footage from the TDC break-in again and again. The intruder entered the room at 3:52, went straight to the first tall filing cabinet and opened the drawer. He did a quick scan of the contents, pulling out one file, then putting it back before moving on to the next drawer. He performed a similar scan of each drawer, moving quickly, as if searching for something obvious that he did not find. He didn't read the contents of any file folder, and unless he was a speed reader, wouldn't have had time to read the title of each folder. He pawed through the drawers of a desk and looked through two other file drawers. At 4:03, he exited the room.

Enlarging the images was no help in identification, proving that the image was blurry as well as grainy and ill lit. Which begged the question of how the intruder had managed to determine anything about those files, since he wore no headlamp and carried no flashlight. From the height of the door, Hud was able to determine that the intruder was approximately six foot two—Dane Trask's height. He wore gloves and a knit hat, a long-sleeved dark jacket, possibly a windbreaker, and dark slacks, possibly jeans. He kept his head down so that it was impossible to tell much about his features. Even Audra probably wouldn't be able to identify her father if he was, indeed, the man in this video.

He closed the file and sat back in his chair. "Any luck?" Beck asked, looking up from his own desk, across from Hud's.

"Nothing. I need to talk to Larry Keplar again." He stood. "If anyone is looking for me, I'll be at TDC headquarters."

Chapter Fifteen

Hud didn't go into TDC's building, but parked near the entrance to the employee parking area and waited. He had been there an hour when Larry Keplar strolled out and headed toward the back row. Hud started his engine and drove slowly, arriving just as Keplar was unlocking the door of a white Jeep. Hud rolled down his window. "Hello, Larry."

"Hello, Officer." Keplar glanced toward the building, as if checking to see if anyone was watching.

"I wanted to talk to you about that security video you gave me," Hud said.

"Is something wrong?" Keplar swallowed, his freckles dark against his very pale skin.

"I just need to clarify some things."

"Now? Here?"

"It doesn't have to be here," Hud said. "Is there someplace else you'd like to meet?"

"You know Newberry's?" Keplar fiddled with his key fob.

"Sure," Hud said. "Why don't we meet there?"

"Okay." Keplar jerked open the driver's door of the Jeep and dived in. Hud waited for him to pull out, then followed him to Newberry's, a combination convenience store/tavern/gas station/post office near the lake. Keplar parked at one end of the gravel lot and led the way into the dim interior lit by neon beer signs and smelling of ancient cigarette smoke, even though smoking had long been banned in bars.

He took a seat at a booth along a side wall and Hud slid in across from him. When a middle-aged waitress in a pink sweatshirt and jeans appeared to take their order, Keplar asked for Bud Light, and Hud ordered a Coke. A country tune began playing somewhere near the back of the bar, and Larry slouched lower in his chair. He had discarded his tie on the drive over and rolled up the sleeves of his white dress shirt. "What did you want to talk to me about?" he asked.

"I was wondering if you figured out how your intruder bypassed the security system," Hud said.

"No." He looked up to accept the beer from the waitress and took a long pull. "I never met Dane Trask, but people say he was really smart. Still, I didn't find anything showing the system had been messed with. That sort of thing usually leaves some kind of electronic fingerprint, so to speak."

"And you didn't find anything?"

"Nothing. No blank spaces or destroyed data or time gaps or anything."

"Nothing suspicious at all?"

Keplar took another long sip of beer. He wiped at a drop of moisture on the table with his thumb. "Mr. Ruffino told me not to talk to the police or the press," he said.

"When was this?"

"After you left yesterday."

Hud sipped his drink, letting the silence expand between them. He had a sense that Keplar wanted to tell him something. "You're not obligated to tell me anything," he said. "But there's no need for anything you do say to get back to Mr. Ruffino."

The door opened, and two men came in. Keplar started, then relaxed as they took seats at the bar. Not fellow employees, Hud guessed. "The only thing odd was, the camera lens in the file room looked as if it had been smeared with Vaseline," Keplar said.

"Do you think the intruder covered the lens with the Vaseline?" Hud asked. That would explain the blurry, distorted image.

"Maybe. Maybe he wanted us to know he was there—that's why he let himself be filmed in the file room—but he didn't want anything that could identify him."

"Walk me through everything that happened after the break-in at headquarters," Hud said. "Your part in the whole aftermath."

Keplar finished his beer and set the glass down on the coaster. "I got to work yesterday morning at nine, and Mr. Ruffino called me to his office maybe half an hour after I got in. He said he thought someone had been in the file room the night before and I needed to check all the security footage."

"Did he say what made him think someone had been in the files?" Hud asked.

"No. And I didn't ask. When the VP tells you to do something, you do it."

"So you looked and found the footage showing some-one in that room at 3:52, is that right?"

"Right. I noticed what poor quality the footage was, so I went to the file room to check the camera. It looked like someone had smeared something sticky—like pe-troleum jelly or something—all over the lens. They had tried to clean it off, but there was still some residue."

"And there wasn't footage showing an intruder anywhere else?" Hud asked. "You checked all the other feeds?"

"Yes, and the entrance logs."

"Did any of the other cameras show signs of having been covered or tampered with?"

"No."

"Had anyone entered the building around that time? Say, between midnight and 3:52?"

"The system showed that one person checked in at 3:45. They used a generic card—the kind we give to vendors or visitors. They have to surrender them at the front desk. Each generic card is coded with a number we can match to the guest and vendor registry, but this card wasn't linked to anyone. In fact, it was a brand-new card, made just the day before."

"How do you make a card?"

"It's a little machine—the same kind they use for hotel key cards. You swipe the blank through the reader and it codes the metallic strip to unlock one or more doors. If someone forgets to turn in their key, we can void that key remotely."

"Has that happened lately? Someone forgetting to turn in their key?"

"No. I checked."

"So you don't have any idea who used the card?"

"I assume it was the intruder—Mr. Ruffino is sure it was Dane Trask." Keplar frowned. "But anyone using the card should have shown up on the security feed for the front entrance—that's the entrance they used."

"I know you said you didn't find any irregularities. But if you were going to bypass the system, how would you do it?" Hud asked.

"You can buy technology that will interfere with the

system," Keplar said. "Disrupt the feed for a few seconds. If it was only a few seconds, it would be harder to detect."

"Where do you buy something like that?"

"There are lots of places online."

"Anything else odd you noticed?"

"Not really."

Keplar had been focused on his system's failure, not the failure of the intruder to find anything worth taking in a quick perusal of files in an almost dark room. "I have to get home now," Keplar said. "My wife will be wondering where I am."

"Your wife worked for Audra Trask," Hud said.

Keplar froze in the act of reaching for his wallet. "She did. Audra fired her."

"Did your wife tell you why she was fired?"

"What does that have to do with anything?"

"What did she tell you?"

"She said Audra resented her because Jana knows more about kids and how to run a day care. She had her own day care center in Kentucky, where we used to live."

"Audra told me she caught your wife going through her desk."

"I don't know anything about that." He pulled out his wallet.

"Do you think your wife would do something like that?"

He counted out bills and laid them on the table. "Look, Jana is a great person. She loves kids, and she loves teaching. She was pretty torn up about having to leave her day care center behind when we moved here."

"Why did you move here?"

"This job is a tremendous opportunity for me. TDC is huge, and this was a big promotion for me, not to mention a big pay increase. Jana's business was profitable, but only barely. It didn't make sense to stay in Kentucky and pass up a chance like this."

"So she took the job with Canyon Critters."

"Yeah. She has all this experience, and she loves kids. But it's been hard on her. Audra is pretty young, and she's not interested in hearing advice from someone like Jana. But Jana can't help wanting to give advice. I thought things would settle down after a while, but I guess they didn't."

"I heard your wife was awarded the contract for the new day care center," Hud said. "The one that was initially given to Audra."

"I'm not even going to comment on that." He slid out of the booth. "I really do have to go now."

Hud finished his Coke, thinking about their conversation. Larry Keplar had moved across the country to take a better-paying job with TDC. He had a wife who resented the move, and probably a bigger mortgage on top of that. He depended on his paycheck, and he depended on TDC for that paycheck. That hadn't stopped him from going against Mitch Ruffino's orders not to talk to law enforcement, but it had made him nervous and not inclined to dig very deep into the mystery of that security footage.

As for Jana's clash with Audra, maybe it had nothing to do with TDC. Coincidences happened all the time in real life, one of the things that made solving real crimes tougher than they usually were on TV.

AUDRA SAT AT her desk and read the article someone had anonymously forwarded to her, a story from the local newspaper's website. Successful Daycare Operator from Kentucky Awarded New Contract for School Facility, declared the headline. The article announced that Jana Keplar, former owner of Sunshine Kids Daycare in Paducah,

Kentucky, had been awarded the contract to operate a day care and preschool on Montrose School District's Canyon Creek Elementary campus. "I'm excited for this opportunity to bring a truly top-tier facility to local families," Mrs. Keplar said.

More paragraphs followed detailing Jana's experience, with no mention of her former association with Canyon Critters Daycare, and no mention of Audra Trask. Audra supposed she ought to be thankful for that.

She closed the file, then squeezed her eyes shut against a fresh flood of tears. Despite the brave front she had put on for Hud, she was struggling not to sink into depression. This morning, after Hud left for work, she had lain in bed, thinking about the days when she could just take a pill and zone out. For a few seconds, the idea had been very tempting.

But she was never going to do that again. She was going to be strong and fight her way through this.

How would her dad handle this? He had been her role model for most of her life, more so than her mother, even. What would he do now?

She hesitated only a moment before she booted up her computer. When it was ready, she looked up a phone number, then punched it into her phone. "TDC Enterprises," a man answered.

"I need to speak to Mitch Ruffino," she said. "This is Audra Trask." She was going to arrange a meeting with Ruffino and have it out with him, face-to-face. She could almost hear her father speaking in her head. "When you need to address a problem, skip the middleman and go straight to the top."

MITCH RUFFINO HAD always impressed Audra as the sort of man who was so concerned with the impression he was making and so focused on always asserting his power that he could never unbend or so much as crack a smile with anyone he felt was beneath him. At the few TDC functions she had attended with her dad, Ruffino had kept himself apart from the others, a ruler overseeing his subjects, watchful for any missteps or slights he might pounce on. Now that she faced him in his office, she saw nothing to change the opinion of him.

She made a point of looking him in the eye and returning scorn for scorn. She had spent her young life disabusing people of the notion that she was weak merely because she was diminutive.

"So you're Dane Trask's daughter." Ruffino looked her up and down. "You don't look anything like him."

She had her father's eyes and chin, if not his stature. And she had his obstinacy. She also had a taste for risk that, while it had gotten her into trouble more than once, in this situation might come in handy. She ignored the chair Ruffino gestured to and stood in front of his desk, her hands resting lightly on this barrier between them. "You and your company have harassed me enough," she said. "You need to stop right now or I'll be forced to take action."

A muscle in his jaw twitched, and his nostrils flared. She watched, the way she might watch a snake, ready to leap out of the way before it struck. "I don't know what you're talking about," Ruffino said.

"I'm talking about the private detective you hired to dig into my private life," she said. "Mr. Salazar."

He had schooled his emotions enough not to react to this, but he shoved back from the desk and stood also. "You can't come in here threatening me."

"I just wanted to deliver that message. I'll leave now." She turned and headed for the door.

"Stop!"

She halted, but didn't turn. His feet shuffled on the thick carpet until he was standing in front of her. "Don't go," he said. "Let's talk."

All graciousness now, he led her to a seating area to the left of the desk, a low sofa and two chairs with a glass-and-steel coffee table. He took the sofa and she sat on the edge of one of the chairs, her purse in her lap. She had a can of pepper spray in there, one her father had given her a couple of years ago, when she'd moved into her own place. She didn't even know if it was any good anymore. Did things like that expire? Mainly, she hoped she wouldn't need to use it.

"Tell me what you want," Ruffino said.

"I told you. I want you to leave me alone," she said. "And leave my father alone. Stop lying about him stealing that money. And stop this ridiculous lawsuit. A judge is just going to throw it out anyway." She was taking risks again, but she was here, so why not go for broke? Her father had also taught her to always ask for what she wanted. If people said no, you really weren't any worse off than you had been before.

Ruffino's eyes narrowed. "How do you know your father didn't steal that money?"

"Because he wouldn't. He didn't need money."

"Everyone needs money. You really are naive if you think they don't."

"My father didn't need more of your money. He made a good salary in his job, and he didn't have any debts."

"That you're aware of."

She shook her head. She really knew very little about her father's financial situation, but she knew his character. "Right now he's living in the wilderness, eating campers' leftovers," she said. "Does that sound to you like a man who cares a great deal about money?"

"No. That sounds like a desperate man. Possibly a deranged one."

She didn't argue; rather, she stood again. "I've told you what I want, so I'll leave now. I know you're a busy man."

"You won't leave until I'm ready. Sit down."

She started to ask if he was going to sit on her to keep her from going, but decided against that. Instead, while she didn't sit, she waited. Something else her father had taught her—don't rush to fill a silence. Other people will often tell you things if you wait.

Ruffino didn't disappoint. "That little school of yours," he began. "I'm sure you could use money to expand and grow."

She looked at him, still silent.

"I see you know the value of not speaking," he said. "That's good. I'm willing to pay for you to continue to keep quiet."

Keep quiet about what? she wanted to ask. But that was the risk she had taken—the gamble that appeared to be paying off. Ruffino thought her father had revealed to her some secret he didn't want anyone else to know. He was offering to pay her to keep quiet.

"Talking to the wrong people could get a person in a lot of trouble," she said vaguely.

Ruffino's scowl deepened. "And I'm telling you that not talking could make you a very rich young woman."

"Did you try making this offer to my father?" she asked.

His expression didn't change. "You strike me as much more intelligent than your father."

She took that to mean yes, he had tried to bribe her

father, and Dane had turned down the money, or whatever else Ruffino had offered.

"Yes," she said. "I'll take you up on your offer." This was a risk, too. What was she going to do if he handed over a big stack of cash? Would that be enough proof for the police to move in?

"You have to do something for me first," Ruffino said.

Her stomach rolled. "What's that?"

"You have to hand over the proof. Your father said he had proof hidden in a safe place. Obviously, he left it with you."

She swallowed hard. "How do I know you'll hold up your end of the bargain if I give you the proof?" she asked.

He smiled, revealing surprisingly white teeth. "You'll just have to trust me."

Chapter Sixteen

"Given everything Larry Keplar told me, I think it's possible that Mitch Ruffino staged that break-in at TDC headquarters in order to add to the urgency of finding Dane Trask, and so that he could quiz us about what we know about Trask and his relationship with TDC." Hud concluded his summary of his interview with Keplar to his fellow Rangers half an hour after he parted company with Keplar.

"Ruffino isn't the man in that video footage," Beck said. "That guy is taller and thinner than Ruffino."

"I think he hired someone to break in, but I think Ruffino set it all up," Hud said. "He would have known—or could have found out—how to make the visitor's key, and he could have given the guy a device to interfere with the security cameras at the entrances, elevators and hallways. He could have smeared something on the camera lens in the file room and wiped it off later. And he was the one who made the decision not to call in the Montrose sheriff and to wait all day, until any trace evidence would have been obliterated, before calling us."

"The biggest thing that stands out to me is that, while the intruder made a show of looking through the files, he wasn't actually looking for anything," Redhorse said. "He didn't turn on a light, and he only made a cursory search."

"Why even bother with paper files?" Dance asked. "I would think anything important at a business like TDC would be on the computer."

"They have paper copies of a lot of signed contracts, surveys and land plats," Hud said. "But even then, I don't think they would keep anything incriminating or valuable in a file room that is accessed every day by dozens of people. Which is another reason this whole thing was a ploy to try to find out what we know."

"Ruffino is worried about something," the commander said. "How do we find out what?"

"Dane Trask knows something," Dance said. "I don't know why he doesn't come right out and tell us."

A knock on the door of the conference room interrupted them. "Come in," Commander Sanderlin said.

Stacy, one of the civilian employees, came in. "Audra Trask is here to see you, Officer Hudson," she said. "I told her you were in a meeting and she said the commander should probably hear what she has to say also."

"Send her in," Sanderlin said.

A few moments later, Audra entered the room. Before she spoke, Hud could tell she was agitated. Her eyes were bright, her color heightened. "I just came from a meeting with Mitch Ruffino," she said. "He tried to bribe me. He thinks my father gave me some kind of evidence relating to TDC Enterprises—something Ruffino doesn't want made public."

Hud stared at Audra, trying to absorb what she had just said. "You went to see Ruffino?" he asked, aware of the anger behind his words but unable to stop himself. "By yourself?"

She raised her chin, defiant though pale, and in that moment his love for her hit him like a punch to the gut. Everything she had endured these past few weeks would have sent a lot of people hiding under the covers, but she was still fighting, refusing to give in. "Somebody leaked the information about my battle with addiction," she said. "Somebody hired that private investigator to look into my background. TDC has been doing everything they can to discredit my father, so it's not unrealistic to believe they're going after me now—maybe as a way to get to my dad. One of the things my father taught me, way back when I was struggling with bullying, was to turn and confront my tormentor. It throws them off guard and forces them to face their actions. And it lets them know you're not going to let them get away with what they're doing."

"So you decided to confront Ruffino." Sanderlin spoke, and Audra turned toward him.

"He's in charge of TDC's operations here, and he was my father's boss," she said.

"Why don't you sit down." Beck stood and pulled out a chair for her. Hud wished he had thought of it first.

Audra sat, purse in her lap. She was still pale, but composed.

"I think we should get your statement on record," Sanderlin said. He nodded to Dance, who went to a corner cabinet and started the recording equipment. Sanderlin recited the date and time and introduced Audra as the speaker. Then he turned to her. "All right. Tell us everything that happened."

She looked around the table at each person, ending her survey with Hud, her gaze steady and, he thought, pleading with him to listen and not be angry. He forced himself to relax and nodded. "Go ahead," he said. "We want to hear what you have to say."

"If you've seen the papers, you probably know that someone leaked a story about my having struggled with drug addiction in the past," she began. "It was an addiction to prescription painkillers, and I went into rehab and haven't had any problems since. So, old news, obviously put out there to hurt me and, I believe, to hurt my father. I already knew someone had hired a private detective to look into my background, and I suspected it was TDC Enterprises, since they've kept up a stream of bad publicity about my father since he disappeared. Then, probably as a result of that publicity, I lost the contract with the school district for the new day care center and preschool that's supposed to share a campus with the new elementary school. TDC is building that school, and I suspect they have some influence with the district. Rumor has it they gave the district a big price break on construction costs. Then, Officer Hudson showed me a child's drawing that was found at a site on public land where someone illegally dumped construction debris. I remembered seeing one of my students with that drawing at the groundbreaking ceremony for the new school. That linked TDC to the illegal dump site—which was also the place where Roy Holliday died." She paused and took a deep breath. "And then someone shot at me and Officer Hudson when we visited the dump site. At first I was terrified, then I was angry. Everything kept coming back to TDC. So I called the vice president of the company, Mitch Ruffino, and asked to meet with him. He agreed right away, which I guess was my first clue that something was up."

She took a sip of water from the cup Hud had slid over to her. No one else said anything, all eyes on her. Hud could think of a lot of things he wanted to say— he wanted to tell her what a risk she had taken, going to TDC. If everything she believed about them was true, confronting them could have put her life in danger. It might still have. But he forced himself to keep quiet. The damage was done, and he recognized the bravery that went along with her foolishness. Maybe this would help them break open this tough case.

"Have you found out anything else about the person who shot at us at the dump site?" she asked.

"They didn't leave anything behind that's helped us identify them," Dance said. "And TDC still denies they had anything to do with the construction debris dumped there. The drawing is a pretty tenuous link, since the argument could be made that it was dropped by the child somewhere else."

"We've had people at the site around the clock since then and haven't had any incidents," Redhorse said.

"What happened at the meeting?" Sanderlin prompted.

"We met in Ruffino's office at TDC. I told him I wanted him to stop harassing me," she said. "At first, he tried to deny that he'd done so. But when I told him if he didn't stop the harassment, I'd take action, his attitude changed."

"What kind of action?" Dance asked.

"I meant legal action, but I think Ruffino thought I meant something else," she said. "When I tried to leave his office, he told me not to go. Then he offered to pay me to keep my mouth shut."

"Shut about what?" Sanderlin asked.

"I don't know," Audra said. "But I didn't tell him that. I played along. I told him I knew talking to the wrong people could make trouble for him. He said if I kept quiet, I could be a very rich woman."

"Did he offer a specific amount?" Redhorse asked.

She shook her head. "No. I asked him if he made my father the same offer, but he didn't answer. I took that to mean yes, he had tried to bribe my dad. Maybe he'd threatened him, too, and that's why my dad felt he had to disappear."

She fell silent, as if contemplating her father in danger. "What happened next?" Hud prompted.

"Ruffino said in order to get the money, I had to hand over the proof my father had left with me. I had no idea what he was talking about. My father didn't leave me anything—certainly not 'proof' of anything. But I played along. I agreed to give him what he wanted in exchange for a lot of cash. And I agreed to meet him Thursday at seven to make the exchange." She looked around at them. "I thought maybe you could be there and record the conversation and maybe I could get him to say or do something incriminating. Something that would prove my father is innocent."

Hud had to bite the inside of his cheek to keep from telling her agreeing to such a meeting was a terrible idea and that there was no way they would risk a civilian like this. But that was only because of his feelings for her. With any other witness, he would have seen this as a breakthrough in the case. The others certainly recognized it.

"Are you sure your father didn't give you anything?" Reynolds asked. "A computer disk? Or one of those flash drives, like he gave Cara Mead?"

She shook her head. "I've been thinking and thinking, but there's nothing. He hasn't even contacted me since he left."

"I always thought that was because he was trying to protect you," Hud said. "To keep you out of whatever mess he'd gotten himself into."

"Whatever the mess is, I'm in it now," she said. "And I want to do everything I can to help."

"Where is this meeting supposed to take place?" Dance asked. "Ruffino's office?"

"No. He suggested we meet at the construction site for the new elementary school. He said it wouldn't look suspicious for either one of us to be there."

"That's good," Knightbridge said. "It will be easier to keep an eye on the situation out in the open, not in his office."

"We can fit you with a recording device and a microphone so we can listen in," Dance said. "And we'll have people nearby if we need to intervene."

"Can you coach me on what to say to get the information you need from him?" she asked.

"We can do that," Sanderlin said. "Though I'd say you did pretty well with him so far, making him think you have what he wants."

"Did Ruffino give you any idea of what he's looking for?" Redhorse asked. "Did he specifically mention a flash drive or notes or something like that?"

"No," she said. "I don't think he knows what he's looking for. He said my father told him he had 'proof' in a safe place. Apparently, Ruffino has decided that means my dad gave it to me. But he hasn't given me anything. I swear if he had, I'd hand it over to you. Whatever it is, it must be pretty incriminating."

"Then why didn't your father hand it over to law enforcement?" Jason Beck asked. "From what we know about him, he doesn't strike me as someone who'd be afraid of a man like Ruffino."

"I know," she said. "I don't understand any of it."

"He must have been persuaded that he or someone he cared about was in grave danger," Redhorse said.

Everyone looked at Audra, and a chill ran through

Hud. "We can't do this unless we can be sure Audra is safe," he said.

"We need to be prepared for Ruffino to want to move to another location once he meets her there." Redhorse said.

"I agree," Sanderlin said. "If Dane Trask left because Ruffino threatened him, or threatened Audra, it had to be a serious threat. Ruffino wants Audra to believe he'll be satisfied with paying her off, but I don't believe it."

"You're saying he'll try to kill her," Beck said.

Audra gasped, and Hud leaned over to put his hand on her arm to steady her. "I think Carmen is right," he said. "It's possible Ruffino—or someone he hired—may have killed before."

"What do you mean?" Audra asked. "Who?"

"I don't have solid proof yet, but I've been going through Roy Holliday's computer files," he said. "The day before he was killed, he had a note to contact MR. His phone records show a couple of calls to a private number with a local exchange. That could be Ruffino. I'm waiting on confirmation of that, but I think it's possible Holliday uncovered something suspicious and confronted Ruffino with it."

"And he was murdered to keep him quiet," Knightbridge said.

"I think it's very possible," Hud said. "We've linked TDC to the illegal dump site where Holliday was dumped. And someone fired on me and Audra the day we visited the site, which is yet another reason to believe Audra is in danger."

"How did the sniper know you would be at the dump site?" Dance asked.

"We talked about it in the hallway at the day care center." Hud turned to Audra. "Jana Keplar could have overheard us and told her husband or someone else at TDC. Ruffino might even have recruited her to keep an eye on you."

Audra nodded. "Maybe that's why she was going through my desk the day I fired her."

"Did anyone follow you here?" Hud asked.

She shook her head. "I headed back toward the school when I left TDC, but when I was almost there, I realized I had to tell you about this. I didn't notice anyone following me here."

"If they were very good, you probably wouldn't have noticed," Beck said.

"I really don't think anyone followed me," she said.

"Let's hope they didn't," Dance said.

"Ruffino thinks you have something your father gave you that proves Ruffino or TDC or someone connected with the company did something illegal," Sanderlin said. "Until he gets his hands on that evidence, you should be safe."

"Should" wasn't good enough for Hud. "Maybe she's safe for now," he said. "But once she hands it over, she'll be in real danger."

"We'll be there to protect her," Dance said.

Audra had gone very still, but now she took a deep breath, the fire back in her eyes. "I want to do this," she said. "I want to stop these people. Maybe then my father can come home."

AUDRA HAD LEFT her meeting with Ruffino shaking, and it had taken a while after she had arrived at Ranger Brigade headquarters for the shaking to stop. She could tell that Hud had been angry at first, upset that she'd taken such a risk, but she hoped her explanations had eased his mind. He seemed calmer, though he didn't say anything until the two of them stood in the headquarters parking lot, next to her car. He kept a hand on her arm, his body tense. "You don't think I should do this," she said.

"It's too risky," he said. "You shouldn't have confronted Ruffino by yourself. Not without talking to me first."

"Why not?" she asked. "I didn't go in there thinking he was going to bribe me. I went to confront a bully, in a public place, with plenty of other people around. I had to let him know I wasn't going to let him intimidate me anymore. That was my battle to fight, not yours."

He slid his hand up to her shoulder and looked into her eyes, his expression so intense it sent a shiver down her spine. "You don't have to fight those battles by yourself anymore," he said. "I can help you—if you'll let me."

She had to look away. It was either that or let him see how much he was getting to her. "I'm not used to leaning on other people," she said. She had worked so hard to learn to stand on her own feet, to not depend on drugs, or her parents, or anyone else.

"Leaning on others doesn't mean you're weak," he said. "And I want to help you."

"And I love that about you." She allowed herself the luxury of enjoying the warmth and strength of his hand on her shoulder before she shrugged it off. "But try to look at this as if you weren't my friend—as if you were one of those other officers." She nodded toward the Ranger Brigade building. "You've got this really difficult case and I come in and offer you a chance to collect some valuable evidence that might help you solve the case. At the very least, I could get proof that TDC has broken the law. There was something they did that my father found out about, that they don't want known. I'd really like to know what that thing is, wouldn't you?"

"Not if it means you getting hurt."

"I won't get hurt." She softened her tone. He looked so miserable—far more upset about this than she was. Yes, she was afraid, but she was also excited to be able to do something to help, instead of tossing and turning at night, worried and helpless. "I'm going to have you and your fellow officers to protect me."

"Your father didn't trust us to protect him," Hud said.

"Well, that's where the two of us are different. He didn't trust people easily, but I'm feeling a lot more trusting since I met a certain Ranger Brigade officer."

He didn't exactly smile, but his expression lightened. "You know what this means, don't you?"

"No, but I'm sure you're going to tell me."

"It means you have a personal bodyguard, at least until we've settled this with Ruffino."

"Do I get to choose the bodyguard?" she asked.

His eyes narrowed. "That depends. Who do you choose?"

"Oh, I was thinking I might ask Officer Knightbridge. He's pretty hunky and has all those tattoos."

His fierce glower made her laugh out loud. "I'm sorry," she said, hand to her mouth. "But the look on your face! I think it's a good thing Officer Knightbridge isn't here right now."

"Where are you headed now?" he asked.

"Home. I'm exhausted."

"I'll be there as soon as I get done here," he said. "And if anything suspicious happens in the meantime, call 911, then call me."

"You're cute when you're bossy." Something about this situation—maybe her own audacity in confronting Ruffino in the first place—had brought out her sassy side. Instead of the panic she probably should have been feeling, she was giddy with excitement, and she couldn't help teasing Hud for being so overly concerned on her behalf. At his dark look, she leaned over and kissed his cheek. "It's going to be all right," she said. "You'll see. Between the two of us, we'll figure this all out. We make a great team."

She got in her car and started the engine. Hud was still watching as she drove out of the parking lot. Maybe she wasn't more afraid because she had faith in him to protect her. No, check that. She wasn't afraid because she had more faith in herself with him backing her up.

Chapter Seventeen

Audra called in sick Wednesday and Thursday, pleading a terrible cold she didn't want to pass on to the children. Brenda promised that everything was under control, and Audra spent the majority of both days in a windowless conference room, trying to memorize the instructions Hud and other members of the Ranger Brigade rattled off. She received guidance on the importance of getting Ruffino to say something that would incriminate him or his company. "Play dumb," Lieutenant Dance said. "Make him explain everything to you. Ask him to explain exactly what information he's worried about you having, or how he could possibly be in any trouble, or how he came up with his plan—anything at all to get him talking in detail about what he or TDC did."

"Won't that make him suspicious?" she asked. "Won't he suspect I'm being recorded?"

"Not if you handle it right." Hud patted her shoulder in what she was sure was meant to be a reassuring manner, but only made her worry more. What, exactly, was the right way to face a man who might be a criminal—even a murderer?

"I'm really nervous," she said. "I'm not sure I can hide that."

"Don't hide it," Carmen Redhorse said. "You don't

have to pretend to be anyone you aren't. Of course you're nervous. If Ruffino comments on it, it's okay to say you don't trust him, or even that you're afraid of him."

"But what do I do when he asks me for the proof my dad left with me?"

"You're going to give him this." Hud handed her a red plastic computer flash drive.

She stared at the Welcome Home Warriors logo on the front. "This is one of my dad's." Dane had handed them out all the time to remind people of the veterans' group he had founded.

"Right," Hud said. "Cara let us have it." Cara Mead, her father's former administrative assistant at TDC. "It's exactly the sort of thing Ruffino will expect your father to have given you."

"While we're on that subject," Officer Beck said, "the first time we interviewed you, you said you had some of these—some your father gave you."

"I do. But I've had them all for ages. I even dug out every one I could find last night and looked at them. They're all full of my own files."

"You mind if I take a look at them, just in case?" Hud asked.

"Sure."

Hud took the flash drive from her. "I'll keep track of this until you're ready tomorrow afternoon," he said. "I'll hand it over before you head to your rendezvous at the construction site."

"What's on it?" she asked.

"Variations of the reports that were on the flash drives your father gave to Cara and to Eve Shea," Hud said. "I corrupted the data, so it won't make much sense, but the files look very technical. If Ruffino insists on taking a quick look, they should be enough to fool him. He probably knows his business, but information in his public bio doesn't indicate the scientific background to decipher technical reports."

"Okay." The four of them—Hud, Dance, Beck and Redhorse—looked so confident. Optimistic even. They were counting on her to get this right. "What about the wire I'm supposed to wear?" she asked.

"It's not actually wired to anything." Redhorse picked up a flat cardboard box that had been sitting in the center of the conference table and passed it to Audra. "Everything is wireless these days. We ordered this just for you."

Audra lifted the box and stared at a turquoise-and-pink-quartz amulet on a thick silver chain, with matching drop earrings. "Jewelry?" she asked, confused.

Dance laughed. "The pendant is actually a sophisticated digital recorder. It should pick up everything you both say. It will also transmit to the van where we'll be hiding, so we can monitor the conversation. If we hear anything that sounds like trouble, we'll be right there, with lots of backup."

"You'll also have a code phrase to repeat if you sense trouble and need help," Redhorse said.

"What's the code phrase?" Audra asked.

"We thought we'd let you decide. It needs to be something that sounds natural in conversation," Redhorse said. "Most people choose some comment about the weather, or something like that."

Audra tried to imagine herself having a conversation with Ruffino near the half-built elementary school. "How about 'It's amazing how quiet it is here this time of day'?"

Hud nodded and typed a note into his phone. "That's good, but we won't necessarily wait for that phrase," he said. "If we hear anything we don't like, we'll make our move. The phrase is in case you see something alarming that we can't pick up from the conversation."

She tried not to dwell on what might constitute "alarming."

"Are you clear on what the plan is for tomorrow?" Dance asked.

"I think so. Hud will be at my house with me to get everything set up, and we'll test the recording equipment there."

"Right," Dance said. "Beck and I will be in a van near your house. After we test the equipment, we'll drive to the neighborhood around the construction site and get set up. We'll also have two teams stationed nearby, at least one where they can keep an eye on the site itself."

She nodded. "At twenty 'til seven, I'll drive to the site and park near the entrance. I'll walk in to meet Ruffino."

"My guess is he'll try to get there first," Dance said. "But if he isn't there, stay inside your car until you see him."

"And after Ruffino and I meet up, we talk, I give him the flash drive and he gives me the money." She swallowed, fear making a knot in her chest. "That's how it's supposed to go, but if he really thinks I know something incriminating about him or TDC, why would he let me just walk away? Why wouldn't he kill me and hide the body, the way he may have done with Roy Holliday?"

"You don't have to do this," Hud said. "We can call the whole thing off now."

"No, I want to do this. I'm just trying to figure out the best way to avoid getting killed."

"That's why we'll be there," Dance said. "If Ruffino tries anything, we'll move in immediately."

"I don't think he'll come alone," she said. "That wouldn't be smart, and he strikes me as pretty smart."

"No, but we'll be prepared to handle anyone he has with him," Beck said.

"But you don't have to do this," Hud repeated.

She took his hand and squeezed. "I think I do have to do it," she said. "It's the only way I see to put a stop to his persecution of me and of my dad."

"I think it's too dangerous," he said.

"It is dangerous," she said. "But if I don't do this, I don't think things are going to get any better. Someone else might even die."

I don't want it to be you. He didn't say the words out loud, but she read them in his eyes. "You ought to know by now that I'm a fighter," she said. "I don't give in easily. I'll be smart, and I won't let Mitch Ruffino get the better of me. My dad and I have that much in common."

He nodded. "I've got your back."

"We all do." Dance put a hand on Hud's shoulder. "Ruffino doesn't know it yet, but he's going up against all of us."

AUDRA STOOD IN front of the mirror in her bathroom and tried to see herself as Mitch Ruffino would—a small woman, wearing jeans and low boots with rubber soles (better for running if she needed to), a pale blue knit shirt with three-quarter length sleeves, and a turquoise-and-pink-quartz pendant with matching earrings. She'd spent some time on her makeup, partly to cover the dark circles under her eyes from sleepless nights since she'd agreed to this risky plan, and partly because she wanted Ruffino to think she was the kind of glamorous, high-maintenance and possibly pampered woman who wouldn't know anything about defending herself. She'd added false eyelashes, heavy liner and dramatic lipstick. She looked ready to go out on the town, not prepared to confront a possible killer. She hoped her appearance would lull him into thinking she didn't suspect he'd double-cross her.

And he would try to double-cross her. She was almost certain of that. Whatever had happened between her father and Ruffino, it had been enough to send her father into hiding. Dane Trask wasn't a man who backed down easily. But Ruffino would have expected Dane to fight back. She imagined a man like him would even be afraid of her father, a former army ranger who was fit and in his prime.

She was counting on Ruffino to not expect a fight from her.

"I've never seen you this dressed up. You almost don't look like yourself."

She turned to face Hud. "I haven't worn this much makeup since a friend and I did one of those glamour photo shoots that were popular when I was in college," she said. "But I'm hoping the glamour will throw Ruffino off guard. If he asks, I'll tell him I plan to go out and celebrate with some of the money he's going to pay me. I'll make him believe the money is all I care about."

Hud put his hands on her shoulders. "You know I don't like this, but I'm proud of you," he said. "And I'm going to do everything in my power to not allow anything to happen to you."

"I know. And that's why I'm able to do this." She touched the pendant at her throat. "Do you know if Dance and Beck are picking up transmissions okay?"

In answer, Hud's cell phone rang. He listened, then said, "Okay," and hung up. "Beck says everything is coming through good, but don't touch the pendant. It creates static, plus you don't want to call attention to it."

"Right." She put her hands at her side. "What time is it?" The day had dragged, waiting for the time that the meeting would start, but now that it was almost here, everything was moving too fast.

Hud checked his watch. "Almost time for you to leave." He walked her to the door. She collected her purse and keys, then turned and kissed him, hard and quick. "I'll be okay," she whispered.

Then she hurried out the door, willing herself not to turn back, not to chicken out. "You can do this," she whispered to herself, but what she heard was her father, telling her the same thing when he dropped her off at the rehab center all those years ago.

She drove to the construction site, keeping to the speed limit and forcing herself not to search for the surveillance van or the Rangers she had been told would be watching over her. There would be officers from the Montrose County Sheriff's Department also, since the school was in their jurisdiction. She turned in at the sign that announced Future Site of Canyon Creek Elementary School.

The school building looked almost complete, only stickers on the windows and a lack of landscaping hinting at work still to be done. Constructed of reddish sandstone blocks, the school blended into the surrounding sandstone boulders, seeming to grow organically from the ground. A low stone wall along the drive separated the pavement from what might be flower beds in the future.

A dark SUV with tinted windows was parked in front of the almost-completed school. Audra turned into the lot, drove a slow circle past the SUV, then back to park in the middle of the entrance drive, the nose of her car facing out. She was blocking the entrance and making it easier for her to drive away. She left the engine running and the keys in the ignition, her purse on the passenger seat, and opened the door.

She was scarcely out of the car before the SUV started

up and drove to within inches of her back bumper and stopped. The SUV's driver, a big blond man in a black T-shirt and jeans, got out. "You're blocking the exit," he said.

She faced him. "I am."

A second big man, this one with closely cropped brown hair, dressed in jeans and a black sweatshirt, got out of the passenger seat. "You need to move your car," he said.

"If that's what you want," she said. "I'll leave. Though I came here to meet Mr. Ruffino."

The back door of the SUV opened and Mitch Ruffino emerged. He was dressed casually in khakis and a green polo shirt, as if he were headed to the golf course after this. "Are you in a hurry to leave already?" he asked.

She removed her sunglasses and fluttered the false eyelashes. "I have things to do," she said. "I plan to celebrate big with the money you're going to give me."

"Only if you have what I want." He moved toward her.

She opened her palm to reveal the flash drive. "I think this is what you want," she said.

He reached for it, but she closed her fingers around it once more. "I want to see the money," she said.

"First, we need to search you," he said. "I want to make sure you aren't recording this. My sources say you're pretty friendly with the Rangers."

For a moment, she was sure her heart stopped beating. Her mouth was so dry, she couldn't speak. *You're not afraid*, she told herself. *You're brash and reckless and tough*. She drew herself up to her full height. "You can search me," she said. "But don't you dare get fresh."

Ruffino looked at the blond. The man stepped forward, towering over her, and patted her down. She kept her expression impassive as he groped her, even as she was inwardly cringing against his touch. He took his time going over her body, but he didn't even touch the necklace.

As soon as he took his hands from her, she stepped back.

"You're shaking," Ruffino said. "Why?"

"Because I don't trust you," she said. "My father is missing, and I'm sure it's because of something you did or said."

"Oh no," Ruffino said. "That's all on your father. He went off the deep end and did something stupid. Now he's paying for it. I'm hoping you're smarter."

She thought of a dozen questions she wanted to ask him—what did you do to my father? What did he say to you? But the Rangers had coached her on what to say. "Tell me about the Mary Lee mine," she said.

Ruffino scowled. "What about it?"

"The paper made a big deal out of the fines you had to pay to the EPA. My father was working on that project before he disappeared. I'm worried there'll be more trouble over the mine."

"We took care of all that," Ruffino said. "We got rid of everything that could be a problem. Even the EPA admits it's all clean now. If your father told you otherwise, he's wrong. We were very careful, and everything would have been fine if he hadn't interfered."

"What about this school?" She gestured toward the almost-completed building.

"Everything is fine here, too. We paid off the people who needed to be paid off."

"All those bribes get expensive."

"Don't call them bribes. And we figured all that into our bid."

"Your bargain bid."

He chuckled. "Wells knew it was worth his while to make a big deal over the bargain he was getting. But there are firms who would have done it for half the price we did. Or not done it at all."

She tried to put together this puzzle, but it wasn't making sense. "Did you tell Wells to take the day care contract away from me?" she asked.

"No. He got nervous and did that all by himself. But don't worry. With the money we're paying you, you won't need to work for a long while." He reached into his pocket and she flinched, expecting him to withdraw a weapon. Instead, he took out a slim leather wallet and extracted a check and handed it to her.

She stared at the check, made out in her name for $300,000. "You're giving me a check?"

"We're going to say it's the proceeds from a life insurance policy we provide for all our executives," he said. "Don't worry. No one will suspect anything."

She had expected a suitcase with bundles of cash, or the key to a secret safe-deposit box, or even the number and pass code to a secure offshore account. An ordinary check seemed so absurd. "How do I know this check is any good?" she asked.

"How do I know this flash drive isn't full of nonsense?" He grabbed her wrist, squeezing hard. "No more games," he said. "Time for you to do what I want. My two friends here will make sure of it."

"That's enough," Hud said from the back of the van where he sat with Dance and Sanderlin, eavesdropping on Audra's meeting with Ruffino. "We've got him admitting to bribes. We need to get Audra out of there before she gets hurt."

"Wait," Sanderlin said. "If we handle this right, we

can avoid letting Ruffino know we're onto him and avoid exposing Audra to more danger."

"She's not a professional," Hud said. "She shouldn't even be in there."

Sanderlin remained calm. "Listen," he said.

"I don't want just the money," Audra said. "I want the contract for the day care center back."

"You don't need that contract," Ruffino said. "You can do whatever you want with this money, especially if you're smart about investing it."

"It's a matter of pride," she said.

"Your father was proud, too, and it didn't get him anywhere. Trust me, you don't want to work around here."

"Why not?"

"Nothing. I mean, the risks are minimal. People exaggerate the effects of that kind of radiation. Really—you're probably getting more exposure from dental X-rays. That's why we took all that material up to the mine, instead of reusing it at the building site. We were actually making it safer."

"What is he talking about?" Dance asked.

"Radiation?" Audra sounded as puzzled as they were. "How can you be sure it's all gone?"

"We can't be sure it's all gone, but it's nothing for you to worry about. And if you're worried about testing, we've taken care of all of that. Everybody who matters is on our payroll. Everything will be fine. And you need to keep your mouth shut about this, or you'll jeopardize the whole operation."

"How big an operation are we talking about?" Audra asked.

"Good," Dance said. "He went off script, but she's following right along."

"Maybe I want to be part of the operation," Audra said.

Hud and Sanderlin exchanged glances. That definitely wasn't part of the script.

"What could you do for us?" Ruffino asked.

"I own a day care center. Can you think of a better cover? No one would suspect me of anything."

"Interesting," Ruffino said.

"I need to know more," she said. "What role would you allow me to take?"

"I'd have to talk to people above me. But you might be onto something."

"I want—"

But they never got to hear the rest of her sentence. Gunshots—very loud and very close—crackled over the speakers, followed by terrifying silence.

Chapter Eighteen

Audra staggered back, blood from Mitch Ruffino's head sprayed across the front of her shirt. She gaped at the blond man, who had shot Mitch Ruffino. "Why did you do that?"

In answer, he turned the gun on her.

She stared, trying to register in vain what was happening. But some primitive part of her brain—the part desperate to survive—took over. She launched herself over the low rock wall, bullets exploding shards of granite around her. She scrambled on her hands and knees into a culvert, desperate for cover as shouts rang out behind her.

More shots exploded, and it took her a moment to realize the bullets were no longer striking near her. Heart in her throat, she crawled to the edge of the culvert and peered out. Men dressed in black fatigues, with shields and helmets, swarmed the area. The two bodyguards lay on the ground, the blond silent and still, the other in handcuffs, blood running from a wound in his arm.

A white service van skidded to a halt at the front bumper to her car. The back doors opened and Hud raced out. "Audra!" he shouted.

"I'm over here!" But the words came out so weak he didn't hear her. She managed to back out of the culvert and stand, her knees aching. "I'm over here," she tried again.

A man all in black, face concealed by a helmet, swiveled and pointed a rifle at her. "Don't shoot!" she screamed, and tried to raise her hands in the air. She felt weak and stupid, and tears streamed down her face.

Then Hud was by her side, one arm around her shoulders, holding her up. "Where are you hurt?" he demanded. "We've got to get you to an ambulance."

"It isn't my blood," she said. "It's Ruffino's." She turned to look at the vice president of TDC, who lay faceup and blank-eyed in the glaring sun.

Hud pressed her face into his shoulder. "Don't look," he said.

"The blond man—his bodyguard, I thought—shot him," she said. "One minute we were talking, and then the man just shot him. And he tried to shoot me."

Hud pulled away far enough to look her up and down. Some of the blood was on his uniform now, and the sight made her woozy. "I need to sit down," she managed.

He led her to her car, opened the door and helped her sit in the passenger seat. Commander Sanderlin approached. "How are you doing?" he asked.

"I don't know." It was the best answer she could give. She was still trying to absorb the idea that she could have been shot, but wasn't.

"The ambulance is on its way," Sanderlin said. "We'll have the EMTs check her out." He was talking to Hud, and she listened with the detachment of someone overhearing two strangers at the next table in a coffee shop.

Sanderlin leaned into the car to address her again. "Do you have the check Ruffino gave you?"

The check—she looked down and realized she was still clutching the check in her fist. It was torn and smeared with dirt and blood. She uncurled her hand and held it out to him.

Hud ran a finger over her bleeding palm. "Your hands are pretty beat up," he said. "Your knees, too."

She looked down and was surprised to see holes in the knees of her jeans, the skin beneath raw and streaked with dirt. "I think it was digging through all that loose rock and concrete," she said. "Trying to get away."

She began to cry then. She couldn't help it. The sheer awfulness of everything that had happened hit her. "I'm sorry," she apologized between sobs.

Hud held her, patting her back, making soothing noises. "It's okay," he said. "It's all going to be okay."

Sanderlin left and the EMTs arrived. They cut away the torn jeans just above her knee, cleaned her wounds and gave her a tetanus vaccination. "You're going to be pretty sore for a few days," one said. "But you should be okay. See your doctor if there's any sign of infection or you start to run a fever."

She nodded. Really, all she wanted right this minute was to take a shower, put on clean clothes, and climb under the covers and sleep away this whole nightmare.

That wasn't going to happen, though. As soon as the EMTs left, Commander Sanderlin returned. "We need to get your statement about what happened," he said.

She wanted to say no. But she had promised to help them, and this was part of helping. "All right."

"I'll drive your car to headquarters," Hud said. "After you've given your statement, I'll take you home."

"That's the most wonderful thing you could have said to me right now." She even managed a smile, though she could still feel the tears walled behind the thinnest of panes of glass, which might shatter any moment. She had never been the weepy type and hated feeling this way now. But maybe this happened to anyone who had

seen men shot right in front of her and who had almost
died herself.

Ranger headquarters was quiet and almost empty,
a sharp contrast to the construction site, which had
swarmed with people. Hud led her to the conference
room, which was so familiar to her now, then filled a
glass with water and set it in front of her. "I'm going to
get the recording equipment set up," he said.

Commander Sanderlin came in. "I know you're probably feeling pretty rough right now," he said. "But we need
to get all the information you can give us. It's important."

She nodded. "Of course."

"We have the recording of your conversation with Ruffino," Sanderlin said. But we need you to fill in the vi-
suals—facial expressions, gestures, all the subtext we
weren't able to see."

"I'll do my best." She took a drink of water. "I'm still
in shock," she said. "I'm not sure if I trust my memory."

"Just do the best you can," Hud said. He sat by her
side, and Sanderlin took the chair across from her, on the
other side of the table.

"Start by describing everything that happened after
you left your house," Sanderlin said. "Then we'll go back
over everything and clarify anything that needs it."

So she described driving to the construction site, finding Ruffino waiting, and everything she could remember about their exchange. When she got to the moment
where he had been shot, she faltered. "I never saw the
bodyguard draw his weapon," she said. "I was talking to
Ruffino and one minute he was there and the next minute..." She shook her head, the horror of the moment
once more replaying in her mind.

"What happened then?" Sanderlin prompted.

She drank more water, not wanting to remember, but

forcing herself to do so. "I asked why he shot Ruffino, then he aimed the gun at me. I was frozen in place, but I guess some part of me—the part that wanted to survive—took over. I dived over that wall and scrambled into the culvert. I don't know why. It would have been easy for one of the two men to follow me, but I just wanted to get away from the bullets. And then I guess the SWAT team showed up, and everything was okay." She closed her eyes. "Thank God it was okay."

Sanderlin glanced down at a notebook she hadn't even noticed until now. "A little before he was shot, Ruffino said something about radiation levels. What did he mean by that?"

She shook her head. "I don't know. Did he mean radiation at the mine? Isn't that what my father was trying to get people to pay attention to?"

"The initial reports TDC submitted to the EPA—the ones your father supposedly authored—showed very low levels of radioactivity at the Mary Lee mine," Hud said. "The same levels you'd find in most rocky areas around here, and not enough to pose any danger. But later measurements your father took, after the mitigation work began, showed much higher levels of radioactivity."

"And the EPA fined TDC for falsifying their initial reports," Audra said. "And TDC blamed my father. But then later, the EPA declared the mine site okay. I remember TDC had a big press conference to announce that all the toxic stuff had been cleared."

Hud sat back. "I've been going over all this in my head," he said. "When Ruffino was talking about safe levels and everything being taken care of, I wonder if he wasn't referring to the mine, but to the school?"

"You mean there was radioactive material at the school?" Sanderlin asked.

Hud nodded. "TDC donated the land for that school. What if they did it not because they were especially civic-minded, but because they discovered it was hot and they needed to get rid of it? They dug up as much of the radioactive rock as they could and hauled it up to the Mary Lee mine, where they planned to gradually get rid of it as part of the mitigation process."

"But my father figured out what they were doing," Audra said.

"Right," Hud said. "And he either confronted Ruffino with his findings, or Ruffino or someone else at TDC found out that he knew the truth, and they threatened him—or they threatened you—and Dane decided he'd be better off going into hiding and fighting TDC covertly."

"Then what did they do with the radioactive rock after they removed it from the mine?" Audra asked.

"They dumped it on public land," Hud said. "In the Curecanti Recreation Area. We thought it was construction debris all along, and it was, but most of it, maybe all of it, was stuff they had dumped at the mine, then hauled to wilderness land."

"Ruffino said they had bribed people. Inspectors, maybe. Regulators." She rubbed her temples. Her head throbbed, making it difficult to think.

"It sounds like TDC has spent a fortune in bribes," Sanderlin said.

"How can they afford to keep it up?" Hud asked. "It's not like they made that much profit from building the elementary school. They didn't get anything but a tax write-off for the land they donated. The fines the EPA levied ate into their income from the mine cleanup."

"I think something else must be going on," Audra said.

The two men stared at her. "Ruffino talked about an operation," she said. "He said if I talked I could ruin 'the whole operation.' And when I suggested working with him, using my day care center as a cover, he said he'd have to talk to the people above him. Does he mean Terrell, Davis and Compton?"

"You may be onto something," Sanderlin said. "It could be the two men who accompanied Ruffino to the meetup with you weren't so much there as bodyguards, but to keep him from saying the wrong thing. He may have been killed to silence him."

The queasy feeling washed over her again. Hud's hand on her shoulder steadied her.

"Thank you for your help." Sanderlin slid back his chair and stood. "We may have more questions later, but Officer Hudson can take you home now."

Neither she nor Hud spoke on the drive home. She sat in the passenger seat of her car, welcoming the numbness, afraid of the storm of emotions that might wash over her if she allowed herself to feel. Hud pulled into her driveway, and she got out of the car and followed him up the walk.

Once inside, she was about to head to the bathroom when he took her hand and pulled her close. "I love you," he said. "I should have said it before, but I can't wait any longer. I love you, and I was so afraid for you this afternoon—and so proud, too."

The words surrounded her and melted into her and soothed her like a healing balm. She looked into his eyes and saw how much he meant to her with those three little syllables, and in spite of everything, she couldn't help smiling. "I love you, too," she said. "I can hardly believe it happened, in the midst of all of this chaos, but I do."

"Believe it," he said, and kissed her—a long, deep kiss that made her feel as if she were floating above all the horribleness of the last few hours.

AUDRA INSISTED ON going in to work Friday morning, over Hud's objections. "I'll do much better if I focus on the children and my job, instead of sitting here brooding." She kissed his cheek and gathered her purse and messenger bag. "And I really think the worst is over. You'll see."

Hud didn't share her optimism, and said as much when he reported to Ranger Brigade headquarters. "If Ruffino was only acting at the behest of others, Audra won't be safe," he told the commander when everyone had gathered for the morning briefing. "We need to go after Terrell, Davis and Compton. I have a hard time believing Ruffino orchestrated all of this without them knowing about it."

"Terrell, Davis and Compton have issued a statement saying they had no knowledge of any of this and are appalled, horrified, etcetera," Sanderlin said.

"You don't believe that, do you?" Hud asked.

"We don't have any evidence showing their involvement," Sanderlin said. "The man who survived the shooting, Alex Ballantine, says Ruffino hired them as bodyguards because he said he had a meeting with a 'dangerous, shady character' and needed protection. Ballantine said Ruffino told them he was being blackmailed by this person and was afraid."

"So why did Ballantine's partner kill Ruffino?" Dance asked.

"Ballantine says the other man—Derek Capshaw— was just a guy he knows from the gym they both belong to. He says Ruffino pulled a knife on Audra and Capshaw must have decided on his own to protect the woman, who they both figured out pretty quick wasn't a threat."

"Audra didn't say anything about a knife," Hud said.

"Ballantine says she may not have seen it. And she's probably in shock."

"So where is the knife now?" Beck asked.

"If must have been lost in the scuffle," Sanderlin said.

"I think he's lying," Hud said.

"He's sticking to his story," Sanderlin said. "And he's coming up clean—no record for him or Capshaw."

Hud started to object again, but Sanderlin continued. "The bottom line is, this isn't our case anymore," Sanderlin said. "The shooting happened on county property, and it's their jurisdiction. They're probably going to press charges against Ballantine, but as far as they're concerned—and as far as the evidence shows—this was all Mitch Ruffino's doing. He was in charge of both the mine cleanup and the school construction, and TDC's statement emphasizes that he had complete autonomy. TDC is an international company, and the partners do not oversee day-to-day operations of their various offices."

Hud exchanged looks with others around the table. Some of them clearly shared his frustration. "Our job is to locate Dane Trask," Sanderlin continued. "That hasn't changed."

"When we find Trask, what then?" Dance asked.

"Maybe he'll having something to tell us," Sanderlin said. "Maybe he won't. But we have to do our job."

As far as Hud was concerned, he had a new job now—protecting the woman he loved.

He met Audra at the school at the end of the day. "How did it go?" he asked. "Any hassles from the press?"

"None. The news stories only mention that Mitch Ruffino was killed in 'an altercation at the school.' No mention of me at all." She smiled. "I'm hoping it stays that way. I'm guessing TDC will do everything they can to hush up this whole episode."

"You look pretty cheerful," he said. He had expected her to still be distraught and worried.

"Take a look at this." She motioned him over to her desk and pulled up a website on her computer.

He leaned in to get a better look. Montrose ISD Cancels New Elementary School Project read the headline. He skimmed the article that followed. The school district was halting construction due to "cost overruns and population projections that the school is not necessary at this time." According to the article, TDC had agreed to refund the money the district had paid so far and dismantle construction. The district thanked TDC for its cooperation and civic-mindedness, and cited the move as an example of the district's commitment to fiscal responsibility.

Hud looked at Audra. "That didn't take long," he said.

"I think TDC is very anxious to rebuild their reputation and make this all go away," she said. "Oh, and I received these this morning." She led him into the outer office, where a large flower arrangement took up much of a side table.

"Who sent those?" Hud asked.

"TDC! Along with a note apologizing for Mitch Ruffino's behavior and reassurances that they had nothing to do with any of this. They offered to assist me in any way they could."

"Assist you with what?"

"They didn't say. I think they're anxious to ensure I don't sue them. Oh, and of course, they're not suing me anymore, either. That was apparently Ruffino's doing, as well."

"Do you believe them?" he asked.

"I think I do." She touched the petals of a large red rose. "We've said all along none of this really made financial sense. And Ruffino has always been the one speaking out against my father, not Terrell, Davis or Compton."

He slipped an arm around her. Maybe she was right, and he'd been letting his emotions, and his suspicious nature, get in the way of common sense. "If the new elementary school won't be opened, then the new day care center won't, either."

"I should feel bad for Jana, but I don't really," Audra said. "I hired a new teacher today for her class—one of the moms who has been subbing wants the job. And our new anti-bullying curriculum starts next week."

She smiled up at him. The woman who had faced down death yesterday, who had seen her reputation shredded in the last week, had bounced back to this happy, optimistic person making plans for the future. "You're incredible, do you know that?" he asked.

"My dad taught me to focus on the things I could control and to look to the future," she said. "I resented his advice a lot when I was younger, but I guess I took it to heart after all."

"We're still looking for your father," he said.

"He's bound to hear about Ruffino's death soon," she said. "If he hasn't already. He'll be back, I'm sure of it." She hugged him close. "There's something else I'm sure of, too."

"Oh, what is that?"

"I'm sure that you're the man I'm meant to be with."

"Is that more planning for the future?"

Her eyes met his, full of warmth and an optimism he

found infectious. "I'm ready to put all this behind us,"
she said. "If you're willing."

"I'm willing," he said.

*   *   *   *   *

THE PROSECUTOR

NICHOLE SEVERN

To my husband: for managing to keep me from going insane during quarantine so I could write this book.

Chapter One

Jury benches had the potential to hide a lot of things.

Old wood protested under his knee as Deputy United States Marshal Jonah Watson crouched to slide his hand under the first bench before the judge and court personnel would take their seats in as little as fifteen minutes. The courthouse was made up of over thirty-nine courtrooms, and he and the other four marshals on his team would search and clear every single one of them.

After seven years of new construction due to age and seismic instability of the old courthouse, the new Multnomah County Central Courthouse had become the nerve center for the Rip City Bomber to meet justice. After triggering four bombs set throughout Portland and murdering thirty-two innocent civilians over the course of the past year, Rosalind Eyler was scheduled to face a jury of her peers to answer for the blood she'd spilled. For the lives she'd destroyed. The sick frenzy of the largest case Oregon District Court had ever seen had already begun. Protestors lined the courthouse perimeter calling for their idol to be found innocent, the media digging for details police had yet to release for the next big story in time for the six o'clock news. There were too many variables in a case like this, too many potential threats.

"I didn't realize you'd be part of the team assigned to clear the courtroom today." And in the center of it all, the all-too-enticing—and all-too-frustrating—senior deputy district attorney prosecuting the case, Madison Gray. Sleek black hair waved down around her shoulders as Jonah pushed to his feet. Her dark green blazer and knee-length skirt accentuated the darker undertones in her skin and highlighted the caramel swirls in her eyes. Sharp features and even sharper heels contributed to her controlling nature and bluntness, but it was the large, soft roundness of her midsection that'd claimed his attention now. Six months pregnant. With his baby. "I specifically requested a special assignment of the east Washington district US marshals to lend us deputies for judicial security."

"Now, why would the district attorney agree to that when he has a former FBI bomb squad technician right here in Portland at his disposal?" He hadn't worked as a unit chief in the hazardous devices school for the Bureau for more than half a decade, but the two years of hands-on training in the middle of a combat zone in Afghanistan had given him all the experience he'd need for the rest of his career. Military ordnance, hand grenades, homemade bombs, thermite. He had the knowledge and the attention to detail required to analyze, investigate and re-create any explosive—improvised or not—he'd come into contact with before joining the marshals service.

The only one he hadn't known how to deal with was the explosion of fire in Madison's gaze when he'd suggested they raise their baby together after she'd told him she was pregnant.

At the time, he'd brushed off her rejection and distance as their one night together all those months ago had turned into something neither of them could walk away from, but five months had gone by, and here she stood, just as adamant. No matter how many times he'd reached out, she'd declined his calls, avoided him in the courthouse hallways and ignored his effort to do the right thing. She wanted to raise this baby on her own and expected him to sign away any rights that came with his role as sperm donor when their baby was born.

She lowered her voice. "You're not supposed to be here."

Jonah crouched to search the next section of the jury bench. The preliminary hearing would start in less than ten minutes, and he hadn't gotten a chance to clear the tables where the deputy prosecutor and the defendant with her counsel would be seated. "What's the matter, Maddi? Afraid the media will see us in the same room together and magically figure out I'm the one who got you pregnant?"

"Why don't you say that a little louder? I wasn't sure the judge heard you in his chambers." Manicured fingernails with a metallic gold polish dug into the freshly stained wood edge of the jury box. "This is the biggest case of my career, Jonah. I can't make any more mistakes. Do you understand?"

A mistake. So that was what she was calling that

night they'd been together. Well, it beat not knowing anything at all, he supposed. This conversation had already beaten the record for their longest by two full minutes in the past five months. Jonah couldn't help but revel in the fact that despite all the self-confidence and control she kept in place when she prosecuted a case, he was still able to get a rise out of her. He swept his hand under the last section of the bench and climbed to his feet before dropping out of the jury box. At six foot three, he towered over her small frame, but she held her ground as he closed the distance between them. "Don't worry, Counselor. You just do your job, and I'll do mine. Speaking of which, I need to make sure nothing except my good looks are going to put you and the rest of the people in this courtroom at risk."

Her attention broke as a door off to the left of the judge's bench swung open. Fury slipped from Madison's expression, stiffness entering her neck and jaw, and Jonah turned to face the woman at the center of the Rip City Bomber trial. The defendant herself: Rosalind Eyler. Two sheriff's deputies flanked her on either side, the brightness of her red Multnomah County Corrections uniform stark against their dark green. Equally red hair blended into the fabric around her collar and draped down her back as the steel links between her wrist and ankle restraints rattled with each step toward the defendant's table.

Battle-ready tension thickened the muscles down his spine as Rosalind and her escort shuffled closer. Madison had made it clear the night they'd spent together— the night that'd resulted in new life forged between them—was nothing more than a mistake she'd happily avoid if given a second chance, but that wouldn't stop him from keeping a psychopath out of her orbit.

A sly smile tugged at Rosalind's thin lips, accentuating the heavy-handed spread of freckles over the bridge of her nose. Green eyes, almost the same color as Madison's blazer, brightened. Deep smile lines forged a path from the middle of her face outward. If it weren't for the fact the woman had been caught dead to rights with the components used to build her devices, Rosalind Eyler would've been just another pretty face.

"Madison, how lovely to see you again. I see you've been busy since the last time we spoke." That destructively humorous gaze dipped to Madison's baby bump, and every cell in Jonah's body caught fire with protective fury. Rosalind turned those deceptive eyes on him, and the hairs on the back of his neck stood on end. He'd met plenty of mass killers—terrorists—in his line of work, but none of them could compare to the woman sizing him up right then. No remorse. No guilt. Only pure pleasure. "Congratulations."

Jonah fought the urge to look at Madison for confirmation. There was no way in hell the Rip City Bomber knew he was the father of Madison's child. "Excuse me?"

"Thank you." The deputy district attorney smoothed her hands over the bump, cradling the underside of where their child rested as another man strolled through the door Rosalind had entered the courtroom through and took position at her side.

Pristine suit, lean muscle, slicked hair with a predatory expression cemented in place. Defense attorney. "Ms. Gray, I do hope you're not speaking with my client before today's proceedings. You know as well as I do any communication between the district attorney's office and my client needs to come straight through me."

"Relax, Harvey." Rosalind's attention threatened to burn a hole straight through Jonah's head, refusing to let up before she redirected her half smile toward Madison. "I was congratulating Madison on her pregnancy and giving her my best. I've heard the delivery can be one of the most traumatic events of a woman's life. I do hope she makes it to the finish line in one piece."

Jonah curled his hands into the center of his palms to counter the pressure building in his chest. "What the hell is that supposed to mean?"

A wave of growing voices echoed throughout the room as bailiffs led families, media and law enforcement personnel through the large wooden doors at the back of the courtroom and into the gallery.

"That's my cue." Rosalind stepped carefully in the direction her police escort led her. "Nice to finally meet you, Marshal Watson."

Sheriff's deputies led the bomber to her chair behind the defendant's table and helped her sit down. Rosalind's attorney took the seat beside his client as Madison straightened her shoulders, gave Jonah nothing more than an irritated glance and headed for the prosecution's table.

Court was about to proceed.

Rosalind watched him every step of the way as Jonah headed for the gallery. That casual smile of hers worked to pierce through the wall he'd built to ignore any distraction that'd keep him from his duty, but the Rip City Bomber couldn't get inside his head. Madison was already taking up too much space in that regard. Taking his seat directly behind the prosecution's table, Jonah automatically stood as the judge entered the courtroom, eyes forward. He'd cleared the courtroom in time for Rosalind Eyler to answer for her crimes, but the fact Madison had taken the case—putting herself and their baby on the front line of defense against a mass murderer—sent a warning straight to his gut.

"You may be seated," the judge said from the raised bench. Four large television screens installed above the grilled sections of wall where air and heat entered came to life as he took his own seat. "The People versus Rosalind Eyler on charges of bombing of public spaces, thirty-two counts of first-degree murder, use of explosives and malicious destruction of property resulting in—"

A cell phone rang off to Jonah's left, near the two television screens taking up the east wall of the courtroom. Slightly muted, probably stuffed down at the bottom of the purse of one of the women toward the end of the pew. Someone hadn't gotten the message to silence their device.

"Whoever brought a phone into my courtroom had better have a damn good reason." The judge stared out over the gallery in expectation.

Seconds passed, the ringing continued, but no one in the gallery moved to silence the device. Low murmurs swept through the gallery. Three hard strikes of the judge's gavel against solid wood echoed through the spacious room. Jonah craned his head back to get a better sense of where the ringing originated and stood, instincts on high alert. He'd cleared every inch of this courtroom, but something told him nobody in the gallery was moving because the owner of the cell phone wasn't present.

The ringing wasn't coming from someone's bag.

"Order!" The judge struck wood with the gavel again, but Jonah could focus only on the sound seemingly bleeding through the wall.

No. The slight electric echo placed it behind the grilled section of a new HVAC unit crews had installed during the new construction. Understanding hit, and Jonah twisted around. He lunged over the partition of wood separating him from Madison. "Everybody get down!"

A burst of fire and debris thrust him straight into the prosecution's table and knocked the oxygen from his lungs. Blazing heat and pain licked across his neck, the back of his skull and arms as the explosion spread fast and took down anyone in its path. Screams echoed throughout the courtroom. Jonah hit the floor beside the table where Madison had been seconds before.

Then it was quiet.

NOBODY SHOULD'VE KNOWN.

The ringing in her ears momentarily drowned out the panicked rush of movement all around her. A groan escaped her lips as she lifted her head. Senior Deputy District Attorney Madison Gray pressed her palms into the hardwood floor. Fragments of concrete and splintered wood bit into the overheated skin of her hands as time seemed to stretch in a distorted, hazy fluid.

The pristine courtroom where she'd been prepared to present evidence against Rosalind Eyler, the Rip City Bomber, had been replaced by fire, pain and blood. She forced herself to focus on the defendant's table as bystanders struggled to escape the massive space. The sheriff's deputies who'd escorted Rosalind into court hauled their charge from the floor and headed for the holding cells in the room adjacent to the judge's bench. Protocol. They couldn't risk the defendant escaping, but even through the haze of trauma, Madison caught the recognizable smile deepening the bomber's laugh lines on either side of her mouth as Rosalind looked back.

Madison collapsed back to the floor as the strength in her arms gave out. She rolled onto her back, her legs twisted one way, her upper body another. The fire alarm screeched louder each time the back doors swung open into the main corridor of the eighth floor. Frantic movements in her lower abdominals kept her conscious. Her baby. She had to check her baby. The explosion—the bomb—had detonated close enough there was a chance she'd sustained internal bleeding without realizing it. The assignment for this courtroom hadn't been released until this morning. Nobody should've known this would be the location of the Rip City Bomber's preliminary hearing. Nobody should've been able to place an explosive device without the US marshals knowing.

"Jonah." His name strained in her throat. He'd been the closest to the blast. The deputy had lunged over the bar in an attempt to protect her from injury. Only he hadn't been fast enough. He had to be here. He had to be alive. Madison battled to get to all fours. The ringing in her ears ceded, but in its place came a wash of terror and panic. The gallery had been demolished, sobs echoing off the paneled walls. Black scorch marks and flames climbed the bench where the judge had been sitting mere seconds ago. She swiped at a line of warm liquid running down the side of her face, hand shaking. Blood.

And there on the other side of the table, the father of her child. Unconscious.

Madison licked dust-covered lips as she stretched one hand forward, then brought her knee up to follow. On hands and knees, she crawled around the prosecution's table until she could slide her fingers into his palm. "Jonah, get up."

He jerked into consciousness, his hand clasping hard around hers. Black-singed ends of hair curled at the base of his neck and around his full beard of light brown thickness. Alarm flashed in iridescent blue eyes at the sight of the aftermath still unfolding around them. Thick ropes of muscle hardened as he pushed upright. "Madison."

"I'm here." Relief coursed through her. He was alive. As far as she could tell, he hadn't been too injured. She tugged her hand from his, falling back onto one hip, and held on to the solid curve of her baby bump. She couldn't breathe, couldn't think. Someone had triggered an explosion inside the very same courtroom where

Rosalind Eyler was scheduled to answer for what she'd done, but Madison didn't have time to investigate why, how or when. "I... The baby."

His gaze immediately dropped to her lower abdominals. He reached for her in the same moment and, without hesitation or consideration for any injuries he might've sustained from the explosion, scooped her into his arms. It didn't matter what'd happened between them, how many times she'd declined his calls or how often she'd gone out of her way to avoid him in their professional interactions. Past experience and his case history said she could count on him to care about this baby. Debris crunched under his boots as he maneuvered around the unrecognizable bench he'd been sitting on before the blast. "I'm going to get you out of here. Hang on to me."

Reality sped into focus as the fire alarm shrieked in her ears. Heels clicked on polished tile behind them as Jonah pushed through the damaged courtroom doors and into the corridor. Courthouse security shouted from the bank of elevators and directed them toward the stairs. The elevators had gone into automatic lockdown. Rubble slid across the floor and slammed into the baseboards as victims of the explosion stumbled from the courtroom. The dark green color of her skirt-suit had turned an ash gray, tiny holes pockmarking the hem on one side. This was supposed to be her big case, the one that'd put her in line for the district attorney. This was the case that would've proved she'd risen above her past, but now her chance was gone. Disintegrated in the leftover ashes of that tinderbox.

Emergency personnel raced toward them from the stairs.

"Issue an evacuation of this building! I want all the top floors cleared as fast as possible. That bomb could've damaged the structural integrity of the entire courthouse." Jonah gave orders without slowing. The command in his voice neutralized the panic clawing up her throat. This was what he did for a living. This was what the FBI had trained Jonah for domestically and in Afghanistan for two years. When the entire world threatened to collapse around her, he'd fallen directly into his element to be the voice of calm and reason, and she couldn't help but latch onto that strength and try to take some it for herself. "I counted twenty-six injured, eight dead and no sign of the judge or the bailiff."

Eight dead? So many lives destroyed. How could this have happened? Why?

The answer burned on the tip of her tongue as Jonah ran toward the stairs. The Rip City Bomber. Rosalind Eyler was connected somehow, and Madison would prove it. As soon as the EMTs cleared her and the baby's health, she'd get in touch with the district attorney. She'd get the bomb squad to analyze the scene and bring new charges against the defendant to make sure Rosalind never saw the outside of a prison cell for the rest of her life. The same sentence Madison's father should've met all those years ago.

New determination chased back the terror that'd taken control.

"Put me down." Madison pressed her palm into Jonah's chest, the fast-paced pounding of his heart in rhythm with hers. She had enough strength to get herself downstairs and checked by one of the arriving EMTs. He needed to be here. He needed to help as many people as he could, and she could take care of herself. "I can walk from here."

"That bomb detonated less than fifteen feet from where you were sitting, Maddi." He easily kept pace down seven floors of courthouse stairs with her added weight. The scent of smoke and something she couldn't identify clung to the deep brown corduroy of his jacket. Nothing like the rich cinnamon spice she'd missed these past few months. "There's no way in hell I'm giving you the chance to run before I make sure you and my baby are okay for myself."

My baby. Those two words sunk like a rock in her stomach. Despite the fact he was indeed the father of the life growing inside her, she'd committed to raising this child on her own after the birth—physically, financially and emotionally. Just because they'd made a baby together didn't mean she needed to rely on him for help or security. But because he'd defended his argument to carry her with the safety of her and the baby in mind, she couldn't offer a rebuttal without throwing her priorities into question. She cared about this baby. There was no argument to be had, but his concern worked under her skin and scratched at her independence. She'd gotten this far on her own, and she sure as hell wasn't one of his damsels in distress to be saved.

Cold Portland air shocked every inch of her exposed

skin as Jonah kicked open the lobby doors and maneuvered her through. Fire and police vehicles condensed
onto the scene as panicked civilians crowded the perimeter the Portland Police Bureau had established and
pointed up the side of the building. Madison followed
their gazes. Dread pooled at the base of her spine where
Jonah's hand supported her. Black smoke and bright
flames escaped what she could see of the massive hole
the bomb had created, and air crushed from her lungs.

Fifteen feet. She'd been only fifteen feet away from
the blast and somehow survived an explosion that'd
ripped an entire hole in the side of the Multnomah
County Central Courthouse building. Gravity increased
its hold on her body as the reality of that thought bled
into focus. This didn't make sense. If the bomb had
been strong enough and positioned well enough to blow
a hole through several feet of concrete and steel, how
had she walked away and eight others hadn't?

Jonah's grip strengthened around her back and alongside her thigh as he rushed her to the closest ambulance.
"I have a survivor. Deputy District Attorney Madison
Gray, age thirty-three, multiple head lacerations, possible internal bleeding and six months pregnant. You
need to make sure she and the baby are okay."

Red and blue patrol lights blurred in her vision as
he hauled her into the back of the ambulance. Within
seconds, emergency staff had a blood pressure cuff
strapped around her arm and an oxygen mask in place.
Her breathing echoed back to her through the mask. Her
heart rate spiked as the facts of the explosion lined up in

her head, but the heaviness of Jonah's gaze anchored her enough to drown the uncertainty clawing up her throat.

"You're going to be okay. I promise." Jonah wrapped a calloused hand in hers at the side of the gurney. Instant warmth shot through her at that single touch, the same warmth that'd led to her getting pregnant by him in the first place, and the world tilted on its axis. From the added oxygen or from him, she didn't know. "I'm not going anywhere."

Static interrupted the sense of peace his confidence instilled deep in her bones. A female voice penetrated the small bubble he'd somehow created between them and the violent chaos outside the ambulance walls. "Deputy Watson, I need you to meet me on channel two."

Extracting his hand from hers, Jonah peeled the radio strapped to his Kevlar vest from his chest and turned the dial. Compelling blue eyes shifted out the back of the ambulance, and in an instant, the spell was broken. The one that had the ability to convince her to let him get past her guard again, that she could trust his intentions. "Glad to hear you survived, Chief. What do you have?"

Remington Barton, Jonah's deputy chief. Madison had met the woman only a couple of times during judicial security assignments and testimony proceedings, but each encounter had been ingrained in Madison's memory. The former New Castle County sheriff held her own in a job dominated by the opposite sex and rarely backed down without a fight. For her deputies, for her witnesses and anyone else lucky enough to be brought under her protection. "An anonymous source has just taken credit for the bombing."

Jonah compressed the push-to-talk button. "And?"

The deputy chief didn't miss a beat. "The call confirmed Deputy District Attorney Madison Gray as the bomber's target."

Chapter Two

I do hope she makes it to the finish line in one piece.

Rosalind Eyler's words spoken mere minutes before the explosion ripped apart that courtroom echoed on repeat in his head as Jonah lunged out the back of the ambulance. The radio's casing nearly buckled under his grip as he studied the perimeter of onlookers and civilians beyond the caution tape marking the scene.

"Jonah." His name pierced through the oxygen mask covering Madison's nose and mouth, drawing his attention back to her stretched out on the gurney. Lines of dirt and debris sharpened the angles of her face. Her hair, usually smooth and without a single strand out of place, was frizzed and more textured than a mere twenty minutes ago.

The mother of his child was the target of a bomber.

The Rip City Bomber case was the biggest the state of Oregon had ever seen in domestic terrorism. Every detail, including the fact Madison had been assigned as the lead prosecutor, had been made public, but there were details the district attorney's office hadn't released to the media. The device he'd heard had been wired with a cell phone to trigger the detonation. Whoever'd set that bomb had to know the layout of the courtroom, where the prosecution's table would be positioned and the minute the preliminary hearing had started in order to achieve full destruction. The only way the bomber would've known the exact moment to detonate was if they'd been close enough to ensure their target was in range.

Only something had gone wrong.

The blast had mainly diverted to the outer wall of the building. Jonah memorized every face in the crowd, every officer and EMT on the scene. The bomber had failed in getting to Madison, which meant there was a chance they'd try again.

His blood pressure rocketed into dangerous territory. He had to get her out of here. For the sake of her life, their baby's life. Jonah closed the distance between him and the back of the ambulance, his right shoulder blade screaming with the slightest jerk of his arm. The sight of one of the paramedics with his hand pressing into the exposed, flawless curve of Madison's belly tugged at something under Jonah's rib cage. He strapped his radio back onto his Kevlar vest. "How is she?"

"She's stable. No sign of internal bleeding or fetal distress," the EMT said, "but we should still get her to the hospital to do an ultrasound and make sure mother and baby are in the clear."

"Can she be moved to a different location?" he asked.

"Jonah, no." Madison pushed upright, the set of that perfect mouth rigid as though she could read his mind.

"I'm not going into protective custody. I need to be here. I need to finish what I started."

Every second she was out in the open was another chance the bomber had of taking away everything Jonah had fought to protect. Madison had made it clear she intended to raise this baby on her own when she'd walked away all those months ago, but that wouldn't stop him from doing whatever he had to do in order to keep her and their child alive. The EMT hadn't answered. "I said, can she be moved?"

"Yes." The emergency technician backed himself into the side door of his rig, eyes wide. "Her vitals are fine, but, Marshal Watson, you're bleeding. We should take a look at that wound on the back of your shoulder."

"That's the least of my problems right now." Stepping up into the back of the ambulance, he pressed his hand beneath Madison's elbow and urged her to get to her feet. "Deputy District Attorney Gray, you are officially under US Marshal protection for the duration of the investigation into today's attack, and I'm getting you out of here."

"Like hell you are." She wrenched her arm out of his hold, that caramel-brown gaze molten. Every ounce of the independent, self-confident and controlled woman he'd been battling with the past few months rose to the surface as though he were one of the defendants she prosecuted in the courtroom. She stood on her own. "Rosalind Eyler killed thirty-two people in the past year. Thirty-two people who won't ever get to see their families again, and I'm the only one who can make sure she pays for that. If I'm going anywhere, it's back to get the bomb squad here to prove to the DA we should add this attack to the charges I'm bringing against her." She maneuvered past him to step down from the ambulance. "I've got a job to do, and there's nothing you can do to stop me."

Moving fast, Jonah pulled his handcuffs from the pocket at the back of his vest and wrapped one cuff around her hand clutched to the ambulance door. He secured the other end around his own wrist as she turned on him, then pulled her deeper into the back of the rig. Tugging her wrist up between them, he stepped into her. "You've made it perfectly clear you want nothing to do with me these past five months, Maddi, and there's not a damn thing I can do about that. But whoever targeted you knows who you are. They know where you work, where you live, what car you drive, who your friends are, that you're six months pregnant and your daily routine. They've watched every public interview you've given and figured out how desperate you are to prove yourself on this case. They'll know your next move and the one after that, and they're going to find out they failed in killing you today. Unless you come with me right now, they're going to try again." He lowered his voice low enough to keep his next words between them. "So I'll make it clear to you now, Counselor. You might think your job is so important to you that you would risk our baby's life, but I'm not willing to take that chance."

He'd already lost too much.

The small muscles on either side of her throat flexed as she swallowed. Hardness in her expression shallowed. Seconds passed, maybe a minute. "How do you know? How do you know whoever's behind this has gone to that much trouble to dig into my life?"

"Because that's exactly what I would've done." He'd investigated enough improvised explosive devices to determine the state of mind of the bombers behind them over the years. Ranging from Middle East combat zones where the devices were meant to cause as much damage as possible for a cause, to homegrown terrorists sending a message as he'd assisted state and local bomb techs, Jonah knew without a doubt whoever'd targeted Madison had made this personal. This attack hadn't been about a cause or killing as many people as possible. It'd been about one person: Madison. As much as he wanted to suit up and be part of the bomb technician team that would be assigned to assess the threat in the rest of the building, he needed to be here. For her. He wasn't FBI anymore. He was a US marshal, and his judicial security had just become a witness protection assignment. "I need you to trust me. If you want to get out of this alive, if you want our baby to make it out of this alive, you're going to have to do exactly as I say."

Her shoulders rose and fell with exaggerated breath. She nodded.

"Good. Take your heels off and hand over your phone. We're headed for my SUV parked around the corner. The bomber most likely knows what kind of car you drive. Move fast but don't run, stay low and keep hold of my hand at all times." He dug the handcuff keys from his pocket and twisted the cuff off his wrist, then hers. A sudden high-pitch protest of Velcro ripping free filled the back of the ambulance as he hefted his Kevlar body armor over his head and maneuvered the thick vest onto her shoulders. He pulled the fasteners tighter at her sides. "Use me as a shield if you have to."

Madison removed her shoes, long fingers wrapped around the heels in one hand, then unpocketed her phone from her deep green blazer and handed it over. "You think whoever set off that bomb is here? You think he's watching me?"

"I'd rather take every precaution and be wrong, than take none and have the bastard surprise us. IEDs come in a lot of shapes, sizes and forms, and there's no way to know if the bomber has set any other devices until the bomb squad is on scene and can clear this entire block." Powering down her phone, he intertwined his hand in hers. "We have no idea who we're dealing with, Maddi, and until we do, I need to get you off the grid and into hiding. That means no phone calls, no email, no messages or contact with your friends, family and coworkers. As of this moment, you're under the protection of the United States Marshals Service. It's the only way I know to keep you safe."

Madison's gaze shot to his as she clasped his hand. "Okay, but there better be dill pickle chips when we get wherever you're taking me."

"I think I can manage that." Jonah tightened his hand around hers and fell into the mindset he reserved for high-risk operations. Any time he'd approached a suspicious package, backpack, a pressure cooker on the side of the street or been assigned to gather evidence after an explosion outside American bases across the ocean, nothing mattered but the objective. In Afghanistan, it'd been to collect as many pieces of evidence as he could and re-create the device in a controlled environment to figure out how it functioned. Right now, it was getting Madison to safety. Nothing else could get in the way. "Three. Two. One."

They stepped from the back of the ambulance and headed straight for the perimeter of tape the Portland Police Bureau had secured around the scene. She struggled to keep up with his long strides as he wound her through the crowd of spectators and police. "Not too fast. Don't draw attention to yourself."

"I think the burn marks in my dress will do that for me." She kept her head down and a tight grip on her heels, but she was right. They wouldn't be able to hide the fact they were covered in ash and blood for long. The faster they left the area, the better.

"You're doing fine." He checked back over his shoulder mere feet from the corner of the courthouse, focused on the familiar car parked four spaces down. Madison's. Twenty more feet and they'd be in range of his SUV. "Just keep—"

The second explosion hurled a fireball and blast wave straight into the sky between buildings. Jonah pulled her into him, covering her with his own body as much as he could as glass and small chunks of cement rained down on top of them. Fire engulfed the parked vehicle they'd passed mere seconds before, the same car he'd recognized a split second before it'd gone up in flames. Dust and debris clouded the air. Another round of panic echoed around them as he straightened, Madison's gaze fixed on the same vehicle. Hot air burned down his throat and into his lungs. "I see you drove to work today."

"THEY PUT A bomb in my car." Madison was barely able to say the words. Who would do this to her? Who would target her? Who would try to kill her? The soft vibration of tires against asphalt did nothing to calm the chaos churning through her. She held on to her heels a bit tighter than necessary as Jonah drove them over the Morrison Bridge. Deep blue water spread out on either side of them, beautiful and entrancing, but she couldn't focus on that right now. Couldn't focus on anything other than the fact if he hadn't taken her into protective custody, she would've gotten in that car to drive to her office. She would've died trying to prove Rosalind Eyler was behind the attack in the courthouse. "If they'd planned on the first device to kill me, why set another one in my car?"

"Backup plan," he said. "Must've been tracking you—visually or electronically—and figured out you'd survived the first explosion. They had the second one waiting for you, to finish the job. Only they hadn't counted on me taking you to my vehicle instead."

None of this made any sense. She was a deputy district attorney. She couldn't deny the cases she'd prosecuted had made enemies over the years, but the line was ten times longer for her boss. Although, trying the Rip City Bomber case as she'd nearly died from a bomb in the same courtroom as Rosalind Eyler was too much of a coincidence to ignore. The only question still out of reach was motive. If she found the motive behind the attack, she could narrow down the suspect, whether that was Rosalind herself, someone close to the bomber, possibly a family member of one of the victims. Once she had a motive, she could secure her future. For her and her baby.

"Thank you for getting me out of the building. There were a lot of other people that needed help, but you made sure I made it to the ambulance." But it hadn't been about her. Not really. She slipped her hand over her growing baby bump. *You might think your job is so important to you that you would risk our baby's life, but I'm not willing to take that chance.* Jonah's accusation twisted the knife in her heart deeper. Because when she'd found out she was pregnant from their one night together, she'd instantly thought of her career. Of how a baby would change the plans she'd set for herself over the next five, ten, twenty years. How this small, precious life she'd become accustomed to over the past few months would derail her chances of being elected to district attorney down the line. She hadn't thought of the impact her decision would have on the child they'd created together, hadn't even thought of Jonah or what he might want. "You were wrong before. I do care about this baby. You have no idea how much. I would never put its life at risk for the chance to get ahead in my job."

Those hypnotic blue eyes she'd fallen prey to over the years remained fixed out the windshield. He hadn't told her where he planned to take her, hadn't spoken much at all unless it'd been about the scene they'd left behind, and the air between them grew thick. His grip slid down the steering wheel as they crossed to the other side of the bridge. "You're right. I don't know how much you care. You've been keeping me at arm's length ever since I told you I wanted to be involved, that I intended for us to parent this baby together."

The knot of guilt that'd formed the moment she'd said those words all those months ago spread like a wildfire. She'd done this to them. She'd taken their friendship—one built on years of him escorting her to and from the courthouse, playful banter and mutual attraction—to the next level, then turned her back on him the instant she'd seen those two blue lines on the pregnancy test. Not only had she severed the connection between them as lovers, but she'd destroyed their relationship as friends, and he deserved better. He deserved to know why. "It's not about you, Jonah. It's… It's about not being forced to rely on someone other than myself. Not being trapped in a situation neither of us can escape from."

"And you believe because we'll be raising this baby together that you'll be bound to me for the rest of our lives?" He directed the SUV onto the 26, taking them east toward Mount Hood. Snowcaps hid the sharp curve of the peak she'd become familiar with since relocating to Portland five years ago, straight out of Berkeley Law, but that still gave a deep sense of wonder and order she craved. "It took two people to make that baby, Madison. Stands to reason it'd take two people to raise it."

Madison. Not Maddi. That one simple change managed to disrupt the emotional calm she'd been trying to hold on to since Jonah had placed himself between the bomb in the courtroom and her. The logical part of her brain said he'd only been protecting his offspring that happened to be inside her body. But the other part of her, the part that missed what they'd had together before she'd learned of the pregnancy, was working hard to convince her he still cared about her. That he'd gone out of his way to make sure she walked out of that courtroom alive. Not because of the baby but because he missed what they'd had, too. "Twenty-three percent of all kids in the country are raised in single-parent homes. Statistically, they might not have the same advantages as a two-parent home, but I make enough money to support us, especially if I'm elected to DA when my boss steps down in a few months. The Rip City Bomber is a career-changing case guaranteed to position me as a front-runner for his job."

"I know what your job entails. I'm the one who escorted you to and from the courthouse every day until you asked for another marshal to take over my assignment. Early mornings, late nights, mountains of takeout and long hours." The city bled to countryside the farther he took them out of the city. "Do you think it's going to get any better when you're the district attorney? Are you even going to be able to take time off to recover from the birth?"

"I've already hired someone to help me when the baby comes." She stared out the passenger side window. It wouldn't get easier. If anything, the long hours and exhaustion would get worse, and she'd still have an infant to care for when she came home. Her child would have to be with a caretaker throughout the day, but the alternative wasn't an option. Not after she'd witnessed what her mother had been through all those years. "I'm not saying it'll be easy, but it's still my decision to make."

His exhale filled the silence between them. "You're right, and I'll respect that decision as much as I don't see the reasoning behind it, but you need to know you don't have to do this alone."

Yes, she did.

"My father was abusive. He drank. He got addicted to drugs, and when he'd come off his high, he'd take it out on my mother." Madison stared out the window. She couldn't remember the last time she'd taken the opportunity to get out of the city. Tall, green pines and light-faced rock streamed past the window, but she couldn't focus on the beauty of any of it. "He could barely hold down a job, but he was adamant she wasn't allowed to work. He needed to know where she was, who she was talking to and what she was doing at all times, leaving us with barely enough to get by or have food on the table. And that's the way he wanted it."

"You never talked about your family when I asked," he said.

"I'm not ashamed of the way I grew up. I'm the woman I am because of what I went through. It took a lot of self-awareness and healing for me to realize it, but I'm proud of the fact I worked harder than anyone else in my class. I made sure I had the opportunity to get out of there the moment I graduated high school by keeping my grade point average the highest of all my classmates, applying for scholarships, working as many jobs as I could. I put everything into getting into law school because I didn't want to be trapped in that life. With him. Like she was."

"Your mother." His voice dropped low, unleashing a flood of renewed illusions that taking her into protective custody was something more than protecting his child.

"He controlled every aspect of her life. He made the rules. He made sure she couldn't leave no matter how bad it got. She tried. Some of my clearest memories are her waking me up in the middle of the night, my bags already packed. We'd spend a night here, a night there, at some crummy hotel in the city thanks to a few bucks one of her friends had thrown our way, but the money always ran out. And she'd go back to him." Madison forced herself to take a deep breath. She had to detach from the pain and move forward more analytically. She'd made a mistake in letting herself imagine there could be more between her and Jonah, and now they'd slipped into an intimacy neither of them could recover from. "I never planned on this pregnancy, Jonah, but the thought of being tied to the father of my child scares me. I don't want to end up like my mother. I don't want to be helpless and controlled. I don't want to give anyone the opportunity to have that power over me. Raising this baby on my own is the only way I can see to make sure that never happens."

The tendons along his neck bunched, revealing the power and strength beneath the thin layer of his T-shirt, as he slowed the SUV. Shadows engulfed them on either side as they took the next unpaved road deeper into the wilderness but within minutes vanished. A large, majestic cabin sat off to the left of a wide clearing surrounded by the tallest trees she'd ever seen. Beautiful landscaping of shrubbery hugged up against the deck and well-maintained grounds. Countless windows and a skylight reflected warm spring sun, inviting and golden. Sharp angles and beautiful wood blended perfectly with the surrounding forest, and an instant feeling of peace washed through her. It was beautiful. The SUV slowed to a stop, and she reached for the door handle.

"I'm sorry all that happened to you growing up, Maddi. I can't imagine how scared you must've been living in that house, but I'm not your father." Jonah shouldered out of the SUV, hand on the door. "The only thing I care about is the safety and happiness of you and that baby. I just wish you'd give me the chance to prove it."

Chapter Three

This wasn't how it was supposed to be.

Taking Madison into protective custody should've been easy. She'd been in danger, and he had the skills to get her out of it. Simple as that. Whatever'd happened between them wasn't supposed to get in the way of their current arrangement, but as she'd revealed the past she'd been keeping to herself all these years, his protective instincts had taken control. He wasn't her father. He'd never go out of his way to control her or their child, never intimidate her, hurt her or trap her in an unbearable situation. Having her walk away from what'd he'd considered the most intense and fulfilling friendship of his life had ripped him apart, but she didn't want the past to repeat itself. Didn't want their child caught in the middle of a toxic environment if things between them hadn't worked out, and he had to respect her decision.

Jonah unloaded his supply bag from the back of the SUV, then paused before hiking up the small incline toward the front door of the cabin, his shoulder on fire. But he couldn't accept never seeing his child once he or she was born. Never having the opportunity to hold the life they'd created together, to be there for their first word, first step, first day of school. To sing their baby to sleep or watch them drift off in his arms. He'd missed out on a lot of that when his son, Noah, had been born. He'd been stationed overseas with the FBI, and when he'd returned home, it'd been too late. "This way."

"If I would've known this place existed the night we slept together, I would've insisted we come here instead of going back to my house." Heels still clutched in one hand, Madison studied the tall rise of the front of the cabin with floor-to-ceiling windows reflecting fading sunlight back into her face. Dried ash and blood clung to flawless warm-colored skin, the rips in her panty-hose revealing scrapes and a longer laceration across her shin, but right then, she was still one of the most enthralling women he'd ever met. "It's beautiful. Quiet."

A laugh escaped up his throat. "Comes with an indoor hot tub, too."

"Get out of my way. My feet are killing me." She marched past him, one hand beneath her growing belly, the other swinging her heels for momentum up the incline. Lean muscle flexed along the backs of her legs as she took the stairs up to the front door. Pushing inside, she slowed slightly beyond the entrance. "I should've agreed to protective custody sooner."

"It's mine." The air-conditioning cooled the stinging skin along his neck as he closed the door behind them. After setting his duffel bag on the bench that made up part of the mudroom, he armed the alarm panel just inside the door. Amazement smoothed the hard set of her mouth, and he couldn't help but memorize the effect. "I bought it before the Bureau assigned me to Afghanistan. Doesn't get much use nowadays since I've relocated closer to the city, but you'll be safe here. Top-of-the-line security system installed by the premier security company in the country, remote location and no connection to you, the DA's office or the marshals service. Whoever's targeted you won't be able to find you here."

"May I...?" She motioned into the main living space.

"Be my guest." He followed in her path as she took in the twenty-foot ceilings, the wood-burning stove he'd gated off to keep small fingers from getting burned. Watched as she ran her fingers over individual books stacked on the shelf off to their left. A light-colored wood made up the grand staircase leading up to the bedrooms over a kitchen built with the same stain on the cabinets and island. Skylights cast pink rays across the prosecutor's face, highlighted the darkness of her hair. He could still see this place as the family home he'd meant it to be when he'd purchased it, but knowing now what he did about Madison's past, he wasn't sure that'd ever be a possibility. "There are four empty bedrooms upstairs for you to choose from, but the main is the only one that has an en suite bathroom. You should have everything you need in there if you want to clean up."

She turned to face him, running her palms down her hips. "I don't have any fresh clothes."

"I keep some shirts and sweats in the closet in case I leave directly from work to come up here. You're welcome to help yourself to anything you need while I put together something for us to eat." He headed for the pantry, making a mental list of the provisions he had on hand. "I don't have dill pickle chips, but I can have another deputy pick up some bags and pack you a few items from your house—"

"Jonah, what are you doing?" Soft footsteps reached his ears a split second before long, delicate fingers wrapped around his arm. She dropped her heels at her feet and turned him toward her. "How long were you going to stand there and bleed until you said something?"

"In case you didn't notice, I had more important things to worry about at the time." In truth, he'd planned on taking a look at the wound in the smaller bathroom while she cleaned up in the main. No need to stress her or the baby out more than she already was, but it was obvious he wasn't going to be able to hide it from her any longer. He let her move him toward the large circular dining table where he'd imagined hosting family dinners and holidays and took a seat. The pain in his shoulder reignited with white fire around the wound. The shrapnel had penetrated past clothing and skin, but not enough time had passed to put him in danger of going into shock.

"For as much as you lecture me about not raising this baby alone, you sure don't apply the same concern to yourself." Her hand slipped from his arm, and he felt the distance in a gut-wrenching kind of way. "Where's your first aid kit?"

"Under the sink." He motioned his chin toward the kitchen island.

She didn't wait for permission, turning her back on him to disappear behind the cabinet, but even that moment of not having her in his sight line raised heated awareness of her. Within seconds, the caramel-colored eyes he'd envisioned their baby to inherit settled on him as she approached with the white-and-red kit in her hand. "Take off the shirt."

The request hit him square in the chest. "Don't have to sound so disappointed about it. I seem to remember there was a time you couldn't wait for me to get my shirt off."

A small laugh bubbled past her lips, and the world threatened to slip right out from under him. He'd missed that laugh. Missed her, if he was being perfectly honest with himself. Jonah peeled his shirt over his head, careful of the small piece of metal that'd torn through the muscle in his shoulder. The days he'd been assigned to escort her to and from the courthouse were some of the memories that stuck in his mind the longest. He'd been at her side not only as part of his protection detail, but also because he'd genuinely gotten comfortable there. He'd looked forward to hearing her talk about her day, wanted every detail she could reveal about the cases she was working on and strived to learn more about her. Time had no meaning when they'd been in the car together, and if he'd realized one morning she'd request another marshal to take over his detail, he would've gone out of his way to memorize every detail of those long hours he'd taken for granted.

"Yeah, well, don't get any ideas of something like that happening again." Madison pressed her thumb near the wound, and he sucked a cold hiss of air through his teeth to counter the sharp attack of pain. "Sorry. I'm not a doctor. I'm not exactly sure how to do this."

Better to feel the pain than feel nothing at all. He had to remember that. "Sanitize your hands with the rubbing alcohol pads in the kit and clean around the wound as best you can. You'll have to remove the shrapnel with the tweezers."

She did as instructed. Calm. Collected. Controlled. Everything he wasn't as he recalled how the damn piece of metal had gotten there in the first place. She was alive. She was safe. She was a target, and he wasn't sure how he was supposed to feel about that. He'd already lost too much. He couldn't lose her, too. A metallic ping registered off the surface of the table. "It's out. Now what?"

"Now you hand me the gauze and tape and rest while I check the security system and make us some lunch." He stood, overshadowing her by more than a foot and a hundred pounds. Despite their differences in size, she'd taken on far more dangerous predators in her line of work without a single crack in that confident expression. Predators like the Rip City Bomber. Madison Gray had risen above a past determined to break her in every way. As long as he'd known her, there was no blockade she couldn't get through, and damn, if he didn't admire her for it.

"Suit yourself." She handed over the roll of tape and gauze and turned away from him toward the grand staircase leading up to the second level. Halfway between the dining room table and the stairs, she slowed. Hesitation bled into her stride. Sections of damaged hair slid across her back as she turned to face him. "You put yourself between me and that device in the court-room, knowing you'd take the brunt of the blast if it hadn't diverted to the outer wall of the building. Was that because you were trying to protect me? Or protect the baby?"

Bits and pieces of memory flashed across his mind. Holding his baby boy for the first time, the smile on Noah's face as the infant had felt and heard his own stomach growl, Jonah counting the number of chubby leg rolls and squeezing each one of them to make his son laugh. There'd been so many of those moments and not enough at the same time. He never should've accepted the assignment to Afghanistan. Maybe if he hadn't—if he'd stayed—Noah would still be here. But now the hardened deputy district attorney in front of Jonah was asking him if he'd put his own life in dan-ger for their child or for her, and he couldn't ignore the hint of past vulnerability breaking the evenness of her voice. "I didn't want to lose either of you."

Not again.

THE SUPERFICIAL CUT across her head stung as Madi-son ran a brush through her wet hair. White marble gleamed across the two-sink vanity stocked with fresh towels, fragranced lotions and a single bottle of cinna-mon-spiced aftershave. Turquoise tile surrounded the spacious walk-in shower and the wall behind the free-standing tub, white hexagon tiles heating under her feet. This bathroom—this cabin—had been built and deco-rated with every luxury she could imagine. From the massive wall of windows in the master bedroom right down to the color of the wood running the length of the entire structure. There was an atmosphere of comfort here, so thick she could see herself on solid ground. Steam clung to the wood-framed mirror over the sink she'd chosen to use to put herself back together. Only she wasn't sure that was possible this time.

Small scratches stood bright against the backdrop of the deeper olive tones of her skin, down her neck, across the backs of her hands. She could still feel the heat of the blast that'd singed across her arms. Parting the luxurious robe she'd found hanging from a hook beside the shower, too big for her, Madison curved her palms over the protruding bump of her belly. Not a scratch. Not a bruise. How much worse would her injuries have been if Jonah hadn't been there? Would she have been able to get herself out of the courtroom if another marshal had taken the judicial security assignment this morning? The answer was already on the tip of her tongue as she recalled his expression when she'd asked if he'd risked his life for her or for their baby. It'd been as though he'd taken the weight of the entire world on at that moment and could barely keep himself upright. Seeing the reserved, practical marshal who'd saved her life—who'd been her friend for so long—break in front of her had crumbled the defensive strategy she'd prepared for herself faster than the attack had. Right then, the walls she'd built to keep herself and this baby safe from dependency had cracked, and she wasn't sure, when it came to Jonah, she'd ever be strong enough to repair them.

Madison hugged the oversize robe around her tighter, hints of that cinnamon-spiced aftershave tickling the back of her throat, and stepped back into the master bedroom. The cathedral ceiling stretched overhead as she paved a trail across the pure white comforter and sheets expertly tucked over the king-size bed with her fingers. She didn't know what it was about this room in particular, how she was supposed to feel being here. She and Jonah weren't together. They weren't lovers. They weren't friends. Why would he bring her here? The United States Marshal Service had safe houses all over the state. He could've taken her to any number of them, but he'd brought her to a place that obviously meant more to him than he'd let on before. Was this where he intended to raise their baby if she'd agreed to him being part of her life?

Dressing in an oversize pair of sweatpants and a T-shirt she'd found in the massive walk-in closet, Madison skimmed the rich gray carpet with her bare toes. Aches and pains stiffened her steps as she circled the large master bedroom. It was perfect in every way. Spacious, welcoming, warm with the fireplace in the corner. The white trim and gray walls soothed the nervous energy skittering up her spine and urged her to fall back on the bed to rest. To stop the constant analysis of each and every moment she and Jonah were together, stop trying to read between the lines and questioning his motives, stop fighting and just…be. When was the last time she'd let herself be still?

The entire cabin was a representation of everything she'd imagined as a child, but reality had never allowed for such dreams. Survival won out over fantasy every day her mother allowed herself and her only daughter to take the abuse her father had handed out. As if they'd deserved the pain for merely existing.

But Madison wasn't that scared little girl anymore.

She'd taken scholarships to put herself through law school, worked harder than any other classmate to get herself on the path to district attorney and vowed never to let anyone get in her way or hold her back. The truth was she couldn't stop. Not until she proved herself. To her father, who'd promised she'd always be useless, helpless and have to rely on him to get through life, to anyone who'd looked her in the face and told her she'd never have the determination, talent or drive to follow through with her dreams. That they were impossible for a woman like her. One mistake. That was all it'd take, and her future would be ripped out from under her.

It wasn't this room asking for her to give in. It was the man who'd brought her here, the marshal she'd put aside everything she believed in for the smallest chance of experiencing what it would feel like to be cared for.

Madison wrenched the bedroom door open harder than she intended and ran straight into a mountain of muscle on the other side. Warmth shot through her as she clasped onto his arm to stabilize herself. Jonah. Strong muscle flexed under her hand, and her mouth dried as memories of how those muscles surrounded her six short months ago lit up in her brain. She stepped back. "I didn't realize you were outside the door."

"I wasn't spying on you if that's what you're worried about," he said.

She hadn't thought of that. "Well, I wasn't until now."

"I wanted to bring you something to eat. I'm not sure if anything makes you nauseous or sick right now, so I tried to stick to some basics I had in the fridge. I got you some strawberries, cashews and crackers." His deep, rumbling laugh invaded the cracks in the wall she'd had to hide behind each time she'd run into him in the courthouse. Jonah stared down at the plate in his hand. "I didn't have any of those chips you like, but I had some dill pickles in the fridge. Thought you might like those, as well."

He'd done all this for her? She reached for the plate, that same heat coiling in her belly charging up her neck and into her face. She couldn't think of a single instance where someone had made her a full-blown meal, not even as a child. She'd mostly lived off of whatever'd she been able to barter from her school friends. Clutching the plate to her middle with both hands, as though she could use the glass as a shield against him, she leveled her chin parallel with the floor. "Thank you. For everything. Not just the food."

"It's the least I can do seeing as how you're one of the few people who can have me fired." He leaned against the door frame with that gut-wrenching smile she couldn't get enough of in place. The way he was looking at her right then… It almost felt as though the past few months hadn't happened, that nothing had changed between them, and a comforting familiarity washed through her. She'd missed that, but more than that, she'd missed him. That smile of his, the way he always seemed to be trying to read her mind. The slide of his hand against her arm when he'd tried to stop her from going ahead of him while he was assigned to escort her out of the courthouse. At first, she'd withdrawn into herself and battled to keep her distance, but after a while, she'd come to crave that touch, that connection to him.

Then she'd found out she was pregnant.

Madison carved a dent into her index finger with the edge of the plate he'd handed her. "Have the police been able to trace the caller who took credit for the bombing?"

"Call came from a burner phone purchased about thirty minutes prior to the bombing from one of the electronics stores around the block. Paid in cash. No security footage and the phone has been turned off," he said.

"It's untraceable." She'd prosecuted enough cases to know the phone would be a dead end, but it wasn't nothing. There was a chance—however small—that when the bomb squad analyzed and re-created the device, they'd be able to follow the incoming call to the phone used to detonate the bomb. Perhaps the bomber had made a mistake in using the same phone to trigger the device and make the call to take credit for the devastation. "How many dead?"

An emptiness slipped into his gaze, and her heart jerked in her chest at the rapid change. So different from the swirl of blue she'd gotten used to when he looked at her, but she couldn't blame him either. Lives had been taken right in front of them, the echoes of their screams still clear in her head. "Eight so far. Victims who were sitting closest to the device in the gallery. Some media, a few family members. Twenty-six wounded, one in critical condition."

"Have the marshals been able to find the judge or the bailiff?" Getting a new judge to take on this case would alter the timeline of sentencing the Rip City Bomber for what she'd done. Madison couldn't afford to have the case take another year, and Rosalind Eyler deserved to rot behind bars sooner rather than later.

"Turns out the bailiff saved the judge's life. Got him out of there right before the bomb detonated." Jonah straightened, suddenly so much…bigger than she remembered. "I checked that entire courtroom and the schedule, Maddi. The preliminary hearing time wasn't announced to the public until an hour before court proceedings started. There was no way someone outside of the case could've gotten into that courtroom to plant the device in the HVAC system."

She nodded, still clutching the plate in her hands. It wasn't his words she had to focus on but the meaning, too. Whoever'd triggered that bomb had intimate knowledge of her, her schedule and the case. Only a handful of people were privy to that information, but no one she would've suspected to try to kill her. She couldn't forget the bomber had called to take credit in the Rip City Bomber's name, too. Why? "The HVAC system would've been put in during the courthouse's construction. The crew finished a month ago. Whoever planted the device only would've had access to that location if it'd been open."

"I'll have my team look into the contractors and their

employees and anyone who might've toured that courtroom up until it was finished." He reached out, taking her hand between both of his, and her stomach flipped. "In the meantime, we can't discount the possibility Rosalind Eyler has wanted you dead from the beginning and will do whatever it takes to walk free. Either way, I'm not going to let that happen."

Chapter Four

Jonah shoved the tablet away from him across the coffee table. Heat crawled up the back of his neck from the wood-burning stove a few feet behind him. After scrubbing the hollows of his eyes with calloused palms, he set his elbows on his knees.

According to Deputy Marshal Dylan Cove—the newest marshal in the Oregon division—the construction crew who'd been contracted to build the new courthouse had all checked out. Each and every single one of them. As a former private investigator out of the east, Cove had the ability to dig past the surface. He was more than capable of uncovering the truth, but nothing had jumped out at Jonah as he reviewed the deputy's report. Not a single worker on that job site had a connection to the Rip City Bomber as far as Cove had been able to tell. No financial struggles. No blackmail material. Nothing that got Jonah closer to finding who'd targeted Madison and his baby. "Damn it."

"And here I was under the impression only Marshal Reed believed he was a superhero, what with him wearing those shirts all the time." Madison's sweet voice, so clearly tinted with exhaustion, soothed the frustrated energy climbing up his spine. She was supposed to be resting, taking it easy. But one thing he'd learned about Madison Gray over the years was that she didn't know the meaning of slowing down. From the moment her feet hit the floor in the morning to the minute she closed her eyes at night, she'd dedicated her entire career—her life—to serving justice. Same as he had, but their shared professional interest was only one of the things that'd brought them together.

Jonah interlaced his fingers, driving them down the bridge of his nose, then to his chin as he raised his gaze to meet hers on the open second-level landing. "I'd tell you you're supposed to be sleeping, but I've known you long enough to know I'd probably have a high heel thrown at my face if I dared question your work habits."

"This basketball you so elegantly implanted in my uterus makes it hard to sleep anymore." Long fingers curled over the edge of the banister, the sweats and T-shirt she'd picked out from his closet hiding the lean figure underneath. Having pulled her hair back, she accentuated the scrapes and bruises along her cheek, head and neck, and his gut clenched. "His late-night dance parties ensure I have to use the bathroom in thirty-minute intervals."

Jonah's hands dropped between his knees as he stared up at her. Shock held him in place as the past rushed to meet the present. "Did you say 'his'?"

Rolling perfect lips between her teeth, Madison took to the stairs until she stood in front of him. A rush of heat that had nothing to do with the stove behind him exploded from his chest. "I found out a few weeks ago. I didn't want to wait. I'm… We're having a boy."

"We're having a boy." He couldn't believe it, but more important than that, for the first time she'd included him in the pregnancy. She wasn't having a boy. They were. "That's…" He didn't know what to say. Jonah stepped into her, wrapping her in his arms. Rigidity infused the muscles down her back a moment before she relaxed into him, and the world, the investigation, the fact they'd barely walked out of the courthouse alive this morning faded. The sweet scent of peach tickled the back of his throat, instantly throwing him back to that night they'd taken their friendship to the next level, and his gut tightened.

She settled back onto the four corners of her toes, her mouth a mere two inches from his. Her exhale tangled with his as time froze, stretching into a comfortable beat from one second to the next. Those mesmerizing caramel eyes flickered up to his, and before he had the chance to close the space between them, she rose up onto her toes and set her mouth against his.

His heart stopped as she slipped her tongue past the seam of his lips and reminded his addictive neural pathways how she tasted, but before he had a chance to process what'd changed in these last few minutes, Madison pulled back.

"I'm sorry. I didn't mean… I don't know what I was thinking." A humorless laugh escaped from between her lips as she seemingly forced her hand to slip from his uninjured shoulder. "This day has been…a lot, and

I had no right to try to make myself feel better about what happened by misleading you again."

Again. Right. Because whatever'd happened between them hadn't meant anything, wouldn't ever mean anything, to her. This was another classic example of simply biology. She'd been through hell today and barely survived. Her nervous system was craving something familiar, something soothing, and he had no reason to believe whatever connection they'd had would be anything more than superficial.

"I understand." Jonah stepped back, the feel of her hips still a phantom weight in his palms. Hell. Reality bled into focus. One slip in involving him in this pregnancy didn't change the fact she'd make sure to go out of her way to raise this baby alone. As much as it hurt to know what they'd had together would stay in the past, she'd made it perfectly clear she wasn't willing to make room in her life for him. When this investigation was finished, she and the baby would move on with their lives. Without him. That was what she wanted, and short of meeting her on the other side of a courtroom similar to the one they'd nearly died in this morning, he'd concede to her wishes. "I'm really happy for you, about the baby."

"Thank you." Brushing a stray strand of hair behind her ear, she stepped toward the tablet still glowing from the coffee table and bent to read the screen. "The deputy you asked to look into a viable suspect from the construction crew didn't find anything tangible. No motives, no sudden influx in bank deposits, or connections between the Rip City Bomber and any of them. Nothing more than a few parking tickets and one DUI." She swiped her index finger across the screen to continue through the report. "The chemical composition of the courtroom bomb matches the makeup of the Rip City Bomber devices. Looks like Marshal Cove's leading theory is Rosaline Eyler is trying to sway the jury in her favor. Prove whoever set off those four bombs around the city is still out there while she's behind bars."

Jonah forced himself back into the headspace to work this case and cleared his throat. "You're the one prosecuting the case, Counselor. You've seen the evidence. Investigators logged four empty beakers with ammonium nitrate residue from Rosalind's laboratory into evidence after the Portland Police Bureau connected four victims from the bombings back to the pharmaceutical company they worked for. She's a former chemist who ensured anyone who'd used her research to get promoted above her didn't make it out of the explosions alive. Along with twenty-eight other innocent victims. Rosalind Eyler is intelligent, determined and doesn't care how many people she has to hurt to get what she wants, but she made a mistake. She got caught. It's not hard to imagine her work didn't end with that fourth explosion. She wants to finish what she started, and she'll do whatever it takes ensure she can."

"Makes sense." Seconds passed. Maybe a minute before Madison moved. "You know, I've prosecuted over one hundred and fifty cases for the DA's office. I've put away murderers, abusers and drug dealers and made sure every single one of them answered for what they've done."

Crackling fire from the stove highlighted and shadowed the angles of her features as she read the rest of the report. Vulnerability swirled in her gaze as she turned toward him, something he'd never witnessed from the deputy district attorney before. Tears glittered with help from the flames in the stove, and his fingers automatically flexed into fists. Ready to confront whatever nightmares had put them there for her. "Every day I walk out of those courthouse doors, I can't help but wonder if I did enough to make a difference. I wonder if there'd been a prosecutor driven and strategic enough, someone who could see the threat my father posed to his own wife and daughter, that things would've been different. That instead of being afraid for her own life, my mother would've been happy, that she would've had the ability to see that I was right there waiting for her to choose to be with me instead of crawling back to him over and over again. I wanted someone to fight for me. Just once."

Jonah had tried fighting for her—for them—and she'd pushed him away. Didn't she see that?

"I don't care who's behind this." The vulnerability vanished, the prosecutor he'd come to admire in the courtroom taking her place. "I'm not going to let them stop me for being here for my son or for being the prosecutor the next little girl in my situation needs." She took the seat he'd vacated a few minutes ago and pulled the tablet into her lap. "The construction crew might not have any connections to the Rip City Bomber on the surface, but that doesn't mean someone else who had access to that courtroom won't."

This, right here, the late nights, the careful poring over of case files, the orders-in from restaurants around the courthouse… This was Madison in her element. Didn't matter how tired she'd get, how long she'd gone without eating, how many times he'd tried to convince her to take a break, she wouldn't quit until she was positive about the next step she had to take in the case. All those assignments to escort her from the courthouse had started out exactly like this. Dark, quiet, just the two of them. She'd always have a homemade crossword puzzle waiting for him to solve to keep him from getting bored while she worked, but what she failed to realize was that he'd been the one to ask for as many judicial security assignments as he could get. Until one night as he'd walked her to her vehicle, she'd hesitated getting in, turned to face him and pulled him in for a kiss he'd never seen coming. She'd changed everything.

Madison pulled the coffee table closer, never taking her eyes off the tablet screen. It was going to be a long night, and there wasn't anything he could do or say to slow her down. Jonah headed toward the kitchen. "I'll get today's crossword from the paper."

A POP FROM the wood-burning stove ripped her from unconsciousness.

Madison blinked against the onslaught of incoming sunlight through the floor-to-ceiling windows in the main living space. Closing one eye in an automatic attempt to dim the sudden blindness, she searched the living room where she and Jonah had spent a good portion of the night narrowing down a list of suspects motivated to trigger that device in the courtroom. The one she almost hadn't survived. The couch where she last remembered him sitting was empty, a blanket thrown off to one side.

He'd stayed up with her through the night. Just like he had countless times when he'd been assigned to escort her out of the courthouse the past few years. Before she'd ruined everything.

Pushing upright in the chair, she stretched her neck to one side. A power cord now ran from the tablet she'd been working on that had died a few hours into her deep dive into the case. Lucky for her, she'd practically memorized everything she needed to know about the Rip City Bomber investigation and had been able to switch over to pen and paper to keep running through all the new angles. Except there was a possibility whoever'd set that bomb in the courtroom was merely hiding behind Rosalind Eyler's name and not connected to the former chemist at all. At least not directly. Or Rosalind had lied about not having an accomplice to help her get her revenge.

No. There had to be something more going on here. The Rip City Bomber's attacks had followed a pattern. One explosion every month until Rosalind had been caught, and this one didn't fit.

Too many suspects. Not enough motive for any of them, but she and Jonah had been able to narrow down the list considerably by eliminating financial backers of the company hired for the new construction of the courthouse. That still left the possibility the Rip City Bomber herself had been involved, however far-fetched considering Rosalind Eyler had been arrested six months ago. Madison couldn't discount a copycat, a partner or a grieving family member who felt they didn't have any other option to find justice, but a motive for wanting her dead had yet to jump out at them.

"Oh, good. You're up." That voice. His voice. It slid through her, reaching into all the dark corners she'd cut herself off from years ago, and lit up her insides. He set a steaming mug of slightly browned tea on the coffee table, the scent familiar and comforting. Greek tea with lemon and honey. Her favorite. But there was no reason he'd have it here, and this tea wasn't on grocery shelves. "I was worried my online order of dill pickle chips wouldn't get here before you came out of your coma."

"I was snoring, wasn't I?" Running one hand back through her hair, she reached for the mug. Heat tunneled deep into her hands and up her arms, but the embarrassment of knowing she'd once again fallen into a situation where he'd had to suffer through her relentless snoring rose into her neck and face.

"Not too bad." His rich, deep laugh swirled through her as he took his seat on the couch across from her. With his own mug in hand, he looked every bit the man she'd gotten to know after she'd woken up beside him in bed one morning. Quick to smile, playful at times and sexy as hell. So different from the marshal he put on for the world. "Enough for me to remember to add earplugs to my order before I hit Submit."

"I'm sorry. It's worse now with the baby. He's always trying to find ways to evacuate my lungs for more space." A smile tugged at the corner of her mouth, and Madison physically felt the atmosphere change between them. Just as it had that night she'd taken him back to her house. With one lapse in judgment, she'd suffocated what she'd considered her only real friendship and turned it into something neither of them had been prepared for. She adjusted to accommodate the pins and needles climbing up the foot under her opposite thigh and took a sip of her tea. Perfect amount of honey and lemon to bring her back into the real world.

She shouldn't have kissed him last night. She'd just… needed to forget the memories of fire and debris and blood. If only for a few seconds. But she hadn't worked to get away from her father's control only to be trapped by another man, this one with a gut-wrenching smile and a claim to the life growing inside her. No matter how much a deep part of her battled to let her defenses down, to remember what it'd felt like to be the center of Jonah's entire world that night, she couldn't make that mistake again. Her future counted on it.

"I'm used to working through the night, but I'll make sure to keep the snoring behind closed doors as long as we're stuck here together." She stood, mug in hand, as she maneuvered her way back toward the kitchen. "Does one of these massive rooms have a desk I can take over? Might be easier for you to get some sleep if I quarantine myself somewhere upstairs."

Setting her nearly full mug on the cool granite of the kitchen island, she forced herself to breathe evenly as awareness spiked her blood pressure higher. She didn't have to turn around, didn't have to face him to know he'd followed her during her retreat.

"Maddi, we've already tried that, remember? For five months," he said. "But you know as well as I do that no amount of hiding is going to solve anything between us."

She did know that. Because no matter how many times she'd dodged having to speak to him in the court-house, no matter how many times she'd declined his calls, this tension between them wasn't going to fix it-self. She wasn't sure what would, but she didn't have the energy to confront the truth now. "Is that because you'll still be able to hear me snoring through the door?"

Warm hands framed her hips, and it took everything she had left not to lean back, to give in, to…have him take care of her for a little while. She stared at the cup of tea he'd made her, determined to hold her ground. To prove she could. To prove he didn't have this invis-ible, illogical grip on her she'd never be able to escape. His breath wisped across the oversensitized skin of her neck and face. "You snore as loud as a chain saw, but you're not a bear in heat."

Laughter burst from her chest, and the hollow, con-trolled, perfectionistic piece of herself she'd used to drive herself into the DA's office threatened to break. This was how it'd always been between them. Him on one side of a blade, her on the other. Their professional interests had brought them into each other's perfectly balanced ecosystem, but too much one way and she'd tip. She'd lose herself and everything she believed in. He was right before. He wasn't her father, and there hadn't ever been a single moment when she'd feared for her safety—not physically—with Jonah, but the thought of relying on someone else, of depending on them not to hurt her when she'd been wrong so many times before, was too much. Her smile faded as she put her shields back in place. Madison turned in his hands, faced him as she'd face any defendant in the courtroom, and stared up at him. "Tell me why you want to co-parent this baby with me, Jonah. Why do you keep pushing me to see things your way? Why is it important to you? And keep in mind 'because that's the way it's supposed to be' isn't an argument you can win."

A sudden coolness swept across his expression. Not stoic or guarded as she'd expected but something deeper, something that almost…stunned her. His palms fell away from her hips, and he took one step back in retreat. In her next breath, he offered her his hand. "Let me show you."

"Okay." Four simple words, but she couldn't decipher the meaning behind them. Slipping her hand into his, she let him lead her around the base of the massive grand staircase and up to the second level. Light-colored wood branched off toward each of the bedrooms as Jonah tugged her into the wing of the cabin she hadn't gotten a chance to explore for herself. Two bedrooms were positioned on this side of the house.

He headed straight for the only door that'd been closed. Hesitation tensed the muscles across his shoulders and pulled the fresh gauze she'd patched over his wound above the collar of his shirt. "We've known each other a long time, but no one, not even the other marshals in my district, know about this."

Light speared into the hallway as he pushed the door wide and waited for her to step inside. Dust floated like falling snowflakes as she rounded the door frame, so distracting from the rest of the space. Every inch of the room had been meticulously designed. From the white dresser and curtains, to the artwork positioned above a crib on the largest wall. A glider in deep-colored fabric pulled at her attention as she struggled to control her breathing.

A nursery.

"I don't… I don't understand. What is this?" This didn't make sense. Her fingers curled into fists as she took in the smallest details and tried to counter the sudden image of her sitting in that damn glider with their son. Heat flared across her skin as she turned on him. "You built a nursery for our baby knowing I wanted to raise him on my own. This is why you've been pushing me to give in to what you want? Because you already put together a place for him to sleep?"

Had this been the reason he'd brought her here after the attack? All this time, she'd believed he had been giving her space, that he respected her decision, but that wasn't it at all. He'd been waiting for the moment to reveal what he wanted when it came to raising their child. How could she have been so stupid? They'd been friends for years, but she'd never truly known the man standing in front of her. "If you think you can win a custody battle with me in court, you have no idea—"

"I didn't put this nursery together for our son,

Maddi." His voice hollowed as he stared out over the top of her head, and her stomach twisted. "I built it for my first son a few years ago. Right before he died."

Chapter Five

He hadn't told anyone. Hadn't revealed it to the FBI when it'd happened. He'd simply packed up his belongings in the small room he'd taken over at Shindand Air Base seventy-five miles from the Iranian border and gotten on a plane to come home. But he'd been too late. He forced himself back into the moment, back from the anger, the desperation, the loss clawing him to shreds inside. Back into this room he hadn't stepped inside since he'd buried his son. It'd been easy to fall into the comforting black hole of numbness he'd found over the years, to pretend he'd moved on and grieved. Until he'd met Madison.

Color drained from her face, her mouth parted. "You never told me you had a son."

"I don't." The finality of that statement hit him as hard as a punch to the gut and left him just as breathless. Jonah studied the gold animal figures on the dresser he'd spent hours searching for across the city two days before he'd left for Afghanistan. A giraffe. An elephant. This nursery was supposed to be a safe place for Noah. Instead it'd been where he'd died. "Not anymore."

"I'm so sorry, Jonah. I had no idea." Her voice softened, keeping him anchored. Supported. Still dressed in the oversize T-shirt and sweats she'd borrowed from his closet, Madison smoothed her hands over her growing belly and accentuated the roundness of her pregnancy. "Will you tell me what happened?"

"I wasn't here." The last memories he had of his son now were the ones he wanted to forget. The phone call telling him Noah had passed away, the race to the airstrip, the long flight across the ocean. He swiped his hand across his face to keep the grief at bay, to protect himself from feeling that pain again, but the past twenty-four hours had destroyed his defenses. "My entire life I've known I wanted a family. I wanted what my parents had. Not just a marriage but a friendship, someone I could wake up next to every morning and be thankful she was part of my life. Someone I could laugh with and raise children with, but working for the FBI kept me on the road ninety percent of the time. It was hard to meet people in my line of work. Most of the time we're running toward the explosions, not away from them, so that tends to put a damper on long-term relationships. I wasn't ready to give up my career and I'd accepted a life partner probably wouldn't be in the cards for me, but I still felt like there was a part of me missing. So I looked into adoption." He exhaled hard, fighting to gain some kind of control. "Miraculously, a teenage birth mother chose me to adopt her baby. I was there with her when she gave birth. I was the first one to hold him. I got to hear him cry for the first time.

He was…everything, and after a couple of days of observation in the hospital, I was able to take him home."

Madison slipped her hand into his and squeezed, eliciting a similar effect in his chest as he swallowed the swelling in his throat. "What was his name?"

"Noah. We had two weeks together before the FBI assigned me to Afghanistan, and I loved every minute of it. I felt like the missing piece I'd been living with my whole life didn't hurt as much." He lowered his gaze to the floor, watching specks of dust dance between them. "As much as I hated the idea of leaving him with my parents for three months, Afghanistan would've been my last assignment for the Bureau. As soon as I got home, I'd planned on putting in my resignation, and Noah and I could live out here full-time." He nodded. "I was five days into my assignment when my mom called me with the news."

Madison's spine straightened a bit more. "How did it happen?"

He remembered every word out of his mother's mouth, every hitch in her breathing over the staticky line, every sob that escaped her chest. She hadn't been able to even say the words until he'd begged her to tell him what was wrong. "He'd passed away in his sleep in the middle of the night. Peacefully, as far as the medical examiner was able to tell, but she couldn't tell me any more than that without doing an autopsy. Sudden infant death syndrome. Something I hadn't known existed until it'd happened to my own son."

"I can't imagine how much pain you've gone through. I'm so sorry." Releasing his hand, Madison closed the distance between them. She rose onto her tiptoes and wrapped her arms around his neck, her pregnant belly grazing his stomach. A soft kick reverberated through him as he held on to her with everything he had, and his heart jerked in his chest. "Why didn't you tell me?"

"SIDS isn't genetic. There was no reason to tell you until you wanted to know." Jonah closed his eyes as their baby kicked at him again. He hadn't ever had the privilege of watching a chosen partner grow the life they'd created together, and he couldn't seem to let go. In less than three months' time, Madison would give birth to their boy, and it was up to her to decide who'd be there for her. "In truth, I didn't know what to say. I wanted you to see I respected your decision to raise this baby on your own without being pressured into doing something because of my past, but now you know, and I'll understand if that doesn't change your plans."

"You haven't pressured me, Jonah." She slid from his arms, staring up at him with vivid empathy in her light brown gaze. "You saved my life, and I will never be able to repay you for that, but my decision hasn't changed. I'm going to support this baby on my own. As much as I want to give you what you want, to give this baby a home with two parents, I can't ignore everything I've overcome to get to this point."

The back of his throat burned. He'd known, even as he'd recounted what'd happened to Noah, that there was a chance Madison wouldn't change her mind. She was the most determined, intelligent, hardworking woman he'd ever met, and to think she'd budge so easily would've been against everything he'd come to admire about her. "I understand."

"But…" Her gaze dropped toward his chest. "After knowing how hard you fought to get Noah, and hearing how short of a time you were able to spend with him before he died, I'm willing to have my lawyer look into drafting a visitation arrangement."

What? "Why would you do that?"

"As much as I've wanted to keep this baby for myself and have wanted to prove I could do this alone, it took both of us to make him." She smoothed her palms over her stomach, highlighting the small bubble of her belly button being pushed outward by their son. "It was unfair of me to ignore your feelings about our circumstances. He's your son as much as he is mine, and he deserves to know how much his father loves him, even if you aren't living in the same house as we are."

Surprise coursed through him. This was what he'd wanted, what he'd worked so hard for. "Are you sure you can live with that? Seeing me every other weekend, or whatever the arrangement will be, having me in your life?"

"The worst part of growing up in the house that I did with two emotionally immature parents was not knowing if they loved me. I don't ever want our son to have to question if his parents cared about him." She lifted her chin a notch higher to meet his gaze. "My decision had nothing to do with you, Jonah. With all those late nights and long drives to and from the courthouse, you became the only person I've trusted, that I could count on to be there when he said and do what he'd said he'd do. You make me feel safe. Having you there in my office was enough to make me feel anchored, and I'd be lying to myself if I said I didn't want more of that in my life. That night I asked you to come back to my place was everything I'd imagined." A burst of laughter rolled up her throat. "And more, obviously."

He stepped into her, placing his hands on either side of her growing belly, and every cell in his body hummed in satisfaction. Having her here, in this room, with their baby between them. It was…perfect. "Obviously."

"But as soon as I saw the two blue lines on the pregnancy test, I knew that would be the end." Her voice neutralized, an emotional calm sliding into her eyes. "You're not my father. I know that. There isn't a single part of me that believes you'd ever hurt me, but I can't put myself in the position my mother did every time she was forced to crawl back to him. I want you to know your son, Jonah, and I'm willing to give a visitation agreement a try, but I won't let you use our son to force something more between you and me."

"What is that supposed to mean?" Nausea rolled through him. He didn't understand. "Everything we had before the pregnancy, you want to, what…pretend it never happened? That we were never friends, that all those long hours meant nothing?"

"I have to." She stepped out of his reach, his fingers tingling for the warmth from her elevated body heat. Long sleek hair shifted over her shoulder as she took a deep breath. "I'm sorry. The truth is I've missed you. I've missed our late nights together and spending the early morning hours creating a homemade crossword puzzle for you to keep yourself busy with while I work, but I think we were both better off as colleagues than we were as lovers. And I think that's how our relationship needs to stay going forward, especially if you're going to be visiting our son. I don't want there to be any confusion. For any of us."

He'd known not to expect her to change her mind about fully supporting the baby, but to erase an entire two years' worth of inside jokes, horrible takeout and case comparison in an instant was…too much to take. The numbness he'd relied on to get him through the past few years spread, and Jonah willingly fell into the safe space he'd created. "In that case, Counselor, I should follow up with my team and figure out who the hell is trying to kill you."

Jonah turned toward the bedroom door and strode from the nursery.

Counselor.

A stone sank deep in her stomach as she read through the Rip City Bomber case files on her tablet, Jonah's expression still engraved in her mind. He'd lost a son, a baby she'd had no idea existed, but the cold hardness etched into the finer lines of his face when she'd cut off the possibility of them being more than parents churned queasiness in her stomach.

She couldn't focus on that right now. A bomb had detonated in the courtroom where she'd been prosecuting the biggest case of her career, and she'd gotten no closer to narrowing the suspect pool than she was a few hours ago. She'd run through Rosalind Eyler's connections, acquaintances, every suspect she could possibly think of—twice—and had come up empty. If the Rip City Bomber had set the device herself, how would Rosalind have done it? How would she have pulled those strings from behind bars? The words on the screen blurred in Madison's vision. She set the tablet on the king-size bed she'd spread her paperwork out on after her conversation with Jonah, hints of that cinnamon spice wafting in the air.

Having the marshal assigned to protect her—the father of her baby—this close had warped her sense of self-preservation the past twenty-four hours. Every touch, every inch closer, had hiked her physical awareness of him into overdrive until all she'd felt was him. Not the deputy US marshal who'd been assigned to clear that courtroom. Not the special agent trained to analyze and re-create IEDs in Afghanistan for the FBI. But Jonah. The man who'd treated her with such care the night they'd conceived their son, the one who'd laughed at her horrible jokes, who'd gone out of his way to make her the perfect cup of tea downstairs after a long night of reviewing the case. The man who'd trusted her above all else with the knowledge he'd lost his son after a mere two weeks of parenthood.

She wouldn't apologize for making her needs for complete autonomy when it came to supporting their child clear, but if she was going to get any closer to uncovering who'd targeted her with that bomb, she needed his help. Sliding from the bed, Madison crossed the massive bedroom and descended down the grand staircase into the living room, her heart in her throat.

Movement registered from the kitchen table where he'd set up multiple files and notepads. Muscle corded across Jonah's shoulders through his T-shirt as he put pen to paper, and her insides threatened to melt as phantom sensation surfaced in her fingertips. "The bomb squad has been able to recover and re-create most of the device from the blast. They're still pulling evidence from the rubble and, in some cases, the victims who were closest to the epicenter. If they pull enough together, police might be able pull fingerprints from the individual components."

"You want to be there." She read it in the slight acceleration of his words, the difference in tone from what he'd used with her upstairs, the focus he expended not to face her, and she didn't blame him.

"Protecting you from whoever set that device and blew up your car is my assignment," he said. "I just do what I'm told."

"And you're regretting pulling me into protective custody after our last conversation." She hadn't meant to say the words, shouldn't have cared about the answer, but there it was. The truth. How could he not knowing he had the expertise to work and possibly solve the bomb investigation but was resigned to staying here with the mother of his child he'd never have a future with? If she were in his position, she wouldn't want to be here either.

"The construction crew and investors backing the contractors were all cleared of motive. There are only two people who benefit having the Rip City Bomber's case thrown out of court, and one of them is the only person allowed access to Rosalind Eyler as long as she's behind bars." Jonah shoved the chair away with the backs of his knees as he stood. "Her lawyer, Harvey Braddock."

Shock replaced the regret that'd brought her downstairs. "You think her defense counsel built and triggered that device during the preliminary hearing?"

"He's a suspect worth looking into, but no one has been able to locate him." Jonah turned ice-blue eyes on her, and the skin of her scalp prickled with the intensity of his focus. "Marshals have surveilled his office, checked the hospitals and morgues, and have been watching his town house downtown. There's been no sign of him since the explosion."

"That doesn't make sense. Rosalind specifically hired Harvey because he's the top criminal defense attorney in the state. He puts in long hours and doesn't stop until he wins or the court makes him stop. He wouldn't up and leave without at least getting another associate to replace him." Madison rolled her lips between her teeth and bit down, a habit she regressed to when she lost herself inside a case. "Besides, killing me with a bomb doesn't automatically get the case thrown out of court, and the caller who took credit for the bombing did so in the Rip City Bomber's name. They wanted us to believe she's behind it. Not convince the jury she was innocent. Harvey wouldn't have wanted any more evidence stacked against his client than he was already up against."

"The only way we're going to make sure is if we find him. You've gone toe-to-toe with Harvey over the years in court," Jonah said. "Any idea where he'd go if he was trying to lie low?"

"We're not friends. Most of the time we only speak when we're in the middle of arguing a case against each other." Snippets of conversation bled into her mind as she tried to recount the discussions between her and opposing counsel from over the course of her career. She lifted her gaze to Jonah, immediately aware of his proximity, and folded her arms across her chest to counter the sudden need to step into him. "There was one time in the past few weeks Harvey talked about getting out of the city once the Rip City Bomber trial concluded. Couldn't wait to show off the beach house he'd inherited from his grandmother to his girlfriend. I'm not sure about the location, but there's a chance the bombing scared him enough to figure who he's really defending and didn't see any other option but to run."

"Any idea who the girlfriend is?" he asked.

"No. He never mentioned her name. At least, not that I can recall." There had to be another way they could locate Harvey. If for no other reason than to make sure he hadn't been injured in the blast. "Can't you get GPS off of his phone?"

"My team already checked. The phone's off." Jonah shook his head, crossing powerful arms over his chest, and an image of all those muscles surrounding the infant in her belly traitorously wormed into her head. "Either the battery died, or Harvey removed it knowing that was the first step we'd take to locate him."

She didn't answer. As much as she'd preferred to work alone, instant satisfaction coursed through her as the past couple of minutes settled between them. She'd missed having someone to talk her cases through with, someone who'd be bound under the same expectations as she was under the law. Someone on her side.

Silence stretched between them, the muscles across her shoulders releasing one by one as she unfolded her arms. Was this how it would be between them from now on? Him on one side and her on the other once their baby was born? Her chest knotted tighter. She'd agreed to have her lawyer draft a visitation agreement, but doubt clutched her insides the longer they stood there. She'd set the boundaries between them for a reason. Why then was it so hard to hold up her end? "How's your shoulder?"

"Is that what you really want to talk about? You've never been one for small talk or social rituals, Maddi. Don't start now." Ringing pierced through the sound of her pulse pounding behind her ears. Had to be his phone. He'd taken hers back at the scene when he'd whisked her into protective custody. Jonah strode to intercept the incoming call, unfolding his arms as he brushed past her. He answered, putting the phone on speaker. "You've got us both, Chief."

"There's been another bombing," Remington Barton said.

Ice shot through Madison's limbs, her gaze locked on Jonah as he turned toward her. For a split second, she couldn't think, couldn't breathe, and she imagined her expression reflected in his. Another attack. She battled for a single word to fall from her mouth. "Wh-where?"

"Harvey Braddock's home." The deputy chief spelled

out the details quickly, her voice even and efficient, and Madison couldn't help but absorb a bit of that calm herself. "Portland police and the FBI's bomb tech are already on the scene. Looks like Mr. Braddock—or someone who'd been using his garage to assemble the device—made a mistake." One second. Two. "One that killed them."

"Harvey?" Madison couldn't believe it. Not after she and Jonah had just walked through all the reasons Rosalind Eyler's attorney should've been innocent. He had no motive other than to introduce reasonable doubt into the case, and taking credit for the courthouse bombing in the Rip City Bomber's name ensured that wouldn't happen. There was something she wasn't seeing yet, a key piece to the puzzle that'd been left out. She closed the space between her and the phone, her arm brushing against Jonah's, and his hand visibly locked around the edges of the phone. "Are you sure it's him?"

"The resulting fire is making it impossible for us to confirm. We don't have all the details or a motive yet, but there's no mistaking someone was building a bomb in the detached garage behind Mr. Braddock's home when the device went off. It's possible he caught someone in the act of trying to set him up, or he'd known the case against Rosalind Eyler wasn't going to end in his client's favor and he'd taken to upping his chances of a win. That'll be up to the FBI to find out." Chief Deputy Barton sighed. "Either way, Harvey Braddock just became the FBI's number one suspect for the bombing at the courthouse, but the bomb squad is short on manpower. The fire department is trying to control the blaze, but it looks like the composition of this device burns hotter and faster than the last one. Only they're not sure with what. The FBI is asking for you, Jonah. You're the one in the state who has the most experience with IEDs."

His eyes shifted to hers, her heart in her throat as the logical part of her brain ran through the angles of what that meant. "I'm not leaving Madison without protection."

"I don't have anyone else who can take over her detail," Remi said. "Not with two bombings in less than forty-eight hours and a manhunt beginning for Harvey Braddock."

Jonah raised the end of the phone closer to his mouth. "Then she's coming with me."

Chapter Six

He caught sight of the flames a block from the scene.
There was no way he'd be able to get close to that garage until the fire department could control the blaze,
which only left Madison out in the open longer. Not a
risk he wanted to take, but Remi had been right. He was
the only bomb tech within a few hundred miles who'd
had experience with this kind of bomb, and he couldn't
ignore the call.

"I've never seen anything like it." Madison stared
out the windshield as thick black smoke hit the SUV.
Police waved him through the perimeter they'd created
at the end of the street, civilians lining the other side of
the caution tape. "What kind of chemicals burn so hot
it's impossible to put them out with water?"

There weren't many compounds that were that in-
cendiary, but, judging on the slightly acidic burn in the
back of his throat and the spread of the flames as they
neared the target scene, he'd narrowed it down to one.
Jonah pulled to the curb, threw the SUV in Park and
pinpointed the garage where firefighters battled the
flames spreading up the main house and consuming

the neighbor's yard. Bright orange embers smoldered in patches over the driveway. Damn it. "Thermite. Nearly impossible to extinguish, even under water. It can burn through pavement and melt engine blocks, but it doesn't really have the capacity to create a blast radius as large as that one. Whoever built the device must've added another explosive charge to increase the diameter. It'll be hours before they can get those flames under control."

Hours they didn't have.

"How would someone have gotten their hands on enough thermite to create…all this without suspicion? And how would Harvey not have known it was going on in his backyard?" Eyes wide, Madison surveyed the scene with astonishment in her voice. "I thought there were restrictions on the public being able to get even the smallest amounts."

"Harvey would've known, which means he might be the bomber we're looking for after all." Jonah shouldered out of the vehicle, locking his jaw against the pain shooting through his wound, and rounded toward the cargo space. He hefted the hatch overhead and grabbed for the toolkit left over from his days in the FBI. Screwdrivers, drill bits, flashlights and body protection. He wasn't a bomb tech anymore, but muscle memory had already taken control.

The passenger side door slammed closed, and before he had a chance to tell Madison to stay in the SUV, she was at his side. Every five-foot-four stubborn, perfectionistic and beautiful inch of her. "The device in the courthouse didn't have thermite in it."

"Our bomber is testing explosive charges." He hauled

his Kevlar over his head, a groan escaping up his throat from the piercing fire in his shoulder. He dropped the weight fast and clamped onto his shoulder with a hard exhale. There hadn't been enough time for the EMTs to assess the shrapnel wound at the courthouse, but sooner or later, he'd have to have Deputy Finnick Reed, a former combat medic, take a look at the damage. "Damn it."

Warmth pierced through his shirt as Madison rested her fingers on either side of his arm to take a look at the wound. "You've bled through the gauze. You should've gotten stitches, but you had to be your insanely responsible self and whisk me off to safety instead."

He laughed. "I take it you wanted me to risk you and the baby while I sat in the back of an ambulance to take care of a minor wound."

"Your Kevlar doesn't think it's minor. Here." She took the brunt of the load from his vest and helped him maneuver it over his head. Trailing a path down his chest with one hand as he strapped the vest into place, she stepped back. "Guess there's no point in asking you not to go in there, am I right?"

"Careful, Counselor. It almost sounds like you might actually care about what happens to me." He unholstered his sidearm, released the magazine and checked the rounds to counter the sudden need to assure her he'd done this dozens of times and survived. "The FBI asked for me because they know I'm the best at this kind of work. If we're going to find out who tried to kill you at the courthouse, I have to know what we're dealing with, and right now, that looks a hell of a lot like desperation. Which is the worst kind of bomber there is. There are no patterns, no rules they're trying to follow, and they escalate quickly. That means more destruction and more innocent lives at risk."

"Desperation?" Her mouth parted. "Who'd be desperate enough—"

"Watson, the chief and the feds are waiting for you to walk them through this particular device's composition while the firefighters try to get this damn thing under control." Deputy US Marshal Dylan Cove hiked his thumb over his shoulder as he pulled up a few feet short of Jonah and Madison. Dark hair and a beard, the color of natural oil, accentuated the haunted gleam of the former private investigator's eyes. Ropes of muscle struggled to tear in two the thin gray shirt he wore under his cargo jacket. As the newest member of the Oregon marshals division, Cove mostly kept to himself, but the past had been clearly etched in his body language and guarded expression. Older than any of the other deputies in the office, the man obviously had some inner demons he still needed to work out, but he made a hell of a marshal. When it came to personal relationships, on the other hand, it seemed only Remington Barton had the power to calm that storm. "Remi wants your prosecutor friend here to stay away from the target scene." Cove's dark gaze cut to Madison. "I can watch her."

"I told the chief Madison stays with me, and I meant it," he said.

"Jonah, it's okay." Her hands were on him again, pulling him back to her side rather than letting him hold his position between her and Cove, and his heart rate dipped back into normal levels. "You might be comfortable running toward the explosions, but I'm not. I'll stay in the SUV, and I'll be here when you get back. I'm sure Deputy Cove is more than capable of keeping me safe."

"Fine." Acceptance ran through him. As much as he didn't like the thought of leaving her safety in the hands of another marshal, putting Madison in proximity to an ongoing burn site wasn't ideal either. He stepped into Cove and lowered his voice. "There are dill pickle chips in the back seat if she has any cravings, and fruit and water in the cooler. She's my witness, and if anything happens to her while I'm working this scene, I'm going to hold you personally accountable."

Dylan Cove smiled, then slapped Jonah's uninjured shoulder before bringing him in a few more inches. "You're going to want to check that concern of yours, Watson. Your personal feelings for your witness are showing." Two more pats on his shoulder and Cove maneuvered around him. The former private investigator rubbed his palms together as he approached Madison, then stretched one hand to lead her back to the vehicle. "Let's see what kind of snacks Deputy Watson packed for you, Miss Gray."

Madison's gaze stayed on Jonah for a few feet before she climbed back into the passenger side of the SUV. Deputy Cove would protect her, Jonah had no doubt. Because if he didn't, Jonah would make sure the newest marshal to their division never worked another assignment in his career.

Shouts and the constant hiss of the fire hoses pulled

him back into the moment. Firefighters had made some progress near the front of the house, but the area around the detached garage where the explosion had originated would be another battle altogether. He caught the attention of his chief deputy and who he assumed would be the special agent in charge on the Bureau side of the investigation. Now that three explosives had been detonated within the Portland city limits, the FBI would want all hands on deck to make sure there wasn't a fourth. Jonah nodded toward Remi as she waved him over and inserted himself into the tight group of investigators. "What do we know so far?"

"Jonah, this is Special Agent Collin Jackson," Remi said.

Jonah shook hands with the agent. "You're the one who convinced the chief to call me in."

"You're a legend back at Quantico," Special Agent Jackson said. "Lucky for us, you've got the experience to deal with this kind of explosive. My team won't be here until morning."

"We haven't been able to get close enough to the garage to collect evidence, but firefighters are making progress. Their only concern right now is to keep the thermite fires from spreading." Remi hooked her thumbs into the shoulder straps of her Kevlar. "Both USMS and the FBI are getting ready to go through the house. We've got confirmation the property belongs to Harvey Braddock, but we can't know for sure the body we spotted inside the garage is him until the medical examiner can get us the ID. There were no other vehicles at the house when we arrived, but that doesn't mean someone else wasn't here before we rolled up. The composition of the two bombs from yesterday and this one are obviously different, but it's too much of a coincidence to believe this explosion and the one at the courthouse aren't linked."

Jonah agreed. There was only one problem. "I initially pegged Harvey Braddock as someone we needed to look into, but his background doesn't show any experience with explosives. No military record or mining. No family members with access to high-burn explosives either, and to create this kind of improvised explosive device, he'd have to have years of training in hazardous materials."

"You're thinking maybe the defense attorney had a partner and that partner killed him, then set off the device to destroy the evidence?" the special agent in charge asked.

"If that's his body in there, sure, or Harvey Braddock wasn't part of the plan at all. He could've discovered or overheard Rosalind Eyler's plans for Madison Gray, and his client instructed her own partner to tie up loose ends, even at the cost of losing her defense counsel." His gut was still telling him the Rip City Bomber was behind this. If they could construct a paper trail back to the source, they'd have proof Rosalind Eyler's attorney—and the Rip City Bomber herself—had targeted Madison at the courthouse. "Any luck on tracing the thermite?"

"One hundred pounds of thermite was stolen sometime last night from a machinery warehouse in northwest Portland." Remi studied the teams trying to put out the fires around the garage. "The shift supervisor called police as soon as he discovered it missing, but most of the Portland Police Bureau officers have been diverted to the scene at the courthouse. We didn't have any reason to break up our manpower for a B&E after what happened downtown."

Jonah studied the pattern of the burns. "We do now."

"What do you mean?" Agent Jackson asked.

"You said one hundred pounds of thermite was stolen." He scrubbed his hand down his face, the heat prickling the exposed skin of his neck. Thermite burned at a temperature around two thousand degrees and destroyed anything and everything in its path. "Whoever triggered the bomb here had to add an additional explosive charge inside the device they'd built to increase the blast zone, leaving less room for the thermite in the container. From what I've seen of this scene and the amount of thermite they're trying to extinguish, the bomber didn't use more than a quarter of what he had on hand."

The deputy chief cut her attention to him. "You're saying—"

"There's a chance this isn't the only device he built," Jonah said.

MADISON TOOK ANOTHER SIP of her water, the heat from the fire burying under the thick collar of her coat and long-sleeved shirt despite the spring breeze filtering through the open door.

Controlled chaos buzzed around her and the marshal Jonah had been reluctant to let watch her. With the passenger side door partly open, she pulled her tablet from her bag and scanned through the files Jonah had forwarded to her one by one. Rosalind Eyler's known associates and family connections, visitor logs from the prison, including those with her attorney's signature, evidence logs from the Rip City Bomber's home, the FBI's extensive profile and interviews with the defendant. She'd been through them more times than she could count. There was nothing here to suggest Rosalind Eyler had kept in touch with a partner or protégé, at least not officially, but the sudden change in MO said this wasn't the work of the Rip City Bomber. Not directly.

Madison raised her gaze to the fire battling for new life every time firefighters thought they'd gotten the blaze under control. Harvey Braddock might've been one hell of a snake in court, but her gut said he couldn't do this. The only thing she'd known him to want more than money was winning cases. Taking credit for the courthouse bombing in the Rip City Bomber's name ensured he'd lose the biggest case of his career.

No. Madison watched the scene through the windshield. Someone wanted her to believe Rosalind Eyler was behind the bombing that'd nearly taken her life and destroyed her car. This one, too. She wasn't sure how Harvey fit into the equation, but having the attorney at both scenes couldn't be a coincidence. Unless... Unless the real bomber was trying to frame the Rip City Bomber for the attack at the courthouse and was using Harvey's garage to push the evidence to reflect that narrative. Harvey could've figured out who'd been trying to set up his client for attempted murder of a deputy district attorney, and the defense counsel had confronted the bomber. Only he'd realized he'd gotten in over his head too late, but that didn't account for the change in composition between the two bombs. None of the devices built by Rosalind Eyler included thermite. Then again... Maybe that was the point.

Firefighters, marshals and local law enforcement rushed between vehicles toward the house, the buzz of the scene transforming into a frenzy. She sat straighter in her seat. Something was happening. EMTs ran toward the fire. Had someone been hurt? Her mind instantly went to Jonah. He was the only technician with enough experience with this kind of explosive. He would've been the first one to suit up and try to get closer to the device. Her stomach dropped. Madison pushed out of the vehicle, her heels wobbling on the uneven pavement. "Deputy Cove, what's going on?"

Marshal Dylan Cove pushed off from the side of the SUV, a water bottle in his hand. Dark eyes narrowed on the frantic upset spreading to the edges of the perimeter. "Good question." He reached for his radio strapped to his vest and compressed the push-to-talk button. "Marshal Cove for Deputy Chief Barton, over."

Static broke through the high-pitched ringing in Madison's ears.

He tried again. "Remington, what the hell is going on in there?"

No answer.

"Try Jonah—Marshal Watson." Pressure built behind her sternum. Jonah had taken point on dozens of

IED disposals and detonations. This was what he'd been trained for, and he was damn good at it. He was fine. She had to believe that. Because the only other option was losing the only person who'd made an effort to give a damn about her.

Cove tried the radio again. Nothing but static.

"Something is interrupting the signal. I can't get through." Concern contorted the deputy's expression. Marshal Cove pulled his sidearm from his hip, released the magazine from the weapon and slammed it back into place. "Get in the vehicle and lock the doors. You don't unlock this SUV for anyone other than myself or Deputy Watson—do I make myself clear?"

"Yes." Sweat built at the base of her neck as she did as instructed, locking herself in the vehicle. Light gray smoke crept along the pavement toward the outer edges of the perimeter where the SUV was parked.

It couldn't have been easy for the bomber to get his hands on this much thermite. Not with so many regulations and restrictions to the public. So whoever detonated this device had to have personal access or they'd stolen it from another source. Madison sat forward in her seat, trying to see through the smoke.

The thermite. Pulling her tablet pencil from her bag, she quickly sketched notes across the digital file on her screen. If the bomber had been at the courthouse scene as Jonah believed, watching to make sure she hadn't made it out of the courtroom alive, they would've known he was with her. With enough research, they could've easily discovered Jonah was the only expert in the field within a hundred-mile radius who'd dealt with thermite in the past, and known exactly how to draw the marshal assigned to protect her out of hiding. With his witness in tow. "It's a setup."

The passenger side window exploded at her right, thick glass cutting across her face and neck as she ducked into the center of the SUV. A scream tore from her mouth. She tried to shield her face with both hands and shoved her tablet between the seat and the middle console. The passenger door swung open. Strong hands ripped her from the vehicle, and she sucked in a lungful of air to scream. A hand clamped over her mouth, forcing her into a wall of muscle. He showed off the detonator in his free hand. "I wouldn't do that if I were you, Ms. Gray. See, your marshal and the rest of his team have just uncovered the second thermite device inside Harvey Braddock's house, and with one press of this button, I have the power to make sure none of them walk out of there alive. You've spent your entire career putting the bad guys behind bars, so I imagine risking innocent lives doesn't sit well with you."

The black ski mask highlighted light green eyes and a narrow face, but anything more than that slipped her attention as bruising pain spread across her face with his grip on her jaw. Quick inhales and exhales hissed through her nose. She tried to shake her head. No. She didn't want that, but the only alternative meant leaving this scene with a man who'd set off three bombs in the past forty-eight hours and killed at least nine civilians.

"Good girl." He leveled his gaze with hers. "Now you're going to do exactly as I say. Nod so I know you understand."

She did.

"Turn around slowly, head toward the back of the vehicle and walk to the end of the block. If you even think about running or signaling one of the officers at the perimeter, the last thing you'll see is that house in flames." He released her. "Go."

Madison turned as he'd instructed and started walking back the way she and Jonah had entered the scene. She kept her gaze down, careful not to make eye contact with any of the remaining Portland Police Bureau officers as they neared the caution tape sectioning off the street from the target scene. Their attention had been diverted to the house, most likely part of the bomber's plan. One wrong move. That was all it'd take, and Jonah would be gone. The fact Harvey Braddock's garage and property were still burning convinced her the man at her back wasn't bluffing. She couldn't let that happen, couldn't risk losing the man who'd pried his way past her defenses with bad jokes and heated kisses.

She'd spent the last five months determined to keep him as far from their son as she could in an effort to satisfy her own insecurities with being able to raise their baby on her own. For what? To prove she didn't need help, to turn herself into a martyr in the name of pride? Jonah hadn't offered to help because he'd been worried their baby would suffer under the care of one parent. Everything he'd done these past two days had shown her he'd only wanted to support her. How hadn't she seen it before now? She'd made a mistake, and now everything they cared about was at risk.

"The black sedan on the right." The trunk popped

open as they came into range of the last vehicle parked on the picture-perfect neighborhood street. "Get in."

What? Madison pulled up short. If she got in that trunk, there were no guarantees she'd ever leave. No guarantees she'd make it out alive, that her son would survive. Panic triggered her flight instinct, and she stepped back into her attacker. She twisted into him and shoved at his chest as hard as she could. Her throat swelled. He latched onto her wrists with both hands and forced her closer to the car. "No. No!"

His arms encircled her upper body, and he hefted her feet off the pavement. Another hand cut off her screams as he hauled her feet over the lip of the trunk. Madison kicked out with everything she had, her heel flying into the middle of the road. This had been a quiet neighborhood until a couple of hours ago when a bomb had detonated a few houses down, and now she was being taken in the middle of broad daylight. Someone would hear her. Someone would see what was happening and tell the police. Rough interior fabric burned the backs of her legs as her abductor forced her into the small, dark compartment. She clawed at him, so consumed with the need to get out that she didn't notice the back of his hand swinging toward her face.

Lightning exploded behind her eyes, and she fell back into the trunk. Pain ricocheted through her head and blacked out the edges of her vision. In a swirl of dizziness, she stared up at her attacker, but couldn't judge how far he stood from her. She blinked to clear her head. In vain. He was going to lock her in. He was going to kill her. Madison tried to sit up, but her balance had been compromised. She reached out. "Wait."

"That's going to cost you, Counselor." He slammed the trunk closed, throwing her into darkness.

Chapter Seven

Jonah crouched in front of the device in full bomb squad gear. The weight of the Kevlar and Nomex increased the tension in his wounded shoulder. Every muscle in his body shot into awareness of the fact one wrong move on his part would kill him and bring this entire house down on top of the team at his back. The device was crude, poorly constructed, but, combined with the container of ammonium nitrate, it'd get the bomber's intended destruction done. The remains of the stolen thermite, a deep red-colored powder, had been packed around the secondary explosive inside a large metal can. With another cell phone acting as remote detonator and a battery duct-taped around the outside of the container, all he could do was try to disassemble the pieces before that phone started ringing.

He set the portable X-ray machine on one side of the device and the phosphorus panel to capture the image on the other to get an idea of anything he might've missed from a visual inspection, and stepped back. Whoever'd designed the bomb had placed it in plain sight. They'd wanted law enforcement to find it, and by setting it up inside the house, they ensured a live technician would have to be time on target. That he would have to approach the package in person.

His earpiece crackled from inside the heavy-duty visor, drowning out the soft whirl of the internal fan built into the helmet. He took the photos, then slowly removed the panel and the portable X-ray machine.

The cell phone screen lit up.

Jonah braced for the same ringtone he'd heard seconds before the bomb had been triggered at the courthouse. He couldn't wait to have the X-rays developed to see what they were dealing with. He had to neutralize the threat now.

The thin balaclava under his helmet absorbed the sweat beading in his hairline as he set down the phosphorous panel and X-ray machine and reapproached the device. He couldn't use the bomb squad's pan disrupter as he had on 90 percent of the IEDs he'd come into contact with to set off the device from a safe distance. Not without possibly triggering a thermite burn, and a mineral water bottle packed with C-4 wouldn't extinguish the chemical reaction either. It'd most likely increase the bomb's blast radius.

There was no playbook in the FBI that would tell him how to neutralize a thermite bomb. He'd have to do this one by hand.

He reached for the grouping of wire leading from the back of the phone into the center of the container. He forced himself to breathe evenly, to stay in the moment instead of worrying if Madison and the baby were safe outside in case he made a mistake. Dylan Cove and the rest of the marshals in his division would make sure she kept a safe distance.

His earpiece crackled again. "Watson…problem."

He was running out of time. Any moment that phone could ring and trigger a detonation ten times as destructive as the one from the garage. He traced the brightly colored wiring with the tips of his fingers. "Remi, say that again."

Static filtered through the radio. This secondary device had been positioned in Harvey Braddock's basement. The signal couldn't get through the foundation cement.

Three wires. Three options to disarm the bomb. One mistake, and he'd never hold his and Madison's son. Never have the chance to become the father Noah had deserved in the first place. Red. Green. Yellow. He unpocketed a razor from his toolkit and sliced the duct tape holding the phone to the container apart. Carefully, going slower than he wanted to go, Jonah peeled the phone from the tape.

All three wires popped free.

His heart shot into his throat. Seconds ticked by, a minute. No detonation. Pulse pounding hard behind his ears, he sat back on his heels. Confusion pushed out the logical answer for a split second, but he couldn't ignore the truth staring him in the face. "It's a dummy."

That didn't make sense. Why trigger a very real bomb in the garage, but set up a dummy in the main house with three times the amount of the stolen thermite?

"Watson…now!" Deputy Chief Remington Barton's

words sliced through the focused haze he'd developed over countless bomb calls throughout the years. Something was wrong.

The device had never been connected to the power supply, which meant…the bomber had never intended to trigger the device. Realization hit, and he shot to his feet as fast as he could under one hundred pounds of Kevlar and Nomex. Walls with black-and-white photos blurred in his vision as he climbed the stairs from the basement to the main level. Sunlight pulled him toward the open back door, where firefighters were still battling patches of the initial blaze. Two Portland Police Bureau technicians converged on him to help him out of the suit as Remington and Special Agent Collin Jackson jogged to meet him.

He pried the heavy helmet from his shoulders—pain shooting through the wound—and stripped the balaclava from his head. Burnt spring air rushed to cool the sweat building at the base of his neck. He shook his head as he handed off the helmet to one of the other techs. "The device is a dummy. The power supply was never connected. The bomber… He set us up."

"I think you're right." Remi cut her gaze to the special agent at her side. "We believe the thermite was specifically used to lure you to this scene, Jonah. You've worked with this composition before, and the bomber must've known that. He stole the thermite from that warehouse last night in an effort to pull you out of hiding. With your witness."

He froze. Madison. His nerve endings caught fire as he pinpointed his SUV. Empty. He scoured the scene, his heart thrown into overdrive, and noticed Deputy Marshal Dylan Cove. Alone. He shook his head. No. "Where is she?"

"She's missing," Remi said.

A high-pitched ringing filled his ears.

"Jonah." Remi's warning tone barely registered. "It wasn't his fault. He used appropriate response when he couldn't get the rest of the team on the radio."

Jonah stripped out of the rest of his gear as rage exploded in his chest. He crossed the property faster than he thought possible and pulled his fist back before Cove turned to face him. He socked the deputy with a strong right hook. The former private investigator collapsed to the ground, but before Jonah had a chance to strike again, Remi and Agent Jackson pulled him back. He lunged again. "You were supposed to stay with her! Where is she, Cove? Tell me where she is!"

Cove rolled onto his side, hand massaging his jaw, as Deputies Foster and Reed helped him to his feet. The newest recruit into the Oregon division wrenched out of the other marshals' hold and faced Jonah with nothing but blood on his mouth and a stiff expression in place. "I don't know. The entire scene had gone into overdrive when you'd found the second device inside the house, but the radios were out. I couldn't get a hold of anyone, including you, to find out what was happening. So I made a call. I instructed her to secure herself inside the vehicle and not open the doors for anyone but you and myself. When I returned to the SUV, I noticed the passenger door open and what was left of the window all over the street. She wasn't inside."

Every word out of the marshal's mouth twisted the invisible knife in Jonah's gut deeper. Madison was gone. He closed the space between him and Cove, Remi's grip on his arm tighter than before. He didn't care what kind of dysfunctional relationship she and Dylan Cove had or what'd happened between them for her to take the marshal's side. He'd spend the rest of his life making sure the deputy never worked a federal case again. "I told you if anything happened to her, I would personally hold you responsible."

Cove held his ground. "I believed you."

"Enough." Remington inserted herself between the two of them. The hard set of the deputy chief's mouth told each of them that was an order, and if any of them took it as anything less, she'd deal with them herself. "We have a very pregnant deputy district attorney missing and a bomber still out there. Blaming each other for what happened won't get us anywhere. Jonah, take Finn with you to search your SUV. There might be evidence in there that will give us an idea who's behind Madison's abduction. Beckett and Cove will gather statements from the officers and civilians outside the perimeter and find out how our suspect managed to slip in and out of this scene without raising suspicion. Stay in radio contact and move quickly. Let's bring her and her baby home as fast as we can."

"It's my baby." Jonah couldn't keep the truth from them any longer. The men and women circled around him had risked their lives for each other over the years. He trusted every single one of them to have his back in the field, only now he needed them to care about Madison as much as they cared about him. He needed them to bring her back. "Madison is pregnant with my baby. She didn't want anyone to know, but I need for you to understand what's at stake for me. I will do whatever it takes to get them back. With or without your help."

"Oh, hell." Beckett Foster, a deputy who'd once carried out fugitive recovery assignment for his own pregnant ex, threaded one hand through his dark hair. The marshal was expecting a daughter in less than a month, and Jonah now understood how insane Beckett had been driven to keep Raleigh and their baby safe from the threat that'd come for them both a few months ago.

The former combat medic and serial killer survivor, Finnick Reed, whistled. "Well, that explains your foul mood over the past few months."

"I'll help you find her, Watson." Dylan Cove stepped into him, then extended his hand toward Jonah in truce. "Even if it's the last thing I do for the marshals service. I give you my word."

Staring down at the deputy's hand, Jonah latched onto the calloused offering and shook. The rage that'd flashed hot and fast fueled a new burst of adrenaline. "Grab your gear."

SHE ROLLED ONTO her left side as the vehicle made a sharp turn. She couldn't tell how long they'd been driving. Minutes. Hours. Time had dissolved to where seconds ran together. Madison groped for something—anything—she could use to pry the trunk lid open, but her abductor had cleaned the space too thoroughly.

Her kidnapper hadn't targeted her randomly. This

had been premeditated from the beginning. As soon as she'd walked out of those courthouse doors on her own feet yesterday, she'd acquired a target on her back. She wasn't going anywhere. Not until the bomber decided otherwise. She traced the wiring from the ceiling of the trunk down to the right taillight. Her mother had smuggled her out in the trunks of random vehicles to escape her father enough times in the middle of the night for her to remember the setup of most cars. Manufacturers were mandated to install emergency release tabs more than twenty years ago due to the high number of accidents that occurred with children locking themselves in trunks, but the spot where she expected the release tab to be sliced into her hand. Her abductor had removed the tab.

"Don't panic." Flipping onto her back, Madison closed her eyes and forced herself to breathe in the small space. She wouldn't run out of oxygen here, but she still had to stay focused. The more adrenaline she used, the less energy she'd have to escape once the vehicle stopped. She was going to get out of here. There wasn't any other option. "Think, think, think."

Feeling along the crease where the back seat met the trunk, she slid her fingertips over cold metal. Seat locks. Relief smoothed the jagged edges of panic. She pulled the first one out.

The vehicle's shocks engaged as the car took another unexpected turn onto uneven road. The back seat fell forward, revealing her masked kidnapper behind the wheel. Dirt kicked up alongside the side of the car through the windshield. Not enough to pinpoint where he'd taken her, but she filed the information for later use in case she had to run. She scanned the car's back seat for a weapon and wrapped her fingers around a heavy piece of metal. A crowbar.

Slowly, keeping her eyes glued to the rearview mirror for any sign her captor was aware of what she was doing, Madison pulled the steel across the seat. A metallic hiss as the crowbar caught on the seat's fabric reached her ears but didn't draw the attention of her attacker. Not yet. The car bounced over rough terrain, and she lost her grip on the weapon. It fell forward onto the floor with a deep *thunk*, and light green eyes locked on hers in the mirror.

"Aren't you resourceful?" He slammed on the brakes, throwing her forward, and pushed the vehicle into Park. Shouldering out of the car, her abductor raced around the driver's side toward the trunk.

The moment he hauled that lid open, she'd be out of time. Leveraging her feet against the floor of the trunk, Madison kicked to thrust herself into the back seat. Metal dug into her oversensitive baby bump halfway through as cold air rushed around her ankles. Strong hands wrapped around her calves and struggled to pull her back through the opening. The crowbar. Her heart thundered behind her ears. Stretching one hand down onto the floor, she searched for the weapon blindly while kicking as hard as she could to throw off her attacker. She caught him in the jaw, and he fell back. She dived for the crowbar with one hand and unlocked the passenger side back door with the other. Dragging herself from the vehicle, she stumbled forward. Foreboding knotted tight in her chest. "What…? No."

Trees stretched in each direction. The crush of the nearby falls filled her ears. He'd brought her out into the middle of the wilderness. The sun had already started trailing across the western half of the sky. In a few hours, darkness would consume this entire side of the mountain and temperatures would drop. She wouldn't survive out here on her own. Not before Jonah and his team of marshals had a chance to find her. Madison rolled the crowbar in her hand, twisting as gravel crunched from behind. She didn't have a choice. The woods were her only option.

Sprinting as fast as she could to the trail leading farther up the incline, she held her large pregnant belly with one hand and the crowbar with the other. She'd kept in shape over the last few months, but her workouts had been more weight centered, not sprinting up the side of a mountain, but she pushed herself harder. The iconic Benson Bridge, surrounded by walls of greenery, a white wall of water and rock, overlooked the lower falls and gave her the only chance of cover. She could make it. She had to make it. For her baby. For Jonah to have a chance to be the father that'd been taken from him after Noah had died.

"You're making this more difficult than it needs to be, Madison." Her captor's voice hissed through the trees. "There's nowhere you can run that I won't find you, and when I do, you're going to wish the bomb at the courthouse killed you first."

Cold blasts of wind and spits of water from the falls

slapped at her exposed skin. Her fingers numbed from her grip on the crowbar, but she couldn't look back. Snow had started melting weeks ago. The incline was slick with water and mud that suctioned at her bare feet. She was out of breath, running out of energy. Her abductor was more physically fit, not pregnant and closing in fast. She couldn't stick to the trail. She didn't have any skills when it came to hunting, but she understood the basic concept of following a prey's tracks. She was making it too easy for him. Her lungs burned, her throat on fire. She wouldn't make it to the bridge at this pace.

Slipping off the edge of the path, she crept as soundlessly as possible deeper into the wilderness surrounding the falls. Twigs and sharp rocks cut into her feet, but she forced herself to swallow the discomfort. She leaned into a tree slightly thicker than her hips and faced away from the main trail. The crown of her head scratched against rough bark as she clutched the crowbar to her chest.

Footsteps echoed off the rocks around her, and a sob built in her chest. From the last remnants of adrenaline leaving her system or the massive amount of hormones singing through her blood, Madison didn't know. She didn't care. Surviving. That was the only thing that mattered. Her kidnapper was closing in, but she wasn't going to go down without a fight.

Filling her lungs with humid air, she let out her breath as silently as possible before creeping deeper into the woods. She kept the tree she'd used as cover between her and the main trail and slipped off her coat. Instant warning charged through her as she set the heavy material at her feet. Temperatures dropped well below freezing out here in the high wilderness after the sun disappeared beneath the horizon, but the color was too bright compared with the shaded greens and deep browns around her. Without it, there was less chance her attacker would spot her on the run. The sound of her breath strained in her lungs, nearly overtaking the rush of the falls. She stepped back, completely focused on the tree she'd left behind.

A twig snapped under her heel.

Movement registered off to her left a split second before a fist slammed into the side of her face. Lightning shot behind her eyes as the ground rushed up to meet her. Foliage and cool, damp earth plastered against her skin. How? How had he gotten through the woods without her noticing? The black ski mask she'd memorized the moment she'd met him slowly came into focus.

"I didn't want to have to do that, Madison, but you're not cooperating at all as I expected." Her attacker's knees popped as he crouched beside her. Brushing a section of her hair out of her face with a gloved hand, he fisted a chunk in his grip and forced her to meet his gaze. "Now the medical examiner is going to be able to tell you were hit in the face, and my whole plan of making your jump from the falls look like a suicide won't be believable. I guess if your body is tossed around a few times, she won't be able to tell the difference. Either way, you're off the Rip City Bomber case."

That was what this was about? That she'd been the prosecutor assigned by the district attorney's office to try the case? The DA had personally handed her the case six months ago with his full support, a career-changing case that would ensure she could raise this baby on her own. Only now, her attacker made it sound as though she'd been targeted because she'd stepped into the limelight.

The bomber hadn't wanted a mistrial from the charges the DA's office had brought against Rosalind Eyler. He'd triggered the bomb in the courthouse to designate a specific prosecutor at the helm, to get her out of the way. Madison locked onto his wrist with both hands to ease the pain spreading across her scalp, but she wasn't strong enough to loosen his grip. There was only one reason someone would go to these lengths to assign a certain prosecutor on the biggest case the state had seen in a decade. The same reason she'd taken on the case in the first place. To use it as a stepping-stone to district attorney when Pierce Cook retired. "You want me off the case so you can be the one behind the prosecution's table when Rosalind Eyler is sentenced."

The list of suspects she carried around in her head narrowed considerably but expanded with the possibility of seventy-two new names. One name for each of the deputy district attorneys in her office. Madison ran through all the prosecutors she'd worked with over the years. "And Harvey Braddock was helping you until you detonated a thermite bomb in his garage to tie up loose ends."

A gut-wrenching amusement filtered into those light green eyes, and Madison braced for the next hit. Her hand brushed against something solid on the ground beside her as her abductor straightened. A phone. He must've dropped it and hadn't noticed it'd fallen from his coat when he'd crouched beside her. "Unfortunately for you, he wasn't the only loose end."

"Don't let the baby bump fool you." She swept the phone into her hand while keeping total eye contact with her attacker. It was an old but successful trick she'd picked up from her father when he'd asked her to be the lookout at the convenience stores around their house. "I'm not going to make this easy for you."

Chapter Eight

There was no way to track her location.

Jonah had confiscated her phone at the courthouse and taken the battery out to keep the bomber from being able to follow her movements. A lot of good that'd done. He'd been the one to bring her out in the open.

He brushed through the shattered glass over the passenger side of the SUV, his instincts on high alert. He had to catalog everything. No matter how small. One piece of evidence was all it would take to tell him who'd put his hands on the mother of his baby. Her tablet pencil stood stark white against the leather of the seat. She must've been working on her tablet when the attacker had surprised her by knocking out the window, but where was it? He hauled her bag from the floorboards and emptied the contents onto the seat. Wallet, car keys for a vehicle he was pretty sure didn't exist anymore, perfume, various shades of lipstick, a brush. "It's not here."

Her abductor wouldn't have taken the device. All the marshals service would've had to do was ping the tablet's whereabouts to narrow in on his location. Jonah ran his hand down between the middle console and the seat. And hit something solid. Tugging the tablet from the depths, he tipped the screen toward him, but was immediately denied access due to facial recognition. A nine-button keypad appeared on the screen. Madison hadn't dropped the tablet when she'd been attacked. She'd hidden it. Why?

Marshal Dylan Cove searched the back seats, the pavement, behind the vehicle, any possible angle their suspect might've approached the vehicle. "I'm coming up empty. You?"

"She hid her tablet between the console and her seat. There's something on here she thought was important enough to make sure I found when I discovered she'd been taken." Jonah slammed the door closed behind him harder than he'd meant. Someone had broken into his vehicle, had put their hands on Madison and taken her from the scene. And it would be the last thing they did in this life. "The company who makes these is well-known for not giving access to their customer's devices, especially to law enforcement. The tech experts won't be able to break into it in time, and I obviously don't look remotely like Madison. I need the passcode."

"Has to be something she uses every day." Cove unpocketed his phone. "I'll call the tech guys to see if they can pull keystrokes off of her work computer and laptop."

"She won't make it easy to guess. Not with confidential case files and documents from the district attorney's office." Which meant no birthdays, no social security numbers, nothing a hacker or opposing counsel could search personal information for to make a guess. "Three wrong entries will lock us out and wipe the memory. Damn it."

They were running out of time. Every minute she was out there was another minute her and the baby's lives were in danger, and he couldn't do a damn thing about it until he figured out the message she'd tried to leave behind for him. She was out there, alone, fighting for her life, and the thought of not finding her in time ripped the deep cuts in his heart wider. He'd already lost her once when she'd cut him from her life. He couldn't lose her again. The hollowness behind his sternum throbbed with the ticking clock. He brought the device up again, cursing the nine-button keypad. This wasn't going to work. He needed another angle, another—

Lines of light blue and white spread out from behind the numbered buttons on the screen followed by deep wells and curves of darker color that hadn't been there a moment ago. Small letters edged the perimeter of the background image. Madison's name, two separate dates, a gray scale and what looked like a bunch of numbers adding up to latitude and longitude. "Women's Healthcare Clinic."

The background photo wasn't a map. It was a sonogram of their baby. Jonah swiped at the screen to get the full picture. The outline of a small gray alien life-form curved around the bottom of the photo. A round head, perfect nose and full lips drew him in before he spotted the six-digit due date typed beside their son's feet. It was worth a shot. The longer they stood here, the higher the chance Jonah wouldn't get to Madison in time. Wouldn't get to his son in time. He tapped the screen to resurrect the keypad and punched in the due date.

The sonogram and keypad disappeared. A white document filled the screen. The Rip City Bomber case file at first glance with notes at the bottom in Madison's handwriting. He turned the device to get a better angle on three words underlined multiple times. "It's a setup."

Shock coursed through him, and he raised his attention to the scene where firefighters had finally extinguished the last of the thermite fires around Harvey Braddock's property. Forensic units had been given the go-ahead to assess the garage and start collecting evidence. All of it, this entire scene, had been made to look like Harvey Braddock had been involved in the attacks and had possibly made a mistake assembling a second bomb if the remains inside the garage turned out to be him, but Madison had figured it out. "She knew this device was to get me into the field and leave her unprotected before he came for her."

A ping registered from her tablet. An incoming message with an attachment. He didn't recognize the number, but that wasn't surprising. Madison had plenty of contacts, private investigators and law enforcement personnel she worked with on a daily basis. He tapped the attachment and a file filled the screen.

A photo of a location he recognized. He wasn't sure how to explain it, couldn't possibly convince anyone else, but his gut said the message had come from Madison. She must've gotten a hold of her abductor's phone. "Cove!"

Jonah wrenched open the driver's side door of his SUV and climbed inside. Dylan Cove collapsed into the passenger seat. In seconds, the engine growled to life. Jonah shoved the vehicle into Drive and ripped out of the neighborhood with a cloud of burnt rubber behind them. Grip tight on the steering wheel, he pushed past the legal speed limit as he wound between Portland traffic and headed toward the highway out of town. He tossed the tablet into Cove's lap, the photo from the unknown number stretched across the screen. "Multnomah Falls."

"You won't get there any faster if you're dead, Watson." Cove latched onto the handle above his head as Jonah wrenched the wheel to climb onto the highway on-ramp in front of another car.

"Watch me." Tires on asphalt droned in his ears, but his head was far from the miles of road in front of him. He should've known the thermite explosive had been set up to lure him and Madison to the scene. He should've seen it before now. Madison had. Right before the bastard had abducted her.

A deep well of desperation honed his senses into hyperfocus. He'd already lost one child because he hadn't been there. He couldn't lose another, couldn't lose Madison. This wasn't just about the pregnancy or his fear of reliving the past. These past eighteen hours of her falling under his protection, of having her this close, had resurrected those first tendrils of feelings he'd closed himself off from when Noah had died. She'd done that. She'd helped pull him above the secrets of his past and breathe renewed love and excitement into the life they'd created together. Something he'd never imagined he'd feel again. Without her, he would've drowned in the hollowness Noah's death had left behind, and he wasn't going to let anyone take her from him. Ever.

"The trailhead to the lower falls is up ahead." Cove unholstered his weapon, checking the safety. "The photo was taken close to the bridge over the falls. If he's got her higher up the rocks, he'll see us as soon as we hit the trail. What's your plan here?"

"You take the main trail. I'll come up through the trees on the south. We can cover more ground that way, but believe me, if I know Madison, she'll make damn sure we know where she's at." Jonah pulled the SUV over and slammed the vehicle into Park. His boots hit the ground, and he brought his sidearm up. The heaviness of the steel tugged on the wound in his shoulder, but he bit back the pain. He couldn't afford any more mistakes. Not with Madison's life in the balance. Cool mist settled against his neck and face as he and Cove closed in on the trailhead.

Elongated shadows stretched across the dirt trail. The sun was setting. Five—ten—more minutes at the most and they'd lose the small amount of light outlining the path in front of them. Jonah slowed, crouching behind the largest rock blocking his view to the river. The steady rush of the falls drowned out any other sounds around them. The perfect location for an ambush. High sight lines, spotty reception, plenty of trees and rock for cover. So different from the bare landscape of Afghanistan. No sign of their bomber or Madison along the higher rocks or on the bridge, but that didn't mean they weren't out here. Radios wouldn't do them any good. They'd have to revert to signals.

Her message had come through a little more than thirty minutes ago. Was he already too late? Unclipping his phone from his vest, he brought up the trail map of the area. Jonah tapped Cove on the shoulder from a few inches behind the marshal. He motioned to the slick, well-worn main trail with two fingers, then nodded his intentions to take up the lesser-known path approximately fifty feet to the south of where they were standing.

Cove understood and fell into a steady pace along the main trail while Jonah diverted to the south. Thick trees and roots would slow him down, but nothing would stop him from getting to Madison. He headed straight into the trees with the trail map fresh in his head. If he hiked farther up the incline in this direction, he should hit the lower falls bridge before Cove's hike from the main trail. His boots sank a few inches at a time as he wound through overgrown trees and dead branches. His lungs burned with exertion with the added weight of his vest, but he pushed forward. He had to get to her. That was all that mattered.

A scream pierced through his loud breathing, and he locked on movement from the bridge. Two figures shifted through the trees, and Jonah pumped his legs as fast as they could go up the side of the mountain. "Madison!"

Twenty feet. Ten. He was almost there.

"Jonah!" His name tearing from her throat out of fear rocketed his pulse into his throat. She twisted out of her abductor's arms from the center of the bridge and took one step toward him as Jonah burst from the tree line.

Just before her attacker pushed her over the edge.

GRAVITY DUG ITS CLAWS into her muscles.

Madison reached for the marshal she'd trusted to save her a split second before her kidnapper pushed her over the side of Benson Bridge. The tops of the trees ringed her vision as she stared up in the sky, her scream cut off by the thundering beat of the falls six hundred feet below.

Seconds distorted into a full minute as the world slowed. She was falling, with no chance of survival once she hit the river.

"No!" Jonah had been running toward her, but he'd been too late.

She stretched out both hands, her fingers skimming down cold steel and concrete as panic charged through her. Her fingers spasmed at contact of the inner arch beneath the bridge, and Madison latched on for dear life. She'd caught herself. Her bare feet swung beneath the bridge—back and forth—as momentum and gravity combined forces to pull her free. The edge cut into her hand as she tried to adjust her grip on the frame, but she wouldn't be able to hold on for long. She wasn't strong enough. Her bulging belly brushed against the girder as she set her head back between her arms. Hot tears slipped down her face and into her hairline, immediately cooling with the help of the wall of water below her. "Jonah!"

The sob clawing up her throat was swept away in the

rush of freezing water. He couldn't hear her, couldn't see her without looking directly over the bridge. There were two other arches to her right. If she could swing her feet onto one of them, she could slide across the girder to the rocks on the other side.

Her fingers were losing friction as water collected on the underside of the bridge. She adjusted her grip, kicking wildly to push momentum up her body and into her hands. Reverberations pounded through her from the bridge. She stared straight up and caught sight of two outlines throwing fists as the sun dipped beyond the horizon. Shadows chased across her vision from the dwindling light.

Jonah landed a hard right kick to her attacker's chest, forcing the masked bomber who'd taken her toward the center of the bridge. He blocked an incoming kick to his shin but failed to dodge the solid punch to the right side of his face. Her abductor followed through with an elbow into Jonah's head, and her marshal slammed into the side of the bridge above her. "Madison, hang on! I'm coming for you!"

Her abductor's shadow solidified behind the marshal. Dying sunlight glinted off a small piece of steel.

"Jonah, look out!" Her right hand tensed around the steel support girder as she loosened her left to reach for him, but she couldn't reach him.

Jonah straightened, his head thrown back onto his shoulders, as the steel disappeared into his side. His guttural scream cut through the constant pound of water on rock below and echoed off the rocks around her.

"No!" Her blood ran cold as he stumbled back, out

of sight. Madison blinked through the mist of water sticking to her face, but she couldn't see him. "Jonah!"

One hand slipped from the girder, and the whole left side of her body plunged to drop. The phone she'd taken from her abductor fell from her pocket and disappeared into the raging waters below. Jonah was hurt. She had to get to the other side of the bridge. Her hand ached from the weight tensing her frozen fingers. She could do this. She had to do this. For Jonah. For her baby. She angled her head up toward the top of the girder and hauled her dislodged hand back into place. The tears dried as she focused every ounce of energy into sliding across the beam. Cold steel aggravated the cut at the base of her fingers as she pushed one hand over a few inches, then followed it with the other. The shape of the arch dipped down, and her fingers slipped along the wet metal until she hit the divider built between the arches. Her heart shot into her throat, but she'd managed to slide a few feet closer to the edge of the rocks.

Two feet of steel separated her from the next arch to her right. She'd have to move one hand at a time and pray she was strong enough to hold on.

Heavy footsteps pounded across the bridge, and she looked up in time to see a third shadow separate from the tree line and collide with her attacker. "Watson, get to Madison! I'll hold him off!"

Recognition flared as Marshal Dylan Cove caught the bomber around the middle and hauled him across the bridge, all the while taking hit after hit to the top of his spine. Another round of fists flew before they fell out of sight onto the other side of the falls, but she didn't hear Jonah respond. Had Cove been too late?

Her hands hurt, every muscle in her arms shaking under the pressure. She had to keep moving, had to get to him—

"Maddi, take my hand!" His command claimed every cell in her body as Jonah stretched over the side of the bridge and down toward her. Crystal-clear blue eyes targeted her with nothing but determination, and a flood of sobbing relief washed through her. He was alive. He was going to get her out of here. "You can do this. I know you can do this."

Madison increased the pressure on her right hand—her dominant—in hopes of taking advantage of the added strength, but her fingers immediately slipped from the steel. She held on with her weakest hand as desperation lightninged through her veins. The tendons in her wrists ached, threatening to give out at any moment. She couldn't hold on much longer. One wrong move and she'd be lost to the falls forever. Her arm spun in the socket as her body swung away from the bridge. "Jonah!"

"Hang on, Maddi. I'm coming for you." His words were drowned from the gush of the rapids below. He disappeared from above her, and desperation turned to outright fear. He was going to try to get to her from the mountain of jagged black rocks and overgrown trees leading up to the bridge from the river, but she was still too far from the wall.

"Please." Numbness climbed into her fingers as circulation cut off due to her added weight. She still had to clear the divider before Jonah would be able to reach her, and it was now or never.

Vibrations rumbled beneath her grip as the fight on the deck of the bridge went into overtime, but she couldn't focus on Marshal Cove and her abductor right then. She was going to die if she didn't get across the underside of the bridge. She kicked out in order to face the steel girder once again. Her shoulder screamed in protest as she engaged muscles she felt like she hadn't ever used to shorten the space between her free hand and the other side of the divider, but she slowly inched her hand to the top of the girder. Latching on, she ignored the discomfort of the steel pressing into the top of her belly and locked her jaw against the pain tearing through her back.

The trees to her right bounced as Jonah climbed out onto a small ledge created by the natural erosion of the falls. Water gushed across his boots and the bottoms of his jeans, but right then it seemed he had attention only for her. "I'm right here, Maddi. I've got you. You're going to be okay. Just a little farther, and you'll be in my arms."

A little farther. That was all. Madison tried to convince her left hand to lift from the steel, but her right hand was already slipping down the arch of the second girder. She couldn't move. Not without letting go completely. There was nowhere for her to go but down. "I can't. There's too much water to get a grip."

"You're going to have to jump to me," he said.

He was insane. "I can't hold on any longer."

"Maddi, look at me." The compulsion in his voice

dived deep past skin and muscle, straight into her bones to where she didn't feel she had a choice but to do as he asked. "You didn't come this far to throw it all away now. I know you're tired. I know you're hurting, but you are the strongest, most intelligent and most stubborn woman I've ever known. I want our son to grow up knowing his mother doesn't just put bad guys behind bars but that she stares fear in the face and tells it to go to hell. I want you to be the one he looks up to when he gets older, but to do that, you're going to have to jump to me."

"Okay." She nodded, more trying to convince herself than agreeing to his plan, but she didn't have any other choice. Not if she wanted to get out of here alive. If she released her left hand and held on to the girder with everything she had with her right, she could swing herself toward him. And trust him to catch her. "Okay."

"That's it." Jonah braced to catch her.

Prying her left fingers from the steel, she held her breath as she swung down and to the right, and at the last second released her hold altogether. Momentum propelled her straight toward Jonah, but she was dropping too fast. She hadn't created enough of a swing to thrust her onto the rocks. Madison reached out for him, the world threatening to slow again as gravity took control.

Jonah latched onto her wrist. "Gotcha!"

Her feet dangled freely above the rapids as she craned her head to look up at her rescuer. The veins in his arm battled to escape from the pressure of holding on to her. Jonah hauled her up and secured her in the circle of his arms, and she collapsed into him. Minutes had felt like hours as death had closed in, but against his chest, time sped up. "I've got you, Maddi. You're safe."

"Thank you." She set her forehead against his chest, reveling in the rhythmic beat of his heart. Tremors racked through her, and he hugged her closer. Right where she needed to be. "You're hurt. I saw him stab you."

"A blade wasn't going to stop me from getting to you," he said.

A scream echoed off the rocks around them, and Madison twisted her gaze up to the bridge's deck. "Marshal Cove."

Jonah's grip tightened around her. "Come on."

They raced up the rocky incline and curved around the edge of the bridge. Hand secure in hers, Jonah maneuvered her behind him, using himself as a shield against the abductor who'd tried to kill her. Both Marshal Cove and Jonah faced off with the masked kidnapper. "Your sick game is over, you bastard, and you're going to pay for every life you've taken these last few days, including the attempted murder of a deputy district attorney."

A deep laugh punctured through the exhaustion dragging Madison down now that she wasn't struggling to save her own life. "The game isn't finished, Marshal. Not by a long shot."

Her abductor threw himself over the side of the bridge.

Chapter Nine

Bright lights and pain increased the pressure at the back of his skull as the emergency room attending stitched the hole in his side. Jonah set his head back on the uncomfortable pillow and squeezed the edge of the mattress. He bit back a groan as the doc threaded the needle through the edges of his wound again. No painkillers. Nothing that would impede his decision-making and reflexes. There was too much at stake since he'd nearly lost Madison over the side of that damn bridge. He held his breath against the next wave as his stomach churned. "Any sign of him?"

"PPB hasn't come up with anything yet. No body. Not a single shoe to go off of. Remi is coordinating with Search and Rescue and their canines to see if the SOB managed to survive." Deputy Dylan Cove's voice softened at the mention of their chief deputy, but Jonah let it slide. Cove iced the split in his lip in his corner of the curtained section of Providence Point Medical Center's ER. Setting the ice pack in his lap, he tested the swelling with his free hand. "Who the hell throws themselves six hundred feet into freezing water like that?"

"Someone with a death wish, and when I find him, his wish is going to come true." Jonah tried to relax as the attending sewed the last stitch into place and wiped the area clean of blood. He tugged his shirt into place after a fresh piece of gauze had been taped over his side. The attending slipped out of the curtained-off area, leaving him and Cove alone. "Whoever he is, he's dangerous. Not only to Madison but also to civilians. He's already set off three bombs and killed nine people. Who knows what else he has planned."

"You make it sound like our bomber survived that fall." The marshal looked a little worse for wear than when they'd started their hunt for Madison at the Multnomah Falls trailhead, but if it hadn't been for the deputy who'd let her slip out of his protection before, Madison wouldn't be here. Jonah owed him.

"I'm not going to discount the possibility." No matter how slim the chances Madison's abductor had survived that fall, Jonah wouldn't take the risk of letting his guard down. Not until he was sure. He swung his legs over the side of the bed, the muscles around his shoulder reminding him to take it slow. "Have any of the victim statements, interviews of employees from the courthouse or neighbors around the second scene given us any new leads?"

"Considering I was getting knocked around by a masked bomber on the deck of that bridge, I wouldn't know. Forensics got their hands on the abductor's vehicle abandoned outside the trailhead, but so far they've only confirmed it was reported stolen three days ago. Last I heard, Reed and Foster were still canvassing Harvey Braddock's neighborhood on foot to see if anyone noticed suspicious activity. I'll check with them and the local cops for updates as soon as this room stops spinning." Cove pushed to his feet, ice pack at his side as he rubbed his bristled jaw. Bruising had already developed across the swollen section of his cheek where Jonah had punched him at Harvey Braddock's property. "Where's Madison? Hard to believe you'd leave her side after what went down."

"I had Remi take her to get checked out by Madison's doctor on the third floor while I got stitched up, and make sure everything is okay with the baby." His insides still hadn't gotten the message she was safe. They were coiled so tight it was hard to breathe.

"Aren't you supposed to be there for that?" Cove asked.

He wanted to be. He wanted to make sure she was okay, that their son was okay. Wanted to hear the heartbeat and see the life they'd created kicking on the ultrasound monitor. All the things he hadn't gotten to do when Noah's birth mother had been pregnant with him, but the fact Madison had gone out of her way to ensure she would be the sole parent to their son knotted a thick band of hesitation inside. She'd spent the past five months keeping Jonah at arm's length. A few hours of terror wouldn't change her mind. He wasn't sure anything could. A humorless laugh jarred the new stitches in his side, and he pressed his hand over the fresh gauze to keep the pain at bay as he set his feet onto the stark-white linoleum floor. "I'm pretty sure my face is the last thing she wants to see right now."

Someone had taken her right off a scene created to divide Jonah's attention and thrown her over bridge. He almost hadn't made it in time. If she hadn't grabbed onto the girders, she would've died right in front of him and taken their son with her. He'd promised to protect her, and he'd failed. An apology couldn't make up for that, yet part of him wanted nothing more than to be in that room to make sure she'd really survived.

"You won't know until you ask." Dylan Cove slapped Jonah below his injured shoulder, then disappeared beyond the curtain.

Jonah bit down on the sting exploding down his back. If the marshal hadn't been there to hold off Madison's abductor while he'd rushed to pull her to safety, Jonah would've given him a matching bruise on the other side of Cove's face for that. But the deputy had a point. Assuming Madison wanted to shoulder on her own the emotional chain reaction of what she'd gone through was an excuse to protect himself against her constant rejection to be part of her life.

Sweeping the curtain aside, he located the elevators to the left and hit the ascend button. Within two minutes, the car settled on the third floor and the doors parted. He stepped out onto the maternity ward floor, the most secure in the building, and flashed his badge to the two nurses at the front station before moving through the double doors. Remington Barton stood outside one of the rooms farther down the hallway, and she immediately turned to face the possible threat. That was why he liked her. Always aware. Always prepared for the next threat. No matter where or who it came from. He motioned to her with his chin in greeting. "How is she?"

"Bruised, shaken, but she's holding it together." The chief deputy rested her right hand on her weapon as she studied the corridor before locking intense blue eyes back on him. "How's Cove?"

"Bruised, shaken, but he's holding it together." He couldn't stop the smile tugging at his mouth. Of all the marshals under her watch, she wanted to know about Dylan Cove first. "And here I thought you'd be worried about me."

"You can take care of yourself. Cove, I'm not so sure about. Good luck in there." Remi maneuvered around him, walking down the way he'd come. She'd made it only a few steps before she turned back. "Can I give you a piece of advice, Watson? Don't let this one go. She needs you more than she's letting on."

"Maybe you and Cove need to talk about your own problems instead of mine," he said.

With a fading smile, she gave him her back and headed down the hallway.

Jonah wrapped his hand around the door handle leading into Madison's hospital room. The past few hours had been the most desperate and terrorizing of his life. He set his forehead against the door, a soft, echoing rhythm reaching his ears. He pushed inside. His eyes adjusted to the dim lighting, instantly locking onto the bright glow of the monitor on the other side of the bed. Madison had pushed her shirt—torn and dirty—high above the roundness of her perfect belly. Resting both hands to her sides, she was the queen he'd built her up to be in his head. Stunning, regal. "Hey."

She turned caramel-colored eyes to him and smiled. "It's the heartbeat."

The obstetrician shifted the jellied wand over Madison's stomach and pointed at the screen. "And there's the heart. No sign of brain trauma or heart problems. You're going to have a completely healthy baby boy."

"No." Madison turned back toward the monitor. "We are."

The movement on the blue-and-black screen compelled Jonah to close the distance between them. He automatically sought her hand with his as he crouched beside Madison's bedside. Strong legs kicked out every few seconds on the monitor, insanely small fingers each outlined by thin lines of blue, and the tightness in Jonah's chest released. "That's our son."

"Everything looks great." The doctor hit a couple of more buttons before a roll of shiny white paper fed from the machine. She handed the sonograms to Jonah with a smile. "I'll give you two a few minutes. You're welcome to get dressed when you're ready, and I'll see you in a few weeks for our next appointment."

"Thank you," Madison said.

He wasn't sure if the obstetrician left, if she'd closed the door behind her or how long he sat there with the printouts in his hand. Jonah had focus only for the bandaged hand wrapped in his. Deep cuts crossed the undersides of her palms from holding on to the bridge. Because of him.

"You figured out the password to my tablet." She smoothed her thumb over the back of his hand in small circles.

"Our baby's due date. Didn't think your device could've fallen between the seats from a struggle. You had to have placed it there, which meant you were trying to tell me something before he took you." Jonah closed his eyes, the heat of rage stirring in his gut. "I'm sorry, Maddi. I almost lost you out there, on that bridge. If I'd gotten there a split second later—"

"You didn't." She pulled her hand from his and raised both of hers to frame his jawline. Forcing him to look at her, she brushed her fingers along his beard. "I'm here. I'm alive. The baby is okay. You saved us, Jonah, and not for the first time. There wasn't anything you could've done to stop him from taking me. Whoever he is, he's planned this from the beginning, and we've been one step behind."

He slipped his hand over her belly, feeling warmth and movement and every ounce of emotion he had left after the hell they'd been through. "I don't want to lose you again. Either of you."

Madison shifted across the bed and pulled him on the mattress beside her. Setting her head against his shoulder, she grazed her fingers down his arm. "You won't."

HE WAS ASLEEP beside her, and the big picture she'd had all these months of what the future would look like had slipped from her mind.

Madison studied the strong curve of his eyebrows, the shadows cast across his cheeks from long blond lashes, the perfect shape of his mouth that'd molded to hers so easily. They'd come straight from the hospital and collapsed into sleep, but the last time she'd been in this position—waking up beside him in a tumble of sheets—she hadn't realized she'd been pregnant. Now, with the fullness of her belly between them, his hand strategically conformed to the shape of her pregnancy, she was all too aware she'd made a mistake. She'd tried to keep him from being part of their son's life. Only if it hadn't been for him putting himself between her and that device at the courthouse or rushing to save her on that bridge, she wouldn't be here at all.

The rise and fall of his back, the ripple of muscles across his shoulders, gave credence to a leashed strength she'd never witnessed before those horrifying minutes on the bridge. He lay facedown, his pillow forgotten on the edge of the bed. Reaching out, she lightly traced the patch of gauze on his bare shoulder, and her insides clenched with awareness. Heat seared her fingers and burned through her veins, but the attraction between them had changed over the past few days. Deepened. Strengthened. Chased back the nightmares.

He'd been stabbed fighting for her life, yet the pain had slid from his features in sleep. No investigation. No life-or-death scenarios. No resentment for how their child would be raised between them. Right here, in this bubble they'd created away from reality, it was the two of them. She couldn't remember the excuses she'd created to keep her from putting herself in her mother's position as she studied him. Leaving her raw, vulnerable and exposed.

"That tickles." One startling blue eye opened, but she didn't pull her hand away. He'd brought her back to the cabin in the mountains, a stronghold against the outside world, but that didn't protect her from the danger gripping her heart in a vise. Didn't stop her from stupidly wanting more than this…arrangement between them. "How long have you been staring at me?"

"I lost track of time. For a while there, I thought you were dead." His laugh rumbled through the mattress and past her defenses, raising goose bumps on the backs of her arms. She brushed his hair off his forehead and revealed a darkening bruise at his temple. Jonah had come for her when she'd lost hope in those last moments before her attacker had thrown her over the bridge. She shouldn't have been surprised, but the thought of a man—her father—helping anyone but himself had colored her vision for so long. It almost made her feel as though the marshal who'd taken her into protective custody had done it for her. Not out of desperation to keep himself from losing another child or failing his assignment. Made her feel as though he cared. "I didn't want to move in case I woke you, but now I can't feel my legs, and I have to go to the bathroom."

"Okay." He pushed his hands into the mattress to sit up and turned toward her. Reaching for her, he gripped the long length of her outer thigh through the sweatpants she'd borrowed from him earlier and increased the pressure along her sore muscles. He massaged the aching muscles running down her legs. "Well, I can only help with one of those things."

As good as it felt to have him touch her, to care for

her, to put her first, Madison pulled her knees up into her chest. "Jonah, stop. You don't have to keep pretending you're in this for more than the baby we made together."

"What are you talking about?" His hand settled against her leg, those brilliant blue eyes sharper than a minute ago.

"You used yourself as a shield to protect me from the bomb in the courthouse, and you raced to get to that bridge in time before I went over, but it wasn't for me, was it?" She smoothed her hand over her belly and lowered her chin toward her chest. "It was for him. Because you didn't want to lose him, and I understand why. I can't imagine how much pain and grief you've gone—"

Jonah crushed his mouth to hers. His tongue breached the seam of her lips, and she gasped as her entire body caught fire. This. This was what she'd needed to cut herself off from the dark, cruel reality waiting for them outside these walls. She'd needed this kiss. She'd needed him.

His fingertips dug into the side of her thigh, keeping her grounded and on cloud nine at the same time. She kissed him back with a wild desperation she hadn't let herself feel in so long, granting him access to the deepest, most self-conscious parts of her. He hiked her knee over his hip to bring them closer, but all too soon, he was pulling away.

Her pulse raged out of control. Her body screamed in protest as he put a foot of space between them, but she forced herself to remove her nails from his muscled back.

"Let me make one thing clear, Counselor. I want you.

I've always wanted you, and the moment that bastard abducted you, I was set on killing him for putting your life in danger. Him and Marshal Cove for being stupid enough to leave you to protect yourself." He cocked his head to the side, sliding his hand beneath the edge of her oversize shirt to graze his fingers along her belly. "We're having a son together, Maddi, but he doesn't detract from what I feel for you. What I've always felt for you. Nothing could. If anything, he's only made me want you—what we had before you took that pregnancy test—more."

Shock stilled the air in her lungs. "You didn't put yourself between me and that bomb because you were afraid of losing him?"

"I won't lie to you. That thought, and all the anger and fear I felt when I lost Noah, crossed my mind, but I did it because I couldn't stand the thought of losing you, too," he said. "All those late nights in your office were some of the best times of my life, but having you here in the cabin in which I intended to raise my family far outweighs the pain I went through when my son passed away. I'll never forget his loss and how his death drove me to join the marshals service, but I can't only hold on to the bad parts of my past. I have to be able to focus on the good parts, too, and that's where you come in."

Wow. She didn't… She didn't know what to say to that. Didn't know how to feel. He cared about her. Not the fact she was carrying his baby but her, and her heart rate picked up a bit more. Madison brushed her thumb across his bottom lip where the skin had darkened after the battle with her abductor on the bridge. She hadn't had anyone fight for her before—choose her—especially not her parents unless her existence managed to get them a larger payout from the government. She wasn't sure how to process the intensity in his expression or where to go from here. She dropped her hand away from his mouth. She'd devoted her entire life to planning for the future, of being independent from everyone, but whatever this was between her and Jonah didn't fit into that plan. What did that mean? "Those were some of my best nights, too."

"Glad to hear it." His smile lit up her insides before he rolled away and sat up on the edge of the king-size mattress. The wound in his side seemed to slow him down, but a sound never left his mouth. Always trying to stay in control, dependable, strong. To pretend the pain didn't get to him. "You should go back to sleep. I need to check in with my division. I'll see if there are any developments from the courthouse or Harvey Braddock's property and check the security system."

She had experience with the need to soldier on, no matter the circumstances. Then she'd been thrown over a bridge because her abductor had wanted her gone from behind the prosecution's table in the Rip City Bomber trial. Curling her battered fingers into fists, she closed her eyes against the onslaught of panic and fear clawing up her throat. Light green eyes flashed to the forefront of her mind. She hadn't recognized her attacker. Not his build. Not his voice. Not the pieces of his face she'd caught glimpses of as she'd struggled to get free of his grip on that bridge. "Police haven't found a body, have they?"

"Search and Rescue took their canines along the trail

to see if they could pick up a scent, but no. No body." He looked at her from over his shoulder but didn't fully face her. "I've got all available officers looking to find him, but with the power of the falls, I'm not sure they ever will."

"Were the tech guys able to trace the phone I used to send the message to my tablet?" If they could trace it back to the seller, that might lead them to wherever the man in the mask had purchased it. They might recover security footage.

"It was a burner, one serial number off from the phone used to take credit for the bombing at the courthouse. Purchased at the same time from the same seller, but when PPB investigated, they found out the security footage hadn't worked for months." Finally, Jonah turned, nothing but guilt and regret contorting his features. "I'm sorry, Maddi. I gave you my word I'd protect you, and when it counted the most, I wasn't there. I left you with Cove because I thought he'd keep you safe, but I should've been there. I should've…"

Her stomach clenched. Lifting herself onto her knees, she crawled across the bed. She wrapped her arms around him from behind and pressed her heart against his back. "Jonah, what happened at Harvey Braddock's house wasn't your fault. You know that. Whoever's behind these bombings, whoever is trying to kill me, has planned every step of this mind game in advance. We're just the pawns."

"You're right. We are just pawns." Jonah lowered his mouth to her arm, planting a soft kiss to her oversensitized skin. He turned into her, and she sat back on her heels. Determination chased back the agony in his expression. "We need to talk to the queen."

Chapter Ten

Jonah had been working this entire investigation with one arm tied behind his back. The bar door ahead of him slid back with a hard thrust as an overhead buzzer alerted the guards of movement. Shiny white tile reflected his and Madison's outlines and the fluorescent lights from above back up to him as they were escorted by the prison's warden into the cell block corridor.

"She's been waiting for you." The warden, the most no-nonsense woman he'd ever met, cast her gaze into each cell as they passed. "Said you'd come crawling to her sooner or later."

"Then she's as delusional as I thought." Women of varying ages, hair colors and rap sheets all wore the same bright orange uniform assigned to them after they'd been sentenced. One by one, Jonah walked past the cells, haunted gazes and violence in the inmates' expressions, and he had to battle the urge to reach for Madison.

She didn't need him to fight her battles. She'd gone up against plenty of monsters in court and come out on the other side stronger and more determined, and right then, he couldn't afford to let his emotions get in the way of keeping her alive. Not when they were about to interrogate a serial bomber who'd been keeping secrets to herself.

The warden paused outside a thick steel door with a slice of window cut into the middle. Through the double-paned glass, a monster stared back from the table in the center of the room. "She's handcuffed to the table, but don't underestimate her. Rosalind Eyler is one of the most dangerous inmates I've ever had the displeasure of holding in my prison. She's under twenty-four-hour surveillance by a guard at all times. When you're done, let him know."

"Twenty-four-hour watches are for inmates who've tried to escape." Jonah's fingers tingled for his weapon, but jail policy had forced him to leave it at the gate.

"If I know anything about Rosalind Eyler, she's been looking forward to this conversation as much as we have." Madison nodded and pulled her shoulders back, accentuating the line of her fresh maternity dress. "Open the door."

The warden signaled to the watch commander.

The buzzer echoed down the corridor once again, and the heavy steel door swung wide. Madison stepped inside first, Jonah right behind her, and they moved toward the table in the center of the bare concrete room.

"I was wondering how many people had to die before you came to see me. What is the body count up to now? Eight or nine?" The Rip City Bomber accentuated the laugh lines etched into the sides of her mouth with a close-lipped smile as Jonah slid the chair out for

Madison, then took his own seat. "Always the gentleman, isn't he, Madison? Probably puts your needs before his own. Nothing like the men who plagiarized my research to advance their careers."

"You know we're not here to talk about Marshal Watson, Rosalind." Madison set her tablet between her and the bomber and swiped through the crime scene photos the bomb squad had taken of the courthouse, Madison's destroyed vehicle and Harvey Braddock's home. "I want to talk about the bomber who has taken credit for three bombings in the Rip City Bomber's name. Do you recognize his work?"

The smile vanished. The corner of Rosalind's left eye twitched slightly, something Jonah would've missed completely if he hadn't been looking for it, and he fought to keep himself from smiling. Rosalind Eyler wasn't happy the spotlight had shifted from her. The Rip City Bomber locked deep green eyes on him, and the hairs on the back of his neck stood on end. This woman had been responsible for the death of thirty-two victims in the last year, and there wasn't a hint of remorse in her expression. She wasn't just a bomber. She'd become a serial killer. "Do you know what the best part of being caught has been, Marshal Watson? Getting to relive every detail of what I did to my colleagues during the trial. It takes a lot to surprise the cops and investigators, but the families? I could live off seeing their pain for the rest of my life."

Rage coiled hot and bubbling in his gut. Rosalind Eyler wouldn't help them. She'd just wanted an audience. Jonah pushed back in his chair and focused on Madison. "We're done here."

"I think you're right." The deputy district attorney gathered her tablet from the table and stood to follow his retreat. They'd made it halfway across the room before another word left the inmate's mouth.

"Wait." Rosalind's voice spiraled tension down his spine.

Jonah and Madison turned in tandem to face the Rip City Bomber. Waiting.

"Show me the photos of the device from the courthouse." Rosalind leaned back in her chair as far as she could with her wrists cuffed to the table in front of her, her bright red hair nearly blending in with the red of her uniform. "I promise to behave."

He nodded to Madison, and they made their way back to the table. Retaking her seat, Madison scrolled through the photos sent from the bomb squad showing off the key components collected into evidence. Bits and pieces of the explosive charge, the switch, fuse, container and the power source draped against a light blue cloth. Jonah recognized each component for what it was, but the process in which individual bombers built their creations was unique. "The first two devices were remotely triggered to detonate with a cell phone using ammonium nitrate as the charge. The same setup you used in the four bombs you set off a few months ago. The third utilized thermite and ammonium nitrate to try to convince us Harvey Braddock is involved when it exploded on his property."

"You're right, Marshal Watson." Those empty green

eyes studied the photo on the screen. "Whoever took credit for this device certainly has done their homework, but they missed one vital piece of the puzzle. I made all of my ammonium nitrate from scratch in my lab, and from the looks of it your bomber went straight to an ice pack."

No concern for Harvey Braddock. Interesting.

"An ice pack?" Madison asked.

"Cold packs are designed with two bags inside, one with ammonium nitrate and the other with water. When you break them open, the two bags mix and cause an endothermic reaction that absorbs heat." Jonah kept his gaze on the killer in front of him. The slight difference in the explosive charge wasn't nothing, but it wasn't the information he'd hoped to learn from the Rip City Bomber either. "We were able to trace the ammonium nitrate Rosalind used in her bombs to her lab because she'd made it herself. Whereas, an ice pack purchase is impossible to trace."

"Unless you know where to look." Rosalind cut her attention to Madison.

His instincts kicked in, and Jonah leaned forward to set his elbows on the table. What the hell did that mean? "You know who's behind these attacks."

Rosalind did the same, leaning across the table. The smile was back as the Rip City Bomber slid her gaze to Jonah. "Have you two picked a name already?"

Jonah didn't answer. He wasn't giving this psychopath an ounce of personal information, no matter what she thought she knew about him or Madison. He was here for information about the bomber who'd abducted the woman beside him. Not to play games. "How did the bomber know what components you used in your devices? That information wasn't made public."

"You're still not sure how you feel about him." Rosalind spoke to Madison as pressure built behind Jonah's sternum. Fluorescent lighting darkened the freckles clustered around her nose and forehead. "You worked so hard to get where you are, all without the help of the people who were supposed to care about you. I bet it's hard to forget all the pain and isolation from your childhood, even harder to let someone get close again. After all, he could be like your father."

Stiffness knotted at the base of Jonah's spine.

"You don't know what you're talking about." The muscles along Madison's jawline ticked every few seconds, her voice dropping to a whisper. Her fingers tightened around the tablet pencil in her hand, her knuckles white.

"Don't I?" Rosalind's eyes grew distant. The chains around her ankles dragged softly against the cement. "You and I aren't so different, Deputy District Attorney. We're both high achievers determined to rise above our circumstances. You in law, me in science. Our entire lives, men have used and abused us for their own gain. My father used me the same as yours used you, and now we're each having to deal with the effects of that trauma by relying only on ourselves. By shutting everyone out who could be a threat to our independence. The only difference is that I had the courage to make sure no one ever took advantage of me again when I killed my colleagues in those explosions. Can you say the same?"

Madison didn't answer.

Jonah's hands shook beneath the table. Rosalind Eyler was nothing like the woman sitting next to him. For every innocent life the Rip City Bomber had taken, Madison had saved lives one hundred times over by putting criminals like Rosalind behind bars. "I'm only going to ask you one more time. How did the bomber know what components you used in your devices?"

Slowly, Rosalind slid her wrists to one side of the table. Her long-drawn-out inhale filled his ears. "Because I told them. It's a shame he couldn't follow simple instructions, though. If he'd angled the device toward the courtroom instead of the outside wall as I'd told him, he'd have gotten exactly what he wanted and so would I."

"What you wanted?" Confusion rippled through him as he studied the woman sitting across from them. They hadn't been able to make a physical connection between the bomber and Rosalind Eyler, but his instincts had proved to be right. The Rip City Bomber knew who'd triggered the explosion at the courthouse and Harvey Braddock's home, who'd tried to kill the mother of his unborn child. Heat flared up his neck and into his face. His voice dipped into dangerous territory. "You made a deal with the bomber before the preliminary hearing. Who is it?"

"Oh, no, Marshal Watson. We're not even close to finishing this game." The bomber sat up straight, an injection of lightness and humor slipping across her expression. The handcuffs at her wrists and ankles knocked against the steel table. "I've got a lot of years ahead of me here, and I quite like the company, but I was willing to make a deal with him so I'll make one with you."

"What kind of deal?" Madison asked.

"I'll tell you the location of your bomber's lab—" Rosalind Eyler smiled again "—if you publicly reduce the charges against me."

FRESH AIR HIT HER square in the chest as Madison stepped out of the SUV in front of Jonah's cabin. She worked to purge the last thirty minutes from her pores, but her mind kept spinning. What the hell had happened in that room? They'd come to the prison to get answers, but she and Jonah had left with only more questions than when they'd started. Rosalind Eyler had given the courthouse bomber the exact components she'd used in four previous devices around Portland and had made some kind of deal with him before the device had been triggered. All for her to give up his laboratory's location to investigators in the end?

It didn't make sense.

There were still pieces missing from this puzzle, and something deep inside warned Madison it'd be too late before she understood the big picture. She combed her hair back away from her face. Her boot heels sank deep into soft earth as she headed toward the front door. "This is all just a game for her. Rosalind Eyler's not giving up the laboratory's location out of the goodness of her heart. She knows she's looking at spending the rest of her life behind bars, and she wants to cause as much chaos as possible before we shove her in a dark corner and forget her name."

"Makes me wonder what kind of deal she struck with the bomber, and how the hell he was supposed to hold up his end with his partner behind bars. She gives him the list of components of her devices in exchange for what?" Jonah maneuvered around the front of the SUV and jogged to catch up with her. He slipped his hand between her rib cage and arm to keep her from slipping. "Keeping the Rip City Bomber's name alive and horrifying?"

Madison slowed before they reached the front door, her hand still wound around his arm. Interesting theory. "Rosalind never claimed she was innocent. Not from the moment she was arrested to when she was scheduled to appear at the hearing. What if making deal after deal gives her a way to relive the bombings, to see how many people she's hurt? You heard her in there. The Rip City Bomber is the kind of woman to feed off other peoples' pain. We're closing in on her partner, and maybe that's not acceptable to her. She wants to make the game last as long as possible. She wants to be recognized as the opponent she is, even if she has to do it from behind bars."

"You think her offer to lead us to the bomber's laboratory is another way to make the game last?" Soft puffs of air crystallized in front of Jonah's mouth in the high elevation, but the memory of how his mouth had taken hers in a flood of release stronger than she'd ever experienced before countered the chill.

"I think she'll do anything to hold on to the spotlight

this trial has cast on her. No matter who she hurts in the process." Madison reached up, skimming her fingers along his jaw. His perfectly maintained beard bristled against her skin and shot a charge of desire through her. Ice blue turned into molten waves in his eyes before he caught her hand in his. Tingling sensations spread from where his thumb rubbed small circles into the back of her hand. "I just don't want you to be one of the people Rosalind hurts."

"I'm not going to let that happen." Keeping her hand in his, Jonah inserted the key into the front door and twisted. Warm air replaced the coolness prickling her skin as he pulled her inside. He tossed his keys onto the side table to their left, closed the door behind them and set the alarm panel in less than two breaths before tugging her into his chest. He slipped his hands to her hips, pressing her baby bump into his lower abdominals, and stared down at her. "I've already lost everything I cared about once and barely survived, Maddi. I'm going to fight like hell to make sure it never happens again."

She believed him. The grounding sensation of safety spiked through her as she lifted onto her toes and pressed her mouth to his. No matter how many times she'd pushed him away over these past five months, he'd never turned his back on her. Never gave up on her, on them. The tightness of his grip on her hips said he wouldn't start now. Electricity singed across her nerve endings with every stroke of his mouth against her, building a knot of frenzy inside.

She'd tried. She'd tried to keep herself from depending on someone else, but Jonah had made it so easy.

He'd saved her life, put her needs above his own. He'd sacrificed his own desires to give her what she thought she wanted when it came to raising this baby on her own, and she'd fallen deeper into the trap. She'd started relying on him.

A rush of fear surfaced and vacuumed the air from her lungs. Everyone she'd ever relied on had disappeared. Her father, her mother when she'd died. Her friends, family. No one had stepped forward to fight for her. Rosalind Eyler and she did have one thing in common. In the end, Madison had to realize nobody would ever be coming to save her when she'd been a kid. She'd had to save herself, but the emptiness she'd tried to use as her greatest strength couldn't support her anymore. Not when Jonah had given her an anchor to hold on to, and every cell in her body revolted at the thought of losing him, too. She tangled her fingers in his hair and broke the kiss, out of breath. She needed to know, needed to hear the words. "Jonah, promise. Promise me you won't stop fighting for me. No matter what happens, don't give up on us."

Us. The concept of being tied to another person had scared her her entire life after what she'd witnessed her mother go through. Only now, that fear had transformed into something else entirely. Hope.

"I'll never stop fighting for you, Maddi. Never." He crouched, lowering his mouth to her throat, and hiked her legs around his waist. He headed toward the grand staircase leading to the bedrooms on the second level. Pale wood and neutral furnishings passed in a blur before he laid her across the end of the king-size bed of the master. Slower than she could stand, he slipped his fingers beneath her calves and unzipped her boots from top to bottom. They landed with a thud beside the bed, and he straightened, every inch the marshal she'd admired since the moment they'd met. Standing above her, Jonah ran his palms over her belly through the fabric of her dress. Small kicks from their son registered on one side. "You are so damn perfect. Why the hell would I ever stop fighting for you?"

She couldn't help but smile, setting her palms over his. "Because you know I'm out of your league."

"You got that right." His laugh charged through her, straight into her core, and her insides melted. Leveraging his hands on either side of her head, he brushed his mouth against hers. "Don't move a muscle."

How could she? He'd rendered her helpless in the best way imaginable. Madison sank into the mattress as the rush of water filled her ears. Steam tendrilled from the open doorway leading into the bathroom after a few minutes before cutting off abruptly, and she pressed into her elbows to sit up. "Jonah?"

Sleeves rolled up to expose strong forearms, he left the confines of the bathroom and reached for her. He took both of her hands in his and pulled her off the bed into the length of his body. "Turn around."

She narrowed her gaze on him. She didn't understand this game, but the deepest part of her—the one she'd ignored far too long—trusted him. Trusted he wouldn't hurt her. She turned in his arms, giving him her back. Heightened awareness overwhelmed her senses as he trailed a path of kisses along her neck from behind. He wrapped one hand around her front, cradling their son, while he tugged the zipper to her dress lower. Heated desire shot down her spine at the brush of his shirt against her bare skin. Cocking her head to one side, she gave him access to the most vulnerable parts of her. Physically. Mentally. Emotionally. Jonah Watson, the reserved, quiet, loyal marshal who'd put himself between her and the bomb at the courthouse, lit parts of her she'd cut herself off from feeling all these years, and the constriction in her chest loosened.

"You've held yourself together for so long, Maddi. You've spent your entire career taking care of everyone else. It's time you let someone take care of you for once." His whispers tickled the oversensitized skin of her neck and shoulders as he slipped her dress down her arms. Cool air rushed to replace the heat he'd generated beneath her skin as her dress fell in a pool at her feet. Leaving her in nothing but her bra and underwear— exposed—Jonah entwined his hand with hers and led her into the bathroom.

She followed ghostlike wisps of steam to the source, the large soaker tub he'd filled with full pink-tipped lotus flowers floating across the surface. Gravity worked to bring her to her knees as she took in the beauty of the added candles and colorful crystals positioned around the edge of the tub. Self-consciousness drained the longer she fought to speak. "When did you…" Her gaze cut to his as thick emotion stuck in her throat. No one had ever drawn her a bath before. No one had gone out of their way or seemed to care about her the way he did. "You did this for me?"

"You've spent nearly your entire life feeling unloved and forgotten, Maddi, but I never forgot you. No matter how many times you pushed, I couldn't walk away. You gave me something I didn't think I'd ever feel again after I lost Noah. You gave me hope for the future." He framed her face between calloused palms, stroking her cheeks with his thumbs. Blue eyes studied her from forehead to chin. "And I'll spend every day of the rest of my life proving I'm the one person who will never stop choosing you."

She couldn't think, couldn't breathe. Her lips parted as he pressed his mouth to hers in another adrenaline-inducing dizziness of desire. She fisted his shirt in her hands and pulled him toward the bathtub.

Chapter Eleven

Everything he'd ever wanted rested on the other side of the bed. Madison's long dark hair fell in silken waves over her pillow and framed the mesmerizing brush of pink in her cheeks. Night had fallen, only punctures of moonlight coming through the wall-to-wall windows stretching across the room. He wasn't sure how long they'd been lying there since he'd brought her back to bed. Didn't care about anything outside of these four walls, but reality wouldn't stop fighting for long.

As much as Jonah wanted to believe the bomber who'd thrown himself off that bridge hadn't survived the fall, his gut warned otherwise. The bombs at the courthouse, the thermite explosive at Harvey Braddock's house… Something he couldn't explain said the dive off the Benson Bridge had been part of the plan, and it was only a matter of time before the killer came for Madison again.

His phone vibrated from the dresser on the other side of the room. Careful not to wake Madison, he slid from the bed, leaving her exactly where she was supposed to be. He silenced the device as soon as he reached the dresser and stepped out into the hallway before answering. "Either you're up late, or you haven't gone to sleep either."

"Who needs sleep?" Remington Barton sounded as exhausted and wound up as Jonah did. The entire division had been called in to hunt for the bomber responsible for nine deaths in the past three days, and if he was a betting man, Jonah would say Remi hadn't wanted to let anyone else take point. "Did you get a chance to read through the bomb squad's report from the thermite fire at Harvey Braddock's home?"

"Give me a minute." He made his way downstairs and collapsed onto the couch. He pulled his tablet onto his lap. His vision battled with the sudden brightness from the screen before he opened the attached file in his email. His stomach rolled. "The body recovered from the garage was confirmed to be Harvey Braddock."

"You reported when you spoke to Rosalind Eyler, she'd revealed her exact components for the bombs she detonated over the past year to the bomber we're hunting, but the prison logs say she hasn't had any visitors aside from her attorney. No mail. No phone calls," Remi said. "I think we discovered how she was able to communicate to the outside."

"Her lawyer." Damn. He'd been afraid of that. Jonah leaned back into the couch. "Rosalind used Harvey Braddock as a go-between, then had her partner kill him and lure me away from Madison all in the same swing."

"She's not just intelligent, Jonah. She was the lead chemist working for the biggest pharmaceutical company in the country." Remi's voice faltered. "Putting her behind bars hasn't stopped her from finishing what she started, and for some reason she's deviated from her MO of working alone and put Madison Gray in her sights. I need you to watch your back."

"I will." The only other option was losing everything he'd fought for since starting the adoption process with Noah, and he couldn't go back to that life. Couldn't survive the isolation, the emptiness. Not after what he and Madison had been through. "I still don't understand how our perp was able to get onto that scene at Harvey Braddock's house. Local PD had the perimeter sealed off and were ID'ing everyone who crossed that line." Tension twisted his insides. "Unless…"

"Our bomber had the clearance to cross that line." Remi sighed. "I'll have Cove reinterview the officers assigned perimeter duty. See if he can pull anything out of the ordinary from their statements. If our suspect is in law enforcement, they'll have access to everything concerning the investigation."

"That's how he's staying ahead of us." As much as Jonah hated to admit it, their new pool of suspects made sense. It explained how the bomber was able to get in and out of the courthouse during construction to plant the first device in the HVAC unit. It explained how he was able to step into and leave the second scene. It explained how the bastard had learned of Jonah's experience with thermite and his background in explosives. The pieces were beginning to fit. All that was left was to fill in the silhouette shadow at the back of his head with a face. Couldn't be any of the marshals from his team. Even with his desire to deck Dylan Cove again, Remi had vouched for the former private investigator on more than one occasion. Jonah trusted her, and he trusted her vetting process for bringing in new marshals. Both Finnick Reed and Beckett Foster had been at his side for the past decade. While the past six months had changed their lives drastically with Beckett's daughter on the way and a new wife on his arm, and Finnick head over heels with a new crime scene photographer who'd once been his witness, that left the PPB officers assigned to perimeter security. And one other person. "How well do you know the special agent who was at the Braddock scene?"

"I don't." Surprise notched Remi's voice up an octave. "All I know is the Bureau assigned Special Agent Jackson to support the local bomb squad with the investigation. I figured you knew him considering you both worked for the FBI's hazardous devices unit a good chunk of your life, and the scene just hadn't been a great place to catch up. It's not exactly a social situation."

"No. I've never met him before." He'd worked with an entire team of agents—dozens from all over the country and outside of it—but Jonah was positive he'd never met Special Agent Collin Jackson in his life. Didn't mean the agent wasn't in Portland on a valid assignment or that he'd lied about his reasons for being on the scene, but Madison's life was worth finding out for sure. "I know most of the agents still working in that unit. Where is he now?"

"Here, at the Second Avenue station running through the same report I sent you." The low hum of voices and ringing phones filled the line. "He confirmed the thermite found at the house and the amount stolen from the warehouse two nights ago are a match, and that Harvey Braddock is the victim firefighters pulled from the garage. Agent Jackson is trying to put the pieces of the device from the garage back together. Hopefully we'll be able to pull prints from one of the components to get a lead on Rosalind Eyler's partner."

"Keep him there while I check into his background, Chief." Footsteps padded down the grand staircase behind him. Hell, he hadn't meant to wake her. "I'll check in with you in the morning."

"Jonah, wait," Remi said before he was able to hit End. "There's something else."

His heart beat steadily in his throat as he raised the phone back to his ear. "What is it?"

"Search and Rescue recovered a stash of clothing and a ski mask a few feet from a set of tracks leading up from the bank of the river." Silence grew heavy around him as Jonah waited for the fist around his lungs to ease. "I'm having forensics comb through the evidence, but preliminary tests have me convinced Madison's abductor survived that fall after all."

The nightmare wasn't over.

"Thanks for letting me know." He ended the call and craned his neck up to watch Madison stop at the bottom of the stairs. "Sorry. I didn't think I was talking loud enough to wake you."

"You weren't, but the bed got cold without you in it." She closed the distance between them, sliding onto his lap with one arm snaking behind his neck. He couldn't help but wrap her in his arms as she rested her head against his shoulder. Turning the tablet to face her, Madison scanned through the document. "The medical examiner identified the body recovered at the scene. Harvey Braddock was involved."

Shock wove between her words, and his stomach revolted. According to her, Madison and Harvey hadn't exactly been friends on opposites sides of the courtroom, but neither of them had had any real ill will toward the other. Not until now. "USMS believes he was acting as Rosalind Eyler's messenger between his client and the bomber, and when they didn't need him anymore…"

"They killed him." Her shoulders rose on a strong inhale, and before he had a chance to tighten his hold on her, she slipped from the circle of his arms. The tablet screen highlighted and shadowed the angles of her expression as she swiped through to the next page of the document, lost in the investigation. How many times had he watched her like this? Her with her focus drawn to the case in front of her, him waiting for her to come back to the present and remember he was there.

It'd been in quiet moments like this in the middle of the night in her office where she'd let him get to know the real her. Not the deputy district attorney trying to win the latest case thrown at her by the DA, but Madison. The woman who bit her bottom lip while analyzing the next pattern, who stayed up late and woke up early to fight for the innocent, who found little value in small talk and other social rituals and strangely remained calm in any situation. The woman who'd somehow broken through the numbness he'd carried all these years and made him feel again. Not just the good parts of life but the ugly, too. In less than three days, she'd untangled years of grief and rage tearing him apart from the inside and expected nothing in return. Hell, that was why he'd fallen in love with her.

His breath hitched. Love.

In an instant, Madison pegged him with caramel-brown eyes as though she'd sensed the realization that ripped the air from his lungs. She lowered the iPad to her side. "You told your chief to keep someone at the station while you look into his background before I came downstairs. You have a new suspect?"

"Special Agent Collin Jackson," he said.

"He would've had clearance to the courthouse during construction." Her outline shifted in the dark, the roundness of her baby bump catching the light from dying embers in the stove. Unsettled energy rolled her fingers into her palms. She seemed to want to pace, walk it out, talk this new theory through, but the attacks had taken too much from them both. "Could explain why he was able to get past the officers at the perimeter of the scene at Harvey Braddock's, but I don't recognize his name. As far as I know, he hasn't been involved in one of my cases before now. What makes you suspicious of an agent?"

"He told Remi he worked for the Bureau's hazardous devices unit, but I've never met him before either, and I don't recognize his name. That gives him opportunity and the know-how he'd need to build those devices." All of which was easy enough to confirm with a few calls, but it was only three in the morning in Washington, DC. His suspicions would have to wait until sunrise.

"You think he's lying," she said. "That he's the bomber?"

"I can't say for sure yet." Jonah pushed to his feet. He'd spent the past five months apart from her. He couldn't keep his distance anymore. "But I'm not discounting the possibility our perp is law enforcement, no. There's too much at risk to make that kind of mistake."

"There's only one problem with focusing solely on law enforcement." She turned the tablet screen toward him. "The police and the FBI aren't the only ones with access to this investigation."

"THE MAN WHO dragged me up to those falls wasn't interested in a mistrial for the Rip City Bomber case. He wanted me out of the way, but not to guarantee a win for Rosalind Eyler. I think he wants to prosecute the case himself." From the moment Jonah had pulled her off that bridge, she hadn't been able to slow down long enough to process what'd happened in that terrifying hour she'd been abducted. Only the soft sizzling of the dying fire in the stove reached her ears this late at night. Without aches bruising the muscles in her body and her head finally clear of the physical tension between her and Jonah, Madison had the headspace to analytically sink back into this case. Into her safe space. Her comfort zone. "There are seventy-three deputy district attorneys in Oregon, and every single one of their careers would change with a case like this on their résumé. We need to focus our efforts on them."

Embers cast dim orange shadows across Jonah's face as he stared down at her. Even in the dark, the concern etched into his expression picked her heart rate up. He'd done nothing but take care of her since the first bombing, despite the hell she'd put him through since she'd read that positive pregnancy test. "We've been operating under the assumption that the man who took you and the person who set off those bombs are one and the same. What if they aren't? What if there's another threat out there I haven't seen coming?"

"You haven't. My kidnapper specifically pointed out I should've died in that explosion, but I didn't. Because of you. No matter what happens, we both know you've done everything in your power to keep me safe. I trust that, and I trust you." She stepped into him as much as her swollen belly would allow and framed his jaw with both hands. "According to the caller taking credit for the bombing, the device in the courthouse was meant for me. I think without Search and Rescue finding a body in that river, we need to consider all the possibilities, but we've been looking for motive and now we have one. Narrowing our suspect pool to the other deputy district attorneys in the county gives us the bomber's motive for targeting me, explains how they could've gotten into the courthouse during construction and how they have continuous access to this investigation."

Silence settled between them as her theory became reality.

"You're right. They haven't found a body." Jonah seemed to tense right in front of her. "But they did find a stash of clothing hidden along the riverbank and footprints coming straight out of the water."

Air stalled in her lungs. Quick flashes of memory lightninged across her mind. The light green, hate-filled eyes of the man who'd taken her, the feeling of his hands on her arms as he'd tried to force her over the bridge. How much stronger he'd been than her, desperate. He was still out there, still hunting her. Whoever'd built those bombs was intelligent, adaptable and dangerous, and nothing like she'd gone up against before. "He must've had a change of clothes, maybe some supplies, waiting for him as part of his escape plan. He's never going to stop, is he? Not until I'm dead or I give up on everything I've ever worked for."

"He can't find you, Maddi. Nobody knows you're here. Not even my team." Jonah shifted between both feet and latched onto her arms. "I made sure of that when I took the battery out of your phone and put you into protective custody. Even with all the access this SOB has to the investigation and the connection he shares with Rosalind Eyler, he can't get to you."

"I hope you're right." She smoothed her hand over her hardening stomach. "For both of our sakes."

"I'll hold off on accusing Special Agent Jackson of terrorism and focus on the other deputy DAs, but I'm still going to talk to my unit back east and ask some questions about why he's here and why I've never heard of him." His hands drifted to her wrists, lightly holding her in place. "Who's next in line to take the case to trial if you're not able to do it?"

"That choice isn't up to me." She'd worked with only

a handful of the other deputies over the years within the county's boundaries, but none of them fit the profile of the man on the bridge. The DA had handpicked her to prosecute this case because of her track record. Ninety-five percent prosecution rate, the highest in the state. The governor had even recommended her to receive the Charles R. English award from the American Bar Association for her distinguished work in the field of criminal justice. "It's at the discretion of the district attorney, Pierce Cook."

Jonah's eyes narrowed on her, hiking her nervous system into overdrive. "This is the biggest domestic terrorism case Oregon has ever seen. Why didn't Cook want to prosecute the case himself?"

"When I met with him for this assignment, he told me he's planning to announce his retirement next month, and he wanted the public and the media to see a strong prosecutor dedicated to bringing this case to the finish line." She'd asked Pierce Cook the same question when he'd brought her into his office the day she'd been assigned this case. She'd met the DA only a few times since she'd come to work for him, but she'd been excited at the prospect of taking on the Rip City Bomber. Now her life—her baby's life—had been put at risk because of it. A knot tightened in her gut. "I haven't talked to anyone in my office since the bombing in the courtroom and you taking me into protective custody. He might've already had me replaced. The justice system doesn't stop just because of attempted murder on the prosecutor."

"The DA hasn't replaced you. Otherwise the bomber

wouldn't have reason to finish what he started. I'll have Remington and Cove pay a visit to the DA, see if they can come up with a list of names who match your abductor's profile." Pulling her into his chest, Jonah threaded one hand through her hair as she set her ear over his heart. Right where he needed her. "We're going to get through this."

"How can you be so sure?" Confidence had come easily for her since she'd pulled herself from that fear-filled life she'd been born into, but now... Madison would have to borrow some of his. She'd have to depend on him to get her through this. The muscles down her back stiffened one by one at the thought, but for as long as she'd been fighting to trust and rely on only herself, the panic never came. Because Jonah would never hurt her. Not intentionally. Without him, she would've died in that courtroom or in her car when she'd tried to leave the scene. She wouldn't have made it to the other side of the bridge. She wouldn't have gotten this far, and the fear she'd hung on to of being in the same situation as her mother—as being trapped by someone who was supposed to care about her—didn't seem to have quite the same meaning anymore. She counted off the steady beats of his heart and closed her eyes. "He could be right outside these walls, waiting for us to make a mistake."

"I don't make mistakes, Maddi," he said. "Especially not when it comes to you."

"Smooth talker." Her mouth tugged into a smile, and suddenly, the past, the divide between them, the fear, none of it seemed as powerful as she'd believed. This moment was for the two of them. Uncertainty and insecurity weren't welcome, and she was able to fully take a breath for the first time she could remember since leaving Los Angeles behind. Because of him. Because of his goodness and dedication to put her first. They'd been friends for years, but in that moment, she could imagine him as more. Not only as the father of her baby but also as a partner.

The low-pitched echo of a ringing phone pulled her back into the moment.

"Don't move a muscle." He spun her around by the hips, keeping one hand on her as he dipped to reach for the phone, and read the screen. The lines between Jonah's eyebrows deepened, and an instant tension filtered through the muscles across his shoulders. "It's Remi."

She couldn't read Jonah's expression. "Why would that matter?"

"I told her I'd catch up with her in the morning. She'd only call me if it was urgent." He slid his thumb across the screen and put the phone at his ear. "Something's wrong."

Worry carved through her the longer he listened. Jonah let his hand slip from her waist, leaving her cold and alone right in front of him. She couldn't make out Remi's words, but the moment he locked his gaze onto hers, she knew. Knew something was wrong. Her stomach soured as all the possibilities lightninged through her mind. Another bombing? An assignment gone wrong for his USMS team? Had somebody been hurt or had her abductor gone after another of the deputy district attorneys? Madison interlaced her fingers beneath her baby bump for assurance, but it never came.

An invisible earthquake seemed to streak through her the longer she waited for him to answer.

"When?" Jonah checked his watch. "Thirty minutes ago. Understood. I'll move Madison as fast as I can. I'll be in touch with a new number within the hour."

Move her? Move her where? Why would he need to give his boss a new number? He ended the call, then maneuvered around her for the duffel bag he'd set near the door. "Get your clothes from the bedroom. We're leaving."

"What is it? What happened?" Her heart shot into her throat the longer he refused to look at her. She watched as he double-timed it to the kitchen and threw a few items from the pantry in the bag but didn't answer. He'd transformed into the overprotective, quiet, detail-oriented marshal who'd thrown her into protective custody right after the bombing at the courthouse. Madison reached out. "Jonah, stop. Tell me what is happening."

His pulse beat strong against her fingertips at his wrist, and a hint of the grief he'd hidden behind all these years surfaced. Loosening his grip on the box of granola bars he'd pulled from the pantry, Jonah leveled his gaze on her. "Rosalind Eyler escaped prison thirty minutes ago."

Chapter Twelve

"How…how is that possible?" Madison stumbled away from him, the pink in her cheeks draining from her face, and her grip fell from his wrist.

"We're not sure how yet or why. My team headed to the prison the moment the warden informed the marshals service, and there's an official manhunt in progress for her recapture," he said. "But the evidence says she's been working with the bomber bent on removing you from this case. Rosalind Eyler made some kind of deal with the man who tried to kill you. Stands to reason since he's failed so far, she might be trying to get the job done herself."

"You think she's coming here. For me and the baby." The lack of emotion in her voice grated against his very being. Madison was one of the most hardworking, strategic prosecutors in the state he'd had the pleasure of knowing. He'd watched her win cases with that exact tone of voice interlaced into her arguments, but over these past few days she'd let him see so much more than that. When her internal guards fell away, she was warm, confident and alive. Now the woman standing in front of him had physically, mentally and emotionally prepared herself for the oncoming threat. "I'll get my clothes."

Jonah ignored the constant buzz of warning at the back of his head and encircled his hand around her arm. Pulling her into him, he forced her to look him in the eye. "She'll never lay a hand on you. Understand? I give you my word."

No one was going to take her. No one was going to take their son. No one was going to take his family. Jonah slipped his hands down her arms, waking the nerve endings in his fingers, and a hint of the desire they'd shared notched his body temperature higher.

"I know." The shallow lines around her eyes softened slightly, just for him, as though she'd been reminded of what they'd shared under the sheets in the same moment. "Make sure the next safe house is as perfect as this one, okay?"

"You've got a deal, Counselor." He smiled, releasing her one finger at a time before she turned toward the stairs. "Grab your clothes and meet me back downstairs as soon as you can. We're wheels up in five minutes."

"Aye, aye, Captain." With a half salute, she padded up the stairs and out of sight. Thirty minutes since the prison warden had reported Rosalind Eyler's escape, but that didn't mean that was the exact moment the Rip City Bomber had disappeared. Jonah crossed to the section of wall structuring the stairs and pressed the release for the compartment door he'd had built underneath when he bought the place. A thin, pale wood door matching the rest of the wood grain opened, revealing the wall safe behind it. He pressed his thumb into the reader, and the lock disengaged. Rosalind Eyler was one of the most dangerous criminals he'd encountered throughout the decade he'd been a marshal.

He wasn't leaving anything to chance.

He pulled his backup piece from inside, loaded fresh rounds into the magazine and holstered it under his left pant leg. Closing the safe and the panel door, he hauled the duffel bag filled with their supplies over his uninjured shoulder. They were running out of time. There was no telling what the Rip City Bomber had up her sleeve, but he'd do everything he could to keep Madison out of danger. No matter how long it took. "Maddi, we've got to go."

Her heels clicked on the hardwood as she raced down the stairs with the few items of clothing she'd been able to hold on to. "I didn't want to go on the run in sweatpants."

"Yes, your choice of heels and a skirt was a much better option." He took her clothes as she hit the bottom step and shoved them inside the bag. By the time Rosalind caught word of this place, he and Madison would be long gone, but his heart jerked at the thought of surrendering the house he'd envisioned protecting his family to a serial bomber. Hesitation gripped him hard.

They could go on the run. They could spend the rest of their lives looking over their shoulders if his team wasn't able to find Rosalind. They could move from safe house to safe house with the possibility of making a mistake thick in their throats.

Or they could give Rosalind and her partner exactly what they'd wanted all along.

He and Madison could be safe. They could move on with their lives. They could raise their son in a stable home with the love he deserved. Together. He could keep her safe. "Rosalind Eyler and the partner she made a deal with want you off the case."

She settled warm caramel-colored eyes on him, and every cell in his body hiked into heated awareness. Three days. That was all it'd taken for him to fall in love with her, to envision her as something more than the mother of his child, more than an assignment, a friend. Madison pointed toward the front. "You're very percep-tive. That's why we're leaving, isn't it?"

"What if we didn't have to leave?" he asked.

"What are you talking about? You told Remi you were going to have me moved to another location." Her palms pressed to her baby belly, sleek lines and soft curves tugging at a deeper part of him. He loved her. He was in love with her, and there was nothing that was going to stop him from keeping her safe. Even Madison herself. "Now you want us to stay?"

"I want you to walk away from this alive." Jonah let the duffel bag drop at his feet. He took a step toward her, then another, as pressure built behind his chest. "I want to get to know my son when he's born in a few months, and I want you to recuse yourself as the pros-ecutor on the Rip City Bomber case."

Ice filled her expression, that automatic guard back in place in an instant, and an immediate wave of cold hit him in the gut. Madison stepped out of his reach, taking the last remnants of heat with her. "You know I can't do that."

"Think about it, Maddi. You weren't pregnant when the DA assigned you to this case. You didn't have a baby to worry about or know how far Rosalind Eyler would go to keep you from prosecuting her." He didn't counter her escape. "She's scared. You're the best prosecutor in the state aside from the DA, and she's desperate to finish what she started, but you're not the only one at risk anymore. If we walk out that door, our son will know nothing more than fear and a life on the run. He deserves better than that. You deserve better than that."

"I'm giving him what he deserves by staying on this case, Jonah." The small muscles in her jaw twitched under pressure. "I'm giving him the future I never had. Prosecuting this case will put me at the front of the line for district attorney once Rosalind Eyler is sentenced, and he'll never have to worry about when his next meal will be, if we're suddenly going to get evicted from our house or if we'll be able to afford shoes for him to go to school. He'll have everything, but only if I can see this through."

"Your life—our son's life—is more important than any job, Madison. Don't you understand that?" He curled his hands into fists as the truth exploded through him. He couldn't lose her, couldn't lose this baby. Not again. He'd tried to ignore it. Chalked it up to the adrenaline over these past few days—to everything they'd been through together—but he couldn't deny it now. "I want us to raise this baby together, here, in this house. I can tell you I've never wanted anything more in my life after what we've been through. I can support you and our son. I can make sure you two have everything you need and more. He won't just not have to worry about where his next meal is coming from, but he'll have two parents to be there to support him as he grows up."

She stepped back as though she'd been hit, the breath rushing out of her. Tears glistened in her eyes as she seemed to regain her balance, but he battled the urge to reach out. He read her answer a split second before the words left her perfectly shaped mouth. "I have to go."

"What?" Shock coursed through him. "Where?"

Diving for the duffel bag he'd discarded on the floor beside his feet, she shouldered their supplies and headed toward the front door. Long hair trailed out from behind her as Madison fled.

"Madison, wait." He threaded his hand between her arm and rib cage in an effort to slow her down, before she made a mistake she couldn't recover from.

"Don't touch me." She turned on him, a hardness in her expression that hadn't been there before, and ripped out of his hold. Her shoulders rose and fell in harsh waves. His fingers stung where her shirt had caused friction, but the oncoming pain of having her walk out that door paralyzed him in place. "I've spent my entire life ensuring I didn't have to depend on anyone, Jonah, but that's exactly what you're asking me to do. All anyone has ever done in my life is betray me, try to control me, and I swore to myself I'd never let someone trap me again." Her knuckles fought to break through the back of her hand as she pointed one long, slim finger at him. "Now you want me to give up on becoming district attorney—of proving I can support this baby without you—so you can have a chance to be a full-time father again."

He swallowed as a rush of grief thickened in his chest.

"I'm sorry you lost Noah all those years ago. I can't imagine how much pain you've had to live with because of that, but I am not helpless." She shook her head. "I am not worthless. I've taken care of myself since the day I turned ten years old, and I don't need a white knight to swoop in and tell me what's best for me and my son. I thought you understood that." The tears fell. "Don't come after us, Jonah. We don't need you."

Her son. Not theirs. Jonah held his ground as she wrenched open the front door and stepped beyond the perimeter of safety. Taking his son with her.

SHE WAS SUPPOSED to be stronger than this.

Madison hauled the bag he'd packed full of food and her clothing toward the SUV and threw it into the passenger seat. Her heels wobbled on the uneven ground, but the rift of hollowness and anger only pushed her harder. She'd gone up against the most terrifying and threatening criminals in the state over the past two years. She'd achieved justice for victims and families, got offenders off the streets, and helped children escape the same fate she'd survived all while holding herself in check every step of the way. But the pressure inside was building to unrecognizable levels.

She collapsed into the driver's seat and gripped the cold leather of the steering wheel, not bothering to check the front door to see if Jonah had followed. She'd trusted him with her body, her entire being. She'd started to believe he would be the last person on earth who'd turn what they had into a domestic cage she wouldn't be able to escape. Just like her mother. Madison pulled down the visor and let the car keys drop into her lap. Swiping at the tears, she twisted the key in the ignition and started the engine.

In seconds, she maneuvered the vehicle down the long dirt road heading back to the main highway. Jonah would have to call someone on his team for a ride. Because she never wanted to see him again. As soon as she reached out to one of her contacts in the Washington State USMS division to have her protection detail transferred to a new marshal, she'd call her lawyer. She'd offered to have her attorney draft a custody and visitation agreement when she'd learned about Jonah's first son's death. She'd wanted to help ease the pain he'd carried all this time, wanted to do something good, but now... Now she understood he'd only used his grief to insert himself into her life. Just as he'd tried to do from the beginning.

Had any of it been real?

The promises? The desire? The way he claimed she made him feel? The tightness in her chest constricted her breathing. Had he cared for her at all or had everything he'd done up until now been only for the sake of their child?

The answer settled at the tip of her tongue. Thick trees and endless miles of dirt stretched out to either side of her as she headed toward the highway. Two and a half hours west before she hit the edge of the city. That was all the time she needed to forget the past three days. Forget the way he'd gone out of his way to protect her, to forget how he'd helped fill the void left behind by her parents' selfishness and neglect. Forget how he'd convinced her to fall in love with him. Leveraging her elbow onto the window ledge of the driver's side door, she rested her temple against her palm. "It wasn't real. None of it could've been real."

The only person she could depend on in this world was herself. She'd learned that as a kid growing up in Los Angeles, learned that as a law student and as a deputy district attorney here in Oregon.

"It's you and me. That's all we need, right?" That was all they needed. That was all she'd ever needed, but the ache around her heart tried to convince her otherwise. Straightening, she slid her hand over her bulging bump. "We're going to make it."

She didn't have any other choice.

Turning east onto Highway 26, she pressed her foot onto the accelerator to get up to speed, but the SUV's engine sputtered. Once. Twice. Black smoke streamed out from the edges of the hood, and the speedometer plummeted toward zero. A strong exhale escaped her control as she pulled the vehicle to the side of the road. Moonlight shone straight overhead as she threw the SUV into Park and pulled at the hood release near her left leg. She looked down at her baby bump. "Do you come programmed with car maintenance know-how? Because apparently your sperm donor does not."

Defeat pulled her deeper into the leather seat. An

invisible ache squeezed her chest tighter as she played through the last words she'd spit at Jonah. *We don't need you.* But it hadn't been the truth. Because she'd come to rely on him for more than protection. As more than a rescuer. He'd been safety personified, someone she'd come to trust over her own instincts, a reminder of the good in the world and that she deserved a small piece of it. He'd been…everything.

Right up until he'd broken their unspoken agreement.

She pulled a flashlight from the glove compartment and turned off the car. The edges of the light were sharper than any other she'd used. A tactical flashlight, designed to cause damage if needed and light the way at the same time. Madison waited for a break in traffic before stepping onto the pavement and rounding the hood. She unhitched it and hauled it above her head. Something burnt and sickening dived into her lungs before the smoke cleared. Scanning the caps and knobs—as though she had any idea what the hell made a vehicle function—she focused on one that looked like it might be missing altogether. Heat worked under her blouse from the engine, steam whipping around her as it came into contact with Oregon spring temperatures. The cap was missing, and from the labels on the thick black hose beside the container, it looked like it'd come off the radiator. She peered down into the well but met nothing but blackness. Empty. "You've got to be kidding me."

Another car sped past and the SUV shook slightly. She'd handed over her cell phone to Jonah when he'd taken her into protective custody. She didn't have any way of calling for a tow truck or maintenance, and there were still nearly one hundred miles between her and the city. Technically, there were physically fewer than that between her and Jonah, but she'd walk straight to Portland if that meant never having to face him again. Damn it. She clenched the edge of the SUV's frame. According to him, Deputy Chief Remington Barton required all the marshals on her team to carry emergency supplies and extra fluids for their vehicles. She'd wanted them to be ready for any threat.

Madison wedged herself between the SUV and the highway safety rail to keep from getting hit by an oncoming vehicle and opened the back cargo hatch. Confusion rippled through her. The space was empty. No supplies. No extra ammunition. No gasoline or coolant. That didn't make sense.

Headlights flashed from behind her, and the hairs on the back of her neck stood on end. Jonah wouldn't have taken out his emergency supplies. Not as they were getting ready to move to another safe house. What were the chances of her vehicle running out of coolant in the middle of the night just as she needed to flee the safe house? The supplies were gone. She was stranded. A car door slammed a few feet away, and her heart rocketed into her throat. "Looks like you're having some car troubles. Can I help?"

"No, thank you. I've already called for help." Without being able to see the Good Samaritan's face backlit by blinding headlights, she braved the risk of a vehicle not noticing her on the side of the road and walked toward the driver's side door. She wouldn't be able to drive the

SUV as is, but a layer of steel and glass between her and the man behind her was better than nothing.

"Come on now, Madison," he said over the roar of traffic. "You and I both know you've never been a very good liar. That's what makes you one of the best prosecutors in the state. Your determination to do what's right, even if you're the one who pays the price."

It was him, the man who'd thrown her over the bridge. He'd found her. Fear tensed the muscles down her spine. Hand on the driver's side door, Madison calculated her options for escape. Waving down another car would put innocent lives at risk. Using the SUV as a safe space hadn't worked in her favor at the second bombing scene. Wilderness lined each side of the two-lane highway, but darkness had already fallen. She didn't have time to grab the bag of supplies from the front seat. If she disappeared into the trees, she'd be running blind, running scared and running without hope of the marshals finding her, but it was still her best option.

"There's nowhere for you to run this time, Counselor." He moved in on her, one step at a time. "And no one who's going to save you."

She didn't wait for her abductor to make the first move. Grip tight on the tactical flashlight, she kicked off her heels and dashed straight across the road into westbound traffic. Headlights grew larger a second before a blaring horn screamed in her ears. The pickup truck barely missed hitting her before she fled into the eastbound lane. Loose gravel and uneven pavement cut into her feet as she pumped her legs hard. She cut the power to the flashlight and ran for the guardrail lining the highway, not daring to look back.

Cold steel grazed her thighs as she vaulted over the rail and landed on the other side. Almost there. She just had to reach the trees. He wouldn't be able to find her in the trees. Her heart rate struggled to keep up with her lungs, fingers numb around the flashlight. Dirt bled into thickening weeds ten feet ahead. It was a straight shot. She was almost—

The ground disappeared out from under her.

She lost the flashlight as gravity pulled her down into the steep incline and into a shallow canyon of litter, water and dirt. A scream escaped up her throat before air crushed from her lungs. She hit the bottom on her side, nothing but wide-open sky above her and miles of trees beside her. Salt and copper mixed in a dizzying flood in her mouth. A groan escaped from between her teeth.

Holding on to her belly with one hand, Madison pressed to sit up. Immobilizing pain shot through her wrist and up her arm, and she cried out. Her wrist had possibly broken from the fall. Didn't matter. She had to keep moving. She wouldn't become another victim in this madman's game. She wasn't going to let Rosalind Eyler or her partner win. Not when there was so much to lose.

Gravel crunched under dense footsteps from behind, and she patted the ground around her to find Jonah's tactical flashlight she'd dropped. "I have to hand it to you, Madison. I didn't think killing you would be this hard. You're a fighter. I appreciate that, but you're only making this harder on yourself."

The footsteps slowed as her fingers felt something heavy and cold. The flashlight. She clicked on the power. Wrapping her fingers around the body, she swung around as hard as she could and met her abductor. Strong fingers locked around her wrist and squeezed. The light from the flashlight cascaded across her attacker's bare face, and recognition flared. No. It wasn't… It wasn't possible. "You?"

"Me." He slammed the edge of the flashlight into her face, and everything went black.

Chapter Thirteen

He shouldn't have let her go.

Rosaline Eyler and her partner were still out there, still a threat, and Madison had escaped down the mountain without any way for him to follow. She might've claimed she didn't need him, but he sure as hell needed her.

Three knocks on the front door reverberated through the house, and Jonah wrenched it open harder than he'd meant.

"You don't call. You don't write. Here I thought we were beginning to become friends after I let your suspect beat the crap out of me." Deputy Marshal Dylan Cove stalked through the front door and took in the raised ceilings. "Why aren't any of my safe houses this nice?"

"Madison left in my SUV twenty minutes ago. We need to find her." Jonah tossed his phone at the marshal with the vehicle's tracking data on the screen as he reached for his Kevlar vest. "According to this, she hasn't moved in minutes, and I'm not giving Rosalind

Eyler or her partner a chance to catch up with her. We're running out of time. Where is the rest of the team?"

"Remi is running point on the manhunt for the Rip City Bomber with Reed, Foster and that FBI guy you don't seem to like. Special Agent Jackson." Cove studied the date on the phone. "You get me. You should feel honored."

"Let's go. You drive." Jonah strapped into his vest and holstered his sidearm. In less than thirty seconds, they left the cabin behind and were headed down the mountain. Every cell in his body raced with anxiety. "Where are we at with the list of prosecutors in line to take over the Rip City Bomber case if Madison Gray is unable to perform her duties?"

Cove nodded toward the middle console. "The list is in the file. I took the liberty of pulling phone records, financials and background checks for the top three candidates I got from the district attorney, but I'm not sure what you're hoping to find. All three names came back clean. No visible connection to Rosalind Eyler, no access to the Rip City Bomber case and no evidence any of them has purchased the components to make a home-made bomb in the last twelve months."

Damn it. Their bomber wasn't going to make this easy for them, was he? Jonah skimmed through the file. Two male candidates, one female. He could rule out the female due to evidence and the altercation on the bridge, leaving two males. Cove was right. Background checks, financials, phone records. None of it led to motive for someone inside the district attorney's office, which left Jonah's original suspect, Special Agent

Collin Jackson. He scanned through the next section of documents. "You included the statements Reed took from the officers assigned perimeter duty at the second bombing scene."

The bomber had gotten onto and off the scene without the Portland Police Bureau noticing. Or the bastard had presumed clearance to be there. Jonah read through the account of one of the officers assigned to watch the crime scene perimeter on the east end of the street, where forensics had narrowed down the exact spot Madison had been taken. The SUV bounced along the unpaved dirt road as they headed toward the highway, but that didn't stop Jonah from highlighting a single name as the rest of the text bled away. He turned the statement toward Cove. "This officer states he let only one person under the tape while he was on duty that day, but never saw the man leave. Want to guess who?"

Cove focused on the name Jonah underscored with his finger. "You've got to be kidding me."

"He had the means and the opportunity. I should've seen it before now. I should've known." Jonah pulled his phone from his pocket and dialed the deputy chief. The bomber hadn't been law enforcement at all, but the SOB might as well have been considering his access to the investigation and the Rip City Bomber case. Hell, how had he missed it? And how the hell had the bastard been able to keep tabs on Madison? The line connected, and he put the call on speaker. "Remi, I need everything you have on Pierce Cook. Now."

"The district attorney?" Surprise laced her question, but the remoteness of her voice said she'd put him on speaker, presumably to keep her hands free to get him what he'd asked for. "I need you to be one hundred and ten percent sure about this, Watson. The second I put in this request, I'm going to have the governor on my back asking why I pulled background on the most popular elected official in the state."

He had to be sure. The Oregon USMS division wasn't the only one who'd suffer if he made a mistake. Madison would lose her job completely, lose everything she'd ever worked for. He'd already blown his chance of turning what they had into something more, of them raising their son together. He couldn't ruin this for her, too.

Jonah strengthened his hand around the phone. "Madison told me Pierce Cook is scheduled to announce his retirement in the next month, that he put her on the Rip City Bomber case because he wanted a strong prosecutor to see the case through to the end. But a case like this would put him down in the history books for life. What if assigning her this case hadn't been his choice? His term is coming to an end. Madison's been recognized by the governor for her work. It'd be easy to confirm the governor is the one who assigned Madison the case and not the district attorney as we believed. He could've just been responsible for giving her the assignment."

"I think you might be right," Remi said. "Not only does he have the experience with explosives during his two tours with the army, but I logged into Portland Police Bureau's database to run a background check. He requested their IT department run GPS on Madison

Gray's cell phone three days ago. Just minutes after the bombing at the courthouse."

"I took her phone after she was cleared by the EMTs, but he could've been trying to get a hold of her after he caught wind of what happened. We need something more. Something solid." He turned to Cove as they pulled onto Highway 26. "GPS says my SUV hasn't moved in ten minutes about a mile ahead. Watch out for her."

"Watson, Madison's GPS location wasn't the only data requested that day." Her voice grew distant. "The DA had them track yours, too."

"Which means Pierce Cook knew where his target was all along. He used me to track her. All he had to do was get her alone." His voice sounded distant, even to himself, as Jonah caught sight of red reflective tail-lights off to the side of the road ahead. A knot of dread pooled at the base of his spine as Cove signaled to pull behind the dark SUV. GPS confirmed his vehicle hadn't moved, and from a cursory inspection, there wasn't any movement inside. "She's not here." Blood drained from his face and upper body, suctioning him to the seat. He clutched his phone too tight. "He was waiting for her, watching her. I let her walk out that door and right into the bastard's hands."

Cove didn't respond as he shoved the vehicle in Park and shouldered out of the vehicle.

"Reed and Foster are wrapped up in the manhunt for Rosalind Eyler," Remi said. "Tech guys are working to find a location on Pierce Cook's phone now. I'll send you the coordinates as soon as they get a clear signal and join you as soon as I can. If he's taken her, it won't take us long to catch up. If not, we'll find out what he was doing trying to locate a federal marshal and his witness without going through the proper channels. Either way, we're going to find her, Jonah. This is what we do."

She ended the call as he hit the pavement and unholstered his weapon. With a nod, he signaled for Cove to move in, battle-ready tension pulling at the muscles in his back. Approaching the SUV from either side, he and the other marshal inspected the open hatch, noting the missing supplies he always kept on hand, and the back seat. He wrenched the passenger side door open and froze. Empty aside from the keys still in the ignition. She wouldn't have walked away. Pierce Cook had shattered a window to get to Madison at the second scene, but as far as he could tell, there hadn't been a struggle here. She'd vanished. No phone, no emergency supplies, no sign of her. What the hell had happened here? "Clear."

"Jonah," Cove said.

He rounded the front of the vehicle where the former private investigator stood staring down at the engine, the hood propped open above him.

"Radiator's completely dry." Cove pointed to the section clearly missing a cap. "Every vehicle the USMS owns is serviced before we check them out, no exceptions, but there are a few drops of fluid on the asphalt by my feet. If I had to guess, someone took a screwdriver to the well and drained it dry."

"Not someone. Pierce Cook." Jonah had no doubts now. The district attorney had tried to kill his successor—twice—and had murdered a defense attorney in the process. Now Cook would spend his retirement behind bars. Jonah would make sure of it. He shifted around to the driver's side of the SUV, headlights of their vehicle highlighting a pristine pair of tan heels, and his world shattered. "I've got her shoes here."

Cove crossed the white line indicating the highway shoulder. "So the car overheats, and she has to pull over. She gets out, pops the hood. There's probably smoke, but your lady is intelligent. She realizes the radiator well is empty, and she needs to refill it if she's going to make it back to the city."

"She knows marshals are required to carry emergency fluids for their vehicles, but when she opens the back hatch, she discovers the supplies are missing." Jonah could see the story playing out in his mind, and he locked his hand on the frame of the SUV. She was out here somewhere. Afraid. Alone. He'd been an idiot asking her to resign from the Rip City Bomber case, asking her to give up her one ounce of security in a life filled with uncertainty and fear. As if he'd known what she'd survived as a kid and decided right then and there none of it mattered. She'd believed in him, and he'd failed her. She was a strong, independent woman who'd taken on the deadliest offenders for a single chance to bring justice to the families that depended on her, and he loved her for it. Demanding Madison let go of her dream to become district attorney—to support their son on her own—had been like demanding he simply forget Noah. He'd regret that last conversation between them for the rest of his life. "That's when he drives up behind her. She doesn't have a phone or a weapon. So she kicks off her shoes—"

"To run." Cove stared across the highway, toward the trees on the other side. "Question is, did she run fast enough?"

HER FEET WERE COLD against the cement.

She couldn't take a full breath, as though something heavy was squeezing the air from her lungs. Madison dragged her chin away from her chest, head pounding. Small kicks protested against the heaviness around her belly. The baby didn't like something invading his space, least of all her rib cage. The edges of her vision cleared in small increments as her eyes adjusted to a single bare bulb above her. Her shoulder sockets ached, but she couldn't pull her hands around to her front. She'd been bound by the wrists. Pressing her toes into the floor, she tipped the chair on its hind legs, but her ankles wouldn't move. Her abductor had zip-tied her feet to the frame. Without something to cut through the plastic, she was trapped.

"I was starting to think I might've hit you so hard you were going to miss out on all the fun." From the corner of the room, the outline of the man who'd attacked her nearly bled into the background. His shadow separated from the wall as he took a step toward her into the radius of light. No mask. Nothing to hide now.

Her boss, District Attorney Pierce Cook, settled hard light green eyes on her, and her heart threatened to beat straight out of her chest. He ran one hand through dark brown hair peppered with gray. Thick forehead wrinkles deepened as he studied her, a handsome face she'd come to trust over the years. He'd once stood as the face of justice for the city. Now he'd become one of its worst.

Pierce reached past her right ear and wrapped his hand around the top rail of the chair. He leaned in, too close. "Do you know how many cases I've prosecuted for this city, Madison? How many criminals I've put away over the years? How many neighborhoods I made safe by committing my life to this work? I built a legacy here. Right up until the governor forced my resignation, until he forced me to put you on the Rip City Bomber case. He took that from me, but now I can make it right."

That was why he was doing this? Why he'd killed nine innocent people, including Harvey Braddock, and tried to throw her off a bridge? Anger stirred in her gut as the pieces fell into place. The bombing, destroying evidence of murder at Harvey Braddock's home, how the bomber had seemed to stay one step ahead of US marshals and police. It was all to serve his ego. "Of all the people I believed in, Pierce, you were the beacon I looked up to my entire career. You were the reason I applied for a job in the district attorney's office. You were legendary. There wasn't a single case you couldn't take on and win, and I imagined myself following in your footsteps. I'm the prosecutor I am because of you." She tried to breathe through the weight still limiting her lung capacity, but it took effort. Twisting her wrists inside the zip tie, Madison tried to keep her expression neutral as the plastic cut into her skin. "But now you're no better than the people we prosecute. Murderers, drug dealers, rapists. It doesn't matter how many cases you've won or how many criminals you've kept off the streets. All anyone is going to remember you for is this."

A close-lipped smile slithered across his weathered face. "No, Madison. They won't. Because in about twenty-five minutes, you won't be alive to tell them anything other than the story I've come up with to explain everything that's happened."

Twenty-five minutes? Why—

The bulk on her chest registered again, and for the first time since waking, she realized why it'd become so hard to breathe. The Kevlar vest he'd strapped her into had been tightened enough to conceal the bright red digits counting down across her chest. Precious oxygen lodged in her throat. He'd turned her into a bomb.

"You see, everything I've done, every bomb I detonated, every loose end I tied up, none of it can be connected back to me," he said.

Realization struck.

"You took credit for those bombings in the Rip City Bomber's name. To frame Rosalind Eyler." She tried to swallow. "You're the partner she made her behind-the-scenes deal with before the first attack. She gave you the list and measurements of the components she used in her devices in exchange for what? Had to be something important to Rosalind to give up that kind of information. Reduced sentencing, a chance to finish the work she started with her coworkers? She wouldn't tell us. I think she was trying to protect her partner. Stands to reason, as her partner, you couldn't do that unless you were the one behind the prosecution's table to offer the deal, and that meant you had to get rid of me. You get to step back into the limelight and leave behind the legacy you've always wanted, and Rosalind gets a deal. Everyone walks away happy."

"Well, not everyone." Pierce shook his head. Straightening, he stepped back a few feet as his voice dipped with frustration. "If that damn marshal hadn't managed to catch up with us at the falls, we would've been able to put this all behind us sooner." He drove his hands into his slacks pockets. "Of course, asking you to step down from the case wasn't an option. We've only met a few times, but I've watched your work all these years. I see that drive I have to rise to the top in you. I know there's nothing I could've said or done to make you recuse yourself from the Rip City Bomber trial, but I couldn't let you take this from me."

The puzzle was starting to make sense as she read between the lines of the district attorney's phrasing, but there was a hole in this fantasy. "There's one problem with your plan, Pierce. You failed to consider the fact Rosalind Eyler killed thirty-two people for taking credit for her academic work, and she knows what you've been doing in her name. How do you think she's going to react when she catches up with you?"

A sincere moment of fear turned Pierce's eyes down at the corners. So subtle she might not have noticed if she hadn't been looking straight at him. "If Rosalind's as smart as all those degrees and IQ tests claim, she'll do exactly as I tell her and be grateful her last moments on this earth will be behind bars and not with a needle in her arm."

"Breaking her out of prison wasn't part of the plan."

She had to keep him talking, keep him distracted. Madison pressed her wrists together inside the restraints and put everything she had into creating enough pressure to snap the zip tie. The plastic wouldn't budge. "What about Harvey Braddock? You obviously used his garage to build your devices, but was his murder always part of this plan?"

"Harvey had his uses. If you'd become district attorney, you would've learned there are some things—some people—worth sacrificing in order to win." Pierce crossed to the other side of the room. Shadows clung to the area outside the spread of light around her, but the reflection of the bulb off the rolltop door said this was most likely some kind of storage room. The district attorney rooted through objects spread across a folding table along one wall. He picked one up, studied it, discarded it. Then another as though trying to choose the perfect torture device to threaten her with. "Harvey knew about the deal between me and Rosalind Eyler. He was on board with it. Right up until he learned you were the target. The idiot threatened to go to the marshals, said he didn't want any part of having you killed in order to get his client the best deal." Pierce turned back toward her, and the hairs on the back of her neck stood on end. "He wanted to take his chances with the jury, but I couldn't have that."

The countdown hadn't stopped, red lights demanding her attention from the dark space between her chest and the Kevlar vest. "You stole the thermite to draw Marshal Watson out into the open and kill Harvey all at the same time. Two birds, one stone. You figured the marshal who'd taken me into protective custody would be forced to leave me with someone else while he was on that scene."

And it'd worked. Pierce had gotten exactly what he'd wanted that day, and the only reason she was still breathing was because of Jonah. Because of how far he'd gone to make sure she walked away from this mind game alive.

"I saw the way you two are around each other. The late nights, the early mornings. I found those homemade crosswords you'd make him to keep him busy while you worked. I had to know who'd get in my way, so I looked into him, too. Luring him into the field with an explosive only he had experience with was the only way I was going to get him away from you, and that gave me the perfect opportunity." Pierce leaned against the table, and for the first time, she recognized the dusty objects on the surface.

Phones, duct tape, box cutter, glass vials with residue clinging to the sides. Pieces that, in the right order, could be constructed into a bomb, but this wasn't Pierce's original laboratory. He'd destroyed that with evidence of Harvey Braddock's murder in the garage. The courthouse bomb and the device left undetonated inside Harvey Braddock's home had been built with the ammonium nitrate from ice packs. Here, it looked as though the bomber had made his own, as Rosalind had revealed that day at the prison. The thickness of dust coating the table, in the air, suggested a much older lab. Could this storage container belong to the Rip City Bomber? Police hadn't ever been able to locate it, but

Pierce obviously had. Was this where he'd meant for investigators—for Jonah—to find her body in order to strengthen his plan to frame Rosalind Eyler? As far as she knew, Jonah hadn't even realized she was in danger or that she'd been taken.

"I know Marshal Watson is the father of your baby, Madison. I know how far he'll go out of his way to protect the people he cares about, especially another child after everything he went through losing his first." He pushed off from the table with the roll of duct tape and tore a piece free. Slapping it against her mouth, he ensured no one would hear her. Pierce reached high above her head—to the string beside the bare bulb—and tugged it.

Darkness consumed the space and threw her into a frantic emptiness that reminded her of all those times she'd hidden in strangers' car trunks to get away from her father. Panic sent numbness down her fingers.

Footsteps clued her in to Pierce's movement as he crossed to the rolltop door and hauled it above his head. Dim light flooded through the corridor from the other side, giving her a glimpse of row after row of storage units. The district attorney paused, his expression as dark as the shadows closing in around her. "Only he isn't coming to save you this time. No one is."

He stepped back and started to pull the door down.

"No!" Madison screamed as loud as the tape would let her, but it wasn't enough. She tried to kick out. He couldn't leave her here. "No!"

The sound of a padlock clicked into place.

Chapter Fourteen

"I had a ping from Pierce Cook's phone two minutes ago on the east side of the city, but I lost it a second later. He must've shut the phone off as soon as he arrived, or destroyed it." Static cut through Remi's voice as Jonah and Cove exceeded the highway's speed limits. Jagged rocks and boulders bled into uniform darkness before Portland came into view. "Corner of Stark Street and Twenty-Second Avenue. I'm on my way with backup."

"We're five minutes out, Chief." Cove maneuvered the SUV around a slower vehicle and pushed the engine harder.

"Cove's and my priority needs to be recovering Madison. Taking Pierce Cook down will have to be your job. Just make sure it hurts when you put the cuffs on him." Jonah ended the call and scrambled to remember what was in the area of where Cook's phone had pinged off the towers. Car parts store, apartment buildings, martial arts studio, car rental. None of those was conducive to holding a hostage…or getting rid of a body. The district attorney would need a private location. Somewhere with a reduced traffic of people in the middle of the night. Somewhere nobody might hear Madison scream. "There's a large storage unit facility on the southeast corner of that intersection."

"Perfect location to make sure your victim can't escape if locked inside." Dylan Cove didn't elaborate. The former private investigator didn't have to. "Those storage places have hundreds of units, though, and we don't have time to search every single one of them. We're going to have to narrow this down."

The marshal was right. Every second Madison was missing was another second Pierce Cook had to kill her. They couldn't waste their time focusing on the wrong areas, and time was already running out. They maneuvered into the turnout leading to the storage facility's parking lot, met by a large gate. Cove lowered the window and flashed his badge to the security officer inside the booth positioned outside the premises. "US Marshals. We have reason to believe a victim has been abducted and hidden inside one of these units. We need to search the property." Dylan Cove showed a photo of their perp to the attendant. "Have you seen this guy come through here tonight?"

"Yeah, man. He came through about thirty minutes ago. In a hurry. Haven't seen him leave, though. He's dangerous?" The security attendant's gaze widened, and he hit the button to release the gate. "I need to call my boss."

Cove shot the SUV through the partially open gate, then parked off to one side.

Jonah shoved out of the vehicle, and they both rounded to the rear, gearing up. Jonah pushed through the pain in his shoulder and side and reached for the shotgun case. He loaded three rounds into the stock and added three more to his vest for easy access. His pistol was enough to take down any threat, but he couldn't waste time trying to get inside one of these storage units by hand. The shotgun would do the job. He closed the space between him and the security officer. "Which unit does that man own?"

"I… I have no idea." The attendant slid the phone down his cheek, then pointed off to their right. "But he drove that way."

Hell. Jonah studied the long row of structure after structure. Twenty, thirty, forty units, all barely lit with flickering and worn-out lighting on the outside. It would take time to search them all. Time Madison didn't have. Hauling the stock of the shotgun against his shoulder, he angled the barrel toward the pavement and took up position along the right side of the first row. "You take the left. Open any one of these units if you feel you have cause. Keep your ears open and your eyes peeled for anything out of the ordinary. According to the attendant, Pierce is still here."

Shadows jumped from unit to unit as Jonah kept himself pressed against the wall, stopping at each unit only for a moment before moving on to the next. No cries for help. No sign of her or the bastard who'd taken her. Doubt coiled low in his gut. The cell towers had pinged Pierce Cook's location near this storage facility. Had he been wrong in assuming this was where the district attorney had taken his prey?

A scrape of metal echoed off the steel rolltop doors

and both Cove and Jonah slowed as they neared the end of the row. With a glance at the former private investigator, he signaled for Cove to use caution with two fingers. Jonah was in the dark from this side of the alley. No sight lines, but also perfectly positioned to move on the target quickly.

Cove pressed his back flat against the unit behind him and leaned his head to the left to survey the source of the noise. Straightening, he nodded, then crossed the narrow alleyway to join Jonah on the other side. "Single suspect, looks like Cook, loading boxes into the back of a moving truck. No sign of Madison with him."

"She has to be in one of the units in the next row." Only problem, which one? Moving trucks didn't exactly fit in these narrow alleys, forcing the district attorney to park at the end of the row, which meant Pierce Cook had most likely used a dolly system to get from his unit to the truck. "I don't care what you have to do to bring him down, but I want him alive. He's the only one who can tell us which unit she's in. Understand?"

"Copy." Deputy Marshal Dylan Cove loaded a round into his sidearm and nodded. "Ready when you are."

"Move." Jonah rounded the corner, shotgun raised, and caught sight of their suspect loading the last of whatever he'd come for into the back of the truck. "District Attorney Pierce Cook, you're under arrest. Turn around, interlace your hands behind your head and get down on your knees. Now."

The man at the rear of the truck straightened slowly, his back to both marshals. Dark hair skimmed along the back of the suspect's sweater collar before he turned to face them. Pierce Cook leveled light-colored eyes on them. Confirmation. They had him. "Marshal Watson, I take it this isn't a social call. Now, just so I get this right when I call the governor in the morning to have your badge, exactly what crime are you accusing me of?"

"Murder of nine people, including Harvey Braddock, kidnapping of Madison Gray, attempted murder of a deputy district attorney, three counts of use of explosives in a public area." Jonah took one step, then another. "Want me to keep going? I'm sure the prosecutor at your trial will have a lot more."

"Trial? I'm not going to trial, Marshal. You can arrest me, but I guarantee I won't spend more than an hour behind bars. I haven't done anything wrong." Pierce squared off as though ready for a fight. "I was sorry to hear about what happened to Madison. Almost killed in that courthouse bombing, then abducted by a masked man from Harvey Braddock's home and nearly thrown over a bridge. I can't imagine how awful you must feel considering you were the one who was supposed to protect her and her baby, but the fact of the matter is neither you nor the USMS have evidence connecting me to any of what you just said."

"Where is she?" Jonah strengthened his grip on the shotgun, his instincts focused on neutralizing the threat to his family. To his future.

"I don't know what you're talking about, but I have a feeling you might be too late." The district attorney's mouth smoothed into a twisted smile under a thick beard as he turned back to continue loading the equipment into the truck.

Jonah stepped into the DA's personal space and pressed the shotgun into Pierce's spine. "I said get on your knees and interlace your hands behind your head."

"Are you going to shoot me if I don't comply, Marshal Watson? You want to, don't you? You want to save the damsel in distress from the big, bad bomber, but like I said—you're too late." Faster than Jonah expected, Pierce Cook spun, slamming his palm against the shotgun to divert the barrel down and to the right. A hard kick from the district attorney landed square in Jonah's gut, and he fell back into the marshal behind him.

Both men went down as Pierce Cook disappeared behind the moving truck.

"Stay on him!" Jonah shoved to his feet. Pumping his legs as fast as he could, he maneuvered around the truck and chased after the fleeing suspect already two rows ahead of him. Heavy breathing and pounding footsteps echoed from behind as he and Cove closed in on their suspect. Pierce wasn't getting away. That wasn't how this was going to end. He was going to find Madison alive. He was going to tell her how much of a mistake he'd made. He was going to spend the rest of his life proving he could make her and their son happy without forcing her to give up her independence. "Pierce!"

Sirens and screeching tires ahead redirected the DA down another row of units.

Jonah pointed to the row next to him. "Cut him off!"

Cove branched off to the right to get to Pierce from the other side.

Jonah's heart pounded hard in his chest, his legs going numb from the slap of his boots against pavement. He turned down the row where Pierce had disappeared, weapon drawn, and halted short.

The district attorney stood in the middle of the alley, a large serrated blade pressed to his throat. Pierce Cook's shoulders rose and fell in shallow waves, but it was the woman standing behind him Jonah couldn't take his eyes off of. "Marshal, please. Help me."

Rosalind Eyler slid the tip of her nose up the length of the district attorney's neck as though savoring every moment of fear she could wring out of the man under her knife. "Did you really think you could use my blueprints, my name, for your dirty work and not suffer the same as all the rest of them, Pierce? I've known men like you my entire life. I've killed men like you. You were never going to hold up your end of the deal, and I won't let you take advantage of one more woman."

"Rosalind, put the knife down." Jonah took aim, but even from a closer position, he still risked hitting the district attorney instead of her. He needed Cook alive to tell them where he'd stashed Madison. There was no other option. "He'll spend the rest of his life in prison for what he's done. That's punishment enough. Put down the knife, or I will pull this trigger."

"I believe you." Rosalind settled bright green eyes on him, her smile wider than he'd ever seen it before, then slid the knife across Pierce Cook's throat. The DA collapsed out of her grip and slumped to the pavement. "Oops."

"No!" Jonah kept his gun on her as he ran toward Pierce.

A gunshot tore through Rosalind's shoulder from behind, and she fell forward with the momentum. Dylan Cove jogged into view, gun trained on the fugitive, and kicked the blade the Rip City Bomber had used out of her reach.

Jonah holstered his weapon and pressed the heel of his palms against the DA's throat. Blood trickled up through his fingers as he applied pressure, but the man's eyes remained distant and unmoving. "Stay with me, Pierce. Tell me where she is, damn it. Tell me!"

MADISON FLINCHED AT the sound of the single gunshot.

She couldn't hear anything, couldn't see anything. Was someone out there? Was someone looking for her?

Jonah. His name pierced through the panic she'd given in to for the last few minutes. She forced herself to take a deep breath to get her heart rate under control. Alone, in the dark, she pulled at her bound wrists and ankles for the hundredth time, but Pierce had done too good of a job ensuring she couldn't escape. Five minutes. The countdown ticked off second by second, and there was nothing she could do to stop it. Nothing she could do to save herself or her baby. Tape sucked the moisture from her mouth.

Screaming wouldn't do any good. She'd have to find another way to get someone's attention. She wasn't going to die here. She wasn't going to let the last conversation between her and Jonah stand. He'd asked her to let go of the future she'd worked her entire life to build—to trust him with every ounce of her being that he wouldn't hurt her—and she'd said no. But now she understood the role fear had played in her life leading her to this exact moment. Fear of relying on someone who'd end up hurting her, fear of being that small, helpless girl she'd left behind. Fear of being unloved and used. Every decision she'd made over the course of her life had been out of fear.

Until Jonah. Where the past had filled her with hollowness and isolation all these years, he'd brought light, warmth, commitment. She'd learned to expect the worst of the people who were supposed to care about her, but the emotional, physical and mental neglect had only prepared her to view everyone the same, to distance herself from getting too close. And when he'd asked her to recuse herself from the case, he'd offered nothing but respect, support and space, and it'd scared her. She hadn't been able to see the ulterior motive—still didn't—but now she understood. Jonah didn't have one. He never had.

And she was tired of letting fear build her future.

Ankles zip-tied to the frame of the chair, Madison pressed her toes into the floor and tipped forward. Getting oxygen was still hard, her lungs working overtime from the weight of the vest and the tape over her mouth, but she'd do whatever it took to get out of there. The two back legs lifted off the cement. She tensed against the chair. She could do this. She had to do this. Slowly, one inch at a time, she angled her toes out, then in, and crossed the storage unit toward the table, the rest of her body following.

Four minutes.

Only the sound of her pounding pulse filled her ears. No more gunshots. No sounds of footsteps telling her someone was coming to save her. She had to save herself. An overly loud thump registered as the back of the chair hit the edge of the table, and she set the chair back on all four feet. She'd made it across the unit, but without something to cut through the zip ties, she'd still be here when the clock ran out. Her arms ached from the position she'd been tied in, but it wouldn't be enough to stop her now. What was on the table? Duct tape. Cell phones.

She'd gotten only a glimpse of the rest before Pierce had shut her inside the darkness. Rosalind Eyler and the district attorney both would've needed tools to assemble their devices. Box cutters. She'd noticed the tool before Pierce had locked her inside. That would work, but her hands were still tied. She didn't have time to try to cut through the zip ties or to try to get one of the cell phones to work. Pressure built in her chest as she read the countdown.

Three minutes.

She'd wasted too much time.

"Come on." Both words disappeared behind the tape secured across her mouth. She needed someone to know where she was. Noise. She needed to find something to make noise and pray it was loud enough to draw their attention.

The unit's walls were built of cinder block, but the rolltop door was presumably steel. Steel could be loud when hit with something hard, but to get to the door she'd have to cross the unit again. She rocked forward onto her toes but miscalculated the angle. Falling forward, Madison slammed onto her right arm with the chair on top of her. Her scream lodged in her mouth as the air crushed from her lungs. Her broken wrist from falling down the incline on the highway burned. She couldn't see, couldn't breathe, and the panic flared. Rawness tore along her throat as sobs took control. Trying to rip her other arm free of the tie, she rocked back and forth against the floor. The chair knocked against the cinder blocks.

She stilled. The sound could be enough to draw whoever'd shot that gun.

Two minutes.

Madison bit back the pain in her arm pinned between the chair and the cement and rocked the frame into the cinder blocks. Once. Twice. She closed her eyes, losing count, as tears streaked across her face. She wouldn't look at the countdown again. Couldn't let that be her last memory. She'd think about Jonah instead, about their son, their future. She'd think about how happy they would've been if she hadn't been so afraid of letting go of all the hurt and pain. The tears dried.

Distorted voices reached through the darkness. Then again.

Opening her eyes, Madison moaned through the tape. She rocked the chair back into the wall harder, accompanied by her pathetic attempt to shout for help. Metal protested in her ears, then a loud bang right before the rolltop door screamed along the track. Several holes had been punctured through the steel. Fresh air rushed into the unit as two outlines took stock of what was inside.

She tried to crane her head up, but managed only

to strain the muscles in the back of her neck. Another shout for help died at her lips.

"Maddi!" The largest of the two outlines collapsed at her side and made quick work of the zip ties. Her un-injured hand immediately went to pull the tape from her mouth as Jonah cut through the ties at her ankles, and a surge of warning shot through her. "I've got you. I've got you."

She sucked in as much air as she could. "Bomb... Vest. Get out."

"I'm not going anywhere without you, damn it. Not again." Cutting her loose from the chair, Jonah pulled her into a sitting position against the wall, his cinna-mon-spiced aftershave diving deep into her lungs. He'd come for her. Even after she'd told him she didn't need him, he'd come for her. "Somebody get that light on. I need to be able to see what I'm doing so I don't blow us all to hell."

The light burst to life overhead, and Madison closed her eyes against the brightness. Someone else was in the unit. A woman. His deputy chief?

The sound of Velcro tearing filled the space as Jonah exposed the device Pierce had strapped to her chest. "Pierce can't hurt you anymore. He can't hurt anyone anymore. Okay? He's gone."

Pierce was dead?

One minute.

Her pulse rocketed into dangerous territory. They didn't have enough time. As much as she hated the idea of the district attorney finishing what he'd started,

Madison couldn't be responsible for bringing two US marshals down with her. "Jonah, you have to go."

"Don't move." He worked fast, examining each wire running from the cell phone duct-taped to the small plastic container near her chest, then moved on to the next. This was what he'd been trained for. This was what he did best, but not even the most experienced bomb technicians were fireproof. "The bastard added a bunch of dead wires to confuse anyone who might've found you in time."

"I'll order everyone back." Remi's voice brought Madison's attention up to the deputy chief angled over Jonah's shoulder before the marshal called to the growing scene outside the door. "Active explosive! I need everyone to evacuate behind the perimeter. Now!"

"I can't cut you out," Jonah said. "He's got the wires running down through the vest."

"Jonah, you're running out of time." She couldn't be the reason he died.

"No, I'm not going to lose you. You're not dying in here today. Understand?" He locked mesmerizing blue eyes on her, and the entire world fizzled into nothingness. In that moment, there was only the two of them. That was all they needed. Nothing else mattered. He pinched what looked like a blue wire between his index finger and thumb. "Do you trust me?"

No hesitation this time. No fear. "I've always trusted you. I love you."

"I love you, too." Jonah pulled the wire free from the device. The countdown on the LED screen stopped for a moment, then flickered before speeding up to twenty seconds remaining. He flipped open the blade he must've used to cut through her zip ties and sliced the Kevlar vest holding the device down the side. He peeled her out and helped her haul the heavy bulk over her head, as she'd done for him back in the ambulance after the courthouse explosion.

Terror stirred in her gut. "What—"

"There was no way to disarm it without triggering the final countdown." He tossed the vest toward the back of the room, latched onto her hand with his and pulled her out of the storage unit. Turning back briefly, he pulled the rolltop door shut. A soft beeping reached under the space between the door and the cement as they ran for safety. He waved toward the marshals standing near the moving truck Pierce Cook had used to abduct her from the highway. "Get back!"

An ear-deafening explosion thundered through the alleyway from behind.

Heat seared across her skin as tendrils of flames and hot air raced ahead of her and Jonah. He wrapped his arms around her, protecting her from the sear of the blast. She ducked her head between her hands as chunks of metal and stone rained down on top of them. Debris bounced against asphalt under their feet. He kept her moving ahead of him. Smoke enveloped them in a thick layer of blackness, but he wouldn't let her stop. Adrenaline drained from her veins as quickly as it'd set in and made every step heavier than the last.

Then the smoke cleared.

Chapter Fifteen

Hell, he'd never hurt like this. Inside, outside and everything in between, but it was nothing compared to the relief making its way through him. Jonah tried to wipe the dried blood off his hands, but ended up only making the mess worse. He tossed the damp rag one of the EMTs had given him into the back of the ambulance and stared out over the scene.

Portland police had already created a two-row perimeter within the storage facility's gates. The owner had been reached and brought down to assess which units belonged to which tenants. With as much damage as the property had suffered because of a federal investigation, tenants would most likely be reimbursed for the whole thing. Special Agent Collin Jackson was already searching the recently extinguished remains of Pierce Cook's storage unit for evidence while firefighters checked the rest of the area for hot spots. The unknown bomb tech hadn't been involved in the plot on Madison's life after all, but Jonah wouldn't ignore the suspicion still nagging him at the back of his mind. Not a single teammate in his former unit back at Quantico had heard of the agent. Could be Agent Jackson was too new to the field, could be something else. Right now, Jonah had more important priorities on his mind. His deputy chief gave orders from under a temporary command tent with Dylan Cove at her side, both Marshals Reed and Foster ready for their next move.

Morning broke over the horizon to the east, casting warm golden light across the pavement, and for the first time in four days, he was able to breathe. It was over. Madison and the baby were safe, and the SOB behind the latest bombings would soon be under six feet of dirt. What that meant for him and the mother of his unborn child, Jonah didn't know. He'd almost lost her for good this time, but he'd managed to stay under complete control when faced with the device strapped to her chest. A straight-up miracle if he'd ever seen one.

His entire life he'd wanted nothing more than to have what his parents had given him inside their small family. Love, devotion, support. He'd had that with Noah for the short weeks after his son had been born. He'd been happy rocking his newborn to sleep for hours and still couldn't get enough when he'd set Noah in his crib. He'd been whole. Up until his mother had called with the news his child had passed away in his sleep, and in a few short months, he'd be faced with that possibility again. Only this time, there was a chance he wouldn't have to shoulder it alone.

Madison smoothed her hands over her growing belly as she gave her statement to one of the uniformed officers off to his right. Long dark hair constructed a waterfall down her back, concealing her face as she laid out the details of what'd happened between her and the district attorney. She and Jonah had managed to escape the blast with nothing more than aches, a few scratches and bruises. He'd been seconds away from moving on to the next row of units when he'd heard the soft pounding behind one of the rolltop doors, and his instincts had told him everything he'd needed to know. He'd found her. Despite the fact she'd been zip-tied to a chair and strapped with a homemade bomb vest, right then Jonah had never seen a more perfect vision highlighted by the spotlights PPB set up around the scene.

His future.

"You've still got a bit of ash on your face." Remington Barton settled against the bumper of the ambulance and stared out over the scene. Sunlight hit light blue eyes just right, nearly making them colorless. Long sleeves brushed against the backs of her hands as she gripped the vehicle's frame, and Jonah caught a hint of a tattoo against her wrist. He'd never known Remi to wear short sleeves. Never known her to talk about her past. Seemed he wasn't the only one keeping secrets from the team. "Sounds like Madison Gray is still in the running for district attorney with Pierce Cook gone. After everything that's gone down over the past few days and having a front-row seat to how far she'll go to prosecute Rosalind Eyler, she's certainly got my vote."

Jonah couldn't take his eyes off the woman in question. "Mine, too."

"Special Agent Jackson was able to pull a fingerprint from the courthouse bomb after the crime scene techs collected all the evidence. It belonged to Pierce Cook."

Remi crossed one ankle over the other. "He used his security clearance to plant the device about a month before the construction was complete. Makes sense, since he and the judge would've been the only two to know which courtroom they'd be prosecuting the Rip City Bomber case in, but we had the bomb squad tear through nearly every inch in the building to make sure. No other devices were recovered."

"He'd been planning on this for a while," Jonah said. "Probably since the day the governor forced Cook to step down from his position and hand the case off to Madison."

"Guess we'll never know. Rosalind Eyler made sure of that." Remi pushed off from the ambulance and stepped up beside him. Gesturing with her chin toward the patrol car at the end of the row, she watched officers load the Rip City Bomber into the back of the vehicle. "They'll add another nine counts of murder, conspiracy and attempted murder to her charges, but I don't think she regrets any of it."

Compelling green eyes locked on him from across the parking lot as Rosalind Eyler paused. A hint of a smile curved at her mouth. Whatever kind of deal she'd made with Pierce Cook wouldn't hold up in the coming months of trial. She'd have to appeal to Madison, and a knot of uncertainty slithered in his gut.

"She's where she belongs. That's all that matters." He watched the patrol car roll past the storage facility gate and turn down the road out of sight. "Madison confirmed Rosalind used Harvey Braddock as a messenger between her and Pierce Cook until the defense attorney learned they planned to kill her. Can we tie his death to either of them?"

A heavy sigh escaped from Remi's mouth. Out of exhaustion or defeat, he wasn't sure. He'd never seen his deputy chief so...burdened. "The thermite burned any kind of DNA evidence left behind. The medical examiner only had so much to work with, but cause of death was narrowed down to blunt-force trauma to the back of the head with a crowbar recovered at the scene. The fire made it impossible to match fingerprints to Cook. The ME will release the body so the family can claim him, but we can't charge a dead man with murder, and we can't prove Rosalind Eyler was involved. All we have her on is conspiracy."

"She's not talking." Jonah shook his head. The woman was going to spend the rest of her life behind bars for what they could prove against her. Why stop talking now?

"Not to us, but she seems to like you." Remi patted him on the shoulder, and he flinched against the pain from the shrapnel wound. "Sorry. Forgot you've already survived another bombing before today. Good work on this case, Watson. You saved a lot of people's lives. Can't imagine why the FBI let you get away."

"I left because of my son." Stillness swam through him as the past he'd been trying to hide surfaced. He waited for the shame, the anger, to rise, but facing the possibility of losing Madison and this new baby to forces outside his control had only hammered the truth deeper. Now there was only acceptance. Peace. Love.

"I had a son before I quit the FBI. Noah. He would've been four now if he hadn't died."

Remi didn't answer, the weight of her attention fixed.

"There hadn't been anything I could do to save him then. He passed away in his sleep while I was assigned overseas. I wasn't there for him, and I've had to deal with that guilt day in and day out ever since." Jonah shifted his gaze to his superior, and the emotional dam he'd built to protect himself from letting that same fear spread crumbled. "Madison's due in a few months, and I have no idea how to make sure it doesn't happen again."

"You can't," Remi said. She stared up at him as the sun climbed higher in the sky, blocking the brightness from her eyes with one hand. "You said it yourself. There was nothing you could do to save Noah, but that doesn't mean you weren't every bit the father he needed you to be. Maybe all you can do is be here for this baby and be here for Madison. They're the ones who need you now. Make every second count while you still have time."

A heaviness lifted from his chest as his deputy chief rejoined the officers going through what was left of evidence from the storage unit. Marshal Dylan Cove turned toward her as she approached, tracing his hand down her wrist, out of sight from the other officers around them, and Jonah smiled. Remi was right. Why worry about the past repeating itself when the present had so much more to offer? He'd always remember his first son. He'd always have those short few weeks between them. Because, if he was being honest, it'd been better than not having any time together at all. Jonah focused on the deputy district attorney who'd claimed his heart and stalked toward her.

The officer she'd been giving her statement to peeled off in another direction as Jonah slid one arm along Madison's lower back and spun her into him. The sling the EMTs had fit around her injured shoulder and wrist scraped along his clothing as she stared up at him, that perfect mouth parting in surprise. Her gaze assessed the personnel around them as she brushed a strand of hair out of her face, but he didn't care about who was watching. "Jonah—"

"I love you, Maddi. You're everything I've been missing in my life. You're the reason I keep taking escort details and lying about how good I am at crossword puzzles. You're on my mind when I wake up and the last person I think about when I go to sleep at night. You're the strongest, most independent woman I've ever had the pleasure of knowing, and I was an idiot to ask you to give up an entire piece of yourself for my own fear of losing you and the baby. I don't want to change you, and I don't need a commitment from you." Jonah lowered himself down onto one knee, her hand in both of his. "If you want to run for district attorney, I'll be the first one to cast my vote. If you want to support this baby on your own, I won't push your boundaries. I promise never to ask you to marry me or demand to be part of this baby's life. Because the choice is yours, Counselor. Whatever you're willing to give me, I'll take it, and I'll always be there for you."

Silence surrounded them, and Jonah realized the entire scene had come to a complete halt. Reed, Foster,

Remington and Cove waited for her response, but Jonah could focus only on her.

A smile brightened Madison's face before she fell into his arms. She crushed her mouth to his, rocking him off balance, and wrapped her uninjured hand around the back of his neck. "Deal."

Three months later

JURY BENCHES HAD the potential to hide a lot of things, but Multnomah County District Attorney Madison Gray had attention only for the inmate on the other side of the courtroom.

Rosalind Eyler—the Rip City Bomber—had made it in once piece to the last day of her trial. Long bright red hair accentuated the lack of color in the woman's face, highlighted the shadows under her eyes. Her deal with Madison's predecessor had fallen through. There'd been no talks of another. Rosalind would spend the rest of her life behind bars without chance of parole. She hadn't personally triggered the bomb in the courtroom three months ago, but being charged as an accessory to Pierce Cook's crimes had brought the grand total of bombing murder counts to forty-one victims. All to be served consecutively. Her new defense attorney, a young woman from Harvey Braddock's firm, hadn't even had a chance.

"The jury finds the defendant, Rosalind Eyler, guilty. Bailiff, please take the defendant into custody so she can make the transport back to Corrections and serve out her days where she belongs. This case is concluded."

The judge slammed the gavel on the base and rose. His dark robe shifted around his feet as he stepped down from his seat and disappeared into the corridor leading to his chambers.

Madison struggled to her feet as murmurs filled the courtroom. Turning to face the gallery, she noted family members of the victims clasping hands, shedding tears and embracing, and the heaviness she'd been burdened with since taking on this case lifted. Forty-one victims, more injured or disabled from the cruel acts of two killers. They would have justice now.

It was over.

The Rip City Bomber wouldn't have the chance to hurt anyone else.

Through the bustling of media and civilians as the courtroom cleared, one face stood out among the rest. A smile automatically curled Madison's mouth wide as the deputy US marshal she'd fallen in love with made his way through the sea of bodies.

"Congratulations, Counselor. You've just prosecuted the biggest criminal case in the state of Oregon." His deep voice penetrated through the buzz around them and filled her with warmth from head to toe. Bright blue eyes leveled with hers as he reached over the bar separating the gallery from the front of the courtroom and smoothed both hands over her nine-month-sized beach ball of a stomach. "Job's done."

"Marshal Watson, I thought I might find you here. How was the gravesite? Did you take the flowers I bought?" she asked.

"It was good." His shoulders deflated on a strong exhale. "I talked to him for a while, told him all about you and the little brother that will be here soon."

"Noah would've been a great big brother." Their son would make his grand entrance into the world any day now, but until then Madison would soak up every moment she could get with the man who'd kept his promise these past three months. No commitment. No custody and visitation agreement. Nothing to complicate or dissolve the connection they'd built since that day at the storage facility. She reached into her bag and pulled a folded piece of paper from the depths. Handing it to him, she memorized the way his eyebrows lifted slightly along his forehead. "I have something for you."

Pulling his hands back from her hips, he unfolded the piece of paper with a deep laugh rumbling through his chest. That gut-wrenching smile she couldn't get enough of outshone the jury's verdict against the Rip City Bomber. Almost. "A new crossword."

"When you got down on one knee, you said you were pretending you weren't good at them. I'd like to see you crack this one." She tapped the paper before she turned to collect her files from the table. A tightening in her belly washed through her, forcing her to hold her breath. Braxton-Hicks contractions. She'd gotten a few throughout the past couple of days, but that had definitely been the strongest of the set. "The reporters are champing at the bit downstairs. Care to escort me to the lobby?"

Jonah swung the gate open for her, the crossword in hand. The sooner he found the answers for every box, the sooner she'd have hers. "It would be my pleasure."

Side by side, they exited the newly refurbished courtroom. Memories ignited of the terrifying moments he'd carried her down this exact hallway after the bombing, but even then she'd known Jonah would do whatever it took to protect her and their son. He intertwined his hand with hers, but another contraction forced her to pull up short. Concern deepened the three lines between his eyebrows as she strengthened her grip around his hand. "Another Braxton-Hicks contraction?"

A flood of sensation pooled low between her legs as the contraction let up. That one had definitely been stronger than the one she'd experienced during court proceedings, and the interval had sped up. She pressed one hand into her left side and felt their son's movement underneath the thick lining of fat and muscle. "No, I don't think so."

"Maddi?" Jonah took position in front of her, framing the baby between both calloused hands. "Tell me what's going on."

"I'm fairly certain my water broke." She took a step forward and cringed against the trickling sensation running down the inside of her legs. "No, I'm definitely sure my water broke. Can you get me to my office, please? I have a change of clothes stashed in my overnight bag."

"We need to get you to the hospital." A combination of urgency and excitement transformed his expression as he took her bag from her shoulder and clasped both of her hands in his. "The baby's coming."

"No. Office first. I need to go to my office." She'd hold this baby in as long as it took. Although the next wave of tightening was already building. "This isn't the movies. Real life says I have at least a couple of hours before this baby shoots out of there."

"And you plan to have that happen in your office?" Clerks, attorneys and security personnel watched them as Jonah helped her shuffle toward the elevator.

"I'm not giving birth in my office, Jonah." She clamped her jaw against the oncoming squeeze from the top of her lungs to the bottom of her torso. Okay. They weren't going to make it to her office. She detoured to the nearest wall and slammed her hand down for something more solid to hold on to. "There's something I have to do first, but I'm pretty sure this watermelon isn't going to let me. Give…me my bag."

He did as she asked, confusion chasing back the excitement that'd been etched into his expression moments before. "What do you need?"

"A pen." An uncontrolled growl ripped up her throat as the third contraction in as many minutes constricted her midsection. "Or a pencil. That will work, too."

He dumped the contents of her bag onto the newly waxed tile and skimmed through everything inside until he'd found her a pen. "You're stopping in the middle of the courthouse corridor while you're in labor. This better be the best-damn-looking pen I've ever seen in my life."

"It's not for me." She had a break between contractions, and a flood of relief wrung the pain from her overtaxed muscles. "It's for you. You need to solve the crossword. Right now." A concerned security guard headed toward them, but Madison waved them off. "We're fine. I'm in labor. Not a big deal."

"You want me to solve the crossword now? Right this second?" Disbelief hiked his voice into the next octave. "You haven't even gotten to the hospital for the good drugs, and you're already hallucinating."

She left the safety of the wall and clenched his shirt in her hands as she dragged him into her. The physical pressure of their son working his way into the world was almost too much to take. They didn't have time for this. She knew that, but the part of her he'd saved that day at the storage facility needed him to do it. He'd kept his word all this time. He deserved to know how she really felt about him. "I will have this baby on the floor if I have to, Jonah. I need you to solve the damn crossword before we go to the hospital. I thought we'd have more time, but we don't. Understand?"

Jonah bit down on the end of the pen cap and pulled the pen free. "Fine. Three across." His mumblings grew fainter as he filled in the boxes as fast as he could, while Madison hung on to his shirt for dear life. Nervous energy skittered up her spine as Jonah's mouth parted. The pen cap bounced onto the floor and rolled away out of sight. He'd finished the puzzle. Her heart skipped a beat, and the pain faded as he raised that dependable gaze to hers. "Is this… Are you serious?"

"I've never been more serious about anything in my entire life. It took me weeks to put together." Madison nodded, reaching for his hand. She stared up at him. Her hair fell behind her shoulder as she prepared for the next contraction. "Deputy US Marshal Jonah

Watson, you are the bravest, most loyal man and most dependable source of safety I've ever had at my side. I fell in love with you long before we made this baby together. You're the rock I've needed my entire life, my everything and the reason I'm standing here today. Before you rushed into my life, I was lost, but you helped me see there's more to a relationship—a marriage—than I ever imagined. I cut you out of my life after I found out I was pregnant, but I never want to spend another day apart again. I love you. So will you marry me?"

His smile slipped. "I promise you, you don't have to do this, Maddi. I'm happy being as involved in your life—in our son's life—as you want me to be. Whatever you need from me, it's yours."

"I need everything, Jonah. I need you. Now. Forever. You're everything I was scared of, and everything I've always dreamed of having, and I want to spend the rest of my life having these moments between us." She kissed him softly. "But if you could give me a quick answer, that would be great, because there's another contraction coming, and I might not remember this later."

His laugh vibrated through her and straight to her toes. "Yes."

"Yes?" Pure elation replaced the past few minutes of pain as he pressed his mouth to hers. Her feet left the ground as Jonah held her against him. She planted her hand against his chest as she settled on the four corners of her toes and smiled up at her marshal. Her life partner. Her everything. "Great. Now take me to the hospital. Noah's little brother isn't going to wait much longer."

Jonah hit her with that brilliant smile all over again and wrapped her hand in his. "You got it, Counselor."

* * * * *

COMING SOON!

We really hope you enjoyed reading this book.
If you're looking for more romance, be sure to
head to the shops when new books are
available on

Thursday 4th
March

To see which titles are coming soon, please visit
millsandboon.co.uk/nextmonth

MILLS & BOON

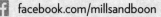

MILLS & BOON

THE HEART OF ROMANCE

A ROMANCE FOR EVERY KIND OF READER

MODERN

Prepare to be swept off your feet by sophisticated, sexy and seductive heroes, in some of the world's most glamourous and romantic locations, where power and passion collide.
8 stories per month.

HISTORICAL

Escape with historical heroes from time gone by. Whether your passion is for wicked Regency Rakes, muscled Vikings or rugged Highlanders, awaken the romance of the past.
6 stories per month.

MEDICAL

Set your pulse racing with dedicated, delectable doctors in the high-pressure world of medicine, where emotions run high and passion, comfort and love are the best medicine.
6 stories per month.

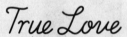

Celebrate true love with tender stories of heartfelt romance, from the rush of falling in love to the joy a new baby can bring, and a focus on the emotional heart of a relationship.
8 stories per month.

Indulge in secrets and scandal, intense drama and plenty of sizzling hot action with powerful and passionate heroes who have it all: wealth, status, good looks…everything but the right woman.
6 stories per month.

HEROES

Experience all the excitement of a gripping thriller, with an intense romance at its heart. Resourceful, true-to-life women and strong, fearless men face danger and desire - a killer combination!
8 stories per month.

DARE

Sensual love stories featuring smart, sassy heroines you'd want as a best friend, and compelling intense heroes who are worthy of them.
4 stories per month.

To see which titles are coming soon, please visit

millsandboon.co.uk/nextmonth

MILLS & BOON

HISTORICAL

Awaken the romance of the past

Escape with historical heroes from time gone by. Whether your passion is for wicked Regency Rakes, muscled Viking warriors or rugged Highlanders, indulge your fantasies and awaken the romance of the past.

MILLS & BOON

MODERN

Power and Passion

Prepare to be swept off your feet by sophisticated, sexy and seductive heroes, in some of the world's most glamourous and romantic locations, where power and passion collide.

MILLS & BOON
True Love
Romance from the Heart

Celebrate true love with tender stories of
heartfelt romance, from the rush of falling
in love to the joy a new baby can bring,
and a focus on the emotional
heart of a relationship.

MILLS & BOON
MEDICAL
Pulse-Racing Passion

Set your pulse racing with dedicated, delectable doctors in the high-pressure world of medicine, where emotions run high and passion, comfort and love are the best medicine.